Midnight Warning

Katharine heard a bell in the distance.

She came awake groggily. Somebody was holding her foot.

She was terrified to open her eyes until she felt the weight on her foot give a stretch and utter a small *meow*. That's when she realized it wasn't a school bell she was hearing, it was the phone.

She rolled over and reached for the receiver, hoping whatever it was hadn't wakened Dr. Flo. She could scarcely get her tongue around the word *hello*.

"Stay away from Bayard Island. What happened to Agnes can happen to you."

"Miranda? This isn't funny!" She heard a click.

Caught between annoyance and relief at being awakened from her bad dream, she snuggled back into her covers. The small cat shifted and began to purr.

Katharine was sliding back into sleep when something occurred to her. That voice had been too deep to be Miranda's.

PATRICIA SPRINKLE

Sins of the Fathers

AVON

An Imprint of HarperCollins*Publishers*

AVON BOOKS
An Imprint of HarperCollins*Publishers*
10 East 53rd Street
New York, New York 10022-5299

Acknowledgments

Four graves lie in a central North Carolina cemetery far from the sea, between two others that span the American Revolution. Their stones bear no names and no dates, but each is etched with a skull and crossed bones. Some people insist the skull simply represented death, but I can find no similar use of the skull with crossed bones. A Carolina legend claims pirates sailed far up the Neuse from the coast, but the Neuse turns northward miles to the east of this cemetery. For me, those grave stones were the mystery that birthed this mystery.

Bayard's Island, the Bayard family, and other characters are figments of my imagination, but this book owes a major debt to *Early Days of the Georgia Tidewater: The Story of McIntosh County and Sapelo* by Buddy Sullivan, and to *The Confederate Privateers* by W. M. Robinson, Jr. I am also grateful to the excellent genealogy rooms in the Smyrna Public Library and the Atlanta History Center, and to the convenience of ancestry.com.

I am also grateful to Norman Burkett of the Bellamy Funeral Home and Randy Carmichael of Carmichael Funeral Home for explaining procedures for the disinterment of old graves, and to Jia Jordan, of the Human Resources Department of Spelman College, for her information about benefits a retired professor would receive. And finally, I must thank my agent, Nancy Yost, for her perseverance in finding this series a home; my editor, Sarah Durand, for her wise editing that made this a better book; and—as always—my husband, Bob, for patience and support far beyond the call of his marriage vows.

Joye Folsom and Jenny-Jill Roberts are as fictitious as other characters in the book, but bear the names of two readers who won a contest on my website. Happy reading, ladies!

Primary Characters

In Atlanta:
Katharine Murray
Tom Murray—her husband
Hobart Hastings—Emory history professor
Dr. Florence Gadney—retired professor of Business,
    Spelman College
Hollis Buiton—Katharine's niece
Posey Buiton—Hollis's mother
Lamar Franklin—genealogy expert

In McIntosh County:
Burch and Mona Bayard—owners of Bayard Island
Chase Bayard—their son
Dalton Bayard—Burch's father
Iola Stampers—owner of a seafood business on Bayard
    Island
Nell Stampers—Iola's daughter
Miranda Stampers—Iola's granddaughter
Agnes Morrison—Bayard Island resident
Hayden Curtis—Burch Bayard's attorney

Sins of the Fathers

Chapter 1

Katharine Murray could have missed the call because of her kettle. The thing was so loud, Tom swore it had started life as a Romanian factory whistle.

"If Susan had listened to you before she bought you, you'd still be languishing in a New York department store," she told it as she reached for the phone.

With Tom gone from Monday through Friday almost every week, she often talked to inanimate objects.

The voice on the other end was deep and well modulated, its vowels rich and round. "Katharine? It's Florence Gadney. I have a favor to ask you. A big one. A matter—" she gave an odd little laugh—"you might say a *grave* matter has come up. I need—what on earth is that racket?"

"My kettle. Isn't it awful? I was just making a cup of tea." Katharine slid the kettle off its burner and hoped Dr. Flo thought she was fixing a midmorning snack. The retired college professor was so efficient she had probably finished her breakfast before the early bird started looking for the worm.

Katharine could picture her sitting on a white brocade couch in a designer pantsuit, for Dr. Flo was not only brilliant, she was also independently wealthy and chic. Hopefully Dr. Flo could not picture Katharine barefoot, tousled, and still wearing the faded red T-shirt and gray knit shorts she had slept in since Tom had had to fly out the evening before.

"What can I do for you?" Katharine asked.

"Well . . ." *Hesitant* was not a word Katharine usually associated with Dr. Flo, but she seemed to be having a hard time getting to her point.

Never in a hundred years could Katharine have predicted Dr. Flo's next sentence, spoken in a rush. "I need to run down to McIntosh County tomorrow morning, and wondered if you'd be interested in going with me. Just for the day."

Katharine held out her phone and looked at it in bewilderment. Why on earth was Dr. Flo asking her? While they knew each another to speak to at the symphony or opera, had served on a few committees together over the years— had even worked together unraveling an old murder case earlier that summer*—they had never been the sort of friends who went away together, even for a day. Their lives touched at very few points.

In her forty-six years, Katharine had never been employed. She had spent over half her life raising two children and taking sole charge of the house while Tom climbed the corporate ladder. Her preferred volunteer activities were tutoring children or teaching ESOL classes. A month before, with her daughter working in New York, her son newly graduated from college and teaching English in China, and her last elderly relative gone, Katharine had begun to wonder what she was going to do with the long stretch of years that lay ahead until Tom's retirement.

Dr. Flo, on the other hand, was childless, and had taught business at Spelman until her retirement. She served on numerous committees and boards, and was a generous patron of the arts. Until her husband's death the prior year, she and Dr. Maurice, a prominent orthopedist, made a striking couple on opening nights—he tall and handsome, almost as black as his tux, and she dainty and sweet-potato gold, wearing a

---

* *Death on the Family Tree*

series of Parisian creations with her hair in a sleek chignon. Even since his death, Katharine suspected Dr. Flo had no concept of what it meant to have too much time on her hands.

"I don't know where McIntosh County is," Katharine hedged, trying to come up with any conceivable reason why Dr. Flo should be inviting her along. "Georgia has so many counties, I do well to remember those in the metro area."

"It's on the coast, between Savannah and Brunswick. Could you drive down with me?"

"That's five hours each way! Surely you mean to stay overnight." After all, Dr. Flo must be seventy.

"No, I plan to drive right down and back. The business I have there shouldn't take more than an hour, so with two drivers, it won't be strenuous." She paused and added with diffidence, "Say no if you can't go. I know this is sudden. Maurice used to say, 'Flo-baby, you expect too much spontaneity from folks. The rest of us need time to mull things over and arrange our calendars.' But if you could go, I'd be grateful. We'd take my car, of course. I thought of you because I would appreciate your insight once we get there."

Katharine had recently raised two teenagers to young adulthood. Anybody who appreciated her insight got her attention. "Insight about what?" She poured water over her tea bag while Dr. Flo explained.

"I had a call this morning from Maurice's cousin Mary, who is visiting her son down in Savannah. She saw an ad in today's paper asking descendants of a Claude Gilbert who was buried in McIntosh County in 1903 to contact an attorney. Mary remembered that my father's father was Claude Gilbert, so she wondered if he came from down that way." Dr. Flo stopped. She often did that in committee meetings to make sure people were listening.

"Did he?" Katharine asked dutifully. Dr. Flo did a lot of genealogical research. She had probably traced her father's family all the way back to a line of African chieftains. They would have been chieftains, of course.

Katharine was surprised to hear her admit, "I don't know. My granddaddy *was* Claude Gilbert and he *did* die in 1903, but my research on the Gilbert branch of my family tree only stretches back to Claude's graduation from Morehouse in 1891. I've never been able to determine when or where he was born, who his people were, or where they came from. He died when Daddy was two, and Grandmother Lucy married again a couple of years later. Her second husband was like a daddy to my daddy, and he was buried with her here in Atlanta, but my birth grandfather is not in the family plot. It's probably a coincidence, of course, but I felt I ought to call and see what this lawyer wanted." She chuckled. "Mary thought maybe Claude left money nobody had claimed— you know, one of those bank accounts people open, then forget." Dr. Flo needed more money like Atlanta needed another Peachtree Street, Road, Circle, or Avenue.

What Katharine needed was breakfast. Her stomach grumbled as she poured a small glass of orange juice and took a sip. *More is coming eventually,* she promised.

"However," Dr. Flo continued, "it wasn't anything like that. The attorney, Mr. Hayden Curtis, represents a developer who wants to build on property where there is a small cemetery, and he needs permission to move graves. Apparently you can't move a grave in Georgia without authorization from the next of kin. The lawyer said he's run the ad for two weeks in every paper from Charleston down to Jacksonville and nobody else has called, which make sense if this is my relative. I am an only child, Daddy was an only child, and so far as we know, Granddaddy was an only child. I don't have cousins that I've ever been able to find on the Gilbert side."

"So what's the problem?" Katharine still couldn't see why she was being invited to drive ten hours to look at a grave. Her insight concerning grave removal was nil.

She took the tea bag out of her cup, added a dollop of milk and sugar, and carried the mug to her breakfast room table. While she sipped, she looked wistfully at a bright yellow butterfly nuzzling the pink buddleia and two hummingbirds fighting over the feeder. Everybody was getting breakfast except her.

"Mr. Curtis says there are actually three graves: the one for Claude Gilbert plus two with the name G-u-i-l-b-e-r-t. In French, that would be *Geel-bear*, but he pronounced it *Gwilbert*. I suppose that's the way it's pronounced down there."

"Do you have French ancestors?"

"Not that I ever heard of. But because this Claude Gilbert was buried the same year my granddaddy died, I am intrigued. In case these *are* my ancestors, I'd like to see the graves before they are destroyed. Could you go with me tomorrow?"

When Katharine hesitated, she repeated, a tad anxiously, "Say no if you can't . . ."

"What's the hurry?"

What Katharine wanted to ask was "What's the big deal?" She hadn't started researching her own family, so she hadn't yet experienced the excitement of finding a sought-after piece in a genealogy puzzle.

"Mr. Curtis says the developer wants to get started and needs the graves moved next week, but Mr. Curtis will be out of town from Wednesday through the weekend. If I plan to see him and sign papers after viewing the graves, I have to go tomorrow. Of course, he's as convinced as you are that I'm crazy to drive all the way down there, but if this is my grandfather's grave, I would never forgive myself if I passed up a chance to see the original plot. However, my reason for wanting you to go is that Mr. Curtis raises all my flags."

For the first time, Katharine felt a flicker of interest. "Why is that?"

"Based only on his hunch that the graves could be related,

he originally wanted to FedEx me documents today to sign and send right back, authorizing the removal of all three graves. He never asked for a single proof that I am Claude Gilbert's granddaughter, nor did he offer proof that the three graves are connected. That makes me as curious about Mr. Curtis as I am about his graves. You demonstrated rare acumen about that situation back in June. I'd like your opinion of Mr. Curtis when I meet with him."

"But he didn't refuse to meet with you?" Katharine couldn't think of any scam that involved moving neglected graves, but scammers were getting increasingly creative.

"Oh, no. He said he could see me tomorrow. Could you possibly come along?"

"May I think about it and call you back?"

"Of course. I'll be here all morning. Just let me know."

How could she possibly go?

Four weeks ago, her house had been vandalized. What the vandals had not carried away, they had destroyed. Since then, she had spent every waking hour on the slow, painful process of reconstructing her home, and she still was far from finished. She spent most of her sleeping hours dreaming about the break-in.

This morning, the reason she was so late with breakfast was that she had lain awake until after two thinking of everything she still needed to do. When she had finally slept, the nightmares, ever vigilant, had returned. She had wakened at dawn dry-mouthed, drenched with sweat, and disoriented, with wisps of dream clinging like cobwebs. When she opened her eyes, she was bewildered to see yellow walls, not taupe, and a floral spread on her bed, not a plaid one. She had struggled to remember what the dream had been, for she was learning that bringing nightmares to light is the fastest way to dissolve them.

Nuggets had returned, spiders among the cobwebs:

* * *

A party. The house looking great. Guests she didn't recognize but who seemed to be having a good time. Standing in the dining room smiling up at the portraits of her children over the sideboard. A hand that shot over her shoulder with a knife. Watching it slash, slash her children's faces while she stood by, helpless.

Reality had surged over her like a tsunami, leaving a desolation of grief in its wake. Her worst nightmares were real. Her children's irreplaceable portraits, painted eighteen years before when Jon was three and Susan five, were gone, their destruction senseless and vicious.

Thinking of those flower faces reduced to ribbons and buried beneath tons of garbage in an Atlanta landfill, Katharine had wept until her pillow was soggy and her body exhausted. Then she exchanged the pillow for the cool, unused one on Tom's side of the bed, and had fallen into an exhausted sleep. Since the break-in, she always slept better after the sun came up.

Grief had gripped her again when she started to wash her face and reached for the soap. What triggered it was such a small thing—the absence of a lopsided clay duck Susan had made in fourth grade, which Katharine had used as a soap dish. When she reached for the soap and the duck wasn't there, she saw again the crumbs of red clay the vandals had ground underfoot. She had pressed her forehead against the beige tiles of the bathroom wall and fought back a shriek.

She was getting used to the mood swings—a sudden plunge from cheerful normalcy to times when she wanted to careen around her lot like a balloon gone berserk. Memories took you like that, sneaking up on you from behind or around a corner. Tom's sister, Posey, the health and exercise guru of the family, recommended three deep, cleansing breaths whenever she felt overwhelmed. Katharine gave that another try, but the only thing deep breathing had accomplished so far was to make her dizzy.

Eating, now—that worked. She had gained five pounds in the past month. She headed downstairs to scrounge up breakfast.

In the kitchen, she had lifted the head of a cheerful pig, reached inside his round yellow shirt, and brought up a couple of chocolate chip cookies she had made the night before. "Don't look so approving," she mumbled through crumbs and chunks of pecan. "You're supposed to remind me of what I'll look like if I keep eating these."

The pig—a whimsical newcomer to the kitchen—beamed a benign benediction.

She had flicked his snout lightly with one finger and ambled to the breakfast room bay window to inspect the impersonation of another beautiful day. She was not fooled by the blue, cloudless dome. In another few hours the sky would be a white haze of heat. Atlanta baked in a midsummer drought, and her own yard was lush and colorful only thanks to the hard work of Anthony, her yardman, and Tom's willingness—and ability—to pay enormous water bills.

Theirs was not one of the largest homes in Buckhead (which one writer accurately called "the most well-to-do and elegant residential area within Atlanta"), but it stood in lovely grounds. That morning, the glittering pool enticed her across the backyard: *Forget the nightmares. Come get rid of your cobwebs with a quick dip before breakfast.*

Why not?

Because she had to buy lamps that day and was already late. There wasn't a lamp left in the house, not one place Tom could sit down to read. He'd remarked on that the past weekend.

With a sigh, she had turned toward the stove. As the kettle shrilled, Dr. Flo had called.

After the call, she sipped the lukewarm brew and considered the invitation. *I could buy lamps today and go tomorrow. Nonsense. You'll never finish the house if you put things off. And who would really care if the house was never finished?*

To still her internal debate, she rose to check out the fridge to see if anything exciting for breakfast had crept in overnight. Nope. Same old same old. "Fix a bagel," she instructed herself. "Bagels take your mind off anything. You need all your concentration to chew and swallow them."

"Breakfast for one coming up," she told the pig as she carried a bagel to the toaster. "Sorry you can't join me." She fetched cream cheese and jam and reached through a hole in the formerly glass-fronted cupboard doors for a plate. "If that glazier doesn't get around to repairing the doors pretty soon," she warned, "I may leave them like this. They are a lot handier."

As she brought down the plate, her mood plummeted again. Her hands shook so badly, she barely landed the dish safely on the countertop. "You like these dishes. You do!" she told herself as she traced the pattern with one finger. "You picked them out."

Only because I couldn't get the ones we had before—the ones we bought in Italy last summer and loved.

She clenched one fist and pounded the countertop. "Deal with it, sweetie!"

She took three more deep cleansing breaths, but how clean can one set of lungs get? By now, hers would probably squeak if you rubbed them.

She placed both hands on her kitchen counter and announced to the pig, "This has got to stop. *Anything* would be better than this."

The pig smiled in sunny agreement. Perhaps he, like Katharine, failed to comprehend how much "anything" can cover.

"I'm going," she told him. "I'm going with Dr. Flo!"

What she pictured was not Dr. Flo's granddaddy's grave. What she pictured was herself floating on wide Atlantic swells, away from decisions and choices and chaos. Excitement rose in her like bubbles in ginger ale. She had grown up in Miami and adored the sea.

She dialed Dr. Flo's number. "I'll go with you on one condition. I'd hate to get that close to salt water without eating seafood, swimming in the ocean, and walking on the beach. If I can get my husband's sister to let us use her cottage down on Jekyll Island, would you be willing to stay a couple of nights?" She held her breath.

"We're in the middle of a record heat wave," the professor pointed out. "You won't want to be out on the beach much. It was a hundred down there yesterday. I checked."

"We can look at the ocean from her air-conditioned living room, we can swim in the morning and just before the sun goes down, and we can take long walks on the beach after dark while sipping chilled wine. I'll furnish the wine."

Dr. Flo hesitated for so long that Katharine thought she was going to refuse, but when she spoke, her voice throbbed with pleasure. "That would be marvelous. I no longer swim, but I love being near the sea."

"Bring your suit just in case," Katharine advised. "The ocean should be like bathwater by now. You may get tempted."

Dr. Flo's rich chuckle flowed down the line. "Warm or not, I don't want to drown in it. I've had my three-score-and ten, but I still hope to live a few years longer."

Neither of them had any idea at the time how difficult that was going to be.

Chapter 2

"Buiton's res-i-dence." The maid gave the last word its full three syllables, accenting the third.

"Hey, Julia," Katharine greeted her. "Is Posey there?"

Julia's voice dropped from formal to family in one second flat. "Hey, Miss Kat. She's just leaving for her class. Lemme see can I catch her." The phone hit the kitchen counter with a click. Katharine heard her booming voice progressing across the kitchen: "Miss Posey, oh, Miss Posey, Miss Kat's on the line."

She got immediate results. "Sorry, I was already in the garage. I can't talk but a minute. I'll be late to class."

That didn't worry Katharine. Her sister-in-law was invariably late, and she wouldn't get out of shape missing an exercise or two. She went to aerobics every day, wearing a series of pastel spandex outfits with matching shoes. She even had matching headbands to hold back her lacquered blond curls. Exercise and Botox kept her looking a lot younger than her fifty-plus years, and people who met her were in danger of dismissing her as a pretty but aging bimbo unless they got a good look at her shrewd blue eyes.

"The way Julia says, 'She's just leaving for her class,' a stranger might think you're a doctoral candidate instead of an aerobics fanatic," Katharine teased, "but this won't take but a minute. Is your beach cottage free for a couple of days? I'd like to go down tomorrow and take Dr. Flo Gadney." Because they used it so seldom, the Buitons let a realtor rent out the house whenever he could.

"Oooh-la-la. How'd you get so chummy with Dr. Flo?" Posey wasn't an intellectual, but she appreciated Dr. Flo's influence in Atlanta's social and civic circles. She would enjoy dropping the information at various venues, "My sister-in-law is down at our place on Jekyll this week with Dr. Flo Gadney."

"We aren't chummy, but she's invited me to drive to the coast with her tomorrow. She has business down there and wants my advice on something." Katharine dropped a modest boast of her own, then grinned at her silliness. "I thought when we were done with business, we could go to Jekyll for a couple of nights, if the cottage is free."

"I don't know, but you can call and ask. Would you like me to do it?"

"No, I will. I mostly wanted permission to use it."

"Of course. You know you don't have to ask."

Katharine knew she didn't, just as Posey knew she always would. Like good sisters, she and her sister-in-law preserved certain courtesies between them.

"Do you still have your key?" When Katharine hesitated, Posey apologized in an embarrassed rush. "I keep forgetting what a mess those thieves made."

It was Katharine's turn to be embarrassed. "They took all the keys from our key board, too. Tom changed our locks, but I didn't think about your keys being on the board." Not only the Jekyll cottage key, but keys to the Buiton's sprawling home.

"If they haven't used the keys by now, chances are they won't, but I'll mention it to Wrens. He'll probably want to change our locks. You know how he is."

Yes, Katharine knew how Posey's big, placid husband was—too easygoing to worry about keys that had disappeared a month before when he had an excellent security system in the house and lived close enough to the governor to get a quick response if anybody did break in, but he was so devoted to his wife that he'd change every lock just to please her.

"Hold on a minute." Posey put her on hold. Katharine presumed she was taking another call until she came back on the line. "The cottage is free and I told the realtor you're coming, so she'll air the place. The hidden keys are in their usual places. Stay as long as you like. They don't have anybody coming in for two weeks. But next time you want to go down, let me know ahead and I'll go with you. I could use time on the beach. Tanning beds make me look sallow."

"It's a deal. And thank you from the bottom of my soul. A few days at the beach ought to help me recuperate from shopping and redecorating. Which reminds me. Do you know if Hollis is home? I'll need to cancel our shopping this week." Katharine danced a private little jig as she said those words. She loathed shopping.

Posey's sigh came from the toes of her exercise shoes. "Oh, yes, she's up in that poky little apartment running the sewing machine. I heard it going when I went out to the car. Why that child won't come downstairs and live with us, I don't know. We've got the whole blooming house . . ."

Hollis, Posey's youngest daughter, had recently graduated from the Savannah College of Art and Design and had asked to live in her family's carriage-house apartment, which had once housed a former family's chauffeur. The apartment was far from the hovel Posey pretended. For one thing, it sprawled over the Buitons' four-car garage and had more square feet than Katharine and two roommates had shared one summer during her college years. For another, since Wrens doted on his three daughters as much as he doted on his wife, the apartment gleamed with fresh paint, Ikea furniture, new appliances, refinished oak floors, and Hollis's own quirky taste in fabrics and paint. Unlike Katharine, none of the female Buitons disliked shopping, so they had completed the redecoration of the apartment in record time.

Hollis, who had studied textiles and fibers, was helping Katharine redecorate her house after the break-in. Katharine wasn't enjoying the shopping, but she was enjoying spending time with her newly adult niece.

"Don't knock her for using the sewing machine," Katharine told Hollis's mother. "She may be sewing drapery for my dining room."

"I wish she'd get a real job."

"Talk to Tom about how real Hollis's job is after he's paid her bill. You could be astonished at how well she's doing."

"Maybe so," Posey sounded dubious, "but her taste in men hasn't improved. Last night she brought a young man in for a drink, and he had the grossest ring in his nostril. I kept wanting to lead him around by it. And he sat right here in our home and told us he is a great admirer of Lenin. I thought Wrens would die."

Katharine suspected that Wrens's blood pressure hadn't gone up a single point. He was accustomed to Hollis's need to shock her parents. She also suspected the young man had been talking about Lennon, the deceased Beatle, not the Russian politician. Most of all, she suspected Hollis was once again jerking Posey's chain, as Katharine had jerked her Aunt Sara Claire's chain back when Sara Claire considered herself one of Buckhead's foremost aristocrats. Hollis could count on the fact that her mother would have a spasm every time she brought home another strange young man.

"So far Hollis has shown the good sense not to get seriously involved with any of them," Katharine pointed out. One of the reasons Posey complained to her about Hollis was to be reassured that the child wasn't fit to be locked up.

"Thank the good Lord for that. Do you want me to call her to the phone?"

"No, I'll call on her cell phone. You go on to class. And

thanks again for the use of the cottage. You may have saved my sanity."

Hollis was, indeed, working on Katharine's dining room drapery. "Are you out shopping for lamps?" she demanded.

"Careful," Katharine warned, "or you are going to start sounding like Aunt Sara Claire. Remember how bossy she was?" She laughed to show she was teasing. She was very fond of Posey's small, dark daughter, who looked far more like her uncle, Tom, and her cousin, Susan, than she did her large blond sisters. Molly and Lolly were traditional products of Buckhead: beautifully groomed young women who devoted their lives to good works, exercise, and reproducing themselves in their own image. Hollis—who since college had refused to be the Holly in that trio of names—accepted no social barriers and few social conventions, and knew every trick in the book to irritate her mother. Katharine found her insightful comments on society and her wide range of interests and friends refreshing. Posey found them infuriating. Of course, as Posey kept pointing out, nobody would ever blame Katharine for the way Hollis turned out.

"I'm not at all like Mrs. Everanes," Hollis objected. "I wasn't trying to boss you. I thought you might be calling to ask my advice about a lampshade or something."

"No, I'm calling to tell you I'm going out of town tomorrow for a few days, so you can take time off. We'll look for stuff for Susan's room later."

"I could look while you're gone."

"You're a glutton for punishment, but I'd be delighted. Go ahead and buy whatever you think will work. But remember, nothing too girly."

"I don't do girly," Hollis informed her with offended dignity.

Katharine was immediately contrite. "Of course you don't. You've done a marvelous job on everything else, and you probably know Susan's tastes better than I do."

"It's not Susan's room anymore," Hollis reminded her with the bluntness that Posey found so mortifying. "We ought to fix it up as a guest room."

Katharine felt like she'd been hit between the shoulder blades. "I guess so," she managed. "Surprise me." She hung up glad she'd be in the ocean by the next day. She needed one thing in her life that hadn't changed.

Chapter 3

The red Jeep in her driveway later that afternoon meant nothing but trouble, so why did Katharine's foot relax on the gas pedal and a little bubble of happiness well up inside her when she turned in her drive and found it there? As soon as she realized her SUV was slowing down, she pressed on the gas to shoot up the hill to the garage.

She had just stopped the car when she heard a shout. "Hey! Just because you drive a Cadillac doesn't mean you *have* to be rude."

She let out a huff that was a mixture of exasperation, resignation, and amusement, then grabbed her purse and refreshed her lipstick.

Hobart Hasting's face appeared at her car window, hazel eyes blazing. He was so winded from running up the hill that Katharine felt a momentary pang. He was her age, after all, and shouldn't be running in that heat. Still, even winded and pink, age suited him. Back in high school, Katharine's fingers had known every line of that face and each wave in that dark hair. Thirty years later his hair was grizzled at the temples and his glasses had been exchanged for bifocals, but the adult was even handsomer than the boy had been.

Which didn't change the fact that they had each married somebody else.

Katharine lowered her window and pulled her sunglasses

down on her nose so she could look over them. "What are you doing here?"

He grabbed on to the car and feigned desperate gasps of distress. "Dying, at the moment. What about, 'How are you, Hasty? Haven't seen you for over three weeks. Have you been out of town?' Do you realize I've been sitting out there roasting for half an hour, waiting for you to get home?"

How like Hasty to blame her that he'd had to wait when he hadn't bothered to let her know he was coming.

She cut the motor. "Do you know I've been shopping for five straight hours and might not have come home for another four?"

"I thought you hated shopping."

"I loathe it." She pulled off her sunglasses and secured them in her purse. Then she opened her door, forcing him to step back, and swung down from her perch in the big SUV. "I'm glad you're here. You can help me carry in lamps."

"Lamps?"

"Lamps. Lamps for the living room, lamps for the den, lamps for Tom's library, two lamps for my study, and lamps for all the bedrooms. I feel like Aladdin, except Aladdin could have rubbed one lamp and gotten a genie to carry the rest. I had to lug every blessed one to the car on my own. Nobody has service these days. And now they have to be carried in."

While she was grumbling she was leading the way to the rear access door. "Voila!" She extended one arm like a ringmaster. "Half the lamps in Atlanta, ready for you to whisk into the house."

He raised his brows above his glasses. "Do I look like a whisker? I rather picture myself as a flowing beard." His fingers made motions down his chest.

"You look more like somebody trying to play two flutes, but why don't you flow with these lamps into the house while I fix us both a drink?" She reached in and hauled out a ginger jar lamp that would sit beside her bed. "Don't you like the bird of paradise on this one? It reminds me of Miami." She started for the kitchen door.

"Did you leave me the heaviest ones on purpose?" he complained.

She didn't answer, for at the threshold she had run into an invisible wall. The white tile floor and gray granite countertops gleamed in afternoon dimness. The kitchen's yellow walls were cheerful, softly mysterious in that light. All the contents of the refrigerator, drawers, and cabinets seemed to be where they belonged. Yet it still took a firm act of will for Katharine to lift her foot and step inside.

"No burglars?" Hasty asked at her heels.

"Not today." She hated that he had seen her pause, hated even more that he understood what made her do it. Was she so transparent? Or did Hasty still know her that well?

"You'll get over it eventually." His voice was gruff. "Or so I hear."

"I hope so. Right now I expect to see a mess every time I come in this door."

She had discovered the break-in when she had stepped through the door one morning, plastic grocery bags cutting into her fingers, and found her newly remodeled kitchen awash in flour, sugar, orange juice, ketchup, broken eggs, and milk. The new glass-fronted cupboards of which she was so proud had been splintered. Glasses and dishes had been smashed. Dish towels and potholders lay amid the muck on the floor, stained with mustard and grape jelly and sprinkled with shards of glass. The seat cushions of her new breakfast room chairs had been shredded.

Hasty prodded her from behind. "Get a move on. These things weigh a ton." She looked over her shoulder and saw that he was carrying two brass lamps so heavy that she had staggered under the weight of one.

Grateful to return to the present, she stepped aside to let

him pass. "Just put all of them in the den for now. I'll sort out where they go later."

She set the ginger jar lamp on the countertop and called after him, "What do you feel like drinking? Beer? Wine? A gin and tonic? Or will tea do?" While she waited for his answer, she kicked off her shoes to enjoy the feel of cool tiles under her bare soles. Her feet were weary, and Katharine never wore shoes unless she had to.

"Tea's fine. Got any cookies to go with it?" He came back empty-handed and headed to the garage again.

By the time he had carried in all the lamps, she had glasses of iced tea waiting on the table along with a plate of cookies. She had made them with double the chips and lots of pecans, the way Tom liked them, but at this rate, there would be precious few left by the time he got home Friday.

Hasty slid into a chair. He never simply sat like other people. "You're looking good."

She felt her cheeks stain with a flush of pleasure. She hadn't dressed to please Hasty that morning when she'd put on beige capris, a soft white shell, a gold chain, and a bronze-toned linen jacket that complemented her hair, but she had thought, as she had brushed her hair into soft layers around her face, "You're looking good, girl." Now she realized it had been Hasty's voice she had heard.

He looked good, too, in white shorts and a sage polo shirt that made his eyes look a soft gray green, but she didn't say so. "To what do I owe the honor of your presence?" She offered him lemon and mint, which he took.

"I got home at noon and felt like a swim." He reached for a couple of cookies.

She grabbed one before he emptied the plate. "The university has a pool. Is it closed Mondays, or doesn't Emory give history professors pool privileges?"

"I like outdoor pools better."

She glanced out toward hers, which looked especially inviting in the hot afternoon sun, but the memory of a private swim with Hasty in June brought a flush to her cheeks and made her reluctant to try it again without others present. Pools can be very intimate places. "Has your apartment complex filled in their pool and made a flower garden?"

"No, they've filled it with little kids who pee in the water. Hell, Kate, can't I come see you when I get back to town without getting the third degree?"

Hasty was the only person in the world who called her Kate. It was a comforting reminder of her deceased parents and very happy high school years, so she hastened to smooth his ruffled quills. "Of course you can come see me. You are my oldest friend."

"Only two months older than you." He popped his second cookie into his mouth whole.

"You know what I mean."

A gleam in his eye told her he was about to remind her they had once been far more than friends. It was time to include his wife in the conversation. "You were going to bring Melissa and Kelly over. Have they ever come down?"

"No, I went up. And I can characterize the visit in two words: *endless hassles.*"

Although Hasty had been teaching at Emory for a year, his wife and fifteen-year-old daughter still lived in Michigan. His story was that Melissa was reluctant to leave her mother. Katharine was reserving judgment. She hadn't heard Melissa's version yet.

"Are they thinking about moving here?" She wondered if that was the right thing to ask. Wondered if she had any business to be asking at all.

"Not yet. Why didn't you answer my e-mails? I sent you several."

"I don't have a working computer yet."

"Oh." He reached for another cookie and took a big bite. "Yum! Lots of chips and pecans, just like I like them!"

She had forgotten that she began making those cookies to please Hasty. Tom had learned to like them that way after they started dating.

Beyond the window, a robin darted away from the birdbath followed by another. They swooped and darted, circling the yard, then returned to perch by the water.

Hasty stopped munching long enough to ask, "Have the police learned anything about your missing stuff?"

"Not so far." She didn't mean to sound pitiful, but she did.

He gave her a long, appraising look. "You used to always claim that things don't matter, only people matter. How does that play out now?"

She looked down at the table and blinked to keep tears from forming. Even so, her voice was gruff with them. "Not real well. I hadn't realized how many of my things were reminders of people who gave them to me—or special places where we've been."

Hasty reached over and put a hand over hers. "Those thugs didn't just destroy your home, did they? They violated your whole past."

How well he understood. Tears welled up in spite of her efforts. One spilled over and ran down her cheek. He lifted it off with a gentle finger. She turned her head aside and spoke fiercely to curb the rest. "I keep fearing I'll forget some person or place I used to think about every time I picked up a certain dish or wore a piece of jewelry. And I hate the thought that somebody has picked up Grandmother's silver service for a song."

He squeezed her hand. "That's hard. Are you sleeping okay?"

She pulled her hand away to pick up her tea, and took a long, cold swallow to cover her confusion. *You are not a teenager any more*, she reminded herself. *No need to get wobbly just because Hasty takes your hand or reads your mind. He's an intuitive, sympathetic kind of guy.* She would not tell him about the nightmares and could not lie to him, so she looked out the window and said nothing. The birds had returned to the birdbath, where they sat amiably side by side.

When she didn't answer, Hasty suggested, "Why don't you buy a blank book where you can list things you had and what they reminded you of? Then you can remember them whenever you want to." He took the last cookie and chewed it while she thought that over.

"I might. That would take up a heck of a lot less space than the stuff did."

He got up and headed toward the pig. "Hello, Chubs. You got any more goodies?" He took off the head, reached in, and took a handful, and repositioned the head so the snout was facing the outside door. "Guard the place, will you?" He put one hand experimentally through the empty shell of an upper cabinet door. "They broke all the glass?"

Katharine realized he hadn't seen the house since it was vandalized. "Most of it. The man is coming as soon as he works his way down his list to me."

He came back to the table, dropped a couple of cookies before her, and kept the rest. "Have you decided whether to refurnish the place or sell out and move into something smaller? You could, now that the kids are gone."

That changed her mood in a gnat's minute. "The kids aren't gone! Jon will only be in China for a couple of years and Susan comes home from New York every once in a while."

"For a visit, not to live." He took a large bite of cookie and spoke through it. "And who knows where Jon will go when he gets home? Face it—they are gone. You rattle around by yourself in this mausoleum most of the time, while Tom is up in Washington doing whatever he does all week. You've got—what? Five bedrooms here?"

She took a gulp of tea to hide her embarrassment. "Six."

"Six bedrooms upstairs and—" he paused to count silently on his fingers "—seven rooms down here, plus the utility room and more bathrooms than you can possibly use in a day. Not to mention how many acres of grounds?" He didn't really expect her to tell him. "All this for one woman, Kate? What would your parents say?"

That made her lips curve in a rueful grin. Hasty had known and liked her parents, who took their faith seriously enough to live by choice in a smaller house than they could afford and who often bought secondhand so they could give more to others. She had already told him what her mother—who grew up in Buckhead—said when she saw the big stone-and-slate house Katharine and Tom were buying: "Are you planning to open an orphanage?"

"My parents aren't around to complain." She set her glass down with a *click.* "And Tom grew up in and loves this neighborhood. We'll probably live here until we die."

She wouldn't give Hasty the satisfaction of telling him that the week after the break-in, she had begged Tom to sell the house and buy a condo down in Midtown, where she could walk to the theater, the art museum, the botanical gardens, and the symphony. Tom had replied, "I live in a condo all week, Kat. The only thing that keeps me going is the fact that on Friday I can get on a plane and come home to you and this house. It won't be long before all that mess is cleared up and things are back to normal. Besides, I'll be retiring before too long." Of course, "normal" for Tom didn't involve a house that was utterly empty five days out of seven, and except for talking about it frequently, he gave no sign that he planned to retire anytime soon. He loved his work and wouldn't be fifty for two more years. She figured he'd work at least ten or fifteen more—a long time for her to rattle around, as Hasty so elegantly put it, in their house alone.

She came out of her reverie to find him watching the robins, who were having a spat. One splashed the other with a wing. The aggrieved one flew away, circled, and dive-bombed, creating a minor tidal wave.

Hasty laughed as the aggressor flapped angrily away. "That'll larn 'er. "

"Or him. You're no ornithologist. You can't tell the difference any more than I can."

They fell easily into the bickering that used to heat up their high school days.

"Sure I can. The one who started it was clearly the female. There he was, having a pleasant little swim with somebody he liked when, wham! Smacked in the face by cold water."

"There she was, minding her own business, when he plopped down in her bathtub and started telling her what to do."

They glared at each other across the table until he grinned. "Truce?"

She smiled back. "Truce." It was an old, familiar ritual: fighting with Hasty and making up. Both had hot tempers but they quickly cooled. Neither was a seether.

He shoved back his chair and picked up his glass. "Want to show me what you've accomplished so far in getting this place back in order?"

Chapter 4

The worst of the chaos was gone, but his clenched fists and tight jaw showed how shocked he was at what he saw. He stood silent before the empty china cabinet with its missing dishes and shattered glass and whistled in dismay when he saw the slashed sofas and chairs that the upholsterers had not yet picked up.

"You're having to fix all this up by yourself?"

"Of course not. I'm hiring people to do most of the work, and Tom was here two weeks to oversee the initial phase, which involved a horde of workers, a fortune in trash bags, and a big blue roll-off container on the front lawn. But he had to get back to work, so since then I've been—you know." She gestured toward the rooms in their barren chaos and tried to seem nonchalant.

Hasty strolled over to the baby grand piano and lifted the keyboard cover. The finish had survived without a scratch, but when he played a quick scale, he frowned. "Some of the keys don't play."

"The men were looking for something, so they ripped out a few wires, strings—whatever they are."

He played several gapped chords, which jangled her nerves. "Getting it repaired is on my list. I just haven't gotten around to it." She didn't mean to sound defensive, but she'd lived all summer with Tom coming home every weekend and being surprised at how little progress had been made. *Just let them try to do it*, she fumed.

Hasty held up both hands. "Hey, I was just seeing how bad it is."

"Well, don't. I'm not real patient these days with people who wonder why it's taking me so long to get the house back in order."

He looked around and shrugged. "Looks pretty orderly to me. A bit patchy, maybe, but it's not as if you lived in the whole place."

Anger flared up inside her. "I still have to fix up the whole place." She strode around the room, waving her arms and saying the things she had been thinking for so many weeks. "People who don't have to live in this mess have no clue how long it takes to decorate and refurnish a whole house from scratch. I have to find people to plaster, paint, and paper, then I have to nag them until they show up. I have to be here when they come. I have to find people to recover or refinish all this furniture and be here when they come to pick it up. Simultaneously I have to be out in stores buying pillows, sheets, blankets, or mattresses to sleep on. And don't forget towels to dry on and dishes to eat on. Do you realize we didn't have a single cereal bowl when those gorillas were through?"

"Hey!" He held up a hand to stop her, but she wasn't finished.

"This very day I have devoted five hours—*five hours of my life!*—to buying lamps, and you have the temerity to stand there and ask whether I've gotten the piano repaired? Nobody but you even plays the damn thing anymore!"

Furious, she collapsed onto the couch, forgetting that all its cushions were stacked on the floor awaiting the upholsterer. She landed with a tooth-jarring thud.

Hasty slid onto to the piano bench and played a quick arpeggio. "Whew! If you have sunk to swearing, you must be upset. But it doesn't take five hours to buy lamps. You could have done it in two."

"If I bought them only to please myself. I have to think about what Tom will like."

"It's not me you are mad at, then, it's Tom. Tell him about it, not me." He bent over the keys and started playing something that sounded vaguely familiar. He looked over one shoulder and announced, "I call this 'Joplin Minus Certain Keys.'"

Only Hasty could make her feel like crying and laughing at the same time. She retrieved the top cushion from the stack and sat enjoying the odd, choppy music. Of course it was Tom she was mad at. She tried so hard not to bother him with domestic details when he was away, but she was everlastingly tired of trying to second-guess his preferences. She had trekked through half a dozen stores that day trying to figure out which lamps he would like, not because he was hard to please but because when he came home, he would look at each lamp and ask why she had chosen brass instead of pottery or pottery instead of something else, and whether she felt she had gotten the best price for each one.

He probably considered that "taking an interest in the home." To Katharine, it felt like she had to justify every decision she made. Why couldn't he just once come home and exclaim, "Great lamps, Kat! You've got excellent taste"?

Maybe because I've never told him how I feel, she thought as Hasty executed an especially tricky part of the Joplin. *Why should he know how much that frustrates me? I don't know what frustrates him anymore, either. Most of the time we live in totally different worlds. Maybe we ought to talk about that when he gets home.*

A wave of longing for her husband swept over her. How long had it been since they'd had a weekend when they didn't either drive up to the lake—which involved a round of drinks and get-togethers with various friends—or dash through a calendar crowded with things to do at home? How long had it been since they had simply lazed around with coffee and talked about things that mattered to each of them? *We've got to stop filling up our weekends,* she vowed. *We need space and time to do nothing together.*

Did Hasty sense her thinking about Tom? He broke off in the middle of a bar and swung around on the bench. "Have you even started on that room you were fixing up for yourself?" He got up and wandered across the foyer. She got up and followed to gloat over his surprise. "Wow! This is a major improvement."

"It is, isn't it?" She joined him and leaned against the doorjamb to admire the transformation she and Hollis had accomplished.

Formerly called "the music room," it used to be a gloomy mix of dark red and taupe inhabited by unread coffee table books, the seldom-touched baby grand, and a grumpy bust of Beethoven. In its new incarnation, soft peach walls echoed flowers in the Aubusson carpet that covered the oak floor. Sunlight streamed through wide wooden blinds at windows uncluttered by drapery. Mahogany bookshelves flanking the fireplace held her favorite books and a few treasures that had escaped the devastation. An old mahogany secretary glowed against the back wall. A new lateral filing cabinet sat opposite the fireplace next to her new mahogany desk with its green leather chair. The only discordant note was her new computer, sitting in boxes on the floor.

She was basking in the beauty of the room and Hasty's admiration when he spoiled it all by adding, "Now all you have to do is use it for something." He pointed to the computer. "You said you didn't have a computer. What do you call that?"

"I didn't say I didn't have a computer. I said I didn't have a working one. I haven't gotten around to hooking it up yet. But I will—soon." She didn't want him thinking that was a hint.

He nudged the rug with his toe. "They didn't steal this? It's a beauty."

"They stole the first one I bought. This is a replacement. Not quite as nice, but almost."

"Come on, Kate, you saw that other rug how many times—two? three? It was still rolled up when the break-in occurred, wasn't it?"

She gave him a wry grin. "Yeah, but I will forever remember it as the most perfect rug in the universe. It was the first thing I had bought in years to please nobody but myself."

"That's pathetic." He stepped back into the hall and looked into every room he could see from there. "So how long will it take one woman to completely refurbish a house this size?"

The challenge in his voice made Katharine bristle. "I told you, I'm not doing it alone. Tom and I talk a lot, and his niece Hollis—remember her?"

"The one with the degree from SCAD?"

"Yeah. She's been great at helping me choose fabrics and wallpaper, but we don't want to rush it."

He snorted. "Let me guess: she isn't content to pop into JCPenney—pardon me, Bloomingdale's or Neiman Marcus—and pick up the first curtains and bedspread she sees, right?"

"No," she admitted. "We traipse all over town scouring Atlanta for one-of-a-kind furniture, fabrics, and wallpaper to create what she calls 'a unique look.' We have also spent an indecent amount of time choosing dishes, glasses, pictures, rugs, and what few accessories I've bought. We devoted two hours to picking five sets of bathroom cups and soap dishes. Can you believe that?"

"I can believe it's possible. It's hard to envision you doing it."

"Follow me around for a few days," she said grimly. "Furnishing an entire house is an exhausting process, but it does have to be done. I just wish it didn't take so long. The only rooms that are pretty much finished so far are our bedroom, the kitchen, and my study."

He ambled back toward the kitchen door. "Which ought to tell you something."

When she reached the kitchen he was already at the fridge, refilling his glass. He asked over his shoulder, "Do you want more?"

"Make yourself at home, why don't you? But yeah—bring the whole jug." Even with the family gone, she still made tea in plastic milk jugs, a gallon at a time.

She padded back to the table barefoot and stretched out her legs. It was nice to have somebody waiting on her for a change. "What was that supposed to mean, 'Which ought to tell you something'?"

He dropped three cubes of ice in her glass with one hand and poured tea with the other. "The fact that you fixed up those three rooms first implies they are all you really need. Here you are, wasting your precious time and your excellent mind—"

She held up her glass in a mock salute. "Thank you, sir, for the compliment, even couched in insult."

"Come on, do you really enjoy spending days and days on such momentous decisions as—what? Stripes versus plaids?"

She gave a short, unfunny laugh. "Most recently, peach versus blue. Of course not. We both know I hate shopping, so don't make it any worse than it is. I've been doing it for weeks and weeks, and there's no end in sight. But at least I'm getting a break starting tomorrow. A friend and I are going down to the beach for a few days."

"Bully for you." He slid into the chair across from her again, slouched down in his seat, munched a cookie, and considered her with a thoughtful expression. "You know what your problem is?"

"I have a destroyed home."

"No, that's your situation. A problem is usually not the problem, it's what you do with the problem. Your problem—" he waved the cookie in her direction for emphasis "—is that you don't have a deadline. I see it all the time in my grad students. If they are running out of money or have to finish by a certain time—say they have a wife and kids to support, or there's a postdoc program they want to apply for—they buckle down and finish. Otherwise, the process drags on *ad infinitum*. If you had to have this house finished by a specific time, you wouldn't spend five hours buying lamps and you wouldn't let Hollis bully you into traipsing all over town looking for stuff. Folks always work better with a deadline." He picked up his tea like a man who has just had the last word.

"We're getting there," she snapped, furious. "These things take time. How dare you show up after a three-week vacation and tell me I'm not working fast enough?" To her mortification, she burst into tears.

Hasty left his seat and bent over her chair. "Oh, Katiebell." His breath was soft and warm in her hair and she felt the steady *thump thump* of his heart against her head. "I didn't mean to beat up on you. I came to make it all better by taking your mind off things for a little while. But look what I've done."

"It's not you." She sniffed and tried to stop her tears. "It's me. The whole time I'm shopping, I feel like I'm slogging through mud in cement boots. I don't know what the heck I'm doing all this for. I don't even know who cares. And I hate it!" She laid her head on her arms and sobbed.

He gently pulled her up and toward him, cradling her head with one hand while the other rubbed her back in long, gentle strokes. She sobbed out weeks of frustration.

Finally she gave a little hiccup. "I'm soaking your shirt."

"Good. It needed a wash. And you needed a hug."

It felt good to stand there with somebody else holding up the universe for a change.

It felt too good.

"Go get your bathing suit," he whispered, dropping his arms to circle her waist. "Let's swim."

She tingled all over.

Summoning every ounce of willpower she possessed, she pulled away, turned her back, and looked at her watch. "I can't. I've barely got time to dress before going out again."

"Nowhere you have to go would be better than this."

Behind her, Hasty put his hands on her shoulders and began squeezing gently. Outside, the pool still sent out its silent invitation. She knew what Hasty wanted. Was that what she wanted, too?

Of course it wasn't. What she wanted was for Tom to be standing there.

She shook her head. "I can't. One of our favorite artists is opening a show at a Midtown gallery. I need to see if she has anything we could use."

His hands grew still. "You're a dreadful liar," he whispered in her left ear. "You aren't convincing me at all."

"I need to go. I do."

He began massaging her shoulders again and spoke in rhythm. "Can't wait and browse the gallery another time? The event will collapse if you don't show up? Your walls will crumble if they don't get paintings before tomorrow?"

She laughed and broke free. "Yep. All of that is absolutely true."

He shook his head. "You know darned well that the only important thing about that opening is that it provides you with an excuse not to swim with me."

She felt a slow flush rise in her cheeks and silently cursed the genes that had given her auburn hair, white skin, and cheeks that blushed at the slightest provocation. Not that Hasty was such a slight one. He was darned attractive, and Tom was gone far too much.

She shoved back her hair and held it to her neck. "Sorry. If you had called to check, I could have saved you a trip."

He wiggled his eyebrows in his hopeless version of a leer. "Which might be why I didn't call. How about if I go home to change, then take you to dinner and the opening?"

She considered it for at least three seconds. She had to eat, and dinner and a gallery opening sounded harmless enough.

Nothing was harmless where Hasty was concerned. Not right now, when she was so tired and vulnerable.

"Not tonight, thanks. I'll see you out."

As they passed her study, he stepped into the room and peered down at her computer again. "You want us to hook this up right now?"

She was tempted, but that would just prolong his stay. "No, it will get done eventually. *Everything* will get done eventually."

"If you live so long." He turned at the front door. "*Au revoir, hasta luego*, and *auf wiedersehen*. All of which imply that you will be seeing me again. How about a swim tomorrow?"

"I told you—I'm going to the beach tomorrow."

"Which one?"

She remembered just in time that Hasty used to have a habit of showing up during her family's vacations on Marathon Key. Back then she had been thrilled. She didn't want that kind of complication now. "Just down to the coast, with a friend." In Atlanta, that could mean the Atlantic coast or the Gulf coast. They were pretty equidistant.

She stepped back into the house. "See you when I get back."

"When will that be?"

"Thursday afternoon, maybe."

He sketched a wave and headed to his Jeep.

She watched while he backed down the drive, and then she stood for a few minutes longer, enjoying the golden glow of the sun and picturing what might have happened if she had said yes. She saw herself pulling on her new yellow bathing suit, leading the way to the pool, slipping into the water beside him . . .

"It's a darned good thing I'm going to the beach," she told a mockingbird perched on a tea olive near her door. The mockingbird bobbed its head in agreement.

Still, every pore rebelled against returning to the vast, disheveled house behind her. The evening she had planned loomed in a stretch of utter boredom, while her alternative was to stay and work on equally unexciting projects such as hanging pictures or making decisions about upholstery fabric.

She took three deep cleansing breaths. They did have one benefit: they kept you from running screaming through the streets.

Chapter 5

Tuesday, Katherine woke with tears snailing in slimy tracks down her cheeks. One by one she replayed the tattered scenes lingering in her head. *The crunch of somebody grinding her Dresden ballerina underfoot. Splinters of light as the Waterford vase Posey brought her from Ireland crashed against a wall. Her beloved new rug being carried in a fat roll out the front door.*

She listened to the hammering of her heart. "It was only a nightmare," she muttered aloud. "I never really saw them smashing things."

She tried to summon strength to open her eyes. When she did, they met a blank space that used to hold a small landscape Tom had bought her in Greece. A deep, piercing cold penetrated her bones. Shivering in spite of the spread on her bed, she sat up and pounded the mattress with one fist. "Dammit!" she shouted. "This has got to stop!"

She slung back her covers, strode to the window, pulled the blinds all the way to the top, shoved up the window, and lifted her face to the pulsing heat of July. When her bones thawed, she showered and dressed in white capri pants, a lemon cotton shell, and a sheer big shirt decorated with gold, yellow, and turquoise geometric designs. Beach-going clothes.

"I will get over this," she vowed to her reflection as she

dabbed on a little concealer to cover her summer dusting of freckles.

She packed quickly, but before she could leave her room, she had to remove a chair from underneath her doorknob. "Silly," she told herself every night. "You sleep in a house with an excellent security system."

Yeah, a mocking voice invariably replied in her head, *and in spite of that, people got in twice this summer.*

It is not actual safety but the illusion of it that permits any of us to lie down in a hostile world and sleep each night. In the past few weeks, Katharine had accepted the fact that a chair under her doorknob was the only way she would get any sleep at all in the empty house.

"Hi-ho, hi-ho, it's to the beach we go," she caroled as she hefted her small bag in one hand, picked up her yellow sandals in the other, and headed downstairs in bare feet.

An hour later she opened Tom's end of the garage to let Dr. Flo park her five-year-old Volvo where his Lexus stayed the few nights a month it was home. It had not been hard to persuade Dr. Flo that Katharine's SUV would be more appropriate if they had to explore any off-road tracks.

While she loaded her bag, a few groceries, and a cooler into the back, Katharine conducted the conversation she always had with her father when she used the SUV. "See? This will be real practical for driving on back roads looking for a country cemetery."

Sure, her father replied, *but this is the first time you've ever taken it on any back roads, and a number of other vehicles would maneuver back roads equally well, consume less gas, and create less pollution. Most of them would also have saved you enough money to feed a family of four for a year. And hon? Tuck in a shovel. You might need it.*

"Tom bought the car," she muttered as she went to fetch the shovel.

"I beg your pardon?" Dr. Flo, pulling a wheeled suitcase and carrying a smaller cosmetics bag, gave Katharine a curious look.

Katharine flushed as she stowed the shovel and reached for Dr. Flo's case. "I was talking to my dad. He and Mother were big on saving the environment and taking care of the poor, so every time I drive this car, I feel I have to justify it to him, even though he's been dead fifteen years."

"I like it." Dr. Flo gave the shining finish a little pat then looked skyward. "It's real classy, sir."

"You look pretty classy yourself." Katharine cast an admiring look over the petite pantsuit of beige linen. With it, Dr. Flo wore a silk shell in a subdued beige, brown, and white print and tiny beige sandals with high heels. The last few times Katharine had seen her, the professor had favored flowing cotton skirts, cotton tops, and flip-flops. This looked more like the Dr. Flo Katharine had always known—except for her hair. The sleek chignon had been replaced by a short silver afro.

"Thank you." Dr. Flo brushed invisible lint from the jacket. "This is my lawyer-visiting outfit, but I'll swelter in this jacket if I have to wear it long. Isn't this heat amazing?" She dabbed at her forehead with an ecru lawn handkerchief trimmed with white lace. "I'm afraid I have more bags. Marcus always swore I take enough on weekend trips to stay a month, but I never know what I'm going to want."

She carried over a briefcase, a laptop computer, and a Neiman Marcus shopping bag, which she handed over with the caution, "Put that where it won't slide around. It's my grandmother's Bible. You won't believe what I have to tell you about that while we're on the road." She shrugged out of her jacket and set it, neatly folded, on the backseat before climbing into the front.

Once they were underway, Dr. Flo pulled a map from her briefcase. Glancing over, Katharine was surprised to see that her upper arms were flabby in the sleeveless shell. Articles about the Gadneys used to talk about their extensive collection of exercise machines and how they enjoyed exercising together before they left for work.

"Do you still exercise every morning?" she asked as she maneuvered the cloverleaf at Moore's Mill Road to get onto I-75 South.

"Not since Maurice died." Dr. Flo didn't look up from her map. "I got rid of the equipment."

"You shouldn't give up exercise just because he died." As soon as the words were out, Katharine caught her bottom lip between her teeth. Who was she, couch potato *extraordinaire*, to tell Dr. Flo what to do about exercise?

"I gave up a lot of things after Maurice died." The words were clipped and bitter. Apparently a year had not been enough to soften the blow of his unexpected heart attack.

Katharine changed the subject. "What were you going to tell me about your grandmother's Bible?"

That brightened Dr. Flo's gloomy mood. "Right after I talked to you, I went online and found an e-mail from a woman named Lila Perkins. She was responding to a message I had posted several weeks ago on ancestry.com, saying I was looking for information about Claude or Henry Gilbert. Lila had been clearing out her grandmother's things and had found a Bible listing both those names on its family page. She gave an Atlanta phone number, so I called right away. As soon as she started reading names from that page, I knew I'd found Daddy's mother's Bible."

"I thought your daddy was an only child." An only child herself, Katharine couldn't understand why something like that wouldn't have stayed in Dr. Flo's family.

"He was, but Grandmother Lucy had three half sisters by her daddy's first wife, and they never forgave her mother for outliving their daddy and inheriting what little he had. Even though Grandmother Lucy shared with all of them after her mother died, they always felt like she got more than her fair share. So when she died, her two living half sisters came in the house while Daddy was out making funeral arrangements and made off like bandits with things they claimed had belonged to their daddy. My father always believed one of them took his mama's Bible, but none of them would own up to it. Lila, the woman who called, turned out to be the granddaughter of Elouise, the eldest. I went right over yesterday afternoon to look at the Bible and took along samples of Grandmother Lucy's handwriting. As soon as Lila heard what had happened and saw the handwriting, she gave me the Bible. I cannot tell you the thrill it gave me to hold it. It used to stay in Grandmother Lucy's front room, and if I was very good, I was permitted to sit on the couch, hold it on my lap, and look at the pictures. I didn't care about the family page back then, but yesterday I discovered Grandmother Lucy carefully listed the birth and death dates of her parents and Granddaddy's birth and death dates, as well."

"But not his parents?"

"No, but in his father's space she had penciled in *Henri*, spelled with an *i,* and put a question mark after it."

"It's puzzling that she wouldn't know his parents' names."

"The Bible was a wedding present from her second husband. It was too late to ask Granddaddy by then." She smoothed her pants with one palm. "But now, just in time for this trip, I have my Claude Gilbert's birth and death dates. If they appear on Mr. Curtis's stone, I'll have found my grandfather's grave. I feel God must have a hand in whatever is going on."

Given everything else on the divine agenda, Katharine doubted whether God had much time to assist in genealogical research, but she would not burst Dr. Flo's bubble. "Could be," she agreed.

An hour later, spying a sign for a rest area ahead, she remembered she hadn't told Tom she was leaving town. He had attended a late function the night before, so they'd agreed on Sunday that he wouldn't call Monday night.

"I need to make a call. Do you mind if we stop for a minute?"

"You're asking a woman of seventy if she minds stopping by a bathroom? You've got a lot to learn, girl. I could use a drink of water, too."

"There are bottles of water on ice in the cooler. Let me open the back."

While Dr. Flo used the restroom, Katharine stayed in the car and called Tom's office. "Louise? It's Mrs. Murray. Is Tom in?"

"No, he's meeting with two senators this morning."

Louise was always eager to tell Katharine about important things Tom was doing. Katharine wished she were equally eager to inform Tom when his wife called. After leaving a message that she'd be down at Posey's Jekyll cottage for a couple of days, Katharine stressed, "It's real important that he get this message."

"Of course." Louise sounded huffy, but she hadn't promised a thing.

They didn't stop again until time to eat. Stiff and weary, Katharine climbed down and felt the heat hit her like a soft pillow. They hurried into the air conditioning. Katharine ordered a cheeseburger with two milks. Dr. Flo ordered a small salad and drank water.

"No wonder you're so thin," Katharine teased. "Do you have to watch your weight at all?"

"Not lately."

While they ate, Katharine began to worry about her companion. Dr. Flo used to be petite. Now, she looked gaunt. She and Dr. Maurice had been very close. Had she lost her will to live since his death? "Would you at least share a dessert with me?" Katharine urged when she'd finished her cheeseburger. "I'm ordering a hot fudge brownie with ice cream, but there's no way I can eat the whole thing."

Dr. Flo grinned. "Nobody ever knew me to turn down chocolate."

To Katharine's relief, when the dessert arrived and was halved, Dr. Flo cleaned her plate.

Chapter 6

Bright coastal sunlight and the bleached asphalt road were so hypnotic, Katharine felt she and her companion had been journeying forever and would never arrive.

"Do you think we've strayed into the Sleeping Beauty's woods?" she asked. Ever since they had left I-95 a few miles south of Savannah and taken U.S. 17, the primary view had been a dense forest of scrub oaks, sweet gums, and long-leaf pines, with bunchy palmettos along the ground. An occasional cabbage palm stood a stiff sentinel against the chaos.

The professor didn't answer. She was consulting directions written in a small notebook.

Katharine blinked to moisten her eyes. Her lids were heavy, her mind a spongy blur. She concentrated on reaching the next set of heat puddle mirages in the middle of the long straight road and tried not to doze off. "What are we looking for?"

"A filling station. I think that's it coming up on the left. The lawyer said it's easy to miss, and I can see why. What a dreary little place. We turn left right after it."

Not much more than a white box with a flat roof, the store's purpose was identified by two ancient gas pumps and a once-red sign above the door: STAMPERS. No apostrophe denoted possession. Was that an oversight? Or a deliberate attempt not to claim the place?

"Do you mind if we make another stop?" Katharine asked.

"I need a Coke and probably ought to gas up. How far out to the island?"

"Ten more miles." Dr. Flo looked dubiously at the shabby concrete building. "That place looks older than I am."

"They might have a cold drink."

"Don't get your hopes up."

Katharine laughed. "It's your hopes that brought us here, remember? I'm just along for the ride. Maybe somebody in there can tell you about the island."

Dr. Flo brightened. "I'll bet they can."

Their tires crunched onto crushed shells over sand that sufficed as a parking lot. The only other vehicle was a decrepit black Ford pickup parked at the front door. The two gas pumps were too old to take credit cards, but the prices displayed were certainly up-to-date. Katharine pulled to a stop beside one.

Dr. Flo reached for her purse. "I'll get the gas."

Katharine had expected that, since it was Dr. Flo's trip, but she didn't think a woman of seventy should be pumping gas in that heat. "I'll pump, you pay. Go on in and give them ten dollars. I'll just get enough to get us down the road. Prices will have to be lower than this."

Dr. Flo didn't budge. "I'll wait and go inside when you do. You never know how welcome a black woman will be in this part of Georgia."

"Most of the people we've seen so far are black," Katharine pointed out.

"Still . . ." Dr. Flo pursed her lips and said no more.

Katharine opened the door, and a blast of heat bulged like a wave into the car. As she climbed out, mosquitoes whined to meet her. She pumped the gas and would have washed the windshield if there had been water or a squeegee. "Oh, well," she philosophized. "There will be a thousand more bugs smeared on it before we get out of here."

When she had finished, they went inside. The shelves

were sparsely furnished, and the place smelled of decades of bare feet on a cement floor, tobacco, day-old bread, and candy. There was no air conditioning, only two ceiling fans that stirred the air like mush.

At the far end of the center aisle, an open door led into an unlit room. An elderly man stood halfway down the aisle calling toward that doorway, "You might as well come out, Miranda. I know you're in there. And you know what I got to have. Come on out, now. Don't be like this." His skin was the soft dusty brown of pecan shells, his hair a mass of close-clipped gray curls.

When he heard the screened door slam behind the women he gave them a polite "Howdy, ladies," then raised his voice again. "You got other customers out here, sugah, wantin' to pay for gas and maybe looking to buy sump'n. Come on out."

Katharine headed to an old-fashioned Coke box near the door, the kind that had ice inside to cool the drinks. More than half the ice had melted. When she reached in to pull out a can, the water gave her wrist a shock that shot up her arm into an instant headache. Blinking back pain, she let the Coke slide into the ice again and turned toward a small assortment of snacks. There wasn't much to choose from except peanuts, beef jerky, and banana Moon Pies.

Katharine only ate chocolate Moon Pies.

"Are you sure there's somebody here?" Dr. Flo was asking the old man.

"She's in there, all right. She just don't want to talk to me. Miranda!" he called. "Git yourself out here, girl. You got customers."

"Hello?" Dr. Flo called. "Anybody here?"

"Be rat with you," a resigned voice called from the darkness.

In another second, an angel floated down the aisle. At least, that was Katharine's first impression. On nearer inspection, she turned out to be a girl in her midteens with yellow-white hair falling straight from a center part to her waist, hiding most of her face. The angelic effect was enhanced by a dingy white jersey sundress that brushed electric-green flip-flops, but her first words planted her firmly on earth. "Kin I he'p you?" She swiped her hair over her shoulders and tucked it behind both ears, revealing a narrow, pointy face and eyes like pale green water.

"We want a Coke and a candy bar," Katharine told her. "Don't you carry candy?"

"Got Snickers and Hershey bars in the fridge." The girl jerked her head toward an old refrigerator near the door. "Otherwise they'd melt." She returned her attention to the old man. "You know I'm not supposed to sell to you. Git on out, now."

"What am I supposed to say when I get back without it? You know how things is, chile. I's gonna ketch what-fer."

She shook her head and firmed her lips. He shrugged and shuffled out like he hadn't really expected to be served.

Katharine was appalled. She wanted to shake the girl until her teeth rattled. Instead she asked, when the girl looked her way again, "Do you have a restroom?"

"In back." The girl nodded in that direction. "It's clean," she added defensively as Katharine hesitated.

Katharine was embarrassed and annoyed, for she had been wondering that very thing. A door in one corner of the storeroom bore a cheap gold and black sign: LADIES. There was no corresponding door for the other sex. After the dark storeroom, Katharine was pleasantly surprised to find white walls, a cheerful green floor, and a window with a yellow blind. The floor looked recently mopped, and while the fixtures were old and rusty from minerals in the water, they were polished to a soft glow.

She returned to the front to find that the ban on serving blacks only applied to locals. Dr. Flo was sipping a Sprite and chatting with the girl, who leaned, propped up by one elbow, on the register side of the counter.

"Katharine Murray, Miranda Stampers. Miranda's been telling me about Bayard Island." Dr. Flo's eyes sparkled. "Her grandmother runs a seafood business there and used to live on the island, but only two households live there now: the Bayard family and a Miss Agnes Morrison."

"That's right. You want a Coke and a cold candy bar? Just help yourself." The girl nodded toward the refrigerator and the cooler. Self service seemed to be standard at Stampers.

Katherine retrieved a drink from the icy water and took a Snickers from the fridge. "How much?"

When Miranda answered without having to think, and made change without calculation, Katharine figured that must be her most common sale. Did her family actually make money in this crummy store? If so, most of their income must be derived from various lotteries, which had colorful signs behind the register. A Georgia Lottery neon sign—a soft pink peach with bright green leaves in a purple square—was lit in the front window even in the middle of the day.

Winning the lottery was the only, if unlikely, hope most nearby residents had of ever breaking out of poverty.

Katharine peeled her candy and considered the chunk of hard chocolate, caramel, and nougat. It looked capable of pulling out every filling in her head. To let it thaw, she asked, "So you used to live on the island?"

"Not me, my granny. She had to move after lightning struck the trailer. Leastways that's what Mr. Dalt claims. Granny thinks he torched it, but nobody'd ever convict him."

Dr. Flo looked properly shocked. "Why should anybody burn down her trailer?"

Miranda gave an elaborate shrug. "Wanting to drive her out. Mr. Dalt don't want nobody but Bayards on that island.

He keeps pestering her to sell him her land and the business, but Granny ain't gonna sell. The judge gave her that land, and Mr. Dalt and Mr. Burch can't do a thing about it." She lifted her chin and dared them to disagree.

"Who are Dalt and Burch?" Katharine was irritated by the way Miranda flung names around like everybody knew whom she meant.

"Dalt Bayard and his son. It was Mr. Dalt's daddy who gave Granny the land to start up her seafood business."

Katharine took her first bite of cold Snickers and wondered what Granny had given in exchange.

Dr. Flo's attention was still on the fire. "But would he really burn down somebody's house?"

Miranda shrugged again. Katharine suspected she practiced in the mirror. "Sure he would. He's the meanest son of a bitch . . . oh! here's Granny now."

Katharine's was no longer the only Cadillac in the parking lot, but hers was a mere child compared to the red convertible with windswept fins that crunched over the shells outside and parked near a corner of the store. It was too well acquainted with salt air to have kept its sheen, but its white leather seats gleamed.

Its top was down, giving a good view of a woman so brown and weathered, she could have been any age between fifty and seventy. When she climbed out, though, brief white shorts and a tight red cotton shirt displayed a figure that was still stunning. Her hair—as close to the color of Miranda's as a bottle could make it—was piled high on her head and fell in a cascade of curls, and she must have risen early that morning to apply so much makeup. Katharine was willing to bet good money that "granny" was not the way this woman introduced herself to men.

Without glancing inside, she went around to the trunk, hefted out a case of beer, set it on the ground, and reached for another. Her shoes were sensible white running shoes, worn without socks.

Miranda gave her a cursory glance, propped her elbow on the counter again and resumed her gossip. "Mr. Burch, now, he ain't too bad, 'cepting he wants to cover the whole blamed island with huge houses. Have you seen what developers have done over on Shellman's Bluff?"

Katharine and Dr. Flo shook their heads in unison, having no idea where Shellman's Bluff might be. By silent agreement they voted not to mention the reason they were there.

Miranda prattled on, heedless of her grandmother heaving cases of beer like a dock worker. "Shellman's Bluff used to be a lot like Bayard Island—not much there. But now it's full of big old subdivisions of great big houses, it has a golf course, a club house—all sorts of fancy stuff. Hilton Head and places up around Savannah have got too crowded, but they's still a passel of Yankees wanting a place to retire where it's warmer and cheaper than up north, so now developers are buying up land around here, bulldozing all the trees, and putting up mansions. I love the marshes and can see why some folks want to live on them, but they're asking more for them houses than folks around here are like to see in a lifetime. When they cover one island, they move to the next. Pretty soon there won't be any place around here where folks like us can afford to live. God only knows what will happen to the fishermen."

The way Miranda rolled those facts and opinions out of her mouth, Katharine could tell she was parroting grown-ups.

Speaking of grownups, the girl's grandmother was now lugging beer around the building. "Do you need to help her carry that?" Katharine asked.

Miranda shrugged. "She can git it. I'm minding the register. You wanting anything else?"

Dr. Flo headed for the refrigerator. "I might take one of those Hershey bars."

Katharine tugged off another chunk of her hard, cold Snickers and let Dr. Flo carry the conversation. "You say that Burch Bayard is interested in developing Bayard island?"

"He's interested in getting money." Miranda's hair had fallen over her shoulders again, so she shoved it back with careless grace. "Mr. Burch 'n' Miss Mona both want to live rich, but they have already run through what her daddy give her—or so Chase says. Chase is Burch's son." She added that with a careless wave that made Katharine suspect Miss Miranda was rather fond of the young man. "He lives in Savannah most of the time and goes to a private school. He'd be perfectly happy going with normal folks, but his parents want him going to that prep school." She said the last two words in the tone Katharine might have used for *reformatory.* "And then they want him to go to college and learn how to handle the fortune his daddy plans on making building houses."

"He'd do better to learn how to be a lawyer and keep his daddy and granddaddy out of jail." The voice floated from the back of the store, raspy from a lifetime of liquor and cigarettes. "Granny" (Katharine could only think of her that way in quotes) set down a case between the aisles and strode toward them. "You all got everything you need?"

"Miranda's been taking care of us," Dr. Flo assured her.

"Talking your ears off is more like it." She gave a throaty chuckle, and her eyes—the same seagreen as her granddaughter's—darted to Miranda. "Well, I need to get this beer in the cooler."

"Cooter was in here wanting some, but I didn't sell him any," Miranda reported.

"Good for you." Without another word she headed to the back corner.

Miranda waited until she was busy, and then tossed her head again, sending that incredibly light hair cascading around her thin white shoulders. "I was fixing to tell you about Chase's animals. He carves the most beautiful little things. That's what he'd rather be doing than go to school. Look." She reached beneath the counter and brought out a raccoon four inches long, carved of light golden wood. "Isn't that the most precious thing you ever saw?"

Katharine picked it up, noticing that Miranda's palm wasn't as clean as the restroom. "It's wonderful," she agreed.

She handed it to Dr. Flo, who exclaimed, "What an imp behind his mask! And I like the way the tail is slightly curved, as if he's tensing himself to run. Very lively." She handed it back.

More pleased with Dr. Flo's critique than with Katharine's, Miranda addressed herself exclusively to the professor. "Everything Chase makes seems like it's alive, which is strange, because he carves them from dead animals. Everybody in his family is real big into hunting, even his mama, so Chase has grown up shooting, but he don't like to kill things. He hunts some, but he's not a good shot like his daddy."

"His granddaddy is better," called the voice from the back. "Even drunk he can hit a half-dollar on a fence and git a squirrel through the eye."

Katharine was so busy trying to picture somebody doing those two things simultaneously, she missed Miranda's next words. She tuned back in at ". . . brings the animals back to his workshop and carves them. See how real he got the fur?" She stroked the little raccoon.

The moony look on her face strengthened Katharine's suspicion that it wasn't the raccoon she was thinking about.

"One day Chase is gonna tell his daddy he'd rather carve

wood than run a family business," she said with the conviction of youth that anything is possible.

That drew a sarcastic laugh from the back. "Don't hold your breath. When his daddy says, 'Jump!' the only thing Chase asks is 'How soon? How high?'"

Miranda tilted her chin and called in rebuttal, "He's gonna show his folks he can make a living carving wood. He's gonna take some to a craft fair up in Savannah and sell them. Then they'll see. You'll all see. He's gonna make so much money, they won't have to ruin the island."

"Somebody will see, all right. Burch is gonna build those houses and Chase is gonna grow up to be just like him. Only hope of saving that island is if Dalt gets his way." She paused and added as if to herself, "God help me, I never thought I'd hear myself saying that." The woman slammed the cooler case and headed to the back of the store, shutting the door to the storeroom behind her.

"All Mr. Dalt cares about anymore is finding his next drink," Miranda muttered to the grandmother who wasn't there. She turned back to her customers. "You seen that old man who was in here just now?" She scarcely waited for their nods. "That's Cooter Biggins. He lives with the Bayards and works for Dalt. He comes in here sometimes while Granny's down at the dock, wanting me to sell him beer. He knows I cain't do that."

"Of course not. You're too young." Katharine hoped that was the reason, and not, as she had feared earlier, an aversion to selling to local blacks.

Miranda's eyes narrowed and took on a wary look. "You from the police?"

"Heavens, no."

"Well, I sell a little beer sometimes if Granny's not here, but the only reason Cooter wants it is for Dalt. That man would drink twenty-four-seven if Burch and Mona would let him. But they've told Granny if we sell him any, they'll take her seafood-business license. They would, too. The whole family is spiteful that way—excepting Chase." She picked up the raccoon and stroked it gently.

Dr. Flo finished her drink. "Well, we've got an errand to run. It's been nice talking to you."

"Nice talking to you, too. Y'all come back now. And watch out for Miss Agnes, y'hear? You don't want to get on the wrong side her. She'd as soon shoot you as spit."

Chapter 7

After they left Stampers, the roads got progressively smaller and whiter with age, until they were down to a shimmering lane barely wide enough for two cars. It had no line down the center and was bordered by knee-high grass to the edge of the forest on both sides.

Dr. Flo peered down the side of the car. "Don't drive off the edge. I'd guess there are snakes in that grass, and I don't care to make their acquaintance." She peered at the encroaching forest. "It's funny to think Daddy's folks may have once lived here. I'd guess this used to be a rice plantation, wouldn't you?"

"Looks like a barren wilderness to me. It would be brave people who made anything out of this."

"Or slaves. They'd have had a ghastly existence in this heat with all these bugs. But Daddy always insisted his people were never slaves. I can't imagine why they'd have been here. Of course, he also claimed we once had a pirate in the family. Anytime I had a tantrum as a child, he'd roll his eyes and say, 'There's that pirate temper again. Came down in her genes.'"

Katharine had a hard time picturing Dr. Flo as a little girl, much less one with a temper. "Maybe you had a relative in Blackbeard's crew. They sailed up and down this coast."

"I doubt we'll ever know." Dr. Flo rolled down her window to let out a fly that had bummed a ride back at

Stampers. "The only problem with getting bit by the genealogy bug is that you wind up with irritating loose ends and have to face the fact that some of them will never get tied up neatly. How are you coming with research on your family?"

Katharine rubbed her eyes, which again were as gritty as the side of the road. "Not at all, so far. My house got trashed last month, remember? And my computer was stolen. I finally got a new computer last week, but I haven't gotten it hooked up yet. I hope by fall things will have calmed down enough for me to get on to genealogy."

"When you do, you are going to wish you had asked your folks a lot more questions before they died. Look! That must be the church the lawyer mentioned, just before the bridge."

Katharine read the sign in disbelief. "The Church of God Reappearing?"

"That's the one. Where do they get these names?"

Katharine was too busy avoiding a snake slithering across the road to hazard a guess.

Dr. Flo shuddered. "I knew there'd be snakes. This place isn't civilized. But we're close. After the bridge, we go half a mile, then turn right at the twenty-miles-an-hour sign."

They crossed a bridge so short it scarcely deserved the name. A faded sign announced BAYARD ISLAND. "We found it," Dr. Flo said with satisfaction.

Immediately over the bridge was a sign much larger than the first: PRIVATE PROPERTY. NO TRESPASSING. Smaller versions of that sign were posted on a number of trees on both sides of the road as they continued to drive.

"This is a public road, right?" Dr. Flo wore a worried frown.

"I sure hope so." When they saw a dented black mailbox next to a sandy track leading into the woods, Katharine slowed. "Could this be the road?"

"No. Mr. Curtis specifically said to turn at the twenty-miles-an-hour sign. I haven't seen one of those. Wait—there it is. The road is just beyond it."

"Road?" Katharine looked in vain for anything more deserving of the name than two ruts of sand centered by a strip of scruffy grass. She also was not thrilled to see another large NO TRESPASSING sign at the entrance to the track.

Dr. Flo peered into the sky. "Hey, Katharine's daddy, it's real good she has an SUV."

Katharine swung the wheel and felt the back fishtail in sand. The forest grew so close on each side, scrub trees seemed eager to climb in with them. Branches scraped her doors and fenders. "Tom will not be happy if I scratch this car."

"Honey, a man who buys a car designed for rough terrain cannot complain about a few scratches to his paint. You tell him I said so."

"I'll do that."

Katharine's eyes were having trouble adjusting to the constant switch from filtered light under trees to bright patches between them. "Did the lawyer say how far it was?"

"No, but I'd have thought we'd be there by now." Worry puckered Dr. Flo's brow. "You reckon we took the wrong road?"

"There wasn't another one."

As they rounded the next curve, Katharine slammed on the brakes. A man and a boy stood smack in the middle of the track. Each had a gun on his shoulder. Two squirrels dangled by their tails from the boy's free hand.

Every mother thinks her child is beautiful, but this child's mother had reason to know so. Dappled by sunlight, his skin was unblemished and lightly tanned. Thick blond hair was tucked behind his ears and fell to his shoulders. He had wide cheekbones and a rounded chin, and beneath a high forehead, his eyes were a startling blue that looked like chips of sapphire. As young as he was—fourteen or fifteen at the most—he was sensual, dressed for the woods in a long-sleeved khaki shirt, jeans, and thick boots with a sheen of sweat on his face and at the base of his neck. He had to be the Bayard boy. No wonder Miranda was goofy over him.

The other must be Dalton Bayard, Katharine concluded. He and the boy could pose for bookend shots entitled "Before and After Sixty-five Years of Dissipation." Dalton's hair was still thick, but it had faded from yellow to white and hung in greasy strings over his face. He had eyes of the same surprising blue, but his were bloodshot. A road map of red veins marked his nose and upper cheeks. Evidence of past meals dotted the front of his blue chambray shirt. His boots and gray work pants were muddy and stained. Several days' stubble frosted his jaw. But his stance was arrogant as he stood challenging them to explain their presence in his hunting grounds.

When Katharine rolled down the window, the scent of his unwashed body roiled into the car. She tried not to inhale as she asked, "Do you know if there's a cemetery down this road? We're looking for a small family cemetery."

Dalton peered in and narrowed his eyes. When he opened his mouth to speak, what few teeth he had left were the soft gold of rotten apple flesh, stained by coffee, tobacco, and neglect. "Why do you want to know?" His tone was malevolent.

Katharine drew back and found she didn't want to tell him. "Just to look at it."

He looked from one to the other, his head bobbing slightly—a snake choosing between potential victims. "Did you all come from Atlanta in answer to the ad?"

"Well, yes," Katharine admitted.

He looked past her and locked his eyes on Dr. Flo. "You think you got relatives buried down here on this island?"

Dr. Flo spoke across Katharine. "I might have."

He looked at her for what seemed like several minutes

without saying a word. Katharine had the feeling he was putting something through his sluggish mental computer and waiting for results. Finally he waved one hand and spoke in the tone of one repelling a cur. "Go on back where you came from. You got no bidness down here. Go on home, now. You hear me? Go on!"

The boy looked from the old man to the women in the car. Curiosity and surprise flitted across his face in equal parts. He muttered, "Daddy needs those graves moved."

"Your daddy needs his head examined is what he needs. He sure doesn't need to stir up all this mess. You ladies go on home. You can turn around down past the bend, then you come right back out, you hear me? Don't you go messing around where you aren't wanted. Go on, git!" He slapped the car's fender like it was the flank of a horse.

Past the bend they entered a clearing guarded by ancient live oaks with wide, low branches, broad trunks, and a thick crop of hoary Spanish moss. Katharine pulled to a stop near one oak to take her bearings. Even crabgrass grew sparsely there, with sand showing through like a balding man's scalp. In the center, where the sun was brightest, ruins indicated the foundations of a small building. From what was left, Katharine deduced it had been built of tabby—a Low Country construction material made of lime, sand, and oyster shells. On the far side of the clearing a rusting wrought-iron fence marked a square in the wilderness, ringed by cedars so old that their limbs were scrawny and the Spanish moss in their branches flapped like long gray beards. A broad slough flowed at the edge of the dry land, then marshes stretched for miles, brown from the summer sun. Hammocks on the horizon looked like ranges of hills.

Katharine caught her breath in wonder. "No wonder developers want to get their hands on this land. People would pay a fortune to have this view."

Dr. Flo was busy replacing her dainty sandals with beige

walking shoes. "You'd better not be one of them. You'd wake up every morning hearing your daddy saying, 'What you needing that expensive house for, shug?' But if we are finished admiring the scenery and second-guessing dead men, are you ready to roll?" She tied her second shoe and opened her door.

"You're okay to get out even after what he said?"

"Of course. The lawyer told us to come."

"Let me drive closer, then."

Dr. Flo slid to the ground. "You can't drive over that ruin, and at least the grass is short enough to see a snake. I'd guess that's the cemetery, wouldn't you?" She pointed to the fence. "I can use exercise after all that riding." She took her notebook and pen, but left her briefcase and purse in the car. "They ought to be safe here, don't you think?" She headed across the clearing.

Katharine cut the motor and opened her door. As heat rolled over her like a wave, she reached in the backseat for a wide-brimmed straw hat she used for gardening. Settling it on her head, she climbed out into a patch of soft sand. "Yuck!" Grit slid and shifted beneath her soles and a sandspur got lodged under her little toe.

"The mosquitoes are terrible," Dr. Flo called, picking her way through the grass and slapping her bare arms and the back of her neck. "We should have brought bug spray."

Katharine pulled out the sandspur and winced. "I should never have worn sandals. They are already full of sand. I'd go barefoot if there weren't so many sandspurs."

"You can wash later. Come on." Dr. Flo was nearly at the fence.

Katharine trudged across the grass. The crabgrass was laced with other grass—both the kind that grows sandspurs and the variety with small saws on each blade. They clutched and scratched her bare calves and ankles. She yearned for long pants and socks.

"This place gives me the willies." Dr. Flo put both hands on her hips and peered out at the trees that ringed the clearing, hung with trailing vines and moss.

Now that Katharine looked closer, the forest there was mostly sycamores and cedars, with a few cabbage palms and clumps of towering long-leaf pines hung with fat cones. The nine live oaks—she turned in a circle and counted them—must have been planted to mark the edges of the clearing. She slapped one cheek and waved away a swarm of mosquitoes around her head. "We'll be lucky to get out of here alive."

The silence of the place and its utter isolation were making her uneasy, too. She had a sense that something brooded in the shadows around the clearing, waiting to pounce. The live oaks guarded the secrets of whatever once stood on those desolate foundations, and no birds sang on their limbs. When Katharine listened, she didn't hear a single sound except the shrill warnings of cicadas, the slip of her shoes in the sand, and the high whine of mosquitoes. The back of her neck prickled, as if they were being watched, but although she looked, she saw nothing but sand, grass, and trees to her left and marshes stretching for miles to her right.

She trudged another couple of steps, then whirled. From the corner of her eye she thought she saw a scrap of blue duck back into the green dimness. Were the old man and boy keeping an eye on them? "Probably making sure we aren't stealing tombstones," she said aloud to reassure herself.

She was answered only by the scream of a gull, high in the sky.

She joined Dr. Flo near the wrought-iron fence, which was rusty and ornamented by lichens: chartreuse, forest green, and a flat green that reminded her of elementary school bathrooms. She found the small collection of graves both pathetic and disturbing. Most lay within the railing but four Morrisons had been buried outside, to the right of the gate. They were parents, a son, and a daughter-in-law. All had been buried in the twentieth century. The daughter-in-law had only been dead fifteen years.

"Let's get this over with," Dr. Flo said briskly. "This air is humid enough to choke us, and it's a tossup whether we'll die first from malaria or heat prostration."

Katharine scanned the sky, which was almost white with the heat. "Feels like we're building up to a storm, but the only clouds are those little ones away out over the ocean."

Dr. Flo wiped her forehead with one forearm. "Grandmother Lucy would have said, 'It's missing a real good chance to rain.'"

She pushed open the rusty gate with a creak worthy of a horror movie. Katharine tried not to shudder as she followed slowly into the little fenced plot, but as she entered the gate, the hair prickled again at the back of her neck. She turned and peered back at the forest, certain somebody was watching them. Again she thought she saw a flash of blue.

She stared harder, but nothing moved until a jay swooped down from a pine tree and perched on the lowest branch of the sentinel cedar that guarded the gate.

She gave a nervous chuckle. "Silly," she chided herself. "Scared of a blue jay."

Putting her fears into words made her feel better. So did Dr. Flo, who looked very professorial as she exchanged her sunglasses for reading glasses with gold rims. She perched them on the end of her nose, opened her little notebook, and clicked her pen to lower the point.

"Let's start at the front and work back. You take that side, I'll take this one, and we'll meet at the big slab at the far back in the middle. We are looking for Claude Gilbert."

Katharine began to roam, reading inscriptions. Some graves were marked by small stones and some by obelisks three or four feet high. Three had slabs of concrete that covered the entire grave. Two of those rested on tabby foundations, but one was elevated on brick pilings fifteen inches above the ground. She could understand the tabby foundations if the water table was so high it was impossible to dig deep without hitting water. The slab on pilings baffled her, for she could look all the way under it, like under a magician's table.

The slabs held not only the names and dates of the deceased, but messages of love and grief:

LEAVING A WIFE AND CHILDREN TO MOURN HIS PASSING
HER FRIENDS WILL SORELY MISS HER
ONE OF PURE SPIRIT, BELOVED OF THE LORD

The stones and obelisks sat askew in the soft sand. Those made of concrete or tabby had been worn by years of sun, sand, wind, and subtropical storms until they were spotted, pitted, and difficult to read. All were half-hidden by knee-high grass and weeds dotted with wild flowers. They were the only spots of color in that forlorn place: red, white, orange, and yellow.

Who were these people who had lived and been laid to rest without anybody to tend their graves? The only surname she saw inside the fence was BAYARD. All had been buried before nineteen hundred.

Who were the Morrisons, then, who lay outside the fence? Outcasts? Distant relatives? A newer branch of the family who died after the fenced yard was full?

She bent and tugged a handful of grass away from the stone of a child who had lived less than a year, then stood erect to peer across the clearing again. "I wonder what this clearing was for. A house, do you reckon?"

Dr. Flo swatted another mosquito and glanced toward the ruin. "It's small for a house. I don't see anybody but Bayards here, do you?"

"And the four Morrisons, outside."

Dr. Flo bent to peer down at another stone. "This one is so worn, I can't read it. How could anybody identify the person to find the next of kin? But since they all seem to be one family, I guess that won't matter. I can't imagine why my people would be buried here, though. We never had Bayards in our family, that I ever heard of."

Katharine paused at the stone commemorating Marianne Bayard, who had died at sixteen. "So many dead children."A picture of Susan in high school—dark and glowing after a soccer game or before a prom—rose in her mind. "Dear God, protect her and Jon," she whispered to the breeze.

Dr. Flo smacked another mosquito. "It's a wonder any children survived, with all these bugs. I've finished my side, have you?"

Katharine joined her at the slab at the back. It was the largest of all and, because it was marble, its carving was still crisp. Foot-high letters at one end read, predictably, BAYARD. Below were carved two memorials:

TO THE MEMORY OF
FRANCIS HAMILTON BAYARD
BELOVED HUSBAND AND FATHER
BORN 1818
DIED 1870
REQUIESCAT IN PACE

IN MEMORY OF
ELIZABETH MALLERY BAYARD
MOTHER OF CLAUDE
AND WIFE OF FRANCIS
WHO DIED IN THIS PLACE
1892

Dr. Flo copied both inscriptions into her notebook. "Probably not important, but at least here's a Claude mentioned. I haven't seen Claude Bayard, have you?"

"I think so. " Katharine wandered back up her side of the cemetery. "Here. He's buried beside his wife, who died years before he did."

Dr. Flo shaded her eyes to peer across the entire plot. "But where could Claude Gilbert and his companions be?"

As Katharine joined her, she saw a smaller plot behind the first. "Maybe there?" Four graves lay inside a small square. One side was the iron fence. The other three were enclosed by a tabby wall two feet high.

"There he is!" Dr. Flo leaned over the railing and read the stone for Claude Gilbert, carved from fine marble:

CLAUDE GILBERT
JUNE 18, 1869–JANUARY 15, 1903
DEAR HUSBAND AND FATHER

Beside it, a small marble marker sagged sideways. It read, simply,

MARIE GUILBERT
1825–1889

A second small marble stone lay on its back near the wrought iron fence. It read

FRANÇOISE GUILBERT
1871–1878
ANGELS, HOLD HER CLOSE

Katherine felt a catch in her throat as she subtracted. Seven years old and forgotten under all this sand. Yet someone had once cared enough to pay for a marble stone. She stretched one hand through the railings to stroke it. "Who do you reckon she was?"

Dr. Flo was busy flipping back a couple of pages in her

notebook and comparing what was written there with the tombstone for Claude Gilbert. "This has to be Daddy's father. The dates are exactly right. I wonder who the others were. Wouldn't you think it was the same family, in spite of the difference in spelling?"

"Most likely. I wonder who lies under that." Katharine pointed to the fourth grave, which was nearest the marsh and marked by a waist-high marble obelisk on a small square base. Either it had sunk or the sand had blown against it, for it sat so deep that only the tops of letters were visible on its base.

Dr. Flo went out of the fenced cemetery, circled it, stepped over the tabby wall, and bent to examine the obelisk. "I can't read it, but I don't think it's either Guilbert"—Katharine noted with amusement that she had settled on the *Geel-bear* pronunciation— "or Bayard. The first letter is too spiky to be a *g* or a *b*. " She stepped around the obelisk to check the far side, then gave a little cry of surprise. "Oh, my! Come look!"

Her voice was so urgent, Katharine hurried to join her. With one slender forefinger, Dr. Flo traced a faint carving on the obelisk face that looked toward the marsh. As her finger moved around it, Katharine gasped.

Dr. Flo stood up and brushed off her fingers. "I think we've found daddy's pirate. Doesn't that look like a skull and crossed bones to you?"

Chapter 8

Katharine turned toward the gate. "Let's dig a little and see if we can read the name."

She pulled the shovel from the back of the SUV with a quick "Thanks, Dad."

A man spoke behind her. "May I help you with that?"

She jumped, feeling as guilty as if she'd been caught digging up endangered plants in a national park.

"Burch Bayard, ma'am." He lifted a Panama hat with a red band. "Didn't mean to startle you." She didn't believe that for a moment. His eyes were lit with amusement, and if he hadn't wanted to startle her he would have called before he approached. Still, his voice was all courtesy.

She would have known without the introduction that he was the middle generation of Bayards. In him, the family's good looks and breeding had reached their pinnacle. Everything from the logos on his white running shoes, yellow polo shirt, and khaki Bermuda shorts to his well-cut golden hair—falling casually from a side part to the tops of his ears—proclaimed him a wealthy man dressed for a casual day. Lines radiating from the corners of his blue eyes meant he either laughed a lot or was careless when he went out in the sun.

"I'm Burch Bayard," he repeated when she didn't speak. "We must be some kind of cousins." His drawl was soft and sweet. Low Country aristocracy.

"I beg your pardon?" She was still befuddled by the suddenness of his arrival.

He rested an elbow on her car, cocked his other hand at his waist, and smiled lazily down at her. "I can't think of any other reason for your kinfolks to be buried in our cemetery, can you? My lawyer, Hayden Curtis, said you were coming down to look at the graves before you give permission to move them."

"Oh." She glanced toward Dr. Flo, bent over the stones in the Gilbert plot. "They weren't . . ." Before she could finish ". . . my kinfolks," he was talking again.

"I'm delighted to meet you. Always glad to claim a beautiful woman as my cousin, no matter how many times removed."

"I'm not—"

The man suffered from an inability to shut up and listen. "This is my son Chase." He draped one arm casually around the boy's shoulders, a comfortable fit since the boy was so short. "A chip off the old block." He gave Chase a light punch on the arm with his other fist. "I'm mighty proud of this boy. Makes good grades, stays out of trouble, knows how to hunt and fish. Even draws and whittles a little, don't you, boy?"

A soft, embarrassed flush that had risen with his father's boasting deepened to an annoyed red. "Some," he muttered sarcastically, watching his toe make patterns in the sand. His voice was an adolescent buzz saw, vibrating between high and low.

"Look people in the face when you're talking to them, son." Burch eyed Katharine's shovel. "Were you planning to disinter your relatives yourself? I told Hayden to make it clear I'd take care of that."

The image of her helping Dr. Flo dig up coffins and of the two of them trudging with the coffins through the sand, hoisting them into the SUV, and driving off into the sunset was so absurd that she laughed.

His grin widened. "That's better. What were you planning
to dig?"

"Sand, so we could read the name on an obelisk near
Claude Gilbert's grave."

"Let us help you. Chase, carry that for her, will you?"

Chase hoisted the shovel to one shoulder and started toward the cemetery, his gun in the other hand. His hair flopped
on his shoulders as he trudged.

"One night I'm gonna sneak in and cut that hair," Burch
said softly as he fell into step beside Katharine. Their feet
made soft scrunching sounds in the sand.

A breeze had come with the Bayards that temporarily
drove away the mosquitoes.

"Actually, it's—" she began.

Again he gave her no chance to explain. "I had never realized there were folks buried here who weren't Bayards. I've
never read the markers, to tell you the truth. Cemeteries give
me the heebie-jeebies. But the county said I had to make a
census before I moved the graves, so I asked my wife to
come out and make sure they were all ours. You could have
knocked me over with a gull's feather when she found your
graves. Our family has owned Bayard Island since 1754, and
I would have sworn I knew every twig on the family tree. I
can't see why anybody except family would have been buried here, though."

"Maybe they came on a visit and died," Chase called over
his shoulder.

Burch laughed. "Don't make the lady think we have a
habit of killing and burying our guests, son."

Chase stood his ground. "But if somebody died here in the
olden days, they couldn't move bodies far in this heat."

"I suppose that's possible. The family did use to entertain
a lot when it was still a working plantation. Bayard Bluff.
Maybe you've heard of it?"

Burch waited long enough for Katharine to shake her

head, but not long enough for her to tell him she'd simply driven Dr. Flo down.

"It was as fine in its way as Pike's Bluff, Kelvin Grove, or Harrington Hall. Not quite in the league with Retreat, of course . . ."

Katharine presumed those were other Low Country plantations, for she had heard of Retreat, over on St. Simons Island.

"Rice was the big money crop. These tidal marshes were perfect for rice. But we also grew Sea Island cotton, as well."

She tried again to tell him about Dr. Flo before they reached the graves. "Listen—"

Burch didn't hear. "Sea Island cotton is perfect for this climate. It was developed or discovered—I don't know which—by planters who fled to the Bahamas after the Revolutionary War. They were loyal to the king, you know." He laughed. "Folks down here seem predestined to take the losing side of local wars. But when they got to the Bahamas, somebody started growing this high-quality cotton that has a long staple and comes back every year. Somebody else brought it to these parts around the 1790s and it grew well along the coast. There was a lot of money to be made out of Sea Island cotton until the War." He looked over the marshes and said with regret, "But you can't farm this land without a whole lot of hands. Bayard Bluff ran over four hundred at its peak."

Katharine didn't ask which war, or point out that 'hands' was a euphemism for slaves. He still didn't give her a chance.

"Now the land isn't good for much, but the view's spectacular, isn't it? Can you beat that anywhere else in the country? So I figure I might as well develop some of the island so we can enjoy the rest."

"You're a builder?" Katharine spoke without thinking,

then mentally kicked herself. She didn't give a hoot who or what he was, and in that fraction of a second she could have told him about Dr. Flo. Now she had steered his conversational bulldozer in another direction.

"Not yet, but as soon as we get those graves moved, I'm going to be. I'd rather develop the island myself than have some outsider come in here and ruin the place. This way I can pick and choose my neighbors. You might want to think about buying in. I can give you a great price on one of the first couple of houses, and it's going to be a community of good people, I promise. No riffraff. I'm even planning to put a gate at the bridge, once I take back the whole island. There's a little seafood company down the slough right now, but they'll sell out eventually."

Katharine darted a look behind her at the boy to see his reaction. Miranda had sounded like they knew each other pretty well.

He didn't seem to be listening. He was peering up at the flight of three gulls as if memorizing their lines.

Burch rattled on. "The slough is deep enough for boats and there's a channel that's open all the way to the ocean, so I plan to put in docks and maybe even a little marina. Do you like boats?"

"Sailing." She thought wistfully of sun-soaked days on Biscayne Bay.

"The water's too shallow for a keel, but a centerboard could work. You'd have to motor pretty far to get good sailing, though. You'd do better with a motor launch. They can be real sweet." He grinned down at her. "I tell you, cuz, you really ought to buy in."

They had come within ten feet of the cemetery fence.

"I am not your cousin," Katharine said firmly. "If anybody is, it's Dr. Flo."

She pointed across the larger cemetery to the small plot where Dr. Flo knelt, trying to stand Françoise Guilbert's stone erect. She could have been anybody until she stood and turned.

Burch, in the process of lifting his hat, froze. "What the—?"

Chase gave his dad a wary, anxious look.

Dr. Flo stepped over the low tabby wall and came around the iron railing to join them. "Hello. I'm Florence Gadney. It appears that at least one of my relatives shares this cemetery with yours."

She extended her hand, but Burch's hand was fanning his face with his hat. "I think there's been some kind of mistake, ma'am." He was still charming, but firm.

Dr. Flo inclined her head as graciously as if she were chairing a board. "I'm as puzzled as you, I assure you, but one of those graves does seem to be my grandfather's. I don't recognize the others, but now that I have their names, perhaps I can find out something about them. I see you've got the shovel. Good! Let's see who that fourth person is." She headed back toward the tabby-enclosed plot, walking briskly.

Burch grabbed Katharine's elbow and spoke softly. "What is this? You said—"

"I didn't say anything. You never gave me a chance." She pulled away.

A worried pucker appeared between his eyes. "I don't want to hurt her feelings, but the slave cemetery was across the bridge, behind a little church."

"We saw the church, but Dr. Flo's daddy insisted his family were never slaves."

"They sure as hell were never part of our family." Burch glanced toward the woods as if hoping inspiration would fly out. "My dad knows more about this cemetery than I do. He's never mentioned any strangers buried here."

"What about—?" Chase began, then broke off as Burch turned toward him. "Morrisons," he finished lamely, pointing in the direction of the graves outside the gate. Katharine had the impression that was not what he'd been about to say.

"A few Morrisons are buried here," Burch conceded, "but they lived on the island." He rubbed the back of his hair with one palm. "I've got to talk to Agnes about getting them moved, too." He heaved the sigh of a man burdened with trivia in the pursuit of greatness. He raised his voice. "Ma'am, I cannot see how your relatives could be buried in this place."

"The dates match," Dr. Flo called back. "Come and see."

He eyed the rows of tombstones with apprehension while he nibbled his upper lip. A small shudder passed over his shoulders. He took a step back. "I appreciate your coming all the way down here from Atlanta, and I'm sorry you had to make the trip, but—"

Seeing he wasn't coming, Dr. Flo stood beside Claude Gilbert's grave and held out her notebook. "These birth and death dates coincide exactly with those of my father's father, who is not buried in Atlanta with the rest of our family. Barring a bizarre coincidence, I have to believe this is the right Claude Gilbert."

Burch lifted his head like a bird dog that's caught a scent. "Did you say Gilbert?"

"Yes. My maiden name was Gilbert."

"That explains it. I noticed that Hayden misspelled the name of the man in the paper. These are Gwilberts."

"Guil-bears," Chase corrected him, so sloppy in pronouncing French that it came out more like *wheelbarrows*.

Dr. Flo fixed Burch with the look she must have given students who didn't adequately research a paper. "Claude's stone reads *Gilbert*."

"That was probably a misspelling, too."

She drew herself up to her full five-foot-two. "As a former professor, I know all there is to know about misspelling, sir, but a misspelled tombstone is rare. The spelling of names often changed from generation to generation, so it is far more likely that the family simplified it." She swatted away a bee as if swatting Burch himself. "I'll check on the two Guilberts to find out if they were related to me, and I'll let you know. Meanwhile, we need to find out who the person is who is buried under the obelisk. The name is covered with sand. May I have the shovel?" She held out one hand.

Burch gave a curt nod. "Chase, go dig out sand for these ladies."

Chase propped his gun against the railings, shouldered the shovel again, and joined Dr. Flo across the tabby wall. Burch made no move to investigate any of the stones. In fact, as the others gathered around the obelisk, he edged over to a sycamore and propped his back against it.

Dr. Flo showed Chase where to dig. As he bent to work, he slid her several speculative looks out of the side of his eyes. The way he heaved sand away from the obelisk base made Katharine suspect he was mentally shoveling all three adults out of his life.

Eventually a single word was revealed: MALLERY.

"Mallery?" Chase's voice cracked on the word.

"That's ours." Burch made the claim like a contestant on a TV show where the fastest answer wins. "Elizabeth Mallery married Francis Bayard in eighteen-forty."

Katharine doubted he'd had to spend hours in a library researching that. He rolled off the names and date as though he'd been fed family history and bloodlines with his baby formula.

Chase wiped sweat off his forehead and pointed to the large slab. "That's Elizabeth and Francis over there. They lived here during the War."

Burch circled the railing and peered over it at the slab. "Well, what do you know? That slab looks like it's in pretty good shape, too. What do you think, Chase, should I move

them close to the house and make a little Civil War cemetery, with a historical plaque and everything?" He turned to
Katharine. "That could be real picturesque, don't you
think?"

She wasn't about to approve setting up a cemetery as a
landscape feature for his new subdivision. "It would be more
picturesque to leave them right here."

"I can't do that. These are the best house sites I've got at
the moment. They're easy to get to and right on the marshes."
He added to Dr. Flo. "There's no question about Mallery.
He's mine."

She raised silver brows above her glasses. "You had pirates in your family, too?"

Chase lifted his head, but Burch laughed. "Pirates? No,
ma'am, we never had pirates. We did have one naval commander." He took off his hat and fanned himself again. The
breeze had died down and mosquitoes were whining. "John
McIntosh Kell, one of the most successful of all Confederate commanders, was our cousin. He was born down near
Darien."

Dr. Flo motioned for Burch to join her. "Come and look at
this."

It was Chase who stepped around the obelisk and peered
where she pointed. "Cool! Look, Dad, a skull and crossbones!" He traced the design with his forefinger. "Not very
well carved, but . . ."

Burch didn't budge. "Probably the work of kids."

"My daddy used to claim we had a pirate in our family,"
Dr. Flo told him. "I don't know if this is the one."

Burch huffed. "I am certain it is not, ma'am. Like I told
you, the Mallerys were our people, and we have never had
mixed blood in our family. No pirates, either."

"Yet here are my grandfather and a pirate, both buried in
your family plot."

His nostrils flared and his words were clipped, but still

polite. "If you are convinced this Claude Gilbert was related to you, ma'am, I'll take it kindly if you will give me permission to move him. You don't need to bother about the others. I'll take care of them."

He obviously expected them to pick up their shovel and march.

He beckoned with one hand. "Come on, Chase. We need to be getting home, and these ladies have a long drive back to Atlanta. Thank you all for coming." He started across the clearing.

"We'll tell Mr. Curtis what you said," Dr. Flo called after him, "but you'd better not plan on doing any digging yet."

He stopped in midstride, balanced on one foot with the other propped behind him in the sand. "I beg your pardon?"

"Obviously we disagree about whether these graves are connected to my family, but I don't think there can be any doubt that they are connected to each other. Therefore, I cannot give permission to move Claude Gilbert without research to clear up who the others are."

"Hell, lady!" He whirled, snatched off his hat, and slapped it against his thigh. "I don't give a damn who *any* of those people are. I just want to move them out of here so I can build houses. I'll put them in a good, safe place. I promise. I'll even let you know where. So please stop by Hayden's on your way home and sign that damned paper."

"I'm sorry, sir, but it's not that simple. Although you are convinced Marie and Françoise are not my relatives, I believe they may be. If that is the case, I am the only person on earth who can authorize their removal. I am willing to do the research to determine whether they are or not, and then I'll be glad to let you move them if I have that authority, but the research will take time. But if you turn out to be right and they are not related to me, you cannot move them without searching farther for the next of kin. Either way, you are going to have to postpone your plans."

He kicked a piece of shell so hard that it lifted high into the air before it fell.

Katharine wanted to kick him. She said in what Tom called a Southern Sugar voice, "If these were my relatives, Dr. Flo, I'd sure hate to move 'em from where they've been all these years. It's such a *chah-ming* place to be buried." She peered up at the shading oaks and pretended not to notice the strangled sounds Burch was making.

Chase was running his fingers over the carving. "It really *is* a skull and crossbones. No doubt about it."

"Of course there's doubt," his father snapped. "Never take anything or anybody at face value, son. How many times have I told you that?" He came back a few steps and glared at Dr. Flo. "Are you going to let me move that grave?"

"Graves, Mr. Bayard. I am going home to look for evidence that the two Guilberts are my relatives. If I find it, I will be glad to give you permission to move all three. I am not trying to be obstreperous. But that is all I can promise you today."

Burch's chest heaved with frustration. "I didn't have to advertise, you know. I could have claimed they were all my relatives and been done with it." He shook a fist toward the far side of the clearing. "That meddling old woman—" He broke off after that cryptic beginning. "Come on, Chase, let's go." He headed toward a break in the forest Katharine hadn't noticed before.

"What was this space?" she called after him. "The clearing. Was it the original plantation house?"

"We *live* in the original plantation house," he shouted, not bothering to turn, "and this is my island. I am going to develop it and I want those graves out of here. Fast! I'm fixing to bring in bulldozers next week."

He strode off without another word.

Chase gave the two women an apologetic little shrug. "He's really needing to get started, you know. He's got a loan and signed contracts and stuff, so it costs him money every day he can't build." He picked up his gun. "That used to be a church over there, until Papa Dalt needed wood to fix the barn."

He pointed to the edge of the forest. Katharine hadn't noticed the old man until then. He seemed to be arguing with Burch. At first the others heard shouts rather than words, but as the voices notched higher, phrases were clear.

". . . don't stir up trouble . . ."

". . . chance I've got . . ."

". . . let the dead stay buried . . ."

". . . aren't gonna care . . ."

". . . more than bodies."

Their voices dropped again for a couple of beats, then the old man shouted something that ended, ". . . over my dead body!"

The younger bent toward him, punctuating every word with a finger pointed at his father's chest. "If necessary, that's exactly how I'll do it!" He dashed between two clumps of cabbage palms and vanished.

The older man turned and yelled at the women. "I told you to git outta here!"

Chase loped to him and shoved him into the woods.

Katharine shuddered. She had been embarrassed by much of what had gone on with Burch, and the collective sins of her race pressed heavily on her. "I am so sorry about that."

"Honey, if I let my feelings get hurt by every bigot I meet, I'd be a seething mass of self-pity. I had already figured out that this must be a white cemetery. Black folks around here couldn't afford wrought-iron fences back when these people were buried. And you see how my folks lie outside the fence?"

"That could be because there wasn't room inside. Claude and the four Morrisons are the only ones here buried after 1900."

"Marie was buried in 1890 and Françoise in 1878, but they aren't inside, either. Neither was Mallery. I'm not surprised the Bayards are upset that graves on their lily-white island might belong to African Americans. I only wish I knew why my grandfather was buried here."

"Could they have been family servants?" Katharine suggested tentatively.

"Not likely. Marie was born in 1825, so she would have had to be a slave."

"Maybe they were white." Katharine scratched a pink welt on her arm. "You're pretty light."

"I have a picture of Daddy's father, and he was darker than I am. I take after Mama's family. Her parents were so light, they could pass for Italian or Spanish."

Dr. Flo's maternal grandfather, George Whitcomb, had been a cultured, well-to-do mortician. He and his wife had been fond of long cruises in their later years. Katharine noted that Dr. Flo—a stickler for good grammar—had not said, "They could have passed" but, rather, "They could pass."

Dr. Flo bent to Françoise's headstone again. "Bring that shovel over here and help me right this poor child's stone. Maybe we can dig a hole deep enough to stand it up until I can decide what to do with these folks."

Dr. Flo was holding the stone and Katherine was shoveling dirt around it when the shot whizzed over their heads.

Chapter 9

They hit the ground. Katharine had her face pressed into the sand when she heard a gruff voice. "What the dickens do you think you are doing?"

Keeping her head low, she peered between two uprights of the iron fence. A tall, stocky woman with a bright pink face strode toward the cemetery. She wore denim overalls, a man's long-sleeved white shirt, and heavy work boots. When she stopped near the gate, a fat basset hound plopped his rump at her heels like he was prepared to stay all day.

The woman's back was to the light, and sunlight caught wispy curls escaping from a white crown of braids and made a nimbus around her head.

There was nothing saintly about the shotgun pointed in their direction.

Katharine knelt and raised both hands, wincing as her left knee found a sharp piece of shell. "Setting this tombstone back up." Her voice shook. "It had fallen over."

Dr. Flo climbed stiffly to her feet. She brushed her pants and said angrily, "Look at what you made me do. I'll have to get these cleaned."

"Better to pay a cleaner than a funeral home," Katharine muttered. "Raise your hands."

Dr. Flo expelled an indignant huff. "Raise my hands nothing." She glared toward the woman with the shotgun. "Ms.

Agnes Morrison, I presume? We've heard about you. What do you mean, firing at two unarmed women?"

"Protecting my property and my family graves." The woman's voice was placid.

"We were told this is Bayard property."

"You must have been talking to Burch. He's never checked the deed. I keep telling him this land from the slough to the road was given to my granddaddy by Ella Bayard. Not a court in the state would say different. Burch can't do a thing with this land unless I agree to sell, and I don't intend to see my part of the island covered with houses so long as I have breath to oppose it. Don't aim to see you here, either, so git!" She jerked her head toward Katharine's car.

"But we—" Katharine began.

The woman took another step in their direction. "I'm gonna count to fifty. If you aren't both in that car before I finish, you're gonna walk limping. I won't kill you, but you might wish I had. Go on, now. Git! One, two, three—"

They were halfway to the car when she burst out laughing. "Hey!" she called.

They turned.

She gestured with the tip of her shotgun. "You forgot your shovel. I'll stop counting while you come back and get it."

Katharine trudged back and picked up the shovel, hating the moment when she had to turn her back on that crazy woman and her gun.

Dr. Flo stood beside the front fender of the SUV like a child playing statues, one foot ahead of the other, her weight on the forward foot, not moving.

"What's the matter?" Katharine called. Then she heard a dry rattle, like beans in a plastic cup. She froze, too.

"Get on in that car," Ms. Morrison ordered, coming closer.

"There's a rattler." Katharine could hardly speak the words. "I can't see it, but I can hear it. I think it's near Dr. Flo."

Katharine did not hear the old woman move, but in a moment saw her inching forward on the toes of her boots. The basset stayed at her heel and whined.

The rattle sounded again. Ms. Morrison was lifting her gun when Katharine heard a shot. A three-foot snake flew into the air and flopped to the ground. Its head was gone.

Dr. Flo collapsed against the car and covered her face with her hands, shaking like a small brown leaf. "Dear God! Oh, dear God!"

Dalt Bayard stepped from beside a live oak trunk and grunted. "Shoulda let him kill her and get it over with, but I never could resist a good, clear shot." He spat and wiped his mouth with the back of his hand. "Now git off my proppity, the whole blooming lot of you. Git!"

"Thanks," Katharine called, as much to rile him as anything.

He trudged toward the woods with no sign that he heard.

Ms. Morrison helped Dr. Flo into her seat, offering comfort in a gruff, awkward way. "You weren't bit. Be grateful for that. I'd have gotten him if Dalt hadn't shot him first. But they can shake you up some, can't they?"

Katharine wanted nothing but to get in her car and drive away, if her legs would let her move, but now the woman wanted to chat.

"You folks interested in old cemeteries?" She spoke to Katharine across the car.

"No, but Dr. Flo thinks some of those graves belong to her family."

She peered at Dr. Flo with new interest. "No bull? Those Guilberts are yours?"

She gave it the French pronunciation.

Dr. Flo took a deep breath and exhaled all of it before she nodded. "I believe this Claude Gilbert was my grandfather. I don't recognize the other two, but I'm going to check them out. Do you think they were French?"

"Our family always pronounced the name that way, but I have no idea why. I don't want to offend you, but I wish I could see Burch Bayard's face when he finds out you are Claude's granddaughter."

Dr. Flo had recovered enough to give a shaky laugh. "He already did. He's trying to graft Marie and Françoise into his family to keep me from claiming them, too."

"But you're sure they're yours?"

"I'm pretty sure about Claude. It's possible the others weren't related, but . . ."

"Highly unlikely. The county has other cemeteries they could lie in if they weren't kin."

They had forgotten Katharine was there, but the mosquitoes hadn't. As she stowed the shovel in the back of the SUV she smacked three that left smears of blood on her arm.

Ms. Morrison addressed her as she climbed into her seat. "Where are you heading after this? Do you have time to run down island? There's somebody I'd like you to meet."

Katharine looked toward Dr. Flo, waiting for her to demur, but the professor said, "I didn't give Mr. Curtis any specific time we'd be there. I just said we'd come after we visited the cemetery. I'd like to see the island, since we're here."

Ms. Morrison reached to open the back door of the SUV. "If you don't mind if Samson and I ride along . . ." She didn't wait for approval. Katharine watched in dismay as the overweight basset struggled to climb aboard. Tom had a strong aversion to dogs in the car, and she could smell that dog from several yards away. Ms. Morrison bent and hefted him onto the seat. "There, boy. It's a bit high, isn't it?" Her face was flushed from the exertion, but her breathing was regular. She put the shotgun in the floor and climbed in.

As Katharine started the engine, she had a momentary memory of herself standing in her kitchen—was it just yesterday morning?—thinking that anything would be better than nightmares and shopping. Shotguns, rattlesnakes, and smelly basset hounds had not been remotely what she'd had in mind.

Neither were chiggers, but from the way her ankles were burning, she'd picked up a few. She reached down to scratch. Dr. Flo asked softly, "Are you all right?"

"Except for bites. Are you okay?"

"I guess so." Dr. Flo picked stickers from the legs of her dress slacks. "This place is crazy. Bugs, snakes, guns—I sure am glad you came."

"Two are usually safer than one."

"White is safer than black. Burch Bayard expected a white woman to claim the graves."

Agnes Morrison laughed behind them. "He sure did."

"He kept calling me 'cuz,'" Katharine admitted, "but I'd rather Dr. Flo was related to him than me."

"I'm not related to him, girl. He's pure alligator on one side and water moccasin on the other. Besides, like I told you, I don't have Bayards on my family tree. Thank the good Lord." She laid her head back and shut her eyes.

The rest of their way through the forest, the only sound was Samson wheezing. His odor was so strong that Katharine bypassed air conditioning and opened the windows.

"Turn right," Ms. Morrison instructed when they reached the asphalt road.

The road down island was a mass of twists and turns. Katharine didn't know whether it had been laid out by a drunk or to avoid marshy ground. They saw no signs of habitation until a low house appeared, sitting under the branches of a wide oak. A cream Mercedes, a silver BMW, and the decrepit black truck they'd seen at Stampers sat near two sandy ruts that comprised the drive. Behind the house was either another slough or more of the one that bordered the cemetery.

Katharine slowed. "Is that the Bayard place?" She couldn't keep the surprise out of her voice. Hollywood has set the standard for "plantation house," so she had expected a two-story porch held up by columns, attached to a huge white house. This house was plain, not excessively large, with a screened porch on four sides and dormers in a gray tin roof. The best thing it had to offer was a view across the slough and miles of marsh.

"Bayard Bluff," Ms. Morrison confirmed.

"It's not very big, is it?" said Dr. Flo.

"This was a rice plantation. The hot, muggy climate used to breed malaria and yellow fever, so before air conditioning, rice and sugar planters didn't stay on their property except for January and February, the coolest months. Their primary residences were in Savannah, Charleston, New York, or Philadelphia, so they didn't bother to build big like cotton planters."

"New York and Philadelphia?" Katharine was skeptical, but willing to give the benefit of the doubt to a woman who had a shotgun in her car.

Ms. Morrison's chuckle was deep and strong, like her voice. "Yep. Lots of folks don't realize it, but a lot of plantations—and their slaves—were owned by Yankees."

"I didn't know that," Dr. Flo admitted. "Were the Bayards northerners?"

"No, their main house was in Savannah until Dalt's daddy, Asa, took over from his daddy, Hamilton. He sold the Savannah place and moved down here full-time, thinking he could make a living farming. He couldn't, of course. The land was never good for much once rice and Sea Island cotton were done. By now it's good for nothing. But the Bayards are prideful men. The way they say "Bayard Island," you'd think it was Manhattan. So Asa and then Dalt muddled along for years growing a little and mostly living off their wives. Bayard men always marry money. Worthless as Confederate dollars, the lot of them, but they look good in a tux. Rich debutantes flutter around them like flies on honey. Get equally stuck, too. Take Mona—smart, rich, she could have had her pick of men. Instead, she wanted Burch and his romantic island plantation." Ms. Morrison laughed. "She got what she wanted, poor soul."

"Do they live down here with his dad?" Katharine asked, looking in her mirror for one last glimpse of the house. Had Mona seen the "plantation" before she married?

"No, Burch has never gone in for farming. He and Mona bought another place in Savannah—with her daddy's money, of course. They live up there most of the time. Turn at that road to the right."

A road—once paved but now pitted with potholes—led to the slough. A shrimp boat and a small motor launch lolled gently at a long weathered dock. A large shed and a small concrete building had once been white before wind and salt burnished them to a dingy cream.

The buildings certainly didn't improve the ambiance of the island. Neither did the rusted white refrigerated truck with STAMPERS SEAFOOD lettered in blue on its side. Two men, black as ebony, were loading it. The air smelled of fish, shrimp, and the marshes they lived in. Katharine inhaled deep gulps, wishing she could bottle that odor and take some home.

An elderly Ford van, oyster shell gray with a disability tag, was pulled close to the concrete building, which had a sign on the door: OFFICE. Ms. Morrison climbed out, helped Samson down, and started in that direction. Dr. Flo followed Ms. Morrison, but Katharine stayed behind long enough to examine her ankles. Sure enough, five pink bumps had raised. She gave them a good scratch before she went inside, hoping she could find grease or butter soon.

A woman was greeting Ms. Morrison and Samson while stubbing out a cigarette in an ashtray that already overflowed. The fuggy chill came as a shock. Katharine's toes curled inward while her lungs caught and held, unwilling to take in the acrid air. How could one small air conditioner, set high in the wall, generate so much cold? How could one small woman exhale so much smoke? Since nobody was talking to her, Katharine looked around. The office contained two straight chairs, a filing cabinet, and a desk—all older than she was. The concrete floor was bare, increasing the chill. Katharine shivered, especially when she noticed that the woman wore a white tank top that hugged her skinny body and high little breasts.

Like "Granny," she was tanned and weathered with bottle-white hair, and she kept her lipstick shiny and her blusher fresh. Her face, however, was a generation younger and far prettier. Her hair was cut square and blunt to frame her thin face. Her eyes—blue, not green—were nearly hidden by long bangs.

She had been reading a paperback novel when they arrived. It lay, facedown and open, ready to pick up again.

It was when the woman bent to scratch under the basset's soft ears that Katharine noticed she sat in a wheelchair. Samson flopped down beside one wheel like he'd been there before.

Ms. Morrison remembered her manners. "Folks, this is Nell Stampers, one of the owners of Stampers Seafood. And these are—sorry, I didn't get your names."

You were too busy shooting at us, Katharine thought while Dr. Flo introduced them both.

The woman put out a nicotine-stained hand and her sharp eyes took in Katharine's clothes with a flicker of envy. Her mouth curved in a professional welcome. "You all looking for fresh shrimp? The boat just came in."

"I could use some for supper." Ms. Morrison pulled five dollars from her overalls pocket and laid it on the desk. "Is Iola around?"

"She was here earlier, but she's gone back to the store."
Nell nodded toward the door. "Tell Tick to weigh out your
shrimp. How much do you ladies need?" She named a price
and the tilt of her chin dared them to claim it was too high.

Katharine shook her head. "I'd love to get some, but we're
on the road."

"We got Styrofoam coolers you can buy for a couple of
bucks, and we'll pack it in ice."

"Then I'll take five pounds." What they didn't eat at Jekyll
she could pack again and take home.

"I'll tell Tick." Ms. Morrison walked heavily through the
door. Samson lifted his head to watch her go, but didn't
move.

Katharine was certain she and Dr. Flo had been maneuvered here for a purpose, but what was it?

Chapter 10

Nell picked up a key chain with a yellow seahorse dangling from it and ran the seahorse back and forth through her fingers while she contemplated her visitors. "Miranda called and said you all stopped by the store. She figured you were looking to buy one of the houses Burch is set on building."

"Oh, no," Katharine protested. "We were looking up family graves."

Nell's eyelids flickered. "Chase says Burch has to move their family cemetery and needs permission for a couple of the graves. Those the ones you were looking at?" She waited for Katharine's nod, then asked warily, "You kin to the Bayards?"

"No. They were Dr. Flo's graves."

Nell looked from Katharine to Dr. Flo like she thought they were trying to put something over on her. She narrowed her eyes, making it clear she wasn't about to step into the trap.

"A Gilbert and two Guilberts," Dr. Flo added. "Have you ever heard of them?"

"Never heard of anybody on this island except Bayards, Agnes, and us." She lit another cigarette and exhaled a cloud of smoke. "There's an old slave cemetery behind the church just over the bridge."

Dr. Flo tilted her chin. "My people were not slaves." Her voice was soft, but firm.

"Well, I don't see how the graves could be yours. The Bayards—well, let's just say they have always been real rigid about some things." Nell took another drag and muttered on the exhale, "Bastards, every last one of them."

Dr. Flo pressed her lips together and inhaled sharply, but did not reply. Instead, she moseyed over to the large front window, which was so crusted with salt it looked milky, and stood with her back to them. Katharine felt like the professor had abandoned her to carry on the conversation. "Chase seemed nice enough," she said, for lack of any other topic.

Nell stubbed out her cigarette like she was grinding somebody into the ground. "Yeah, but like Mama keeps reminding Miranda, God visits the sins of the fathers on the children to the third generation, so Chase is likely to reap what the rest have sown. There hasn't been but one generation of Bayards yet who did right by other folks."

Appalled by the theology, Katharine objected as tactfully as she knew how. "I don't think that generation thing is a threat, do you? I can't see God sitting up in heaven waiting to zap the grandchildren of people who sin."

"That's what the Bible says: 'The sins of the fathers will be visited on their children to the third generation,'" Nell spoke with the kind of conviction it is useless to argue with, "so Chase isn't out of the woods yet. Not by a long shot."

Katharine turned toward the door. "I guess I ought to go get my shrimp." Dr. Flo could do her own talking if she wanted to know more about the island. Katharine hadn't buried any ancestors there.

Nell opened her top drawer and took out a flat white envelope. "Agnes will get it for you, but you pay me." It was more command than suggestion.

Katharine reached for her wallet and handed her three bills.

"Plus two for the cooler," Nell reminded her. She added Agnes's five and stuffed all the bills into the empty envelope. Was that a day's income? How did the family manage to survive?

Nell restored the envelope to its drawer and waved Katharine toward one of the visitor chairs. "You all might as well sit. When Agnes and Tick get to talking, she tends to be a while."

When Katharine perched on the bare steel, she felt chill seep through her pants. Dr. Flo remained by the window, peering out at its impressionistic view of the dock. Nell lit up again. Katharine looked at the ashtray and wondered how much Nell would save in a year if she smoked her cigarettes down to the filter.

Nell blew a perfect smoke ring toward the ceiling, watched it rise, and spoke as if talking to herself. "Anything you want to know about this island, I can tell you. Daddy farmed for Dalt and Asa Bayard, and his daddy did, too."

What Katharine really wanted to know was where she could find a spot to thaw out and whether Nell had anything salty and greasy to kill those blasted chiggers. She would have made a polite excuse and gone outside, except Dr. Flo turned for an instant and sent a silent message.

Katharine wasn't sure what it meant, but she interpreted it *Keep her talking.*

"Agnes said Burch doesn't farm."

Nell shook her head. "You can't make the kind of money Burch and Mona want by farming. This land has been raped by Bayards for two hundred and fifty years, just like the rest of us. It can't put out like it used to." She took a couple of puffs.

"What does Burch do instead?"

Not that she cared. Katharine tried to remember the path that had led her from her own house and all she had to do back there to this isolated seafood business on the edge of nowhere, discussing the private lives of people who were no more real to her than soap opera characters. The journey seemed as hazy as the office air.

Nell gave a bark of a laugh. "Do? Burch? Nothing, to speak of. He dabbles in real estate a little, but he doesn't sell much. I don't know why he thinks he can build and sell houses. Mona, now—" another drag on the cigarette "—she's a decorator up in Savannah and does real well—or so Chase says. I've never had any call to hire her, myself." She looked around the barren little office and gave another raspy smoker's laugh. When Katharine didn't join in, she added with a touch of venom, "She doesn't make enough to support them in the style to which they intend to remain accustomed. I can tell you that."

Since childhood, Katharine's mother had instilled in her a distaste for gossip. She had heard more than enough about Burch Bayard and his wife. "When did you all start this business?" She wished Agnes would come back so they could get on with their own agenda. First on her list was a bottle of water and fresh, hot air.

"Around thirty years ago, when I was five. Not long after my accident. Mama had bought that little store up on U.S. 17 the year I was born, and she was running it while Daddy worked for the Bayards, to supplement what Daddy made. Then a tractor turned over on Daddy and me one morning while I was riding in his lap, 'helping him plow.'" Her fingers sketched the quotes. "Daddy got killed and my back was broken, so I couldn't ever walk again." The hand that stubbed out another half-smoked cigarette trembled.

"How awful!" Katharine pictured the man on the tipsy tractor holding his little girl, feeling the machine lurch beneath him and begin to roll. What must Nell's memories be like?

Nell took a deep breath of plain air—if the air in the room could be called plain—and exhaled before she continued. "It *was* awful, but good came out of it. Mama took Dalt and Asa to court and several witnesses testified that Daddy had been telling anybody who would listen that the dadblamed tractor was pulling to the right and likely to tip. Judge Whaley decided in our favor and awarded us a real good settlement. The Bayards couldn't come up with cash, so Mama asked the judge to make them give her ten acres on the slough and build her a dock and a shed to start this business. Her daddy had two boats and was wanting to retire, so she and her brother went in together. He bosses the crews and she and I run the packing and shipping end of things. I keep telling her we could do better down in Darien, but she won't leave the island. We get by."

From the decrepit state of their buildings and trucks, it looked to Katharine like they were barely hanging on, but appearances can be deceptive. For all she knew, this was one of the most lucrative seafood operations on the eastern seaboard.

"How did Dalton Bayard take the decision?" Dr. Flo inquired without turning around.

Nell gave her a surprised look, as if she had forgotten the professor was there. "Kicked up a real ruckus. Threatened to appeal and everything, but Mr. Asa wouldn't let him. Mr. Asa claimed they didn't have the money for a lawyer, but folks say the judge had some kind of hold over the family. Afterwards, though, people said it was a good thing Judge Whaley was already planning to retire. Once he'd crossed the Bayards, he'd never have won another election in this county."

Katharine picked up on something she had said earlier. "You don't want to be on the island?"

Nell grimaced. "Not really. I'd rather work where there are other people and places to go for lunch. Besides, like I said, I think we could make more money somewhere else, but Mama is as bad as a Bayard about this island. All my life

Dalt has been coming by here pestering her to sell—he plumb hates us having a piece of his precious land—but Mama's like a barnacle. She's attached herself here, so here she's gonna stay, come hell or high water. Of course, now that Burch is talking about developing the island, I find myself in two minds. I don't want to spend the next thirty-five years here, but if we left, that would be like giving in to the bulldozers and a second Yankee invasion." She shrugged with a laugh. "I guess I'm as bad as Mama."

Tires crunched on the gravel. "Oh, drat, here she is now. I thought I'd got her out of my hair for the afternoon. Lately she rattles back and forth between the store and this place like a cat that's lost its kittens."

The woman they had seen at the store opened the door and stomped in. "You got today's deposit ready?"

Nell reached for another cigarette and took time to light it before she replied. "Not yet. I figured you weren't coming back and we could make the deposit on our way home. Where did you hare off to?"

"We needed beer down to the store. I bought some and put it in the cooler."

Nell gave a little snort. "For the tourist rush?"

"Don't you be pert, missy." The older woman seemed to notice the others for the first time. "I'm Iola Stampers, since my daughter don't have the manners to introduce us. Weren't you down to our store, earlier?"

Katharine offered her hand. "Yes, we were. I'm Katharine Murray and this is Dr. Flo Gadney."

Dr. Flo turned from the window and moseyed over to join the party. "Nell has been telling us about how you won a lawsuit and started this business."

Iola heaved a sigh that was far more dramatic than her daughter's. "It ain't been easy, I can tell you that. We've had a lot of trials and tribulations in our lives, but the good Lord has preserved us through them all."

"Miranda mentioned that you all had a house burn down."

Iola nodded with another sigh. "Yep, except it was a double-wide. It used to sit right over yonder—" she motioned toward a solid wall "—looking out at the marsh. Convenient for Nell and her chair. We had a ramp and everything. A real pretty place, too, and quiet excepting for those pesky gulls. But it burned while Nell and I were picking up a few things in Eulonia one afternoon. Dalt Bayard told the insurance folks he saw it get struck by lightning, so they put it down to that, but I didn't see no lightning out this way when we was in town. Fortunately, we hadn't sold our house, so we went back there, but I'd rather be closer to the business. May bring in another trailer one day."

"Dalt will kill you," Nell warned, pulling a stack of checks from a drawer.

Iola grinned, showing two gaps where upper incisors used to be. "I'd like to see him try. You work up that deposit while I talk to your guests. Would you like to sit?" She motioned to Dr. Flo.

"No, thank you. We've been riding all day. I'd rather stand. You take the chair."

Iola sat while Nell turned on her calculator and started entering checks. "I already told them I wish you'd sell up and move off this godforsaken island," she told her mother.

Iola crimped her mouth. "What I wish is that you'd do the work you get paid to do. I need that deposit."

Nell crimped her own mouth in fair imitation of her mother. "You'd have had it if you had stuck around. You won't get to the bank before it closes anyway." With a little flounce she bent over the keys.

Katharine was embarrassed. She'd been raised to keep family battles private.

Iola slid down in her chair and stretched out her long bare legs, marbled with varicose veins. "I can tell you one good thing about us keeping this land. It kills Dalt Bayard a little bit every day, knowing we own it."

"Killed Mr. Asa, too," Nell murmured without looking up, explaining to the others, "He died not six months after the trial." She picked up the cigarette without looking in its direction, and put it unerringly in her mouth while her other hand punched in numbers. Katharine wondered if she ever got burned.

Iola nodded and explained to their guests, "He got shot while hunting and died before anybody found him." She let that sink in, then added, "Some said he shot hisself, because he couldn't stand to have his son on his back all the time." She gave Katharine a quick, penetrating glance and lowered her voice to a whisper, "Some said Dalt shot him because his daddy let go of land."

"Mama!"

Iola shrugged. "Wouldn't put it past him." She spoke to Katharine. "He's meaner'n the devil hisself and twice as proud. What's he got to be so proud of? I ask you that. Old drunk, never spends a penny these days on anything except liquor. Chase told Miranda that Burch asked Dalt to let him mortgage Bayard Bluff, to get him started on that building project, but Dalt said he'd see him in hell first. They don't exactly get along." She slewed her eyes toward Nell.

Nell refused to be goaded again. She took time to blow another smoke ring and watch it rise before she said, "Just because you're family doesn't mean you have to get along."

Iola shrugged. "No, but family is family. You stand together in times of need. Chase says Burch and Mona are scraping the barrel these days. He ain't sure they'll even have enough to send him back to that lah-ti-dah school next fall. And Chase says his other granddaddy—Mona's daddy, who is a big-wig developer out in Texas somewhere—well, he won't give Mona another red cent, either, until Burch sells two houses. The old man gave Mona a right good bit of money when they got married. He was an oilman before he got into land development, and is really loaded. I mean, really! But Chase says he thinks a man should support his own family."

Katharine couldn't tell whether Iola was talking to Nell, to her and Dr. Flo, or a bit of both. What she could tell was that Chase talked too much family business outside the family.

Nell looked up and shook her head. "If he thinks a Bayard is gonna support his family, that particular Texan isn't as smart as they all let on to be."

Iola grinned and announced to their guests, "Bayards don't work. Anybody 'round here could have told him that, if he'd bothered to ask before he let his daughter get hitched up to one. Never was a Bayard to work, even if his family went hungry."

"They ran a plantation. And farmed," Katharine pointed out.

Iola reached for Nell's cigarettes. As she lit up and blew twin streams from her nostrils, Katharine wondered how long it took a person to asphyxiate on secondhand smoke.

"They never run nothing," Iola informed her. "They hire others to do the running while they drink and party."

"And they marry money," Nell added.

Iola nodded. "That's one thing Bayards do real well, marry money. But they don't work. If somebody would give Burch a job where all he did was party and let other folks work? He'd be in hog heaven. I figure the reason he wants to build these houses is that he fancies hisself walking around in a yellow hard hat watching other people work, then having neighbors around to party with. But don't expect him to dirty his hands."

Dr. Flo spoke again. "But he is willing to sell off some of the island when he needs to. That sounds wiser than his father."

Nell snorted. "Don't you believe it. That's Mona's doing. When it comes right down to it, Burch will bleed over every square inch he sells."

"And Dalt will fight him every inch of the way. He don't want a bunch of strangers living in his backyard."

Katharine was confused. Was Iola championing the man she'd been accusing of murder not a minute before?

"But it's Burch's land?" She hadn't meant to ask. She hadn't even meant to speak. Something about the island—its people and its stories—was drawing her in against her will.

"Half of it is," Iola corrected her. "Asa wrote his will leaving half the island to Dalt and half to Burch. He knew Dalt wouldn't share with Burch in his lifetime, and lordy, that man may live past a hundred."

"Eighty his last birthday and still as chipper as Mama," Nell contributed. "Of course, she's no spring chicken."

Iola clamped her lips around her cigarette and glared at her daughter.

Nell laughed. "Well, she's not a winter chicken, either. Mama gets along pretty well for an old lady of sixty.

"Fifty-nine," Iola said stubbornly. "But Nell's right. Selling land was Mona's idea, according to Chase. She told Burch they might as well get the good out of the land before he loses it to taxes. She even persuaded her daddy to finance the project after Burch builds and sells his first two houses, to show he's serious about it. She'll keep after him until he does it, too."

Nell sniffed. "Mona likes life's little luxuries, and they're scarce on the ground at the moment." She handed her mother a stack of checks and a deposit slip with a flourish. "I like life's little luxuries, too. Why don't we sell this place and get ourselves a life?"

"Because nothing would please the Bayards more." Iola snapped the answer without thinking, but then she leaned back in her chair and waved her cigarette like a parody of a star of the gilded age. "Of course, I might be persuaded to sell when this land is worth a million an acre and I can retire in style." She gave a raspy laugh. "Like that's going to happen. What's really gonna happen if Burch builds his houses is that the county will up the taxes until folks like us—" she eyed Katharine's diamond, a full carat that had belonged to Tom's grandmother, and flicked her eyes toward the door, like she was remembering the new Cadillac "—ordinary folks won't be able to pay. We'll have to sell out for whatever Burch will give us."

Nell blew a puff of smoke her way. "Which is a good reason to sell out to Dalt now."

"I wouldn't sell to Dalt Bayard if he was the last man on earth. You know that. Besides, this land is right on the water. It ought to bring in a lot more once the place starts developing."

"Like you'd ever sell it for it to be developed." Nell looked at Katharine and curled her lip. "Mama keeps threatening to donate the land to the county for a park, but I'm not gonna let her do it. This business is all we've got, and I've worked as hard as she has at building it up."

Katharine was wondering how she could get out of further involvement in what was obviously an ongoing battle when Dr. Flo stepped forward with a contribution. "Burch's development is going to be put on hold for a while, anyhow, until I can research graves we looked at this afternoon."

"Is that right?" Iola blew out smoke and regarded Dr. Flo through the haze.

Dr. Flo nodded. "There's nobody else can give him permission to move them, and I won't until I'm certain they belong to my family."

Iola picked up the checks and stood. "More power to you. I'd best be getting to town with these, even if Nell has been so slow that the bank is like to be closed. Good to meet you."

"You know good and well you'll use the night depository," Nell called after her.

Iola's raucous laugh floated back as the Cadillac convertible roared to life.

Nell clasped her hands before her on the desk and took a deep breath. "What did I tell you? Can't sit still for more than ten minutes. Shall we see if Tick has your shrimp ready?" She bent to pat the fat dog beside her wheel. "Wake up, Samson. We gotta roll." She waited until he lifted himself and waddled toward the door, then wheeled herself around the desk. As she led the way out the door, she told her guests cheerfully, "So help me, I'm gonna kill Mama one day."

Chapter 11

The contrast between the frigid office and the outdoors was so intense, Katharine felt like she was strolling into hell. Ms. Morrison (Katharine still could not think of her as Agnes) settled herself and her shrimp on the backseat with Samson and the shotgun at her feet. "You all talk to Nell and Iola some?"

"Some." Katharine eased out of the lot, aware that her own shrimp rested in a skimpy Styrofoam cooler in back, its lid so unsteady that the whole thing could topple at the first curve. Tom would really be thrilled to come home and find the car smelling like shrimp plus dirty dog.

Ms. Morrison laughed. "Then you know all there is to know about Bayard Island. I'd wager they told you every blasted secret anybody's had on the island for the past fifty years."

Dr. Flo chuckled. "Just about." Even Katharine, concentrating on not spilling the shrimp until she could get them into something more solid, smiled.

"I thought they would. There's no better way to learn about the island than from the Stampers, especially if they are together. What one doesn't tell you, the other will, for spite if nothing else. They tell you about Bert's accident?"

Dr. Flo nodded. "And their fire. It sounds like their family has had it rough."

Katharine was having it rough, too. Her chiggers were

driving her crazy. Once she got past the twisting part of the road, she pulled up her left leg and scratched her ankle, hoping the other two were so engrossed in conversation they wouldn't notice.

"Right rough," Ms. Morrison agreed. "I appreciate Iola and Nell hanging on like they do. If they close down and sell the property, I'll be the only thing standing between this island and ruin." She reached up and laid a big hand on Dr. Flo's shoulder. "I hope you'll think long and hard before you give Burch permission to move your graves. I know I have the deed to that property somewhere. I've been looking through Granddaddy's papers, but I haven't found it yet. You could buy me time." Without waiting for an answer, she told Katharine, "That's my mailbox on the left. You can drop me off there."

No house was in view down the sand and shell drive.

"She's going to have a ways to walk," Dr. Flo said softly.

The forest grew close to the drive, but Katharine figured it couldn't do much more damage to her paint than the trip to the cemetery already had. "I'll drive you home. You have Samson and the shrimp." *And the shotgun*, she mentally added.

"I'd be grateful," Agnes accepted without fuss.

The roof came into view first, tin gleaming through the treetops—but that was all Agnes's place had in common with Bayard Bluff. This house was small, shaped like a *T* and built of boards and battens that had never known paint. Katharine suspected if she went inside she would find the living room and a bedroom on each side of a wide front hall with bedrooms above them, and an eat-in kitchen and storeroom in the wing at the back. The space over the kitchen was a screened-in sleeping porch. The side of the house faced the drive so that the front porch—also screened— could face the slough, which glided past like a water snake broad enough for the small motorboat tied to a weathered dock. Fishing poles leaned against the rusty bark of a cedar in the front yard. Four hens and a rooster scratched in the sandy yard between the house and the slough, in the shade of live oaks laden with moss.

"This is charming!" Dr. Flo exclaimed.

Katharine doubted that the fastidious professor would ever want to live there. The whole place looked like a hotel for bugs.

Agnes dismissed the compliment, but with an undertone of pride. "It's comfortable, but it's not as old as Bayard Bluff, which was built in the seventeen nineties. Ours wasn't built until 1874. I think some branch of the Bayard family lived here before it was deeded to granddaddy. Will you all come in and have a glass of tea?"

"I'm not sure we have time." Dr. Flo sounded regretful. "It's already past four, and we still have to visit an attorney down in Darien and get to Jekyll."

"It won't take long," Agnes countered, "and I'll give Katharine butter to put on those chiggers. Looks like she got quite a few."

Katharine was embarrassed that her surreptitious scratching had been noticed, but admitted, "I'd be grateful for butter. And tea. My throat is parched from smoke."

Agnes gave her rumbling laugh. "Nell does fill the place up a bit, doesn't she? But bless her heart, it's about the only pleasure she's got." She climbed down from the car and helped Samson out. He lumbered over to a large oak near the water, where there was a depression in the sand just his size.

"Nell's got Miranda," Dr. Flo pointed out as she climbed down.

"Miranda belongs to Nell's older brother, Jack. He's in jail for selling drugs and not likely to get out anytime soon, so his wife divorced him and took Miranda down to Waycross. She comes up to spend summers with her granny, but if she keeps carrying on about Chase like she's started doing this year, she may not get to come for a while. Iola says she's too old to be keeping up with a teenager's hormones."

"That family really *has* had some tragedies, hasn't it?" Katharine exclaimed.

Ms. Morrison gathered up her shrimp and her gun. "The greatest tragedy as far as I'm concerned is Nell. I taught her in school, and she's real bright. Could have gone to college if she'd gotten a little help, but that was right before the HOPE scholarships came in and Iola said she couldn't afford to help her. Iola suggested that Nell ask Dalton to help—sort of a 'This is one last thing you all could do to make up for my legs'—but all Dalt would agree to was to swap Nell's college education for the ten acres and Iola's promise to get off the island. She wouldn't do that, so Nell's been stuck right here, working in that office six days a week." She sighed, then motioned with one thick hand. "You all come on in, now."

As they trooped from the kitchen down the wide front hall, Katharine gave herself a mental pat on the back. A living room was on one side and a bedroom with a snowy chenille spread on the other. The house could have been gloomy, for the floors were made of wide, unfinished boards and both walls and ceilings were tongue-and-groove boards, but someone had painted the walls creamy white and spread bright rugs on the floor.

Their hostess showed them to comfortable rockers on the front porch and went to fetch their tea. The air felt cooler there—perhaps because of the water and maybe because of a breeze that stirred the moss in the oaks. The hens clucked companionably. A nanny goat and two kids bleated in a pen on the far side of the house, beside a modest garden. Two cats—one large, one small—curled on a table at the end of the porch. They were what Katharine's children used to call "Halloween cats": orange, black, and white.

Dr. Flo rocked gently. "This is very peaceful."

Katharine scratched her ankles and waited for relief. Ms. Morrison reappeared with a big pat of butter on a white crockery plate. "Rub it on thick, now," she instructed. "You want to smother the little buggers. Tea's coming in just a minute." She lumbered back to the kitchen.

Katharine spread butter lavishly on each bite and willed the chiggers to smother.

Ms. Morrison reappeared with a tray holding crystal glasses of sweet tea with slices of lemon and leaves of fresh mint. She passed the tea and handed out dainty cloth napkins. "My grandmother's stuff," she mumbled. "Don't get to use it too often." She sank into a rocker that was rounded to fit her sturdy hams.

Katharine rocked and felt the chiggers' itch abating, content to let the other two carry the weight of the conversation.

"I was just telling Katharine that this is a very peaceful house," Dr. Flo commented.

"I've lived here most of my life, and there's no place on earth I'd rather be. I cannot bear to watch Burch push over noble trees in order to fill the island with strangers who consider it thcir God-given right to exploit the island for their own comfort. It doesn't bear thinking about."

Dr. Flo stirred her tea and sipped it gratefully. "How long has your family lived here?"

"My grandparents moved in in 1892. Whoever had been living here before had recently died, I think. But I don't know what happened to their children."

"Children?"

"Let me show you." She shoved open the screened door and led them down the front steps. The house rested on brick pillars all around. She led them to the one at the right corner of the porch, where concrete or tabby had been smeared over the brick and four small handprints pressed in with the date, 1874.

"I don't know who the children were," Ms. Morrison said as they resumed their seats. "Don't know a thing about the prior tenants. Granddaddy moved here in 1892, like I said. He was the first cousin and great friend of Miss Ella Bayard, who was both Dalton's grandmother and his step-great-grandmother."

"Do!" Dr. Flo exclaimed.

Their hostess beamed at having shocked them. "At seventeen she married Claude Bayard, who was over forty and had a fifteen-year-old son, Hamilton. When Claude died eight years later, Miss Ella waited a year, then married Hamilton. They were apparently very happy together. My mother said they were the nicest Bayards she ever knew. I didn't know him well—he died when I was five—but Miss Ella lived until 1953. We always regarded her as the great benefactress of our family." She rocked and ruminated for a minute.

"Granddaddy was an Episcopal priest, but he was never strong and he had some sort of collapse right after he finished seminary. Miss Ella wanted to help, and she had both money and influence in these parts because her daddy was rich and she had married Claude Bayard. She arranged for Granddaddy to serve a church down the road and to hold weekly services in the Bayard Island chapel, which used to be in that clearing near the cemetery. After she married Hamilton, she persuaded him to deed Granddaddy this house and eight acres, including the land where the church stood."

"They would have had a long walk to church in the heat." Dr. Flo delicately fanned herself with one hand.

Agnes flapped one big hand toward the side of the house where the nanny was bleating. "It's only a skip and a holler along the slough." She took a hefty swig of tea and wiped her mouth with a dainty napkin that looked incongruous in her big, rough hands. "Dalton Bayard may be a son of Satan, but his grandmother was a saint."

"And you grew up in this house?"

"After I was seven. My grandmother died and my parents moved back in to take care of Granddaddy." She laughed. "I've never ventured far from my roots, Florence. I grew up in the house where Daddy did and later taught math where he used to teach English." She looked contentedly at the vista of broad live oaks and ancient cedars, bordered by the ribbon of water.

She had answered one of Katharine's silent questions: how she managed to buy groceries and gas for the blue Honda parked in her yard. With no mortgage and few bills, she should live comfortably on a teacher's pension.

They rocked companionably for several minutes, imbibing the peace of the place. Dr. Flo brushed away a circling fly and asked, "You don't know anything about the Mallery who was buried near the Guilberts, do you, Agnes?"

Katharine hid a smile. Those two had certainly gotten to a first name basis pretty quick. She still had her own reservations about a woman who shot first and asked questions later.

Agnes furrowed her brow. "Mallery. Mallery. Seems like that name is familiar."

"One of the graves is that of Elizabeth Mallery Bayard," Katharine reminded her. "Mother of Claude."

"Yes, but there's something else. Seems like I saw that name once in old papers around here. As a kid I used to spend rainy days rummaging in drawers, because my folks have always been pack rats and I never knew what I might come across. While I'm looking for my deed, I'll see if I can find anything about a Mallery or the Guilberts. How would I get in touch with you if I do?"

Katharine gave her the phone number at Posey's beach cottage and Dr. Flo recited her home number. Katharine shifted uneasily in her rocker when Dr. Flo inquired, "Do you have children? What happens to the land and this house when you are gone?"

Agnes apparently had no qualms about discussing her demise or her estate. "It goes back to the Bayards, unfortunately. That was a stipulation of Miss Ella's grant. From what I understand her son, Asa, pitched a hissy fit when he heard his parents were giving away some of their land, so Mr. Hamilton wrote the deed so that our family could own the land in perpetuity, but could not sell it or leave it to anyone except the Bayards. I watch my back when Dalt's around." She gave a bark of laughter that made the cats look up uneasily and Samson give a low *woof!* She bent to give the dog a reassuring pat before she added, with a twinkle in her eye, "The only thing that ever tempted me to get married was the notion that I could pass on this land to my children. I decided that was too high a price to pay."

Chapter 12

The road to Darien was miles of vine-covered forest inter-spersed with mobile homes. Occasionally somebody had built with brick or stucco, but the prevailing opinion seemed to be, "Why build when you can buy a prefab house already furnished?"

When they reached the county seat, they found Mr. Curtis's office in a strip mall with a plate-glass window lettered in flaking gold: HAYDEN CURTIS, ATTORNEY AT LAW. As they approached, Katharine and Dr. Flo had an excellent view of a blond receptionist's brown part as she polished her nails at the front desk. "Y'all go right on in." She waved them toward a closed door at the rear, multitasking by indicating their way while drying her nails.

When Dr. Flo knocked, a bass drawl called, "Come on in. It's open."

They stepped into a windowless office with avocado shag carpet and gray walls. Katharine felt she had wandered into a cave, especially since the only illumination came from low-watt bulbs in table lamps beside the client love seat and on the credenza behind the desk.

Did Hayden Curtis prefer dim light because his office was furnished in thrift-store chic? Or because he was so unat-tractive? A pudgy little man with rolls of fat bulging over a tight white collar and his belt, he had an abundance of black hair—fluffy on top, curling from his ears, lying like a pelt on the backs of his hands. His eyes, which were on a level with Katharine's own as he stood behind his desk to greet them, were like two shards of coal.

They locked on Dr. Flo as soon as she came in. "Miz Gadney?"

Dr. Flo and Katharine exchanged a quick look. Burch must have called.

"Dr. Gadney." Her voice was smooth as velvet. She looked chic and competent in her beige pantsuit and heels, but Katharine refused to feel underdressed. She had no need to impress a man in a shiny, rumpled suit.

His air conditioning, like Nell's, was low enough to turn Katharine's toes to ice, but beads of sweat stood on his forehead. He pulled a white handkerchief from his jacket pocket and swiped it across his face with one hand while he waved them to the love seat with the other. The office was so small, Katharine's knees touched his desk when she sat.

"Good of you to come." His voice aimed for hearty but achieved only breathy heaviness.

He finally looked at Katharine. "And you are?"

While he waited for her to answer, he folded his handkerchief and restored it to his pocket, making it clear he was only giving her part of his attention. She wondered if that technique was effective in court.

"Katharine Murray." Devilment made her add, "Dr. Flo's chauffeur."

That earned her his attention for an instant. She bent to set her purse on the floor to hide her smile.

"I see. Do you want her present, Miz Gadney, while we discuss this—ah—little matter?"

"I definitely want her present. Katharine has my full confidence." Dr. Flo fixed him with a look that used to dominate classrooms. "We have seen the cemetery this afternoon. And met Burch Bayard." She paused between statements to make a complete sentence of the last.

"I know. He called. He says it's unlikely those graves belong to your people."

"Not at all." Dr. Flo drew the Neiman Marcus bag onto her lap and took out a worn black leather Bible, the once-gold edges faded and speckled. She laid it on his desk and opened it to the page where births, marriages, and deaths were recorded. "If you will turn on that lamp," she gestured to the reading light on his desk and waited until he complied, "and compare these dates with the ones on the gravestone for Claude Gilbert," she laid her notebook beside the Bible, "you will see that the dates for the birth and death of the man in Mr. Bayard's cemetery and for my grandfather exactly coincide. I have no doubt that I have found my grandfather's grave."

He slid a sheet of paper toward her. "So you are authorized to give permission for Burch to move the grave. Just sign here." He indicated the line with his pen and held it out to her.

Dr. Flo shook her head. "There are three other graves that seem to be connected to his, and I am not familiar with those names. I need to do research to determine if I am the person with authority to move those graves." She closed her Bible and notebook and put them away with the air of having had the final word.

He shoved the paper another infinitesimal quarter inch her way. "You don't have to worry about those graves, Miz Gadney. Permission to move the one will be fine." Again he held out the pen.

"Dr. Gadney," she corrected him, keeping her hands in her lap. "And somebody has to be concerned about those graves, if they are to be moved. If they are related to my grandfather, you need my permission to move them. I am the last of his family."

His lips tightened but before he could speak, she added, "You need to know, too, that after Mr. Bayard left, we met

Miss Agnes Morrison. She claims she has the title to that land."

"That woman!" His voice rose several notes. "Meddles in everything. She has no claim to that land. No claim whatsoever." He patted the air with both hands to dismiss Miss Morrison and her claims. With his snout of a nose and hairy paws, he reminded Katharine of a panda. Put the man in the right suit and he'd make a grand panda—plump, hairy, and potentially dangerous.

"She said her grandfather—"

He cut her off with an imperious wave. "Her granddaddy was given land for his lifetime. Since the Bayards have never had another use for it until now, they permitted her family to live there out of the kindness of their hearts, but the land has always been theirs."

Since they came in, he had developed a little wheeze. Katharine wondered if he had asthma and whether they were bringing on an attack.

She entertained herself by considering the difficulties an asthmatic panda might encounter in the wild.

"Miss Morrison was quite emphatic that she has documentation to prove her claim," Dr. Flo said calmly, "but that will be your problem. My only concern is that I must wait to sign anything until I can research the identity of those persons buried in the other graves, to determine if they were my ancestors."

Mr. Curtis interlaced his thick fingers and clasped his hands close to his chest like he held winning cards. "Ma'am, to be blunt, it's unlikely any of them were your ancestors. That cemetery has been in the Bayard family for over two hundred years, and without wanting to overstate the obvious, they are white. Burch Bayard will take legal action against anyone who claims one of his ancestors was involved with a black woman, so unless your ancestor was white, I believe we are finished here." He stood.

Dr. Flo opened her purse, took out an envelope, and extracted an old sepia photograph. "My ancestor was not white. This was him. It says on the back 'Claude Gilbert, 1902.'"

The lawyer glanced at the photo, turned it over, read the name, and handed it back with obvious relief, "Then he is not the man buried in the Bayard cemetery. That tombstone has a misspelling. We are looking for a family of Gwilberts." He pronounced the name as if it were a familiar one.

Katharine stirred in her chair. "Are there other Gwilberts in this county?" She had never heard the name, but Mr. Hayden had said it so confidently that McIntosh County might be full of Gwilberts.

"Not that I know of," he admitted, adding quickly, "Lemme look." He reached in his bottom drawer and pulled out a small telephone book. Either the company didn't put out new books of that region very often or he was sentimentally attached to an early edition, for his was limp and dog-eared. He donned a pair of drugstore reading glasses and thumbed through the pages, licking his forefinger before turning each page.

Katharine motioned for the photo and held it close to the table lamp. Claude Gilbert had been a handsome man, with an oval face and a little mustache, but he looked darker than Dr. Flo.

Mr. Curtis laid down the phone book and shook his head, failing to conceal his disappointment. "The Gwilberts must have died out or moved away."

"Or changed the spelling of their name to Gilbert," Dr. Flo suggested with asperity.

He waved his furry paw again. "I regret that you have wasted your time . . ."

Dr. Flo drew herself up in her chair and said in an icy voice, "I have not wasted my time. I have found my grandfather's grave."

Mr. Curtis's face grew pink and mottled, and spit collected in the corner of his mouth. "Can you prove that your people have any connection with Bayard Island?"

"Not yet. Until today, all I knew about Claude Gilbert was that he went to Atlanta around 1887 to attend Morehouse College, became a lawyer, and remained in the Atlanta area." She paused, then added, "My father was a lawyer, too. He graduated from Emory law school." Her eyes flickered to the unimpressive degree hanging behind Mr. Curtis's desk.

He clasped his chubby fingers so tightly together they turned white. "The fact remains that you cannot be positive that this Claude Gilbert was your grandfather."

"Not positive, yet, but so certain that I am willing to sign to have his grave moved." She took the photo Katharine handed her, restored it to its envelope, and slipped it back into her purse. "However, while I have no idea who Marie and Françoise Guilbert"—she emphasized the French pronunciation— "were, or who the Mallery was who was buried near them, I am convinced that at least two of those graves are connected to Claude's. Otherwise, why enclose them together like that? Naturally, then, I want to do more research before I give permission to move any of the graves. I hope you understand. If the Guilberts turn out to be my relations . . ."

He stood. "I don't think there is any possibility that they are your relations. We don't need to bother you any longer, Miz Gadney. We'll take care of our little problem down here. Sorry you came all this way for nothing."

It didn't take a psychic to figure out what he planned to do.

"We've seen the graves," Katharine pointed out.

His gaze flicked her like a whip and returned to Dr. Flo.

"If those graves get moved without Dr. Flo's permission," Katharine continued in a quiet voice that her children had learned meant trouble, "she will sue and I will testify to what I have heard, both here and out at the cemetery. I am sure Agnes Morrison will be willing to testify, as well. We met her at the cemetery and went home with her to discuss the graves."

Frustration stripped off the thin veneer of manners and revealed the country boy within. With an oath he slammed one fist on his desk. "I shoulda let Burch sign off on all them graves and been done with it. Ain't nobody else's bidness. They're in his plot, on his propitty."

"Then why did you bother to look for descendants?" Dr. Flo's voice was cool and merely curious. Katharine admired her poise. In the professor's shoes, she would have been furious.

Instead, it was Hayden Curtis who was a hairsbreadth from incoherent. "Because we didn't want Agnes stirring up more trouble than is necessary. She pointed out that some graves say Gwilbert instead of Bayard, and she said if we didn't look for their relatives, she'd make a stink." He pulled out his handkerchief one more time and dabbed his forehead, cheeks, and the back of his neck.

With no warning, he slumped into his seat, scrabbled in his desk for an inhaler and stuck it in his mouth. He took several deep breaths with his eyes closed.

"Are you all right?" Katharine asked. "Should we call your secretary?"

He flapped his hand in negation and took the inhaler out of his mouth long enough to gasp, "Give me a minute."

They sat uneasily until he sat back up in his chair and pocketed the inhaler. "Agnes affects me that way. I shouldn't let her get to me, but she does. She's so apt to make a fuss over nothing, but she tends to make such a big one, we couldn't just let it pass. But it's not like you have been tending those graves all these years, or even know who those people are." Having failed with intimidation and threats, he tried pleading. "We'll put them in a place where they'll be taken care of without it costing you a dime. Mr. Bayard will assume full responsibility for all the costs of moving and transplanting them." He clutched his handkerchief in one hand while his other one shoved the paper across his desk so it was right in her face. "All you gotta do is sign right here—"

One forefinger covered with soft black hair marked the place while he swabbed the back of his neck again. Katharine wondered how low the thermostat would have to be to cool his blood. His skin shone with oily sweat.

Dr. Flo shook her head. "I was a professor of business, Mr. Curtis. I taught my students never to sign a paper until they had studied it and considered all the ramifications. Recent lawsuits against top executives in large corporations have demonstrated the wisdom of that. So if you will give me the papers, I will take them home with me, sign them, and mail them back to you as soon as I have satisfied myself that I have the right and responsibility to do so."

He chewed his lower lip. From a lump on it, Katharine deduced he did that whenever he was perplexed, and he must be perplexed a lot. She didn't envy him, caught between Burch Bayard's determination and Dr. Flo's integrity.

He came to a decision. He folded the papers and shoved them back in a desk drawer. "Okay, you win. When you are ready to sign, give me a call and I'll send them to you. I'd give them to you now, except that wouldn't be right, seeing how as somebody else might show up tomorrow also claiming to be a descendent of Claude Gilbert. But if you get positive proof you're his authorized descendant, you give me a call and I'll send them overnight. You gotta do it fast, though—you understand? Mr. Bayard can't wait around." He shoved his handkerchief back in his pocket without bothering to fold it. One corner dangled sloppily like a little white flag of surrender.

"We'll be in Jekyll for a few days," Dr. Flo told him. "I'll get back to you by the end of the week, if possible."

He grabbed up his pen and the back of an envelope. "Where you gonna be on Jekyll? Lemme have a number where we can reach you. I'll have my secretary call if she can turn up information on those other graves. I'm gonna be out of town the rest of this week, but heck, if she finds anything, I'll even have her run it down so you can see it for yourself." He reached for a pen.

Dr. Flo shook her head. "I don't have a cell phone."

Having seen the secretary, Katharine had little faith in her ability to do genealogical or any other type of research, but she gave him the number at Posey's. Better that than Mr. Curtis calling on her cell.

As they rose to go, he reminded them, "Don't wait too long to get back to me, you hear? They's millions riding on this deal."

Katharine wondered how much he personally stood to gain. Was development on Bayard Island his personal ticket out of his dreary little office?

"There is also the dignity of the dead." Dr. Flo rose, but did not put out her hand. "I think you will agree that we owe them that much?"

Mr. Curtis didn't reply. As Katharine followed Dr. Flo out the door, she looked back. The panda had been replaced by an angry little bull.

Dr. Flo was silent until Katharine pulled out of the parking lot and headed south toward town, then she cupped her slender hands over her nose and bowed low over her lap, rocking back and forth. Katharine was startled. She'd been embarrassed for the professor, but had never imagined Mr. Curtis would make her cry.

A gasp and a chuckle made her realize Dr. Flo was laughing. Still rocking back and forth, she clapped her hands to punctuate her delight. "Thought he had himself an old darky grandmother in there, didn't he? Gonna sign that white man's paper and say 'Yessuh, yessuh, glad to have you move my fambly graves. Kin I polish your fu'niture whiles I's heah?'"

Her accent was so droll that Katharine laughed, too. Once she started, she couldn't stop. She laughed so hard she had to pull into a filling station parking lot. They laughed until tears ran down their faces and washed away the whole afternoon. Whenever Katharine was about to regain her composure, Dr. Flo would blurt out something like "Agnes and that shotgun!" or "Just like a wood nymph," or "Wooee—the size of that rattlesnake!" or "My chauffeur," and set them off again.

Finally Dr. Flo took several deep, gusty breaths. "I needed that. And when we get down to Jekyll? I'll tell you what, girlfriend, I might take you up on that swim. I feel the need right now for a thorough cleansing." She brushed her face and the front of her jacket. "Don't want to carry along any microscopic particles of Mr. Curtis that might have stuck."

"One hour and we can be up to our necks in the ocean," Katharine promised.

Chapter 13

When they got back on the road, Dr. Flo brought out her
reading glasses and the small notebook she'd used at the
cemetery. "I sure hope I can find out something about these
Guilberts and where they came from."

"And Mallery the pirate. You won't forget him, will
you?"

Dr. Flo gave a gentle snort. "Let's give Mallery to Burch's
family. I would like to know why he was buried alongside
my relatives, though—and why my relatives were buried
with the Bayard family." She took out a pencil and began to
make notes.

"I wouldn't know how to start looking for something like
that."

"First, I'll go online and check ancestry.com to see if I can
find the Guilberts. Is there an Internet connection in this
house where we'll be staying?"

"Sure."

"Good. Maybe I can find something tonight. I'll particularly want to look at the census data for 1870 and 1880. If
Marie lived in McIntosh County, I should be able to find her
and a good bit about her. By then they were listing the
names, ages, and professions of every member of every
household."

"You can get all that online?" A novice to genealogy research, Katharine was astounded.

"Absolutely. I also want to look up Francis and Elizabeth Bayard, to find out if their entries are near hers. That would indicate they were neighbors, since the census lists households in the order the census-taker got to them."

"I wonder why the husband's memorial said 'Beloved husband,' but hers only said 'Wife of Francis and Mother of Claude.' I'll bet there's a story there."

"That's the kind of thing that is harder to find. The dead can't take their wealth, but they sure do take most of their stories. Genealogy is like real detective work, not the kind you read about in books. Not much violence or sex, just a lot of slogging. You don't expect to get all the answers fast, either. Sometimes you don't get answers at all."

She returned to her notes. "There's one possibility about Marie that may have occurred to you, too."

Katharine didn't want to admit she hadn't given Marie a thought since they'd left the cemetery. "What's that?"

"Francis Bayard was born in 1818 and Marie in 1825. Marie may have been Francis's mistress, and the children their grandchildren, whom she raised. She could have come from New Orleans or somewhere like that."

"Which would mean that Burch might not know all he thinks he does about his family's history. Do you think that looking at the various censuses—or is it censi?—will tell you enough?"

"Probably not. I may have to look at marriage and death records and see if there's a deeds book for McIntosh County showing who owned property back then. There's even a book that lists what is found on the family pages of old Georgia Bibles. If Marie kept her family records in a Bible that got copied in that book, I'll have hit pure gold. And there's always the chance I'll come across a reference book I have never used before. Genealogy is a constant learning curve."

Katharine gave her a teasing glance. "You aren't likely to

find all you need as fast as Burch and Mr. Curtis would wish."

"Absolutely not. This could take weeks, months, even years."

"While poor Mr. Curtis pines away. You are *bad*, Dr. Flo." Her eyes twinkled. "Girl, you don't know the half of it."

As they left the mainland for the Jekyll Island causeway, Dr. Flo looked across the marshes and confessed, "I've never been to Jekyll. I always meant to come, but never got here."

"It's one of the nation's seashore treasures, but developers are hot to get their hands on it. It's got terrific beaches, wonderful riding waves, good golf courses, and an ideal location."

"I'm getting the notion that any location is ideal to you so long as it's close to the ocean."

Katharine arched her back to get the kinks out from driving. "True, but what I meant was, Jekyll is at the far western tip of the curved coastline between Florida and South Carolina, so hurricanes generally pass far out to sea."

"That does give it a certain advantage. We aren't expecting any hurricanes this week, are we?" Dr. Flo sounded anxious.

"Not even a storm. Do you mind if I open the windows now so I can enjoy the air?"

"Go ahead, if you can stand the heat. The wind won't ruin my hairdo." She patted her crisp silver curls. "But can you believe how hot it is, even at the end of the day? My only consolation is that it's hotter in Boston, Chicago, and St. Louis."

"All those places that make fun of the South for being so hot," Katharine agreed. "I'll leave the AC on to cool us down a bit, even if I do open the windows."

She appreciated the cool on her knees even while she enjoyed gulps of thick, humid air redolent of salt marshes and tidal decay. The marshes were not at their best wearing large patches of summer brown and sticky with mud at low tide, but as she watched the rippling interplay between sun and shadows on the grass, she said, "Every time I get back near the ocean, I wonder why I left. To me, that's the smell of home. Isn't it marvelous?"

Dr. Flo wrinkled her dainty nose. "Girlfriend, if this is the smell you associate with home, you had a deprived childhood. Smells like the whole place is slowly rotting away."

Katharine laughed. "I guess it does, a little. Miami doesn't smell like this, anyway, but the keys do. We used to rent a little place down on Marathon every summer, and no matter how hot it was, I always slept with my windows open so I could smell the air. At Posey's cottage I always leave my bedroom windows open at night."

"Inviting burglars?"

Katharine wished she hadn't mentioned burglars. For the first time all day she felt the nightmares crouched and waiting. Determined not to let them spoil her vacation, she said firmly, "But isn't this gorgeous? I feel like I can inhale not only the marshes, but the colors of the marsh and the water and the sky."

Dr. Flo craned her neck and peered up. "That sky seems awfully big and close. Feels like it might crush us."

Katharine laughed. "My mother always said that at the beach, God makes up for the lack of mountains by giving folks an incredible sky."

"Well, I wouldn't mind a few hills to hold it up."

Katharine laughed again as she pulled into a small shopping center near the end of the causeway. She couldn't remember when she'd last felt so carefree. "No hills on Jekyll except a few little ones on golf courses. Sorry. I'm going to run in and pick up a few groceries to supplement what I brought. Do you want to wait in the car?"

Dr. Flo picked up her purse. "Let me come in and pay."

"Nonsense. I won't get much. You can pay tomorrow."

At the checkout counter, Katharine saw a slim woman who looked vaguely familiar. She had fluffy blond curls, soft pink skin that looked like it had never been out in the sun, and well-shaped hands tipped with deep red nails. She smiled. "Aren't you Katharine Murray? I'm Joye Folsum, from the realty office."

"You didn't wait for us, did you?" Beside so much perfection, Katharine was keenly aware of her gritty feet, travel-creased pants and shirt, and the fact that she hadn't put on lipstick or powder since lunchtime. She was appalled if she had kept this woman at her office so late.

"Oh, no, I had other things to do." Ms. Folsum was a multitasking marvel. She managed to swipe her debit card and punch in her PIN while smiling her thanks to the cashier and carrying on a coherent conversation. "But Mrs. Buiton called and told me to expect you, so I went over earlier to check things and make sure the house was aired and ready. You know where to find the family's hidden key, or do I need to get you one from the office?"

Katharine started unloading her own basket. "I know where the key is hidden. Thanks."

"Give us a call if there is anything you need." Ms. Folsum picked up two bags of groceries and headed out the door.

"Did you see that gorgeous woman who left just before me?" Katharine asked as she climbed back into the car. Dr. Flo nodded. "She's Posey's realtor. She made me feel like a frump. How can a woman work this late and still manage to look like that?"

"She hasn't been exploring cemeteries all day." Dr. Flo stretched, arching her back. "This is so marvelous. I've been sitting here thanking God for you. This is the first real vacation I've had since Maurice died."

Katharine gave her a surprised glance. "I thought you'd

been out of the country a lot. I hadn't seen you for ages until I ran into you at the history center back in June."

"No, I was—" Dr. Flo looked out the window as if looking for a word "—hibernating. I don't really want to talk about it."

Katharine tried not to feel hurt that Dr. Flo would pull the curtains of privacy so tightly around her after their camaraderie of the past hours, but reminded herself, *She owes you nothing just because you've had fun together.* Still, she found it puzzling that a woman of Dr. Flo's intellect and social stature could drop out of the Atlanta scene for so long without a single rumor circulating about where she was. Had she had a breakdown? Gone into a serious depression? From all reports, she and Maurice had been very close. Whatever she'd been doing and wherever she'd been, apparently Katharine wasn't to be told.

As they headed up the island in the slanting golden light of early evening, Dr. Flo peered out at the trim brick houses, backyard patios, and well-kept lawns that lined the street. "It's very suburban, isn't it?" she said with a trace of disappointment she couldn't quite conceal. "When you said 'cottage,' I was expecting something in the nature of big wooden houses with wraparound verandas, a conglomeration of mismatched furniture, and linoleum floors nobody minds if you track sand in on."

"Those are all gone." Katharine shared her regret. "Still, brick or stucco houses, vinyl or tile floors, and aluminum windows make more sense when you have to keep a house up in this climate. And while I miss the big porches, I find that air conditioning and modern kitchens are definite compensations."

When she turned into Posey's driveway, she could tell Dr. Flo was still not impressed. She had seen that reaction before. Posey and Wrens valued their privacy, so had built a two-story, *U*-shaped stucco house without a single window facing the street except for matching sets of French doors with small balconies upstairs at each end of the *U*. With a smile, Katharine got out and punched in the code to let them into the garage. Once she had pulled the SUV inside, she fetched the hidden key to the house, but instead of taking Dr. Flo in the kitchen door, she led her across the courtyard to the front door, using the code pad to close the garage door behind them.

When they stepped inside onto the white tile floor, Dr. Flo dropped her bag and gasped. "How lovely!"

"It is, isn't it?" Katharine had seen that reaction before.

The foyer ceiling soared two stories above them, then sloped slightly over the great room to meet a wall of glass facing the ocean. A bridge connected the two sides of the upstairs, its white banisters scarcely noticeable in the expanse of space, especially when—as now—the eastern sky was a rosy reflection of the sunset, spread over a deep purple sea.

The great room flowed into the dining room and kitchen to their right, behind the garage, creating one large space of white walls, white wicker furniture, white cabinets and counter tops, glass-topped tables, and fat down cushions in bright beach colors of hot pink, yellow, turquoise, and orange. Beyond the glass wall, a broad deck was ready for relaxing, outdoor wicker already in place. A wooden boardwalk meandered across sparsely planted dunes to the beach.

Katharine hefted her own bag. "There's a master suite downstairs to the left and four bedrooms upstairs. Two of them face the ocean. I'll be in one of those, and if you like, you can have the other."

"If you don't mind, I'd rather be downstairs. I have always been afraid of fire."

When Katharine got upstairs she flung up the windows so her room would fill with the sound and scent of the surf.

Beyond the boardwalk, the beach was wide and only slightly damp. She called downstairs. "The tide's just started in— perfect for a quick dip before dusk."

Dr. Flo called back. "I've changed my mind. Do you mind if I stay here and see if I can find Marie on the Internet?"

Katharine bit her lip. She respected the ocean too much to swim without at least somebody watching her from shore, but after all, they had come down for Dr. Flo to research her family. "That's fine." She tried to keep the disappointment out of her voice.

She was looking sadly at those perfect waves across the dunes—who knew if they'd be that perfect again before they left?—when Dr. Flo appeared in her doorway in a soft white cotton tank top, white shorts that showed off her slender legs, and red flip-flops.

"I remembered how much you've been wanting to swim. How about if I take a book down and read while you go in? I don't want you swimming alone. But I'm warning you, if a shark gets you, I'll wave and tell him to have a good dinner."

As they headed down the boardwalk, somebody called "Yoohoo!" A perky redhead stood on the deck of the house next door, wearing blue shorts and a white shirt that set off her nicely rounded figure. "Hey, folks. Is one of you Katharine?" Her accent was thick South Georgia.

"Yes," Katharine acknowledged.

"I'm Jenny-Jill Roberts, from Bainbridge. Posey called to tell me you were coming down. I just wanted to say if there's anything whatsoever that we can do for you while you're here, let us know. We're both retired, so we're here pretty much all the time. If you need something, don't hesitate to call us. Our number is beside your kitchen phone."

"Friendly neighbors," Dr. Flo remarked as they padded along the wooden boardwalk and finally reached the soft sand above the reach of the tide.

"A vast improvement over Posey's last ones. They were always yelling about kids making too much noise on the deck, and since Posey has three girls and four grandchildren, they usually bring kids down when they come."

On the hard-packed sand, Dr. Flo chose a spot for her towel. Before she had spread it out, Katharine had dropped her own towel and dashed to the sea.

She reveled in the shock of the water as it splashed over her body, the tang of the salt on her skin, the taste of it on her lips, and the crash of breakers over her shoulders before she got far enough out to ride the waves. "This is better than therapy!" she exclaimed, laughing to herself. She felt moving water stroke away all her tensions not only from that day, but from the past weeks, as well. She glided up enormous waves with a sense she was about to take off and fly, then swooped down to touch bottom briefly before gliding up again. She took deep, restorative gulps of spray-filled air and called a soft, "Thank you," to the listening silence above the descending gray of the sky. "Thank you for the ocean and this glorious day. And thank you we didn't get shot."

She could have stayed in for hours, but as the sun sank behind her she finally admitted it was time to get out. The sky was pearl gray overhead and she could no longer see even a tinge of pink in the west. "There's always tomorrow," she consoled herself as she splashed through the shallows.

When she had showered, she pulled on white shorts and an old T-shirt of Jon's. She never dressed up at the beach unless she was going out. She pulled her hair back in a ponytail and padded barefoot downstairs. "I'm going to light mosquito repellant lanterns on the deck and carry a light supper outside," she told Dr. Flo, who was booting up her laptop at the dining room table. "I've got a bottle of Pinot Grigio chilling in the fridge, a wedge of Brie, crackers, ingredients to make oyster stew, and Rome apples. How does that sound?"

Dr. Flo peered above her reading glasses. "Marvelous. Do you need any help?"

"No, you look for your ancestors."

Dr. Flo had returned to her computer after the first word.

Katharine made the soup and carried everything out to the table, which she set so both could face the ocean while they ate. She didn't bother turning on a light. The lanterns and the glow from the house were enough. She smiled at how industriously Dr. Flo was punching computer keys. She hated to disturb her, but was about to call her to supper when she heard a crow. "I've found Marie Guilbert!"

Katharine grabbed up her wine and rushed inside, surprised at her own excitement.

"I can't find her in the 1870 census, but she was in McIntosh County by 1880. Look!" One slim finger traced a line on the monitor. "She was fifty-five years old, listed as the head of her household, and had two people living with her: Claude Guilbert—with a *u*—and Essie Mae Wilkins. All of them were black." She leaned back in her chair and said with satisfaction, "Put that in your pipes and smoke it, gentlemen."

Katharine leaned closer. "I didn't realize they called African Americans black back then. Does it say they lived on Bayard Island?"

Dr. Flo pointed to two blank squares at the beginning of Marie Guilbert's line. "No, the census form had spaces for addresses, but none of them were filled in for this district. That's not unusual. Folks who lived out in the country might not have an address. However, they are listed in the order in which they were visited, and the Bayards were not their neighbors. I checked."

Katharine bent closer to the screen. "I wonder who Essie Mae Wilkins was. Marie is listed as a seamstress, while Essie Mae is listed as a housekeeper."

Dr. Flo frowned. "That's odd. Black people didn't have

servants in those days." She shifted the screen to the left so they could read the lines to the end. Her finger pointed to another spot on her screen. "I can't make out where Marie or Claude were born, can you?"

Katharine peered at the scrawl. "That particular census taker must have been hired for persistence, not penmanship. I can't tell if the first letter is an *A*, an *H*, or even an *R*." The rest of the short word was an illegible scrawl. She did quick math. "But Marie was forty-four before Claude was born. She could have been his grandmother." She felt a thrill rise up in her at this confirmation of Marie Guilbert as a living, breathing woman with a home and an occupation in McIntosh County. "Maybe they lived in that house on Bayard Island. Maybe it was even built for them, and the handprints are Claude's and Françoise's!" She saw again the little tombstone, fallen and forlorn. "I hope that little girl had at least one day of giggles making her mark on the cornerstone of her new home. I wonder why they lived there."

Dr. Flo gave a genteel snort. "Given the Bayard attitude toward blacks, it's unlikely that the Bayards *let* them live there. Besides, I told you, the Bayards weren't their neighbors. I don't know where this particular census district was. Marie could have lived anywhere in the county."

"Who were the Bayards's neighbors?"

"So far I haven't found any Bayards at all."

"Would this be a good time to take a break and eat? The oyster stew is getting cold, and I don't want bugs to eat the Brie."

Later she refused Dr. Flo's help in putting their few dishes in the dishwasher. "You go see what else you can find."

"I wish I could find the Bayards."

"Check Savannah. They might have been living there when the census was taken."

"Chatham County," she murmured to herself. Katharine heard her clicking the keys. "Here they are!" Katharine joined her at the computer, feeling like gold coins were falling into their hands, one by one.

Again Dr. Flo's finger traced a line. "In 1880 Claude was thirty-two and head of his household. He had a five-year-old son, but no wife. Elizabeth Bayard was living with him, too." As Katharine returned to loading the dishwasher Dr. Flo added thoughtfully, "Elizabeth was only fifty-seven by then, but she'd already been a widow for ten years. At least I had Maurice longer than that."

Katharine was so startled, she dropped a plate and shattered it on the tiles. As she swept it up, she kept thinking, *What if I lost Tom in one more year? What would I do for all the years I had left?*

A moment later, Dr. Flo exclaimed, "Oh, my. Guess who Claude Bayard's housekeeper was."

Katharine dumped the plate shards in the trash and hurried to look. She read aloud, "Mae Ella Wilkins, thirty-six. She must have been Essie Mae's big sister."

"Her mother, more likely. She's sixteen years older. But why would the Bayards's housekeeper's daughter be keeping house for Marie Guilbert?"

"More mystery. How about apple slices to fortify you for the search?"

"Yes, please." Dr. Flo spoke absently, puzzling over the screen.

Katharine brought the plate. "Did you say you checked for Marie in earlier censuses?"

"I did, and I couldn't find her. It's possible that the name was spelled differently—even phonetically—and I missed it, but she wasn't in McIntosh County in 1870 under any spelling I could think of. I'm guessing they moved to Georgia between 1870 and 1880."

"Which would make sense, if Françoise was born in 1871. Poor little thing, she never even made it into a census. She was born and died between census years."

Dr. Flo reached for an apple slice and crunched it morosely. "That could be the epitaph for lots of kids."

"I find it sad to think of people giving information in one census without knowing they will have had a child and lose her before the next one rolls around."

"Or that they'll be dead themselves." Dr. Flo lifted her wine glass in a mock salute. "To ignorance. It's good that none of us knows when death is hovering in the wings of our lives."

They would have cause to remember that remark.

Chapter 14

When the telephone rang, Katharine glanced at the clock on the microwave and was astonished. It was quarter past ten. The day had seemed longer than that.

The voice on the other end was another surprise. "Katharine? It's Agnes. Agnes Morrison. I hope I'm not calling too late, but is Florence still up? I've found things she may want."

Katharine went upstairs to brush her teeth, to give Dr. Flo privacy. When she came down a few minutes later, Dr. Flo said, "Wait. Here's Katharine. Let me ask her to get on an extension so she can hear this."

Katharine went into the master bedroom and brought the bedside phone into the kitchen. Posey always bought portable phones so she could carry them anywhere. Dr. Flo had carried the kitchen phone over to the dining table, as if she was more comfortable in an office setting.

"Would you repeat what you just told me?" Dr. Flo requested.

Agnes complied. "Miranda came over this evening for me to help her with geometry, and after we finished, we had a treasure hunt for those papers. She found them in an old chest in the study. There are several letters written between 1874 and 1879, some written to Marie and others to someone called Dearie. All of them are signed *Mallery*."

"Mallery the Pirate?" Katharine raised her eyebrows at Dr. Flo and felt a thrill go up her spine.

Dr. Flo grinned. "That's as far as we had gotten," she told Katharine. "Go on, Agnes."

"Well, I haven't read them, but one of them was headed Port-au-Prince."

"Haiti? Let me check something." Dr. Flo tucked the phone between her ear and her shoulder and backed up a few screens on the computer. She shifted the page to the far right and peered at the scrawl that had puzzled them before. "Could be," she said under her breath.

"We found Marie in the 1880 census," Katharine explained to Agnes while they waited. "She was living in McIntosh County."

"On Bayard Island?"

"The census didn't say."

Dr. Flo came back on the line. "I believe the 1880 census lists Marie's and Claude's birthplace as Haiti. Katharine and I were having trouble earlier making out what that word was."

"So maybe they came to the States sometime between 1870 and 1880," Katharine added. "To Bayard Island."

"That would make sense," Agnes agreed, "since the letters were left here. Besides, why bury the people on the island if they didn't live here? Well, if you would like to have all these things, Florence, I'll be glad to send them along."

"That would be wonderful!"

"There's also a small baby shoe and a silver locket. The locket is so tarnished and fragile that I was afraid to open it, but since they were both at the bottom of the drawer, they probably belong with the letters, so I'll send them along. You can decide if they belong to your family or not. If not, send them back and I'll put them in the drawer for another hundred years. If they do, keep them. I've been meaning to clean out this place anyway, to save somebody having to do it after I'm gone."

"We could pick them up Thursday," Katharine suggested. "We'll leave here then."

"Don't come out of your way. I have to go to town tomorrow anyway, so I'll stick them in the mail. I almost forgot to tell you my other important news: I found the original deed to this land, the one Hamilton and Granddaddy signed. It doesn't read like I remembered—or as I'd been told. I don't think I ever actually saw it before. You won't guess what it says, Florence."

"You can sell or bequeath the land?"

"No, but neither does it revert to the Bayards. It stipulates that when our family does not want or need the house any more, it and eight acres of land revert to descendants of the family for whom the house was built. Only if none of them can be found will the land revert to the Bayards." Her rich laugh rumbled over the line. "If you can prove the house was built for Marie Guilbert and you are her last living descendant, you may be my heir."

Dr. Flo was startled into a moment's silence, then she forced a little laugh. "That won't do me much good, Agnes. I'm racing you to the finish line."

They exchanged a few pleasantries and prepared to hang up. Before they did, Agnes said in a rush, "If you all have to come back down here for anything, I have two spare rooms. They aren't fancy, but they are yours if you need them." Her tone was diffident. Katharine suspected Agnes wasn't accustomed to issuing overnight invitations.

"Thank you," Dr. Flo replied. "We might take you up on it."

Katharine doubted that. She had a hard time picturing the fastidious professor staying in a house with no air conditioning and a multitude of bugs.

When she rejoined Dr. Flo in the living room, she found her standing at the large sliding glass doors, looking out to sea. She trembled from head to toe. "Did you hear that?"

She pressed her hands against the glass to steady herself. "I may be about to add big branches to my family tree!" She swung away from the doors and began to pace, rubbing her hands. As she passed a big lounge chair, she collapsed into it as if her legs had given way. "They may have come from Haiti. Haiti!" She rolled the word on her tongue like fine wine, then swung her legs up onto a large ottoman, clasped her hands in her lap, and sat silent for a moment as if sinking deep into the roots of her own vine.

"Which means they may have been wealthy enough to afford servants." Katharine fetched them each another glass of wine and lifted hers in a salute. "To your ancestors, whoever they were."

Dr. Flo set her glass untouched on a table beside her. "Maybe that's how they could afford to send Claude to Morehouse. But I wonder where Mallery the pirate comes in."

Katharine offered a tentative—and awkward—suggestion. "Do you suppose Marie—or maybe her daughter—could have been *his* mistress, had his children, and brought them home?"

Dr. Flo's pursed her lips as she considered. "That would make sense, wouldn't it? If Mallery was related to Elizabeth—"

"—a brother, maybe— "

"—and he died, Marie might have brought his body back to his sister to be buried, and Elizabeth let her and the children stay."

"Maybe that's even why Elizabeth and Claude built her a house on their island."

Dr. Flo's dark eyes twinkled. "Hiding the evidence? Could be. Elizabeth probably paid for the house, since the Bayard men have always tended to marry money. Maybe she even paid Essie May to take care of the house, and sent Claude to Morehouse." She sipped wine and chuckled. "Isn't this fun?

We've made up a whole story out of a few lines on a computer screen and a signature at the bottom of letters we haven't even seen. We have no idea how much of the story is true, and may not be able to prove a bit of it."

Katharine settled onto the couch with her feet tucked under her. "That's the only part I don't like about genealogy. I don't want stories that aren't true. I want to *know* about people."

"Get over it. Like I said before, the dead can't take possessions with them, but they can—and do—take most of their stories." Dr. Flo reached for her glass and sipped wine with a thoughtful expression. "Sometimes I hope heaven has a huge bank of television screens where we can watch the life stories of every single person who ever lived. We can finally understand why they did what they did, how they suffered, places where they came this close to being great and missed it." She held two fingers half an inch apart. "And if we come to an incident involving another person we want to know about, we can click to a link to that person's story."

Katharine bent low over her wine. "I hope we get to edit out the parts we don't want other people watching."

Dr. Flo eyed her keenly. "You got something to hide? You're as red as this apple."

"It must be the wine. I've had three glasses, which is two over my usual limit. But I'm feeling real happy about now. We've accomplished something, and I'm glad you invited me along."

"I'm glad you invited *me*." Dr. Flo stretched lazily in the big lounge chair. "You ought to be real glad Agnes is sending me those letters. Otherwise, I might camp out on Jekyll for the rest of the summer. Now I want to go home and get to work on the Guilbert story."

"You know," Katharine mused lazily, "story is one of humanity's basic needs, isn't it? I can picture folks coming back from a mammoth hunt and telling the story: who was brave, who was funny, who got killed, who ran away. I'll bet even back that far, it wasn't enough to drag the carcass back into the cave and announce—"

The doorbell chimed. She sat up quickly, and wished she hadn't. Her head was beginning to buzz. "Who could that be?"

Dr. Flo looked worried. "I hope it's not that dreadful Mr. Curtis. We didn't give him this address, did we?"

Katharine furrowed her forehead, trying to remember. "I don't think so. Besides, why would he be coming so late?"

Her legs felt like Play-Doh as she walked toward the door.

Chapter 15

She peered through the peephole. The security lights, which came on as soon as someone stepped onto the front walk, illuminated Chase Bayard, glowering and biting his lower lip. Katharine recognized that look. It said *I don't want to be here. Mother made me come.*

Beside him a woman shifted impatiently from foot to foot. She stood a few inches taller than he, and had stormy eyes of honcy brown. Her hair, a sleek golden fall to her shoulders, curled on the ends and in tendrils around her face. The color, like Iola's and Nell's, had probably come from a bottle, but had been applied so expertly that nobody could be sure.

She pressed the bell again.

As Katharine reached for the knob, she was painfully aware of her own faded shirt, wrinkled shorts, bare feet, and untidy ponytail. Nobody had mentioned that Mona was gorgeous. Her makeup was impeccable, even at that hour of the night, and she wore a green tank top that showed off tanned, muscular arms—tennis arms that got lots of exercise on country club courts. The tank was studded with gold stars around its plunging neckline, and a small gold dolphin hung from a slender chain on her tanned chest.

Yet even if she had been plain and stark naked, Mona Bayard would have radiated the aura of prep schools, entitlement, and money that distinguishes U. S. aristocrats. As a girl, Katharine used to wonder what it was that made certain girls different from her. She could be dressed in the same sort of clothes and wear her hair brushed in the same long ringlets down her back, yet there was an air about them—a confidence, a casual conviction that the world would recognize their worth and automatically bestow on them its best— that she, with parents who firmly believed in public schools, the equality of all people, and simple living, would never achieve. Posey, Wrens, and their children had it. So did Tom and her own children. From birth they had been part of a tribe that instinctively recognizes one another and drifts together in a comfortable herd no matter where they are in the world. Katharine might now have all the privileges of the upper class, but she would never really belong.

Mona knew that.

Katharine saw the woman's quick assessment as soon as the door opened and the ever-so-slight condescension as she stepped inside. In the next instant she had stuck out one hand and said, in a husky voice with the friendly Texas drawl that is broad and flat like the state, "Hey. I'm Mona Bayard. What a great house!" She strode into the front hall on straw sandals with such thin wedge heels that Katharine marveled she didn't twist her ankles. She flung back her head and peered with admiration at the soaring ceiling and at the far glass wall with its view over the dunes. "Do you own it?"

"No, it belongs to my sister-in-law, Posey Buiton."

"Posey Buiton?" The husky voice warmed with delight. "This is the beach house that was featured in *Southern Living* a couple of years ago?" When Katharine nodded, she asked eagerly, "She's married to your brother?" Katharine saw herself going up a notch in Mona's esteem.

"No, I married her brother."

"Oh." So much for the notch. A brother who could marry Posey would have class. A woman who married Posey's brother had probably made a good catch.

Mona turned around and around, approving the art on the

walls, the bright cushions in the far room, the gallery over the foyer. "Hot damn! I'm in Posey Buiton's beach cottage. I loved that article." She turned to Chase. "Remember, honey? I told you and Daddy at supper one night about a woman in Buckhead, up in Atlanta, who owns a lot of antebellum furniture and a gorgeous beach cottage, as well? This is the cottage." She turned back to Katharine. "I've heard she has an antebellum bed up in Buckhead I'd simply die for."

Katharine didn't believe for a second that Mona Bayard had driven all the way to Jekyll to gush over furniture. A call to Posey would have sufficed for that. Chase didn't think his mother was there to discuss furniture, either. He leaned against the front wall picking a scab on his hand, obviously hoping he was invisible.

The cottage, however, gave Mona the handle she thought she needed to turn their conversation from a talk between strangers into a chat between friends. She moved a little closer and spoke softly. "Listen, I really need to talk to you. Alone. Is there someplace where we can be private?" Her eyes darted over Katharine's shoulder.

The wide staircase hid Dr. Flo from view, but Katharine figured she must still be in the recliner, for she could hear television news. She waved one arm to indicate the open nature of the floor plan. "Not really, as you see. Besides, it's Dr. Flo you want. It's her grave—"

"No, it's you." Mona still spoke barely above a whisper. "I really need your help."

"How did you find me?"

Mona looked toward Chase.

He might be mad at his mother, but he wasn't above boasting to strangers. He shrugged. "I just looked on the Internet for the address to match the phone number you gave Mr. Curtis."

Katharine gave Mona a rueful look that meant *How did*

our kids get to know so much more than we do? Mona wasn't paying attention. She was peering around with an anxious expression. She asked, so softly that Katharine could scarcely hear her. "Where is your—ah—"

"Friend?" Katharine finished for her. "In the living room watching television. We were having a glass of wine before bed. Would you care to join us?"

She knew her invitation would not be accepted. Mona's toes pulsed in her straw sandals. Katharine appreciated the determination that kept her feet planted on Posey's tiles.

Mona lowered her voice even further. Katharine had to strain and move close to hear. "No, I won't be long. I just came to ask you to please convince her to forget all this nonsense." On the last three words, she swept out her right hand as if she were executing a backhand. Katharine wondered if that was her favorite stroke.

"You know— " Mona added when Katharine said nothing, "—about the cemetery and all."

When Katharine still said nothing, she said in a rush, "Hayden did some checking after you all left, and there were some Guilberts from France who came over and visited this area." Her prep school must have taught French. She pronounced the name correctly. "They probably died from yellow fever or malaria while visiting Bayard Island and had to be buried there, because it was too hot to ship the bodies back."

Burch must have repeated Chase's theory to his wife. "When did they come?" Katharine kept her voice pleasant and merely curious.

"What?" For the first time Mona was off her stride.

"When did they come to Bayard Island?"

Mona gave another backhand wave. Did it really keep her troubles away? Katharine felt her own hand itching to try it. She clasped it with the other behind her, to make it behave.

"I don't know." Mona frowned as if trying to remember.

"What does it matter? What does matter is that they were not your friend's people, so she doesn't have to worry about those graves."

"But one of them died in 1878, one in 1889, and one in 1903. Don't you think it odd that the same family would send three members across the ocean so many years apart and all of them would die on Bayard Island? Surely after the second death, the family would have avoided that island like, well, like the plague." Katharine smiled at her own joke. Even Chase's lips twitched.

Mona fiddled with the dolphin on her chest. "That's not your problem."

"None of it is my problem. Let me call Dr. Flo."

Mona dropped the chain and grabbed Katharine's arm. "No! Listen to me!" The dolphin swung wildly as she leaned so close that Katharine could smell the spicy scent of her hair. "You need to convince her to go home and forget all this. If that story gets around—"

Katharine furrowed her forehead. "What story?"

Mona gave an impatient huff. "You know—about that man being her relative. Bayard Island has been in Burch's family for over two hundred and fifty years. There have never been any blacks buried on it. But if people think there were, they'll think one of his ancestors—you know how people are. And the Atlanta papers are always looking for a new scandal. If it gets printed in Atlanta, it will get right back down here in a gnat's minute."

Katharine would have pointed out that Atlanta had enough scandals of its own to fill the paper each day, but Mona surged on.

"Burch doesn't need a scandal when he's trying to develop the island. We have a big developer planning to come in once we get a couple of places sold—" she didn't so much as hint at her own connection to that developer "—but if it looks like there's a scandal, if lies get plastered all over the papers . . ." She stopped and completed the sentence with a pleading look. One hand reached for the dolphin again. If she wasn't careful, she was going to pull him off that chain one day.

Katharine took a step back, not bothering to hide her disgust. "Dr. Flo isn't going to go home and call reporters."

"You don't know that. Look at what happened to poor Thomas Jefferson. One person started a rumor and now all sorts of people are claiming to be related to him."

Her audacity in comparing the Bayard family history to Thomas Jefferson's stilled Katharine's tongue long enough for Mona to hurry on.

"Not that there's any truth in it where Burch's family is concerned. His people would never have fooled around that way. But if the media starts to hint that they did, it could ruin all Burch's plans. You do see that, don't you?"

Katharine shook her head. "All I see is that this is Dr. Flo's concern, not mine. If you'll let me call her—"

"Just think about it, okay?" Mona grabbed Chase's arm so hard he protested, "Ow!" but she dragged him toward the door, still pleading. "You could do everybody a big favor. Burch will take care of those graves and put them in a real good place. She won't have to be bothered at all. Please." On the front stoop she stepped back and wobbled a little on the thin wedge heels. "Tell her we've found proof that these Guilberts came from France and died in a yellow fever epidemic."

"What kind of proof do you have?" Dr. Flo spoke from behind Katharine, then moved to stand in the front door. Her voice was level and cultured, her poise undisturbed. Katharine wondered how much she had heard. She gave no sign of anger except for a faint flaring of her nostrils.

Mona's eyes flickered with surprise, recognizing Dr. Flo as a sister aristocrat.

"Hey," she said in that friendly drawl, "I ought to have talked to you in the first place, but I thought Katharine might be able to explain it to you better than a stranger could." She seemed to have forgotten that Katharine had been a stranger to her fifteen minutes before.

"I don't know what proof Hayden has," she admitted, "but he did find information about Guilberts who came over from France and stayed on the island. We think they died and were buried there because it was too hot to transport them."

Dr. Flo raised one eyebrow. "Do you plan to advertise in France for their descendants?"

That confused her. "I don't think that will be necessary. Burch will sign the papers."

"Burch cannot sign the papers unless he can prove he is a direct descendent. That's the law. Besides, we found Claude in the 1880 census, living in McIntosh County with Marie. Both names were spelled with a *u* at that time."

"So he's not your grandfather." Mona practically gushed with relief.

"Oh, yes, he's my grandfather. I am positive of that. Agnes Morrison called a few minutes ago. She's found letters that may help prove it."

"Oh, Agnes." Mona dismissed her with a gesture. "The older she gets, the crazier she gets. I wouldn't believe anything she said, if I were you."

"I still want to look at those letters. There's a possibility that Claude and Marie once lived in the house Agnes now inhabits."

Mona stared for a good three seconds, trying to absorb all that in. "Were they white?"

She immediately pressed a hand to her lips, as appalled as Katharine that she had voiced that aloud, but Dr. Flo did not seem bothered. "No, both Claude and Marie were black."

"Well, I don't want to be rude or anything . . ."

Dr. Flo interrupted, as unruffled as ever. "All this can be checked, it will just take a little time. Has your husband told you Agnes claims to own the land where the cemetery is?"

"Agnes is three bananas short of a bunch. The fact is, Burch's grandmother or somebody felt sorry for Agnes's granddaddy—who was also a tad peculiar, from what I've heard. She gave him permission to live in the house and let him serve as priest for a pathetic little church that used to stand on the island. To give him something to do, you know? But there is no reason whatsoever for Agnes to still be living there except the goodness of my father-in-law's heart. That church has been gone for years."

Chase spoke hoarsely, startling Katharine into remembering he was there. "Papa Dalt took down the walls and roof and used the wood to fix the barn."

"That's just a story he tells." Over her shoulder Mona sent him a clear mother-look that meant *Don't tell these people family secrets.*

Chase got interested in rubbing out a spot on the front walk with one toe.

Mona continued talking as if he had never interrupted. "Burch hasn't gotten around to telling Agnes she has to move, but it's nonsense for her to claim she owns any of the island. The Bayards would never give away land."

They gave part of it to Iola, Katharine thought. Dr. Flo made a restive move beside her. She could be thinking the same thing.

Dr. Flo tilted her chin. "Be that as it may, until I can determine positively that I am or am not related to the Guilberts, I cannot give permission to move those graves."

"You have to!" In the light streaming from the house, Mona's eyes glowed like amber. "Burch needs to build those houses. He's poured everything we have into that development. We need the money for Chase's school fees." She pulled the boy forward as Exhibit A of their desperate need.

He'd have been more convincing if Katharine hadn't known the price of his sneakers could have bought groceries for a week. "Don't hold Burch up. Please!"

"Perhaps he should consider building somewhere else," Katharine suggested. "There's a lot of undeveloped land on the island."

"Not cleared and with a road already to it. Burch needs that site."

"I won't hold him up one hour longer than is necessary," Dr. Flo assured her, "but I must warn you that unless your husband has firm proof those are *not* my relatives, if he attempts to move any of the three without my signature, I will sue. Is that clear? Good night, Mrs. Bayard."

"You . . . you . . ." Mona lunged.

She grabbed Dr. Flo's shoulders with muscular fingers and shook her as if she were a small rag doll. "You cannot do this to us. Do you understand? You can*not*. We have got to build those houses!"

The silver afro jerked back and forth. Dr. Flo could not pull away. Katharine seized Mona's arms and tried to break her grip, but the woman was made of hard muscle and frenzy.

"Chase!" Katharine cried.

He pounded up the sidewalk and grabbed his mother from behind. His fingers were vises on her forearms. "Stop, Mama! Come on. It's time to go home." His voice was rough, angry. "I have math to study."

Mona grew still. She stared, wide-eyed, from Dr. Flo to Katharine, then pressed both palms to her cheeks. "Omigod! I can't believe I did that. I am sorry! I am *so sorry!*"

Dr. Flo reached up and massaged one shoulder.

"Please forgive me," Mona begged. "I never did anything like that before. But if you just knew—" She stared for a moment longer, then whirled and sprinted down the walk toward the Mercedes parked at the curb.

Dr. Flo went into the house.

Chase gave Katharine an apologetic little shrug.

"Goodnight," she told him.

"Goodnight."

They looked at each other for a moment of mutual embarrassment before he headed toward their car. By the time Katharine returned to the house and shut the door, Dr. Flo had already gone to her room.

Katharine was fast asleep when the phone by her bed clamored for attention. She fumbled for it and muttered a drowsy, "Hello?"

She heard a hissed whisper with a thick drawl. "You are in dangah! Stay away from Bayard Island!"

"Who is this?"

"A friend. Stay away from Bayard Island or your lives will be in danger! You have been warned!" Whoever it was hung up.

Katharine propped herself on one elbow and looked at the clock. It read 11:57. "Chase or Miranda," she muttered. "Had to be."

But no matter how much she tried to tell herself the call was nothing but a prank, she lay awake for more than an hour listening to the surf and piecing together everything that had happened that very long day. It was hard to believe that thirty-six hours before, she had never heard of Bayard Island. Had it only been yesterday that she had told her little pig that she'd prefer anything to nightmares and fixing up the house?

Chapter 16

Wednesday on Bayard Island

Agnes's Honda jolted over ruts in sand and shell while Samson slobbered out the passenger window. Seeing Chase on the road ahead, gun in one hand, she slowed. "Don't you shoot game on my property. You hear me?"

"No, ma'am, but it's not your property. It's Daddy's property."

"That's what he thinks. I've found the deed to that land. We'll see what a lawyer—a real lawyer, not that scum your daddy hired—says about it. But my quarrel's not with you. If you want to come down tomorrow, I'll help you with algebra."

Chase nodded. They both knew he needed help. He'd failed first year algebra and the school had said he'd need to pass a competency test in September or repeat it in the coming year.

If, of course, he got to go back at all.

"I'll probably come in the afternoon." Might as well put it off as long as he could.

"See you then." Agnes flapped a hand out the window as she drove away.

"Cooter, let's go hunting this afternoon." With one horny nail Dalton Bayard scratched his jaw just under his chin. "I reckon it's 'bout time for a shave, first. These whiskers're beginning to itch in this blasted heat."

Mona insisted that Dalt bathe and shave once a week whether he needed it or not, but most of the year he resisted—more out of principle than conviction. In July, though, a bath and a shave felt as good as a dip in the ocean.

He caught a fleeting sight of himself in the mirror and peered again. Who was that old man? How had the handsomest man in McIntosh County—handsomer in his day than Burch or Chase either one—how had he deteriorated to this? Dalt turned his head this way and that, checking out the scrawny neck, jutting chin, pouches under his eyes, and eyebrows that had sprouted until they looked like dabs of Spanish moss stuck to his forehead.

"Getting old is a bitch," he growled.

"Better than the alternative," Cooter reminded him. "You still look pretty good unless'n you open your mouth."

In his eighty years, Dalt had admitted to only one fear. That one, he boasted about: "I'd rather tolerate toothache than face a dentist's drill." Nobody had ever convinced him that dentistry had evolved since his youth into an almost painless process. He knew, though, that he was no longer handsome when he smiled.

He turned from the mirror and headed to the shower. "Might as well take a bath while I'm at it. We going hunting later?"

Cooter hesitated. "Burch ain't keen on you toting a gun when you been drinking."

"I can still outshoot him. But you can shoot today. I'll spot the game."

"Where you studying on going?"

Dalt snickered. "Thought we'd mosey down past Agnes's."

"You know she don't 'low no shooting on her land."

"It's not her land. It's my land. And down there, we might sight us something so big, even you can't miss it."

Mona, sitting on the marsh-side porch with her second cup of coffee, looked up in surprise at tires crunching on their driveway. When her husband mounted the steps, she frowned. "I thought you were going to be in Savannah until tomorrow or Friday."

Burch slung his jacket across one chair and sank into another. He rubbed his head and sighed. She suspected he was hung over. Was he starting in like his daddy? That fear haunted her day and night. She could tolerate almost anything but a drunk.

She looked back to see him studying her. "I thought I ought to come back and check on what you were up to while I was away."

She drew back. "Nothing I shouldn't be."

"Keep it that way. I got a few things to do around here, then I'll be heading back."

"What time will you be home Friday?" She tried to sound casual, but she had an appointment with a Savannah golf pro she desperately wanted to keep.

Before he could answer, Chase came running up the drive, gasping for breath. "Daddy! I'm so glad you're home." He slammed the screened door behind him and fell into a chair, dropping his gun with a *clunk* beside him.

"You know better than to run with that gun." Mona's voice was sharp. An expert shot since childhood, she still shuddered to see a gun in the hands of her son.

Chase panted for a moment, then shook his head. "It's not loaded. Listen, Daddy, I just saw Agnes on her road, and she's found the deed her granddaddy and Papa Dalt's granddaddy signed. She says it gives her the land!"

Dalt stumbled onto the porch from inside, smelling of soap and rubbing his rosy chin. "Nobody ever gave Agnes anything. Dried up old prune, she'd have been a better woman if they had." He cackled at his own wit.

Chase looked from his grandfather to his father. "She's not going to let you build where the old church was. Says that land is hers."

Burch looked from his father to his wife. "Looks like somebody better talk sense to Agnes, one way or another. Any volunteers?"

Nell looked across the lunch table at Miranda. "And where were you last night, missy? When I said you could borrow my van, I didn't mean for you to come creeping into the house after midnight. Did you know she was that late, Mama?"

Iola nodded. "You know I don't sleep until she's in."

"So where were you?" Nell demanded.

Miranda swept her hair behind her ears with a shrug that bordered on insolence. "Over at Miss Agnes's, where I said I'd be. She was helping me with geometry."

"You weren't studying geometry until midnight."

The truth of that made Miranda sulky. "No, we were looking for some old deed. That place of hers is plumb full of stuff, and she got it into her head she wanted to find the deed before she went to bed. We turned out practically every drawer in the place."

"Did you find what she was looking for?" Iola reached for another handful of cold fries. Neither of the women liked to cook, so one of them generally ran into Eulonia and brought back fast food for everybody. That afternoon they sat at a table out behind the store, fanning flies and chewing hamburgers that had gotten soggy on the long ride out of town.

"Sure did." Miranda tossed the pickle from her hamburger onto the sand. "She claims it means Burch can't build his houses in the clearing. She's gonna get a lawyer and take him to court if he tries!" She finished her drink with a strong *slurp* on the straw.

Nell took the last fry. "You know as well as anybody that won't stop Burch long. He'll find a way to get what he wants. Bayards always do."

Miranda huffed. "Gloomy-Gus. I still think it's great."

Iola pushed back from the table. "It's none of our business, is what it is. Time to get back to work, girls."

Nell wheeled herself toward her van muttering, "What would I give to leave this godforsaken place?"

Miranda returned to shelving canned goods, hoping nobody asked Miss Agnes what time she had left the night before.

Agnes was shelling peas on her front porch into a blue bowl that had been her grandmother's. A bucket on the floor held unshelled peas, and a newspaper on her lap caught the pods. When the goats bleated and Samson started to bark, she looked up, curious, then laid the newspaper on the table and stood in surprise. Calling a greeting, she stomped down her front steps to meet the unexpected visitor.

The moss in the oaks quivered at the sound of a shot.

Chapter 17

Wednesday on Jekyll Island

By mutual agreement, Katharine and Dr. Flo did not mention Bayard Island or the Guilberts that precious day at the beach. Dr. Flo's laptop stayed in its case. Dr. Flo, however, grew moody toward sundown. Fearing she might be getting bored, Katharine suggested as they came back to the house after her final swim, "Shall we go out for a scrumptious seafood feast?"

The professor grimaced and shook her head. "I've got a little headache from all that sun and am pretty sore from getting shaken up last night. Why don't you go? I'll just nibble cheese and crackers. I don't feel much like eating."

Katharine was relieved. She had only suggested a restaurant because she thought Dr. Flo might prefer to eat out. Delighted not to have to get beautiful for other people, she pulled back on the shorts and shirt she'd worn all day and padded down the stairs. Her favorite supper was already available in the kitchen: shrimp boiled in beer from Wrens's bar, hush puppies from a mix in the pantry, and a salad.

"Don't you want some?" she coaxed when the shrimp was pink.

"Maybe just a bite. It does smell good," Dr. Flo admitted.

The food seemed to do her good. Katharine was glad to

see her refill her plate. "I don't want you getting sick on me," she scolded, smiling to take away the sting.

Dr. Flo gave her a slight smile in return. "I'm feeling better. Maybe I was just hungry."

They carried bowls of strawberry ice cream to the living room and watched TV. When an actor answered his cell phone, Katharine realized she hadn't checked hers all day.

Hollis had called to report on purchases for Susan's room. Hasty had called, saying, "Hope you're having fun. See you Thursday." And Tom had called three times, saying in obvious frustration the last time, "Where are you? I've been trying to reach you for two days."

She headed upstairs for privacy to talk to Tom.

As she dialed his number, she remembered how she had waited for his calls when he was at Georgetown and she at Agnes Scott. If she had realized then that long-distance dating was setting the pattern for their whole lives, would she have married him?

"Don't go there," she warned as she waited for him to answer.

"Are you all right?" His voice was anxious. He, too, had been affected by their two break-ins. He was more protective than he used to be.

"I'm fine. Didn't you get my message? I called your office yesterday morning and told Louise I was coming down to Posey's cottage until tomorrow, with Dr. Flo Gadney."

"That's odd. I asked her to try the house a couple of times today and she never mentioned you had called."

"Maybe she's getting senile." Louise was twenty-seven.

"She's been real busy pulling together reports."

They had this conversation at least once a month. Tom refused to believe Louise would deliberately fail to give him Katharine's messages. Katharine was convinced she did.

"Are you having a good time?"

"Wonderful. The ocean is fantastic— warm as bath water, with perfect waves. And we had the most incredible afternoon yesterday, too. We met an angel . . ."

"Hon," he interrupted her. "I don't like to cut you off, but I'm in the middle of dinner with some people. Can I call you back around eleven?"

"Call tomorrow night," she suggested quickly. "I'll be back home by then."

She didn't really need to tell him about the pirate's grave, the rattlesnake, the Bayard and Stampers families, or Agnes and her gun. To Tom, they would simply be stories, nothing to do with his life. Nevertheless, she felt sad as she turned off the phone and headed back downstairs.

She found Dr. Flo on the deck. "Isn't that lovely?" She gestured without turning. The rising moon, full and deep orange, shed a golden path across the water. "It's like one of heaven's golden streets. If I had the courage, I'm certain I could step out onto the water and walk straight to Maurice. He'd give me that teasing smile and say, 'Hey, Flo-baby, what took you so long?'" Her voice dropped to a whisper. "Sometimes I miss him so much. We had such fun—and such dreams for our retirement."

Katharine joined her at the rail. "How long did you have together after he retired?"

"He never did retire. He planned to leave his practice soon after I retired, but—" she paused for a moment, as if remembering—"things came up. He kept putting it off. He took off most mornings the last few years, but he . . . he had things he was working on."

Panic rose in Katharine. She and Tom talked about doing so much once he retired: seeing the world, sitting side by side in the evenings with their books, spending a month at a time up at the lake, renewing their scuba certification so they could dive together. Tom wanted to spend hours in his library, reading all the books he'd accumulated over the decades. Would they have time for all that? What if one of those bright young Louise look-alikes in Washington snagged his attention before then? Would she have spent her life waiting for a reward she never got?

Dr. Flo seemed to sense her thoughts. "How long until Tom retires?"

Katharine heaved a sigh full of the heaviness she felt. "Years and years. He's not fifty yet. And like Maurice, he loves his work. He'll probably keep at it as long as they let him, and I don't know how well he'll tolerate being home all the time."

Dr. Flo reached over to pat her hand. "I pray you'll have many healthy years together to do what you want." She turned away. "For now, I'd better say goodnight. We have a long trip tomorrow, and I'm still sore. I cannot thank you enough for all of this." She spread both slender hands to encompass the golden path of the moon, the restless sea, white clouds scudding across a deep gray sky, and the whisper of palms. "I cannot recall the last time I felt so refreshed."

"I cannot thank you enough for giving me a reason to come." They exchanged a quick hug before they separated to sleep.

Katharine sat by her window for nearly an hour, enjoying the water and thinking about the day. She was ready for bed when the phone rang. She grabbed it before it could waken Dr. Flo. A noisy, merry crowd almost drowned out a man's slurred voice. "Ms. Gadney there?"

"Dr. Gadney has retired for the night. Is this important?"

"Real important." The last word tied his tongue in knots, so he repeated it carefully. "Im-por-tant. I know who that woman was."

"Which woman?" Katharine thought she recognized the voice, but the man was so drunk she could not be sure, especially with the crowd behind him.

"The woman in the summa . . . cemma . . . graveyard. My

great-great—hell. I don't know how many. Her cousin. Came to stay. Died. Up 'n' died. Had to be buried. Sad. Was very sad." Katharine suspected he was swaying with the words.

"I thought you said your family never had any mixed blood."

"Mixed blood?" His voice rose belligerently. "I didn't mention mixed blood. Did I mention mixed blood?" He sounded like he was asking somebody nearby. If he was as drunk as he sounded, he'd be falling off his bar stool any minute.

"Where are you?" She didn't know why she asked. She didn't have Mona's number, and wasn't as adept as Chase at finding personal information on the Internet.

"None of your business. That's where I am. But I know who that woman was."

Katharine spoke with slow deliberation. "We know who she was, too. She is in the 1880 census, and she was black. The Guilberts came from Haiti. Are you sure she was your cousin?"

She heard nothing but background merriment on the line, and wasn't sure he understood.

He had understood enough to ask finally, "If she knows who the woman was, will she sign the damn papers?"

"I have no idea. Shall I have her call you first thing in the morning?"

"No. No, no, no, no. I'm in Savannah. Came up yesterday. On business. Boring business. Tell her to swing by Hayden's and sign."

"I'll tell her you called. She'll have to decide what she wants to do."

He lowered his voice, his words thicker and more slurred. "You look like a sensible woman. Lemme level with you. I got a bastard of a father-in-law, okay? A bastard, but he's got big bucks. Willing to help me out with my de—devel—

houses, but I gotta prove it's gonna work. You get me?" He waited for a reply.

"I get you. You have to sell two houses before he coughs up any money."

His voice was sharp and suspicious. "How you know that?"

"Mona told me."

"Oh, Mona. Just like her old man. Hard as nails. Made me put all my money into this. All of it, you understand? Nothing left for my kid's education. Nothing left for booze. Gotta build two houses quick. Can't wait around on some old black lady. Gotta get started. Tell her sign by Monday, okay? Monday at the latest. Gotta—"

"I'll tell her. But what about Agnes? She claims she has a deed to the clearing."

She heard the sound of a glass hitting the bar, as if he'd taken another swig. "Agnes idn' gonna make trouble. I promise you that. So tell that old black lady she better not make trouble, either. You hear me? You tell her."

"I'll tell her," Katharine promised. "But listen, you need to go to bed now. You've had enough to drink. Do you hear me?"

"I hear you."

She heard a sound as if the receiver was hitting something again and again. Had he taken her advice and gone straight to bed without hanging up the phone? She went to bed enjoying the picture of the receiver swinging unnoticed all night. But she lay awake listening to the roar of the tide and thinking about the mess people can make of their lives when they consider themselves the center of the universe.

The roar of the surf in the night blended seamlessly with the roar of the surf in the morning. Katharine didn't realize she had slept until she noticed the glare beyond her eyelids. She lay savoring the sound and a breeze that circled her room. *I haven't had a nightmare since we got here*, she thought drowsily. That thought was followed immediately by, *Is there a word for nightmares that happen while you're awake?*

She stretched, wishing she could stay a month. Was there time for one more swim? She crossed the room to peer over the dune. The sky was a murky blue, as if the air was gathering itself together for a storm, but the waves rolled gently. "I will not think about going home until I have to," she resolved, fetching her suit.

Dr. Flo wasn't yet up, but there were enough people on the beach that she felt safe swimming alone. However, once she got in, she discovered that the incoming tide was meeting a strong wind. Together they broke the waves irregularly and too far out for her to get beyond them to ride the swells. She dodged breakers for a time, but after one crashed right over her and sent her choking and tumbling, she spat out salt water and decided it was time to go in. Several scrapes stung from where she had been dragged along the sand.

She slicked back her hair, draped her towel around her waist, and limped back to the house. Dr. Flo, with a cup of coffee and still in her robe, called from the deck, "Looks like the ocean won the battle."

"You got that right." Katharine turned and peered crossly out to sea. "It looks perfect from here, doesn't it? But it's treacherous when you get close."

Dr. Flo rubbed one shoulder with a wry smile. "Like some folks we could name. I take comfort, though, in the fact that no matter what humans do to the land, they'll never tame the sea. Are you ready for breakfast? I'll fix it while you dress and put something on those scrapes."

Refreshed, Katharine pulled on khaki slacks and a turquoise cotton top. When she got downstairs, Dr. Flo was putting eggs and bacon on the table. For their trip home she had dressed in a full yellow cotton skirt, an orange top that made her skin look like soft burnished copper, and yellow plastic flip-flops. Except for the silver hair, she could have been ten. *Dr. Flo has really gone casual since she retired,* Katharine thought with a smile.

"Burch Bayard called last night," she reported as she buttered her toast. "Drunk as a pole cat and wanting to inform us that he had 'discovered,'" she sketched quotes with her fingers, "that Marie Guilbert was the cousin of his many-greats grandmother."

"Did you tell him what we found?"

"Yes. He immediately changed his tune. Wants you to stop by Hayden's today and sign the papers, since you know who Marie was."

Dr. Flo looked thoughtful as she poured two mugs of coffee. "You know, I think I might as well. I lay awake last night trying to think of any good reason not to sign, and I couldn't think of one." She held up her fingers to tick off facts. "We know Claude Gilbert lived with Marie, originally had the same surname, and they both came from Haiti sometime before 1880. That would explain the tradition that our people weren't slaves. Since Claude's dates fit what I have for my grandfather, don't you think that's enough confirmation for me to claim authority to move all three graves? What Burch does with his island is really none of my business. So if it's not too far out of our way, I'd like to stop by Mr. Curtis's office on the way home, sign the papers, and get it over with. Can you think of any reason why I shouldn't?"

"Nothing except sheer cussedness."

Dr. Flo flashed a smile. "There is that. Maybe I should reconsider."

After breakfast there was nothing left to do except pack the car. "The only thing that makes leaving halfway bearable is that it looks like it's going to storm," Dr. Flo said as she looked regretfully at the water. "Let's pretend they're going to have dreadful weather for a week."

She bought a paper while Katharine stopped by the realtor's to thank Joye Folsom for her thoughtfulness in getting the house ready. As they drove across the causeway, Katharine was amused to notice that even though Dr. Flo no longer taught business, she still read the business section first. They were approaching I-95 before she reached the local news.

She gave an exclamation of dismay. "Katharine, can you believe it? Agnes is dead!"

Chapter 18

"Agnes?" Katharine craned to read the headline: RETIRED TEACHER FOUND DEAD. That was not a wise move while trying to merge into a solid wall of eighteen-wheelers. Her sudden swerve earned a blast from a red truck's horn.

"She was found at home yesterday afternoon, shot through the head. They think the wound was self-inflicted." Dr. Flo lay down the paper and frowned out the windshield. "I can't see her killing herself, accidentally or on purpose. Can you? She was so determined to defend her granddaddy's deed to that property, and she knew how to handle a gun."

Katharine remembered again Burch Bayard's claim: "Agnes isn't gonna give any trouble. I can promise you that." *Burch didn't kill her,* she reminded herself. *He was in Savannah yesterday. He must have heard it on the news, or somebody called him from home.*

Even though Agnes had touched their lives only briefly (and nearly fatally, Katharine added to herself), they were sobered by her death. While Dr. Flo went into Hayden Curtis's office to sign the papers, Katharine sat in the car under a shady tree and thought about the gruff woman with her crown of braids, her overalls, and her spunky determination to live the life she wanted to live.

She jumped when her cell phone rang.

"Why didn't you call me back?" Hasty demanded without a greeting.

"I didn't get your message until late last night. I forgot to turn on my phone before that."

"Is something the matter? Your voice sounds funny."

She didn't mean to tell him, but old habits die hard. In another minute she was pouring out the story to Hasty like she used to in high school. She started with the little store, and then told about the cemetery, the graves, and Agnes shooting over their heads.

"Are you sure she missed on purpose?" he interrupted. "Maybe she's a bad shot."

"I don't know about that, but now *she*'s dead. Somebody shot *her* and didn't miss."

He whistled. "That place is scary. Do they know who it was? And why?"

"Not that we've heard. The paper is calling it accidental, and didn't name anybody, but Dr. Flo and I think it was mighty convenient for Burch Bayard."

"Sounds like it. Stay out of it would be my advice. Let them figure it out on their own."

His bossy tone made her want to argue even if she agreed with him in principle. "I maybe ought to tell them Burch called me last night and said he'd been in Savannah all day yesterday. "

"He could have been trying to establish an alibi."

"You can't establish an alibi by calling somebody and telling them where you were hours before."

"I'd still stay out of it. It has nothing to do with you."

"No, except I sort of liked Agnes. She gave me butter for my chiggers."

"Obviously a princess among women. When are you getting home?"

She felt a spurt of irritation at how quickly he moved past Agnes's death to what she suspected was his real reason for calling. "Sometime this afternoon, I guess. Listen, I have to go. Dr. Flo's coming and we need to get on the road."

Dr. Flo climbed into the SUV and asked, "Talking to Tom?"

Katharine felt a lot guiltier than the call warranted. "A friend. Did you sign the papers?"

"I did. I also told the mannequin in Mr. Curtis's office that I'd like to be present for the disinterment. Do you think she'll remember to tell him?"

Katharine started the engine. "I'd call back Monday and tell him personally."

"I think I'd better."

"Would you like me to come back with you?" As soon as she'd made the offer, Katharine wondered why she had. *This has nothing to do with you,* she told herself crossly. *You've got a lot to do at home, and Dr. Flo has dozens of other friends who can come with her.*

"I don't need to come," she added hastily. "I guess I'm beginning to feel like an honorary Guilbert or something."

"I'd be honored if you would come. Just don't start feeling like an honorary Bayard." Dr. Flo clicked her seat belt. "I just wish I didn't feel like I've let Iola and Nell down. With Agnes dead, they are the only two standing between Burch Bayard and his plans."

Katharine shot her a curious look. "You don't reckon Burch or Hayden Curtis shot Agnes, do you? They were both supposedly out of town, but maybe while we're here, we ought to stop by the police station and tell them what we know."

"It would be the sheriff, wouldn't it, and not the police, since she lived out in the county? But I don't know what we'd tell them. We don't actually know diddly-squat. Certainly no more than the sheriff can find out by talking to Iola and others . . ."

"But—?" Katharine repeated Dr. Flo's unspoken word.

"But maybe we ought to at least drop by the sheriff's office and tell him how she was on Tuesday afternoon and when we spoke to her Tuesday evening. If they have any foolish notion that she committed suicide, they need to know she was healthy and of sound mind the day before she died."

"Sound mind?" Katharine was backing, but she took her eyes off the rearview mirror long enough to give Dr. Flo a quizzical look. "The woman took a shot at us. So you do the talking, okay? I'm not sure I could say she was in her sound mind with a straight face."

They found the police station—a small wing attached to one side of city hall—but couldn't find the sheriff's office by simply driving around. "Shall I stop and ask somebody?" Katharine offered.

"Why don't we go on up to Agnes's? Somebody is bound to still be there we can talk to. It's on our way back to the interstate anyway, isn't it?"

"Basically," Katharine agreed, although she doubted they'd be welcome if the sheriff was investigating Agnes's death.

By the time they reached the island, scudding clouds had turned the sky as dark as dusk. No sheriff's cruiser guarded the road beside Agnes's mailbox. No crime tape stretched across her drive. Although Katharine kept expecting one, no hand of the law forced her to halt as they crunched over the shells on Agnes's sandy drive.

"Surely somebody will be down there." Dr. Flo leaned forward in her seat, clutching her purse so hard that her knuckles were pale.

Katharine didn't answer. The wind was so strong that she had all she could do to steer between agitated trees and avoid branches that grabbed at her car.

They rounded the last bend and found the slough whipped to small waves. Agnes's chickens huddled beneath the porch, hunkered down for the storm. Katharine slammed on her brakes just in time to avoid a fishing pole that flew across the hood.

"I swan," muttered Dr. Flo. "Nobody's here." The weathered house sat as placid and deserted as when they'd brought Agnes home two days before.

Katharine hated to think what the house would look like when it had been unoccupied a few months. Wood is a strange substance. When used, it lasts, but left alone it quickly begins to decay. Within a year or two, even if Burch hadn't bulldozed it, the house that had stood since 1874 would be crumbling, prey to vines and termites.

To dispel those gloomy thoughts she pushed her door open, leaned against the wind, and climbed down. The professor didn't move from her seat. "I wonder where Samson is. He may not remember us."

"I think he'll remember. It's only been a couple of days, and Agnes brought us into the house and gave us tea. Besides, he's so fat, we could easily outrun him." Katharine looked again toward the house, half-expecting Agnes to hail them from her back door and invite them in out of the storm. "It does look like he'd be barking by now, though."

The only sounds were the wind, distressed hens, bleating goats, and cicadas, whose whirr rose to crescendo and fell again. Moss flapped in the trees like flags of warning as they climbed the back steps.

Katharine didn't know why she knocked, but it seemed the thing to do. Nobody came, of course. She pulled open the screened door and tried the knob. The back door was unlocked. "What do you think?" she asked. The first fat drops of rain pattered on leaves overhead.

"I'd say go in. Agnes wouldn't mind and—" The patter became an explosion as a sheet of water fell with the suddenness of a curtain descending. Dr. Flo shoved Katharine inside and followed on her heels, brushing drops from her hair and clothes.

Katharine looked around. "They don't have it taped off or anything, and we couldn't stand out there in all that downpour." Who was she explaining to? Practicing for the sheriff when he arrived? She was resisting a strong urge to tiptoe and whisper in the empty house, and was startled when Dr. Flo switched on the fixture that hung over the table. They both flinched at the sudden glare.

Dr. Flo grabbed a hand towel from a rack near the sink and used it to dry her face. "As long as we're here, I'd like to see if she left those letters lying around."

Katharine hid a smile. Dr. Flo must also have felt a need to justify their trespass.

Before, they had passed through the kitchen so quickly that Katharine had gotten only an impression of the room, but it seemed much the same: a scrubbed pine table cluttered with junk mail at one end, two kitchen chairs, food boxes and jars on the countertop, dishes left to drain by the sink. Agnes had been a slap-dash housekeeper, but things were clean. The only change was that on Tuesday, the cat bowls by the fridge had been full of dry food and water. Now they were licked dry.

Dr. Flo pointed to the dishes in the drainer. "Why would a woman about to shoot herself wash her dishes?"

"Maybe she wanted to leave things tidy?"

"You know good and well Agnes would never kill herself without providing for her animals." Dr. Flo was getting snappy.

"Samson?" Katharine called. "Samson?"

No fat basset appeared, but the smaller of the two cats came from the front of the house and uttered a pitiful *meow*.

"You poor puss." Dr. Flo rooted in the pantry and found a bag of food. She filled one dish, filled the water bowl, and watched with satisfaction as the cat crouched on its haunches to eat. The second cat came running and pushed the first aside. "There's enough for both of you," Dr. Flo rebuked it as she filled the second food dish. "You are just like a big cat we had. He'd eat all the food, too, unless we put out two bowls."

Katharine was getting worried about the dog. Where could he be? She wandered toward the hall, but stopped in the doorway. "I wonder where she died."

"Where she was killed, you mean." Dr. Flo was getting crabbier by the minute, and had clearly made up her mind about that matter.

Seeing nothing in the hall to distress her, Katharine peered first into the living room, then into Agnes's bedroom. Furniture was apparently another thing the Morrisons never got rid of. The bed, wardrobe, dresser, and a couple of living room pieces looked old enough to make Posey and Mona shriek with excitement.

In both rooms, however, all available surfaces had piles of things. They looked like the contents of drawers Agnes had turned out Tuesday evening and never put back. If so, she had not slept in that bed Tuesday night, for it was covered with clothes.

When Katharine prowled back into the hall, she noticed Agnes's shotgun propped against the grandfather clock. Had the sheriff's men found it near Agnes's body and put it back? Katharine didn't know much about police procedure beyond what she had seen on television or read in books, but that seemed unlikely.

Behind her in the kitchen, she could hear Dr. Flo crooning to the cats.

Katharine pulled open the heavy front door, and stepped onto the porch. A gust of wind blew rain through the screen. It had so much force behind it, it stung her cheeks. Rain had already misted a blue bowl of peas on the table and darkened a newspaper beside it, where empty pods lay curling and dead. Only half the peas in a bucket on the floor had been shelled.

Shelling peas wasn't a chore Katharine had done much of or particularly liked, but she couldn't imagine it driving a woman to suicide. She also wondered if a woman was likely to leave the job half-done to go clean her gun.

At the screened door she gagged. The rain had come in from the southeast, across the slough, so the rusty trunk of the cedar facing the house had been protected. On its rough, stringy bark, scraps of gray matter were covered by avid flies. Their buzz filled her ears as she pressed her hand to her mouth, jerked open the door, and lost her breakfast into the gush of water from the roof. She didn't even notice that her head and shoulders were soaked until she lifted her head.

She staggered back to one of Agnes's rockers and dropped into it, pressing her face to her knees. She took long, deep breaths through her nose until, hearing Dr. Flo in the hall, she lifted her head to call, "Don't come out here. They didn't clean up the mess in the yard and the rain hasn't washed it all away."

She spoke with such force that the professor asked, "Are you all right?"

"I will be in a minute. I got soaked, though."

"You can change into something dry before we leave. I'm going upstairs to see if I can find those letters. They aren't down here and I think she'd want me to have them, don't you?"

She didn't wait for an answer. Katharine heard her climb the worn wooden staircase.

In a minute, feeling stronger, she decided to find a towel. After that, if she could walk, she would go upstairs and help Dr. Flo.

An oak Victorian music stand did duty in the bathroom as a towel cupboard. Katharine chose one of the neatly rolled towels—a soft blue one—and did what she could to dry her hair and shoulders, but her clammy shirt clung to her like a shroud.

Where did that image come from? She shuddered as she headed upstairs to find Dr. Flo.

The air in the upstairs hall was so hot and thick, she could hardly breathe. Dr. Flo was in neither of the two bedrooms, and from their dusty surfaces, Katharine concluded that Agnes never used and seldom cleaned them. They, too, were piled with debris from open, empty drawers—artifacts from at least three generations of Morrisons. Staring down at one collection of yellowed, useless envelopes, balls of dingy string, and scraps of lace, she vowed to keep her own drawers and closets cleaned on a regular basis.

"Dr. Flo?" she called in the hall. She got no reply.

When she opened the door at the back of the hall, she saw why. Dr. Flo was opening desk drawers in a small room at the back of the wing, but between them lay the sleeping porch, open to the storm. The rain drummed on the tin roof overhead and fell in torrents from broad eaves. The eaves were wide enough to keep all but a fine mist from coming through the screens, but Dr. Flo could not have heard her.

Katharine stepped onto the porch and saw why the downstairs bedroom had not needed to be cleared of debris. This was where Agnes slept in summer, in a white iron bedstead up among the treetops. The porch had the same happy, haphazard look as the kitchen. Katharine felt goosebumps rising. Was that from the wind? Or from seeing Agnes's comb and brush lying on an old oak dresser amid a dusting of pink face powder?

She began to share Dr. Flo's suspicions as she mentally ticked off indications that Agnes planned to come back: overalls hung from a nail on the far wall; a wrinkled white cotton nightgown slung over the foot of the bed, ready to be put on again; one slipper near the rump-sprung chair in the corner and one under the bed; a book facedown on the night table beside a utilitarian reading light. The book was only half-read.

She joined Dr. Flo. "You were smart to open the windows in here."

"They were open when I got here. Thank heavens for wide eaves, or all this would have been soaked." She gestured to indicate the stacks of papers that filled every surface. As she spoke, a breeze lifted papers on the desk and sent them spinning to join others on the floor that must have traveled by an earlier breeze.

The Morrisons had used this room for a study. It held a desk, a filing cabinet, and bookshelves on every available bit of wall. Somebody had even built shelves over the windows and the door. The desk was so old the varnish had worn off. The books were a jumble of theology, literature, history, and math. Two bottom shelves held stacks of *National Geographic* and other magazines, covered with dust. "Agnes was right about the Morrisons being pack rats," she told Dr. Flo. "I don't think they ever threw anything out."

"Maybe not, but I can't find those letters. I don't see that deed she said she found, either. Maybe she took them downstairs, handier for when she was going to town."

A door slammed downstairs with such force they felt as well as heard it.

The women looked at one another in panic. "Maybe the wind," Dr. Flo whispered.

Katharine's own mind was veering between a murderer returning and an angry sheriff wondering who these women were, leaving fingerprints all over a crime scene. She looked down at her hands in dismay. Why hadn't she thought of that before?"

She wondered if she'd be able to persuade Louise to call Tom, wherever he was, to bail her out of the McIntosh County jail.

Anything was better than standing there waiting. She went

through the porch to the hall and called over the banisters, "Hello? Who's there?"

Chase Bayard peered up the staircase with a puzzled frown. He must have left a raincoat or umbrella in the kitchen, for his tan shirt was dry but his jeans were soaked below the knees. He had to try twice before he got his first word out. "Mi—Miss Agnes isn't here. She—" his voice cracked. He swallowed hard and tried again. "She shot herself yesterday. Did you want something?"

Before Katharine could reply, Dr. Flo pushed past her and descended the stairs. "Yes, we were looking for letters that may relate to the Guilberts in your family cemetery. Agnes called Tuesday night and promised them to me, but on our way home, we read in the paper that she had died. We were going to Darien anyway to sign those papers your daddy wanted, so we thought we might as well run up here and see if Agnes left them where we could find them. I don't suppose you've seen them, have you?"

She stood high enough on the steps that Chase had to look up to her. Confusion and uncertainty flitted across his face. "No, ma'am, I just got here. I saw your car in the yard." He swallowed again and bit his lower lip as if undecided what to say next. Finally he blurted, "Daddy would get real upset if he knew you broke in or took stuff out of the house."

"We didn't break in." Katharine passed Dr. Flo on the steps and joined him in the hall. "The back door was unlocked. And we haven't taken a thing. We did feed the cats."

"Oh, good. That's why I came, to feed the animals. Miss Agnes really loved her animals." He bent to stroke the large cat, which had come through the hall and was sitting with its tail switching. It turned and dashed down the hall. "That one's real wild," he said with an embarrassed flush.

"Do they really think she killed herself?" Dr. Flo asked. "It's hard to believe she would have done that without providing for the animals."

"I know. She must have been real upset about something. Or maybe she was cleaning her gun and it went off. They know she shot herself, because Papa Dalt and Cooter heard the shot, and they got here not long after she'd done it. They were the ones who called the sheriff. He said the last car tracks on her road were hers."

"How did your granddaddy get here, then?" Katharine asked.

"Walked along the slough, same as I did today. It's a couple of miles from her place to ours by the road, but the road bends a lot. Our place and hers aren't even a mile apart along the slough. Papa Dalt and Cooter were out shooting squirrels—well, Cooter was doing the shooting since Papa Dalt was—wasn't feeling good. They heard the shot and came to see who was riling Miss Agnes. She didn't hunt, but she shot at trespassers a lot."

Dr. Flo made a noise between a laugh and a snort. "We know. She shot at us."

His eyes widened. "No joke?"

"No joke. So they found her and called the sheriff, but they didn't find any sign that a trespasser had been here?"

"No, ma'am. Not at all." He knelt down and reached for the little cat, which had crept from the kitchen in search of the conversation. "We're gonna miss her. She was a special lady."

The little cat let him pick her up and cuddled down in his arms like she'd been there before. "Maybe Miss Agnes did provide for the animals, sort of. I saw her on the road yesterday morning and she asked me to come over today. She said she'd help me with my math." He swallowed hard again. "Maybe she figured I'd feed them for her when I got here."

"Surely she wouldn't have wanted you to find her body!" Dr. Flo was clearly shocked.

Chase shrugged. "Maybe she was depressed. She was pretty old."

"Not much older than I am, young man, and I have no intention of shooting myself."

"Yes, ma'am. I mean no, ma'am. I—I don't really know why she did it." He looked miserable.

"When was it that you saw her yesterday?" Katharine asked.

He shrugged. "Sometime around ten. She and her dog were in her car headed somewhere." He peered around. "Have you seen him anywhere around?"

"No," Katharine told him. "Just the cats."

"Will you take them?" Dr. Flo bent to the big one. It approached and wove back and forth under her hand, then darted to the kitchen like it had suddenly realized it was being friendly.

"I wish I could, but Mama's allergic. Would you like them?" His eager expression wiped away the thin veneer of sophistication that young adolescents work so hard to achieve. "We won't be down here much longer and nobody will feed them after that. If you'd like them—"

Katharine stifled a groan. Five hours in a car with two cats was one of her personal visions of hell, but she could see that Dr. Flo was on the verge of accepting. She was reaching out to stroke the head of the little cat in Chase's arms.

To Katharine's relief, she stepped back with obvious reluctance. "I'm not allowed to have pets where I live." She turned to Katharine. "I don't suppose you . . . ?"

Katharine turned away to hide her expression. Apparently Dr. Flo didn't share her aversion to lying to children. Dr. Flo's house was larger than hers. She could keep a hundred cats and scarcely notice. Of course, the Gadneys had a lot of valuable antiques. Maybe that kept Dr. Flo from having cats? But she'd said she once had cats . . .

Katharine realized the other two were still waiting for her answer. "We are away too much to have pets."

"They could die here!" Chase sounded close to tears. "Somebody needs to take care of them." The little cat, alarmed by his outburst, jumped from his arms and darted to the kitchen.

"Your daddy claims he owns them now," Katharine reminded Chase. "If so, it's his responsibility to find homes for them. For the goats and the chickens, too, unless he wants wild animals roaming his new subdivision."

"Yeah, but he'll —" Loyalty stopped him, but he probably knew, as Katharine suspected, that Burch's solution to his newly acquired menagerie would involve bullets, the slough, and chicken dinners.

"You can get feeders that measure out food and water while you are away," Dr. Flo said thoughtfully. "And you have a lovely yard for cats to roam around in."

The little cat crept back into the hall and wove back and forth around Katharine's ankles. Then it peered up and asked, "M*eow?*"

Katharine sighed. "See if you can find some boxes for them to travel in while I get some dry clothes out of the car. I can't travel as wet as I am."

Chapter 19

The storm had subsided to a gentle drizzle. Chase helped her carry the cats' supplies to the car, then he went to feed the goats. Dr. Flo closed up the house while Katharine changed and carried the cats, taped into cardboard boxes with air holes, to the car. She was carrying out the second, the smaller one, when Mona's Mercedes growled down the drive.

"What are you doing here?" she asked as she got out. "And what are you removing from the property?"

Mona was exquisite in a long white skirt, navy blouse, white blazer, and white and navy sandals. Every hair was in place, her makeup fresh. Katharine was acutely aware of her own damp, frizzing hair, her perspiring face, and a stain on her thigh where the male cat had turned over his water as she attempted to put him in the box. Just once she would like to meet this woman looking good.

"We came because Agnes had promised Dr. Flo some letters."

She'd decided to let Mona think they hadn't known about Agnes's death.

"Why are *you* here?" Dr. Flo asked, joining Katharine.

"You must not have heard, but Agnes is dead. I came to see if she had any bits and pieces that might be worth saving before Burch tears the place—ah-ah-choo!" She opened her purse and snatched out a tissue too late to catch the sneeze.

"Ownership of this land is still in question," Dr. Flo informed her. "Tuesday night, Agnes found the original deed, which included a stipulation that when or if the Morrisons no longer required the house, it reverted to the family for which it was built." She drew herself up to her most haughty posture. "It is possible I am the last member of that family. Katharine, may I use your cell phone?"

"Sure." Katharine handed it over.

"Who are you calling?" Curiosity battled annoyance in Mona's voice. She dabbed her nose again.

"My lawyer. I want him to take steps to ensure that nothing can be removed from or done to destroy this property until a legitimate search has been made by the authorities for that deed." She punched in a number, listened, then said, "Rodney? Flo here. I'm fine, but listen . . ." She moved away so the others could not hear. In a few moments she returned. "He is going to file a motion immediately."

Mona turned to Katharine with her forehead wrinkled. "She's not serious, is she? Slaves never lived on this property." She turned her head aside to sneeze again. "Excuse me. The rain must have stirred up pollen or something." She used her tissue to blow her nose.

Dr. Flo pulled her notebook out of her purse and slapped it against her palm. "I have inventoried every room and have asked my attorney to come down tomorrow and do the same. You had better not remove a thing from this house until that matter is settled. You might want to have your attorney make an inventory, as well."

Leaving Mona standing there with her mouth open, she got in the SUV.

"The property is ours. There is no doubt whatsoever about that," Mona called angrily.

Katharine thrust the cardboard box toward her. "In that case, take Agnes's cats. They'll starve otherwise."

Mona backed and clasped her hand over her nose. "No wonder I'm sneezing! I'm allergic to cats. Get that thing away from me!"

"If it turns out you own them, I'll send you a bill for room and board," Katharine warned as she stowed the second cat in the back of her vehicle.

On the way back to the road, she said admiringly, "That was a stroke of genius, calling your lawyer to file an immediate motion, but when did you have time to inventory the house?"

Dr. Flo's black eyes twinkled. "My poker buddies call me Queen of Bluff."

Of their five-hour trip home with two cats alternately yowling and scratching the sides of their boxes, the less said the better—especially since the larger one soon clawed his way out and roamed the car for the rest of the drive. The women ate sack lunches from a drive-through and made only one gas and bathroom stop.

"If traffic is bad, I'm going to need Agnes's litter box," Dr. Flo warned as they reached the outskirts of Atlanta.

By the time they reached Buckhead, Katharine had a throbbing headache and tight muscles in her neck and down her back. She had thought she had left all her stress on Jekyll, but it had crouched on top of the car and ridden back with her like another cat.

After Dr. Flo drove away, she left the cats in the car while she set up the utility room with the food and water dishes and litter box she had brought from Agnes's. "Just like home," she told them as she carried them in and released them. The big cat darted into the small space between washer and dryer and tried to press himself into the wall. The little cat dashed out of the utility room and disappeared.

"You'd better remember your sandbox is in here," Katharine called after her. She propped one elbow on the dryer and asked the big one, "Why on earth did I bring you all home? You're going to want me to talk to you and pay you attention, and Tom is coming home tomorrow and wants to go up to the lake. Can you ride up there and ride back again Sunday, when you haven't even settled in here yet? Are you going to need a cat psychiatrist when this week is over?"

He hissed and puffed up his fur.

She stooped down and coaxed, "Make an effort, okay? Work with me here. I know you miss Agnes. She was a great owner. But I'll do my best. Take a while to get used to the place and relax. I'll be back."

She took a couple of pills for her headache, brought in her bags, and unpacked. Then she called Posey. "We had a marvelous time," she reported, and described most of what had happened on Bayard Island. She didn't mention Agnes's shotgun or her death—Posey was apt to let things like that slip to Tom.

Posey listened with few comments until Katharine mentioned one name. "Mona Bayard?" she said in the tone that meant she was trying to remember something.

Posey's spacey memory was legendary in the family. Wrens often joked, "Sugah, at least you don't have to worry about becoming absentminded when you get *old.*"

Still, if you gave her enough time, she usually dredged up what it was she was trying to remember. This time it took thirty seconds by Katharine's watch. "Is that the Mona Bayard with that *gaw-geous* house down in Savannah—the one everybody was talking about on last year's tour of homes?" Posey's drawl tended to deepen when she was talking about antique furniture and old houses. She adored both. "You know, the one with all that *mahvelous* antebellum furniture?"

"The very same. She asked if you were the Posey Buiton

whose beach cottage was featured in *Southern Living*, the one with all the antebellum furniture. You all are soul mates, definitely, except the way she carried on, they are down to their last dollar and need this island development to pay for their son's private school. I'll keep you posted if we learn anything more."

"You think she might want to sell some furniture?"

"Could be. Call her and ask. I hope never to have to speak to her again. Thanks again for the house."

"Anytime. But don't forget I'm going with you next time you get a chance to go down."

"That may be sooner than you think. Dr. Flo has decided she wants to be present at the disinterment of her ancestors. I told her I'd drive her down if I can."

"Disinterment? You mean when they dig them up?"

"Afraid so. Dr. Flo wants to be sure Burch and his attorney don't try any monkey tricks, like burying them any old where and saying they carried out her wishes."

"I can't see that it matters where they're buried, if she hasn't known about them all these years, but I'll go if she doesn't mind. I've never attended a disinterment. What does one wear?"

"Long sleeves, long pants, and repellant. This one will be in woods where chiggers and mosquitoes abound."

"I can't wear my summer black in the woods!" Her summer black was a Chanel.

"Of course not. Wear slacks with a long-sleeved T-shirt. We aren't dressing up, Posey, we're dressing for survival."

"Still, we ought to show respect. I'll think of something. Let me know when."

After Katharine hung up, she roamed the house trying to decide what to do next. She checked the phone for messages. She held up her new dining room drapery and admired Hollis's handiwork. She thought of calling the glazier again, but couldn't summon the will. Hasty was right. Without a dead-line, it was easy to postpone things that required energy or thought.

She skimmed three days' mail and tossed most of it. She considered the two paintings she'd bought Monday evening and decided she liked one of them. Maybe she should have let Hasty take her to the gallery. He might have stopped her from buying the other picture.

She went back to the phone, trying to remember if there was anybody she ought to call, but she couldn't think of a soul. Feeling at loose ends, she turned on the outside tele-phone ringer and went out to check her yard. Three squirrels played chase overhead, chattering like little boys and fling-ing themselves across incredible distances between branches, landing safe every time. Their gray-brown fur, outlined in gold, was the color of oak bark. "Hey, little guys," Katharine called up to them. They bolted.

She browsed among her borders and pulled deadheads off the daylilies. She strolled down to check her roses, which had been gorgeous when she left.

In her brief absence, Japanese beetles had descended. They had chewed off most of the leaves and burrowed deep into blossoms, leaving them rotting and brown. "Preda-tors!" she snapped in disgust. "Just like Burch Bayard. You'd chew up the whole world, wouldn't you, for your own personal gratification?" Sick at the destruction, she stomped back into the house and called Anthony's wife to ask him to bring beetle poison when he came to mow the following morning.

She fetched her secateurs and removed the rotting roses. While she gathered up the debris, she found herself darting another glance at the telephone ringer. Finally she recog-nized the root of her restlessness. She was waiting for Hasty's call.

"Dumb!" she told herself.

Dumb and foolish, snapped her Aunt Sara Claire's voice in her head. For once, Katharine agreed with her. If Hasty called, he'd want to come over. If he came over, he'd want to swim. If she said no, he'd invite her to dinner. Tired and with a headache still lurking, would she be strong enough to say no?

"I am prolonging my vacation," she announced to a robin.

Chapter 20

She changed into white pants and a coral top, slid her feet into tan sandals, and made herself into the person she wished Mona Bayard could see. "Dr. Flo isn't the only one with ancestors to research," she told her reflection.

The Atlanta History Center was only minutes away. Its library, the Kenan Research Center, was a tranquil place with soft yellow walls and tall windows overlooking a gracious garden. It was also a place where people went for serious research, not to chat. Nobody would expect her to greet or even smile at them unless she wanted to. Accustomed to spending most of her time alone, she needed some time among people without being expected to talk to them.

She left her purse in a locker and, carrying a legal pad and a couple of pencils, headed to the glassed-in genealogy room to one side of the main reference room. Before she reached the door, a gravelly voice said, "Why, hey, Miz Murray. You checking your ancestors again?"

A whiff of stale tobacco and old coffee wafted over Katharine's right shoulder. She turned to see a man about her own height but twenty years older. His face was bronzed from the sun and had a sharp beaked nose. His hair was pulled back into a ponytail that curled in a white ringlet over his shoulder. An anchor tattoo decorated one arm, and his black T-shirt commanded, DON'T BOTHER ME. I'M LOST IN THOUGHT AND IT'S UNFAMILIAR TERRITORY. With the shirt he wore black jeans and workmen's boots that had seen a lot of work.

His smile was full of stained teeth as he held out one hand and said in a North Georgia twang, "Lamar Franklin, ma'am. Do you remember me?"

How could she not? He and Hasty had come to blows in the history center parking lot the previous month due to a foolish misunderstanding. Each had thought the other was stalking her when in fact each was protecting her from the other. Katharine had seldom been so mortified.

Hoping she was hiding her reluctance, she shook his calloused palm. "Of course."

"So, are you back here researching your family? I could give you he'p, if you need it." He walked that fine line between friendly and obsequious.

"Thanks, but I'm just browsing today. I thought I'd get familiar with what's on the shelves in the genealogy room."

"They got all sorts of stuff." He took her elbow and steered her through the doorway. "What county were you interested in?"

Katharine disengaged her elbow. "Fulton, and I can find it."

"Okay." He took a step back and held up both palms. "I get the message. I'll be right over there." He jerked his head toward a table outside the door. "Let me know if I kin he'p you any. Be seeing you." He sauntered off with the swagger of a man who has done another good deed for the day.

The smell of him lingered after he was gone. Katharine moved down the shelf looking for fresher air. She had intended to see what she could find on her mother's family, but her attention was caught by a volume entitled *Early Days of the Georgia Tidewater: The Story of McIntosh County and Sapelo*. Three days ago she had known nothing about McIntosh County, including where it was. Now she reached for the book as if it were the biography of an old friend.

She checked the index first, but found no mention of the Bayards or Bayard Bluff. Nevertheless, she read with fascination about other big plantations that flourished in the region in the eighteenth and nineteenth centuries. When she read that the planters only spent the two coolest months of each year on their plantations, she exclaimed, "Just like Agnes said!"

A man at the next table looked her way. She flushed and mouthed a silent, "Sorry."

I really must stop talking to myself, she thought. *It's getting to be such a habit, I don't notice when I'm doing it.* She had a disquieting vision of herself as an old woman, pottering about Atlanta in deep conversation with herself.

As she read, she wondered which side of the war Yankee plantation owners had fought on—if they had fought at all. She knew that many wealthy Yankees paid poor men to take their places in the Union Army. She also wondered why Georgians who owned plantations in McIntosh County had weathered the war a few miles inland, in Waycross. The author gave no clue as to what had prompted that choice.

A history major in college, Katharine was so interested in what she was reading that she lost track of time. She took pages of notes on what had happened to blacks in the county after the war. She learned that on January 16, 1865, General Sherman issued a special order decreeing that barrier islands from Charleston to the St. Johns River in north Florida were to be set aside as "reservations" for freed slaves. She shuddered at the language, given how American Indians had fared on reservations. Had Sherman really been naïve enough to believe field hands would know how to administer vast plantations? Did he think the land would earn as much broken into small parcels as it did when farmed in vast tracts?

When she read that he had also decreed that all abandoned plantation lands from the islands to thirty miles inland were to be off-limits to whites, she deduced that the measure was more punitive than compassionate or even practical. That meant that former plantation accountants and those who understood not only crop production but also the process of marketing crops were forbidden to offer their expertise to the new landowners, had they so desired. The stupidity of those Reconstruction years appalled her, but were current government policies on a number of issues any wiser?

To her relief, as she continued reading she found no evidence that Sherman's special order or ban on white residents was ever enforced. Instead, the author reported that the 1870 census showed that the county had over a thousand whites, although the majority of the population was black. One interesting chapter was devoted to Tunis Campbell, a black lawyer from New Jersey who came to McIntosh County as the commissioned representation of the Freedmen's Bureau. Soon afterwards, he set himself up as a dictator. During his tenure, blacks were given most of the power in the county. Would that have attracted Haitians like Marie Guilbert to move to McIntosh County? Had she settled on Bayard Island in defiance of the Bayards themselves?

She was reading about Burch's cousin, naval commander John McIntosh Kell—who was actually as important as Burch had boasted—when Lamar Franklin asked over her shoulder, "You interested in naval battles?"

Trying not to cringe at his tobacco-and-coffee cologne, she gave him a curt reply. "Not particularly. I would be interested in pirates if I found any, but I haven't."

"They was some privateers during the War, but that's about as close as you're gonna get to pirates that late in history." Rightly guessing that she had no idea what he was talking about—and that they were disturbing the man down the table—he bent closer and explained, "Those were private ships given permission to capture enemy vessels and share the spoils. I got a book about the subject at home, if you are interested."

"I don't know if I'm interested or not. Did they fly the skull and crossed bones?"

"I don't rightly know, but I'm heading home now to get ahead of the traffic. When I get there, I'll look it up for you." He strutted away.

Katharine finished her research into McIntosh County by checking the index for Guilberts, and discovered she was disappointed not to find any. As she gathered up her notes, she wore a wry smile. At the moment she was far more interested in Dr. Flo's relatives than her own.

Chapter 21

When she reached her house, she was chagrined to find Hasty's red Jeep parked in front of Hollis's black-and-white Mini. "Oh, dear," she groaned.

Ever since Hollis had seen Katharine and Hasty at a restaurant having a perfectly harmless reunion lunch after they'd run into each other for the first time in twenty-nine years, Tom's niece had regarded him as a threat to her uncle, whom she adored. Once Posey had spilt the beans that Katharine dated Hasty in high school, nothing Katharine could say or do would convince Hollis that he was now simply a friend.

Maybe because it wasn't strictly true.

Hollis had a key to the house. Chances were good that at the moment she and Hasty were in the kitchen drinking Cokes while she either grilled Hasty about his intentions with regard to her aunt or sang her uncle's praises. Neither was likely to please Hasty. Katharine was tempted to head back down the drive and go out to supper.

She couldn't. She had cats to feed.

As she pulled into her garage, she reminded herself, "You are a grownup. You can deal with this. All you have to do is imitate Agnes and tell both of them, *'Git!'*"

Sure enough, they were in the kitchen, but on their second round of beers, not Cokes. As soon as Katharine appeared, both started talking.

"I came to set up Susan's room," Hollis informed her, her

dark eyes stormy, "and found *him*— " she jerked her thumb toward Hasty, her emphasis on the pronoun reducing him to something that had crawled out of the slime "—sitting in the drive. I also found a cat in your utility room."

"Did you forget our date?" Hasty demanded simultaneously. "I thought we could swim before dinner. And I brought that blank book you wanted." He held up a slender journal bound in soft blue leather.

"Date?" Hollis swung from one to the other. Her new haircut—mahogany instead of the dead black she'd affected in college—flared out, then settled back against her cheeks.

Katharine dealt with Hasty first. "We didn't have a date. You said you would call."

"I did, but you weren't here, so I figured the drive home was taking longer than you expected and I'd be here to welcome you. You said you'd be back this afternoon." He held out his arm so she could read his watch. "It is officially evening." He stood.

"Come back another time, but call first," Katharine suggested. "The book is lovely. Thanks."

"I'm not going anywhere. I was getting you a Coke."

"She might want a beer." Hollis knew good and well Katharine never drank beer. When she was small, a nasty boy had informed her it was made from horse pee. That was how it had tasted to her ever since.

"She doesn't like beer," Hasty said, ambling to the fridge like he lived there.

Katharine could have throttled them both. Another headache was sprouting at the base of her scalp and working its way up the back of her head.

Hollis watched sulkily while Hasty filled a glass with ice and poured a Coke into it, waited for the foam to go down, and filled it some more. "Did you know a cat got in here while you were away? He's hiding between the washer and the dryer."

Katharine massaged the base of her skull with the fingers of both hands. "There are two cats. While I was down at the beach their owner died and nobody else would take them." Seeing that Hollis had more questions, Katharine waved a weary hand. "Don't ask. It's too complicated to explain. Put it down to my inability to say 'no.'"

An unfortunate statement, given that Hasty was setting the Coke before her and asking, "Do you want a massage? You look worn out." Without waiting for an answer, he put his hands on her shoulders and began to work her muscles hard.

Katharine pulled away. "What I really want are a couple of aspirin. There are some in the upper cabinet next to the fridge."

He fetched them, and she downed them with Coke. Then she closed her eyes, waiting for the throbbing to subside. Now that she had the Coke, she discovered she was very thirsty. She took several swallows and savored the sting in her mouth before she said, "Now I need a minute to catch my breath. We got back later than I expected, since we stopped to . . . get the cats." She wasn't ready to talk about Agnes's house yet. "Then I went to the history center for a bit." She opened her eyes long enough to ask, "Would you feed the cats, Hollis? There's food in a bag on the washer. You'll need to put some in both dishes. They don't share."

Hollis complied.

Hasty again came to stand behind Katharine and massaged her shoulders and neck. She curved her head into the pain. "Oh, that feels good!"

Hollis crouched down, held out a dish of food, and called "Kitty? Kitty?" The big cat did not come out. She swiveled toward Katharine. "What are their names?"

When she saw what Hasty was doing, she put down the cat dish and hurried to the table. "I'll do that. I thought about becoming a massage therapist at one point, and I give great massages."

To Katharine's relief, Hasty stepped back and let her take over, but he gave Katharine a wink as he slid into a chair across the table.

"They don't have names," Katharine said to distract Hollis. "Or if they did, I never heard them. I suppose I'll have to think of new ones. You got any ideas?"

"Live with them a few days. Something will come to you." Hollis dug her strong fingers into the weary muscles. Katharine winced with pain, but it was good pain. Finally Hollis stopped. "That's enough for today. I don't want you sore tomorrow. Do you want to come upstairs so we can hang Susan's curtains and put on her bedspreads? That's what I was planning to do before I found *him* here." She jerked one thumb toward Hasty.

Hasty pushed back his chair. "Let Kate rest. I can hang curtains. I don't even need a stool."

Katharine didn't bother to open her eyes. "That would be marvelous. But if you go out to your cars for anything, be careful not to let the cats out. They aren't used to the place yet. And Hollis? I'll be getting ready for Tom to come home tomorrow, so I won't have time to shop. Or swim," she added for Hasty's benefit.

She laid her head down on her crossed arms like a child at school and dozed while she waited to be called for applause.

They were fast. In less time than it took for Katharine's aspirins to work, Hollis was back. "You want to see the room? It turned out pretty good, I think." Katharine wearily followed her upstairs. After all, the child (she still thought of all her own offspring and nieces as children when she was tired or irritable) had gone to a lot of trouble over this while she was lolling around at Jekyll. She hoped she could muster enough enthusiasm.

"It's great," she said a minute later, and meant it. The room had turned out better than pretty good. Susan was going to like the combination of peach, taupe, and green as much as she had liked the rose, white, and blue she had grown up with, and Hollis had used a combination of striped curtains, solid bedspreads, and floral cushions that made it appropriate for guests of both sexes.

If we ever had guests, Katharine thought wistfully. Her parents used to have a wide circle of friends from all over the world, and Miami's winter weather, combined with the proximity of their Coral Gables home to Miami's International Airport, meant they entertained frequent out-of-town guests. Some years her family had so many folks who stopped by for a quick nap and a bite to eat during long layovers between international flights that her dad had joked, "We may not run a bed and breakfast, but we run a snooze and snack." A wave of yearning for them swept over her. No matter how many years it had been, she was still often taken unawares by moments when the reality of their absence was fresh and raw.

They stayed in the room a few minutes longer while Hollis pointed out special touches and Katharine praised her taste, then they trooped back down. Hollis, Katharine noticed with amusement, stayed between her and Hasty on the stairs.

"Did you see her study?" Hollis asked him over her shoulder. She headed that way and stood in the arch with a glow of satisfaction. "I think it turned out rather well, don't you, Aunt Kat?"

The early evening sun slanted through the blinds and bathed the room in gold. Katharine's new carpet glowed like jewels on the floor. All her favorite bits and pieces on the bookshelves were rimmed with light. A reading chair Katharine had never seen sat invitingly by the window.

"Where did that chair come from?" she asked.

Hollis bit her lip. "Do you like it?"

"I love it. It's just what the room needed to be perfect."

"Good. I saw it in a Salvation Army yesterday afternoon, and that's what I thought, too. You don't mind that I bought it there, do you?"

"Kate loves the Salvation Army." Hasty draped one arm over Katharine's shoulder. "She used to shop there all the time."

Hollis narrowed her eyes and glared.

Katharine pushed Hasty away. "As long as you all are in the working mode, would you put together my computer?"

She sat in her new chair and watched them work. When they weren't competing for her attention, they worked well together. They even managed to laugh a time or two.

"Do you want to stay for supper?" she asked impulsively, having taken a quick mental inventory of her pantry and fridge. "It won't be much—linguini with white clam sauce, tomato and mozzarella salad, and garlic bread—but I've got fresh peaches we can slice over ice cream."

"Works for me," Hasty agreed.

"I'll make the salad," Hollis volunteered. "Do you have basil in the garden?"

A few minutes later Katharine was slicing peaches at one counter, Hollis was making salads at the island, and Hasty was at the counter near the stove lathering slices of French bread with butter and showering them with garlic and parsley. Katharine felt herself beginning to relax.

Her newly remodeled kitchen felt like it used to in the past, when all four Murrays were home and fixing a festive dinner together. This house loved being filled with people. It needed them. So did she.

The temperature was pleasant, so they decided to light a citronella candle and eat down by the pool. "So how did your week at the beach go?" Hollis asked when they'd all filled their plates and wine glasses. "Good swims and lazy reading?"

"Plus old graves and pirates." Katharine told them about Dr. Flo's mysterious graves and the one with the skull and crossed bones. "We think whoever it was must have been buried around the time of the Civil War," she concluded, "given the dates on the other graves in that section of the cemetery."

"Pirates left that coast in the early seventeen hundreds," Hasty objected. "They hung some of them in Charleston and cleared out the rest. Pirates sailed around in the Caribbean for a while after that, but I don't think there were any down there by the time of the American Civil War."

"How about around Haiti?" Katharine asked.

"I don't know a thing about Haiti."

"Do you know anything about privateers? I learned today that the Confederacy had some of those."

"What are privateers?" Hollis asked as she twirled linguini on her fork.

Hasty always loved to lecture. "Countries used to give something called a 'letter of marque' to private ships, granting permission to capture vessels of an enemy nation and promising them part of the spoils. Those who sailed on those ships were called 'privateers.' It was one way of increasing a country's naval power with little or no expense. In the mid-eighteen-fifties, the nations of Europe admitted that privateering was nothing but legal piracy and signed a treaty not to issue any more letters of marque. The United States, however, refused to sign, saying it hadn't issued letters for a long time anyway. That backfired when the Civil War broke out, because one of the first things Jefferson Davis did was start issuing letters of marque to Southern ships so they could help the Confederate navy by seizing Yankee vessels."

"Would they have put a skull and crossed bones on a privateer's grave?" Katharine asked.

"I doubt it. I also doubt you found a pirate's grave. It was probably a skull, a symbol of death."

"There were crossed bones under it," she said firmly, "and Dr. Flo's daddy always told her they had a pirate in the family."

"Not during the Civil War," Hasty spoke in the obstinate tone he was apt to use when corrected.

"There's no point fighting about something nobody can prove right this minute," Hollis rebuked them, but she looked happy that they were quarreling. "Didn't you promise us peaches and ice cream, Aunt Kat?"

They finished dessert as the last minutes of day slid down a pink and gold sky. Fireflies appeared to dance above the lawn. The moon, almost full, rose above the trees. It would have been a lovely romantic evening with the right people. It wasn't half bad with the ones Katharine had.

Hollis waited to leave until Hasty had driven away. "Are you afraid to sleep here alone?" she asked.

"No, I not only have the security system, I also wedge a chair under my door."

"Like that would do any good," Hollis scoffed.

"Don't knock it. It works for me."

But Katharine lay awake longer than usual that night, listening for sounds in the house. She had barely fallen asleep when she was disturbed again by the telephone.

Heavy breathing was followed by a whispered hiss delivered in a false accent somebody had probably copied from a bad movie. "Neffer return to Bayard Island. It iss not healthy for you. You and your friend could die!" There was a pause, then the whisper added, "Do you understand?"

"Go to bed, Miranda," Katharine said crossly.

She heard a gasp, then the phone went dead.

Only after she had hung up did she wonder how Miranda had gotten her unlisted home number.

Chapter 22

Friday morning Katharine put out food and fresh water for two invisible cats, cleaned a litter box that was definitely not invisible, and treated herself to a swim before breakfast. As she stroked up and down the pool she found herself sending up prayers of thanksgiving for the silky water, the peace of the morning, the beauty of her yard, and the joy of having a pool. Then she remembered what Hasty had said earlier: "All this for one woman?"

"I'd share it if I knew how," she muttered as she climbed out.

Anthony was coming through the gate, so she pulled on her coverup and went to meet him. Before she could tell him about the Japanese beetles, she noticed that his smile was wider than usual. "The way you're beaming, God could send the sun on vacation and let you light up the world. Did you win the lottery?" she teased.

"Just about," he told her. "My daughter called last night, and she's jumped through all the hoops. She'll be getting her Ph.D. next month. My little girl is gonna be a doctor!"

If they had been on hugging terms, Katharine would have hugged him. "That is fantastic!"

"Sure is. Her mama was already on the phone when I left, looking for someplace to throw a party. We'd be honored if you'll come. We don't have a date yet, but I'll let you know."

"Have it here."

She didn't know which of them was more surprised by her offer, but when he hesitated, she gestured to the yard. "All of this is as much yours as mine. You've done all the work. Please? I'd be the one who was honored. You can either have a formal party or a swim party, whichever you like. You'd be doing me a favor, too, because you'd give me a good reason to finish the house by then."

"I'll ask Elna," he murmured. But he was looking around like he was already seeing his daughter and friends scattered about the lawn.

"No, I'll ask her. I'll call her when I go in. But first, we've got an awful case of Japanese beetles. Did she tell you?"

He held up a sprayer. "She told me. Let's see what they've done."

"Oh, my," he exclaimed when he saw the shiny green backs among the rotting buds she'd left the day before because they weren't hurt. "If you'd called me when you first saw them . . ." Anthony had never been shy about reproving her for any neglect of her yard.

"I didn't see them until last night," she protested. "I've been away, and the roses were fine when I left Tuesday morning."

"Those little terrors can swoop in and destroy plants before you know it. Let me get at them, then."

Leaving him to his work, Katharine headed inside to change. On her way through the kitchen she called Anthony's wife. Elna sounded reluctant at first, as well she might. *I've never asked them here to enjoy what he's created,* Katharine realized with a pang. She doubled her efforts and made it clear she would be delighted to offer her house and yard as her gift to their daughter for her achievement.

"It would be beautiful," Elna admitted. "If you're sure and Anthony doesn't mind, it would be wonderful. Thank you so much."

"When do you want to have the party?" For the first time, Katharine realized the enormity of what she had offered.

"The last week of August. She said she'll be home by then."

Six weeks. Katharine looked at what she could see of the downstairs in dismay. As she pictured the upstairs, panic started in her toes and surged upward. What had she done?

"That will be fine," she told Elna, proud that her voice didn't even quaver. "You start making your list of people to invite, and I'll get the house finished." They exchanged the pleasantries that oil the wheels of society, and hung up.

"Next time you see your friend Hasty," Katharine told the chubby pig as she robbed him of a prebreakfast cookie, "tell him I now have a deadline to get this house in order, but I may die in the attempt."

That cookie was the last one, so while she fixed and ate breakfast she made another batch, jotting herself a note to remember to get more pecans and chocolate chips. She'd gone through a lot of cookies that week, between guests and taking some down to the beach.

Rosa, the maid, came at nine, headed upstairs to get their room ready for Tom's arrival, and hurried right back down. "You know you got a cat on Mr. Tom's pillow?"

Katharine accompanied her upstairs. Sure enough, the small cat was curled on Tom's pillow, having a snooze. As soon as it saw the women, it streaked out the door.

"Hey," Katharine called after it, "you could at least stick around to help change the bed."

"Mr. Tom ain't gonna like having a cat on his bed," Rosa warned.

"We won't tell him," Katharine suggested. "After you make the bed, close this door."

She peered into the other bedrooms, but the little cat was nowhere to be found.

She went to her study to compile a list of everything she

needed to do so they could leave for the lake as soon as Tom arrived. He wasn't due until four, so when the telephone rang, she was puzzled to hear his voice.

"Where are you?" If he had come home on an earlier flight, she'd have to cancel her hair appointment.

"Still in D.C. I'm sorry, hon, but I'm not getting home this weekend after all. Mitch went to the hospital a couple of hours ago with chest pains."

Even as she voiced sympathy for Mitch, whom she genuinely liked, Katharine felt ice around her own heart. The company CEO was only fourteen years older than Tom. If Mitch could have a heart attack before he got around to retiring . . .

She pushed down that thought and tuned in to what Tom was telling her. ". . . a big do in Chevy Chase tomorrow night that he was supposed to attend, and he has asked if I could go instead." She could tell he was pleased. Mitch had bypassed three men with more seniority to choose him.

"That's impressive! Next thing you know, you'll be senior vice president." Katharine was already mentally packing her bag. "Black tie, I suppose?" She had a new black dress she'd been eager to wear.

"Of course."

She waited for the next sentences, which would be, *Mitch said to send the jet to pick you up. How soon can you be ready?* It had happened before.

Instead, Tom said, "I wish you could come, too, but Ashley—Mitch's wife?"

Trophy wife of thirty, hair like spun honey, wide blue eyes, mouth a perpetual pout smeared with lipstick, figure like . . .

Stop it, she told herself. *Who Mitch marries is no business of yours.* But she had been fond of the homey, practical woman he'd divorced two years before. They'd been married longer than Ashley had been alive. Sometimes, like most corporate wives, Katharine wondered if Tom would come home one weekend and announce that he was trading her in on a newer model.

Nonsense. She and Tom had a solid marriage and still loved and enjoyed each other. She forced her attention back to what he was saying. ". . . a cousin of the woman throwing the party, and she was looking forward to it very much, so Mitch has asked if I will take her."

"Oh."

If Tom had been a woman, he could have read a paragraph into that word: *Bitch! Doesn't mind marrying somebody thirty-two years older, but as soon as he gets laid up, she's on the prowl. I'd wager both our kids that it was her idea for him to ask you to take her. Mitch is so besotted, he wouldn't suspect a thing. But Ashley doesn't want to miss her cousin's party? My foot! She's got enough cousins in Washington to fill a small town, and she never minded going to their parties alone when she was single. Now she not only has to have an escort, she won't put up with Will Sikes's foul mouth, Chesney Jenkins's damp hands, or Tony Sorrel's battleaxe of a wife—who would be sure to come along. Specifically requested you, did she? The best looking and smartest of the four? So help me, if she makes a move on you, you'd jolly well better . . .*

"It's not going to be a real exciting party, anyway," Tom reassured her. He launched into a description of who would be there with what hidden agendas. Katharine hadn't noticed the little cat creep under her desk, but when she tapped her foot in impatience, she stamped on her tail. The cat uttered a cry of terror and took off down the hall in the direction of Tom's library.

"What was that?" Tom interrupted himself to ask.

"A cat. We are now the proud owners of two cats."

"Cats?"

"Cats. Felines. Their owner died. It was real sad."

She filled him in on meeting Agnes by the cemetery—leaving out the gun—drinking tea on her porch, reading of her death, and going back to the house yesterday. "She had promised Dr. Flo letters, but we didn't find them. She even said Dr. Flo might be the heir to her land, but that's a long shot and we didn't find a deed. It breaks my heart to think of that vacant land getting overbuilt with ostentatious houses so a few rich people can retire down there."

"Folks have to live somewhere. Sounds like it also broke your heart to see two cats without an owner."

"Well, it did, and nobody else would take them."

"What are their names?"

"I never heard her call them anything. I'm working on new ones."

"You might consider Impulse and Second Thoughts. But they'll be good company for you. Just keep them off our bed and out of my library, please."

She should have known Tom wouldn't object to cats in principal. Once he had even brought home two kittens for the kids. Of course, he had then taken off and left Katharine to care for them, and had called several times in the following week to instruct her not to let them sleep on beds, pee on rugs, prowl among his precious jade collection, or sleep on top of the books in his library.

She huffed. Really! If he wasn't in the house, he had no say in how it was run.

"Katharine?" he sounded penitent. "I'm real sorry you can't come up for the party."

"I am, too, love, for more reasons than one. You know Ashley's reputation. Be very careful."

Tom laughed. "She's not interested in me." But she could tell the notion flattered him.

"I'm interested in you, and one of my duties is to warn you about the barracudas."

When he'd gotten certified in scuba soon after they married, Katharine—already certified—had gone along for a refresher course. The dive instructor had told them, "Always stay with your buddy. That way, you'll have somebody to warn you about the barracudas."

"Just like in marriage," Tom had whispered to Katharine, giving her hand a squeeze.

It had become a code between them. He would sometimes warn her about a new male acquaintance, "He is closely related to the barracudas." At parties, if some man came on to her too strong, Katharine would cruise up to Tom and murmur, "I've picked up a barracuda."

Tom, however, never thought he needed protecting. "Don't be silly," he muttered over the phone.

Which only showed how vulnerable he was.

But what more could Katharine say? She didn't want him to hang up miffed. She had learned long ago that couples who live apart don't have the luxury of little spats. What would be a minor flare-up at home can become a flaming row by the time one partner carries it around a few days. She racked her brain for a neutral topic of conversation, something that would let them defuse the present one. She couldn't think of anything, but her mouth seemed to have a mind of its own. "Did you ever buy any books about pirates?"

"Pirates?" His voice was suspicious. "As in another ocean predator?"

She laughed. "No, silly, as in sailors who preyed on other ships along the coast of Georgia. I don't remember if I told you about the pirate's grave we found Tuesday."

"If it was a real old grave, they sometimes used a skull to connote death." He still sounded irritated.

"That's what—" she stumbled "—somebody else said. But this one didn't look much older than the Civil War, and it had crossed bones under the skull. I promise you."

"I've got books on pirates somewhere." She could tell he

was finally ready to give up the quarrel, too. She waited while he thought, knowing he was mentally picturing his library, shelf by shelf. Tom's memory was phenomenal, one of the things that made him so good at what he did. He seldom forgot a person he had met or anything he had read. And while he hadn't yet read all the books he'd bought over the years, he seemed to be able to close his eyes, roam his shelves, and read all the titles on the spines.

In a few seconds he said, "Try the second shelf from the top on the right end of the wall behind my desk. I've got something about Blackbeard. He roamed Georgia for a while. There's one about pirates down in the Caribbean, too. I swear, hon, one of these days I'm going to sit down and—"

"—read every book on those shelves. I know." She managed a carefree laugh since he wasn't there to read her face. "But you'd better hurry and retire or stop ordering books, or neither of us will live long enough to read them all. You got another package from Amazon while I was gone."

"It ought to be a biography of Alexander Hamilton. Put it on my desk."

"I already did. And thanks for the pirates. I'll let you know if we find out who the one in the cemetery was. Have fun at the party."

"Thanks. I'll be missing you."

She had succeeded in banishing his bad mood, but as she went to make iced tea for the weekend she would now spend at home, she permitted herself a glower of disappointment. "How is making tea like a good marriage?" she asked the cookie pig. "You have to give them both time and you have to accept that hot water and an occasional burn are part of the process."

While she waited for the tea to steep, she stood at the window watching Anthony mow. Elna was so lucky. He came home every single night.

What makes people leave their homes and families to roam the world in the name of business? she wondered. *Why can't people stick around near where they live and find enough to do?*

It might be heresy, but she suspected it had a lot to do with comfortable hotels, fancy meals, and other perks those travelers had come to accept as their due. It must be nice to leave somebody behind to worry about getting the grass mowed and the diapers changed.

When the phone rang again, Katharine ran to answer, hoping Tom was calling back to invite her up after all. Instead, a raspy voice said, "Miz Murray? This is Lamar Franklin. I looked out that book we were talking about, the one on Confederate privateers, and it has some stuff you might be interested in. I'm coming down to the history center later today. I'll run it by your place this afternoon."

Katharine did not want the man coming by her house, and she doubted that the book would be of much interest, but after he had gone to the trouble of "looking it out" for her, glancing through it would be the least she could do. "Thanks. I'll be here. Do you know where we live?"

"Yes, ma'am, and I got directions from Mapquest."

She hung up and smacked her cheek in disgust. "Stupid, stupid, stupid. Not an hour after promising Elna and Anthony that you will have this house finished and ready to party in six weeks, you have committed yourself to stick around the house all afternoon waiting for a man you don't really know and aren't sure you can trust, who is bringing you a book you don't want to read. You, my dear, need a brain transplant."

"Meow," agreed the little cat, who was watching her from the door.

Chapter 23

She called Hollis to tell her they needed to pick up their pace, but Hollis wasn't home.

She called the upholsterer and told him she had made a decision about fabric. It was true. She had carried the swatches for the living room couch and chairs with her to the phone and made the decision while waiting for him to answer. What she had done was lay them all on the counter, close her eyes, and reach for one set.

"Chairs are for sitting on, not worth hours of agonizing," she informed the little pig. He beamed approval.

"You know what I like about you?" she asked him. "Unconditional love."

The upholsterer agreed he could pick the couch and chairs up Monday and have them back in three-to-four weeks. "No longer than that," she warned.

She called the glazier and informed him if he couldn't get out to her house the following week to repair her kitchen-cabinet doors, she would need to call somebody else. He assured her he would be there Wednesday, at the latest.

She called the painter, who still had three rooms to complete, and told him he needed to get them done within two weeks. Accustomed to having her hesitantly ask, "Could you please come out sometime soon?" he protested at first, but when she persisted, he agreed he could show up on Thursday.

"Early on Thursday," she instructed.

She poured herself a glass of tea marveling at how much she had accomplished in such a short time. Why hadn't she been firmer with all of them weeks before?

The bathrooms still needed towels. She went to her computer and looked up the Bloomingdale's Web site but then, remembering Hasty's jibe, she logged off that site and pulled up the site for the JCPenney Outlet Store. She ordered a dozen sets of towels to match various bathrooms, paid for them by credit card, and gave her name and address for delivery.

Only when she had logged off that site did she feel a shadow of doubt. She seldom bought things over the Internet, and she had never bought towels without feeling them first. *I should have bought one set,* she worried. *Then, if they were okay, I could have bought more.*

It's done, her father reminded her, *and they'll be fine. Thank God you have money to buy towels at all. You're doing great, honey bunch.*

She grinned at the ceiling. "I am, aren't I?

Feeling very accomplished, she headed toward Tom's library. She deserved a little R&R with pirates.

Tom's books confirmed what he and Hasty had said: pirates had been driven out of Southern coastal waters by the early seventeen hundreds, several decades before the Bayards bought their island. Had the first Bayards discovered the pirate grave planted on their new property and decided to locate their family cemetery beside it?

No. That grave didn't look three hundred years old, and it was too much of a coincidence for both the pirate and Elizabeth to have both been Mallerys. Had Mallery families been common in Georgia then? Katharine couldn't recall ever having heard the name.

She headed back to her computer and looked up Mallerys on ancestry.com.

She jumped when the telephone rang, and couldn't believe she'd been working for an hour. As soon as she answered, she heard the excitement in Dr. Flo's voice.

"The letters arrived! Agnes sent them before she died. And I had a message from her lawyer when I got home, asking me to call him. I did, and he said on Wednesday morning she had instructed him to notify me upon her death, and told him she had sent me instructions concerning the property. He didn't know what they were."

Katharine felt her heart skip a beat. "So what were they? And what do the letters say?"

"I haven't opened the envelope yet. As soon as I saw it, I had to call and tell you. I am so pleased Agnes kept her promise before she died."

"I am, too." Katharine understood the impulse that made Dr. Flo call. When you live alone, you can generally deal with the bad stuff on your own. What is hard is having something special to share and nobody to share it with. She was flattered that Dr. Flo had called her. She was getting very fond of a woman she had known only casually a week before.

"Quick, see what Agnes said and call me back."

"I'll do that. And Monday, after Tom goes back, shall I bring the letters up so you can see them?"

For the first time since Tom's call, Katharine was glad he wasn't coming home. "Bring them today. Tom called a little while ago and said he can't get home after all."

"He's not ill, is he?" Having your own husband drop dead in an instant makes you keenly aware it could happen to others.

"Oh, no, he's fine, but his boss isn't." She explained about the party, touching lightly on Ashley when she'd rather have used a cleaver. "I could come down to your place this afternoon, if you like."

Before Dr. Flo could answer, Katharine remembered she

couldn't. "Drat. Somebody's dropping off a book this afternoon and I don't know how to get in touch with him to tell him not to come."

"Why don't I bring them to you?"

"I hate for you to always have to come here. Besides, I want to see your gardens." They had been featured in the *Journal-Constitution* more than once.

"This isn't the afternoon for that. It's best if I come to you. Besides, I know the way to your house and you don't know the way to mine, and your car has had enough miles put on it in pursuit of the Gilbert family history this week. Shall we say around two? I promise not to even peek until then, but it may kill me."

"I sure hope not. By the way, I have some news, too. I've been doing a little research into the matter of pirates this morning. Tom has a couple of books about them that I skimmed through, and I've also been looking up Mallerys on my new computer—which I got conncctcd last night."

"Good for you. Did you find Mallery the Pirate?"

"No. In fact, I'll be interested in knowing what the letters tell us, because pirates were gone before the Bayards bought the island. What is more puzzling, there were no Mallerys in Georgia during the years when Elizabeth was growing up."

"What?" Dr. Flo sounded like she thought she hadn't heard correctly.

"There were no Mallerys in Georgia. I checked the 1830, 1840, and the 1850 censuses, thinking I'd find out who Elizabeth's relatives were, but I couldn't find a single Mallery in Georgia. In fact, I found very few in the South. There were five hundred Mallery listings elsewhere in the United States, mostly in New York and Connecticut."

Dr. Flo gave an evil cackle that startled and delighted Katharine. "So Burch had himself a Yankee ancestress. I wonder if he knows."

"He rattled off his family history pretty easily, so he probably does, but I doubt he'd tell us where she came from."

"Then unless these letters shed some light on that, I doubt if we'll ever know—which means we won't be able to find out where our pirate came from, either."

"Couldn't we check all the male Mallerys in the country in her generation?"

Dr. Flo chuckled. "Yes, but not only would that be tedious and time-consuming, but 'pirate' isn't likely to be listed as a profession in the census, either."

Katharine felt her elation oozing away. "Do you ever get discouraged looking up all this stuff?"

"Frequently. A whole lot of the process is picking the most promising-looking trail and following it until you discover it was the wrong one. Did you find anybody who looked promising?"

She consulted her notes. "Not really. In 1860 two Mallery men lived in Savannah, but John was a carpenter and George was some sort of agent. I couldn't read some of it."

"Some of that handwriting is dreadful." Dr. Flo commiserated.

"No, this was beautiful, but so full of curlicues and flourishes, I couldn't read those two words. Neither man appeared in the 1870 census, so they could have gone to sea as pirates, I suppose—except there weren't any pirates."

"They could have simply moved. What race were they?"

"Nothing was put in that column."

"White, then. The color of normal."

Katharine was embarrassed by her deduction, but forced to agreed with the conclusion. "I don't think they were pirates, anyway. My best guess is that Mallery the Pirate was a relative of Elizabeth's from the North."

"A no-good white man who shamed his family and had to be brought back to a backwater little island to be buried."

"Maybe not," Katharine objected. "Maybe he loved his

sister or cousin very much, repented in the end of all his wrongdoing, and asked to be brought back there to be buried near Elizabeth. If we're making it all up, I prefer stories with a happy ending."

"I keep telling you, girl, in genealogy you seldom get endings at all, happy or otherwise. Trailing threads are the norm. In this case, since it will be next to impossible to figure out where Elizabeth Mallery came from without asking Burch—who probably wouldn't tell us if he knows—it will be impossible to find out if she had a brother, much less a cousin. The biggest question I have about all this is why that pirate was buried with my relations."

"Which the letters might answer. I got one solid thing out of my research into Mallerys: names for the cats. I'm going to call the female Phebe, spelled with no *o,* and the male Savant. Those were members of the Mallery clan in 1850. Can you imaging saddling a little boy with the name *Savant*?"

"It would have been a burden to bear," Dr. Flo agreed. "Are they settling in all right?"

"Skittish, but the little one is currently sleeping on my feet. That's progress, I guess. And speaking of progress, I went to the history center after you left yesterday and found a book on the history of McIntosh County. It had a whole chapter on John McIntosh Kell."

"The one Burch claimed was a famous Confederate naval commander?"

"Yes, and he was. But there were other interesting facts in the book, too. Did you know General Sherman issued an edict that gave all the barrier islands from Charleston to Jacksonville, plus all the land up to thirty miles from the coast, to blacks after the war? No whites were supposed to live there at all." Katharine didn't mention that Sherman had designated the land a "reservation." She was too ashamed of that fact.

"Do! That would have taken in most, if not all, of McIntosh County. You know it never happened. Those plantation owners didn't give up all their land."

"I didn't seen any evidence that the edict was enforced," Katharine admitted. "In fact, the author said there were still a good number of whites in McIntosh County in 1870, and he claimed that some of the plantation owners hired their former slaves and paid them in land. That sounds like they were still around. But there was a black man in charge of the county for several years. He came down with the Freedmen's Bureau and set himself up as a dictator, it sounded like. Whites were terrified of him, but some of the black folks grew pretty prosperous."

"Maybe that's why Marie and the children came from Haiti. Her profession was listed as seamstress. She may have been able to make more money in Georgia, although it looks like she'd have gone to one of the cities where there were more people needing a seamstress."

Katharine was about to ring off when Dr. Flo thought of one more thing she wanted to say. "I found a historic cemetery in Darien this morning that will let me bury my people there, but I still want to go back for the disinterment. I don't trust either Burch or his lawyer, and I don't want them simply moving Claude, Marie, and little Françoise over the bridge to the old slave cemetery."

"I think you'd be wise to be there. Burch seemed in a pretty big hurry, and he might figure you'd never come back to see where they were buried. I talked to Posey, and she'd like to go, too, if you don't mind. Then we can go back to her cottage for a few days more."

"How kind. I'd love that. But do you have time for this, with all you have to do?"

Katharine gave one hurried thought to the house and the next six weeks, and knew she ought to say, "Actually, I can't. I'm sorry." Instead, she was already saying, "You know me—any excuse to get to the ocean."

Dr. Flo sounded pleased. "We'll give Granddaddy a send-off to remember. See you in a little while."

Katharine fixed some lunch for herself and Rosa, and discovered that the little cat was now following her around the kitchen. The big one hadn't come out of his retreat between the washer and dryer.

When the phone rang again, she hoped it wasn't Dr. Flo calling to say she wasn't coming. On the other hand, it could be Tom, telling her to pack.

Instead, the voice on the other end was incoherent. All she could discern was tears and a rush of disjointed words. ". . . ruin everything . . . how could you?"

"Who is this?" Katharine demanded. She looked at caller ID, but the number was blocked.

"Miranda. Miranda Stampers."

"How did you get this number?"

"Chase." She said the name like it was honey. "He knew the name of the woman who owned the house you were staying in down on Jekyll, and so he got her number on the computer, and I called her and said you lost an earring in our store and I wanted to call and tell you I'd send it to you. She gave me your number."

That would have been Julia, the housekeeper, not Posey. Posey, like Tom, always checked caller ID and only took calls from numbers she recognized. Katharine always answered, afraid one of her children or a friend had had an accident and borrowed somebody else's phone.

"What are the chances of that?" Tom once asked.

"If it's one in a zillion and it ever happens, I want to be there," Katharine had replied.

Now she was there with Miranda on the other end, and she wouldn't remonstrate with Julia, because if she actually had left an earring at Stampers, she would want to know.

"What did you want?"

"Look, I'm sorry about the other calls. We—I mean, I thought maybe if you got scared, your friend wouldn't come back to sign the papers. But now Chase's daddy says she already signed and he's gonna start work next week. Next week! He's gonna cut down trees, tear up the clearing, drive away the animals . . ." She burst into tears again.

Katharine knew how Miranda felt. Who in America doesn't feel helpless when developers invade their community, followed by men on bulldozers whose macho delight is to push over as many trees in a day as possible? When Katharine herself saw a formerly wooded lot clear-cut for building, she felt like calling down God's vengeance upon them with curses like, "May your houses never sell and your children go hungry in the streets."

Miranda's pain vibrated over the phone.

"I am so sorry," Katharine told her sincerely. "Dr. Flo doesn't want that property developed any more than you do, but she had no good reason not to sign for the graves to be moved. There is one possibility, though. We got a package of old letters from Agnes, which she mailed before she— died."

No point in bringing up speculations about Agnes's death.

"It's possible that there will be information in there that will give Dr. Flo a claim to that clearing, as well as to Agnes's house. If she has any leverage to stop or even postpone Burch's bulldozers, I'm sure she will use it."

Miranda sniffed. Katharine could see her pushing back that sweep of hair. "Why would she own any of Bayard Island?" Her voice was doubtful, but a sweet note of hope had crept in.

"We don't know. But there's a mystery about her family being buried there at all. These letters might explain the mystery. You sit tight, all right?"

Katharine had no idea what it meant to "sit tight," but

those words still calmed her children when they presented her with a problem she needed time to work on.

Miranda gave an enormous sniff. "Okay. Thanks. I'm sorry I bothered you 'n' all. Well, I better go. A customer walked in."

Katharine was waiting for Dr. Flo when the phone rang again. "Grand Murray Station," she muttered as she went to answer it.

"I know it's almost time for Tom to get there," Hasty said in a rush, "but I wanted to thank you for dinner last night. That was fun."

"It was. And thanks for putting together the computer. I've been using it this morning trying to find Mallery the Pirate."

"Any success?"

"Not yet, but I'm still hopeful."

He laughed. "If you find an American pirate who lived and sailed after the Civil War, you let me know. I keep telling you, there's no such creature."

"I'll let you know. Would you prefer your words with salt or without?"

"Preferably with more of that clam sauce you made last night. I can't remember the last time I had a home-cooked meal."

"Maybe while you were up with your family last week?"

"Oh, yeah. Maybe then. When does Tom get in?"

If he hadn't asked, she would never have told him. At least that's what she told herself. But he had, and she had never been good at lying to Hasty. "He's not coming." She explained, leaving out the Saturday night party and stressing that Tom was staying at the request of his ailing boss.

"So when does he get his sainthood merit badge?" Hasty asked sourly.

"Sometime tomorrow night. Listen, I do have to go. Dr.

Flo is coming over to read letters she received from Agnes, the woman who died."

"How about dinner tonight, since you're all on your own?"

She was trying to come up with one good reason to say no to a harmless dinner—and finding her mind strangely blank—when she was saved by the bell. The doorbell.

"Dr. Flo is here. I can't talk right now. But we may want to have supper together and discuss all this. Let me have a rain check."

She hung up quickly, but thought his last words were, "It's not raining."

Chapter 24

"What a lovely place you have here!" Dr. Flo exclaimed. Katharine was surprised, because from pictures she had seen, the Gadney estate was larger and much more ornate. "And look at the proportions of these rooms. You all must be so happy here."

"We have been," Katharine agreed, "but good proportions is about all the rooms have to offer right now. It's still a bit chaotic."

Scarcely glancing at the disorder in the other rooms, Dr. Flo paused in the archway to Katharine's new study. "This is absolutely delightful. It is where you work?"

Katharine was pleased, for Dr. Flo was the first nonbiased woman to see it completed. When she described the room's transformation, the professor nodded. "I used to tell my students that every woman needs one space in her home that is entirely hers, where she can escape to recharge her spiritual and mental batteries. You will do good things here."

Katharine laughed. "So far all I've done is order online towels and look up the Mallerys."

Dr. Flo patted the monitor. "That was a baptism for your genealogical future." She held out a priority mail envelope. "Is this where we'll look at what's in here?"

"We can spread out better in the breakfast room." Katharine led the way. "The dining room is still such a mess that I cleaned off this table to work on."

Dr. Flo settled herself in a chair and tore the envelope open. "Here goes."

The first thing she pulled out was a legal-sized document. She scanned it briefly. "This is a copy of the deed Agnes mentioned. There's a note attached." She read the note silently, then handed it to Katharine.

Written in a neat, schoolteacher hand that seemed incongruous for such a large, forceful woman, the letter was dated the morning of Agnes's death.

Dear Florence,

I am concerned about keeping this deed in the house with all the hullabaloo on the island at present, so am opening a safe deposit box this morning in Savannah. I also am sending you a copy and the second key, and instructing my lawyer to notify you on the occasion of my death. Please tell him about the box and that he will find the key buried in my sugar canister. If it is not there, it will have been stolen, but the thief will have no way of knowing which bank it fits.

Do you ever feel that some things are preordained in this world? I feel like that about meeting you. It seems I have known you much longer than one afternoon, and I am convinced you will play an important role in preserving this island for a while longer. I hope to see you again.

Agnes Morrison

Only the signature looked like Agnes, sprawling across the page in strong dark letters.

Dr. Flo fished in the bottom of the priority mail envelope

and brought out a small tan bank envelope. "She wrote down the name of the bank and its address on this."

Katharine was scanning the deed for the pertinent paragraph. "Here it is. 'In the event that the Morrisons choose to leave Bayard Island or die without issue, the property—'" she omitted the legal description of the property " '—and the house standing thereon shall revert to the descendants of my childhood friend, Claude Gilbert . . .' Here you are!"

Dr. Flo reached for the deed. "It actually says Claude Gilbert?"

Katharine pointed to the line. Dr. Flo continued to read. " '. . . descendants of my childhood friend, Claude Gilbert, formerly of Bayard Island. If such descendants cannot be found, the property will revert to the Bayard Bluff estate.' Oh, my!" Her voice held wonder.

"Just what you always wanted," Katharine teased. "An unpainted house with a view of a slough, your own nanny goat, a few chickens, and who knows how many palmetto bugs? Not to mention man-eating mosquitoes, a sky so big it could fall on you and mash you, and Burch Bayard nagging you to sell every day of your life."

"How much do you think he'd pay?" Dr. Flo sounded as if she was speaking thoughts aloud rather than replying to Katharine.

Katharine was shocked. "You wouldn't sell to him!"

"I might. I don't want to live there, as you graphically pointed out."

"You could give it to the state for a park."

"I'm not giving anything to anybody right now. This could be a godsend."

"God wouldn't give you land like that to sell to a developer."

"That's how little you know. God knows what I need, and right this minute, a liquid asset is something I could really use."

"But—?" Katharine stopped and simply stared.

Dr. Flo bent her head and closed her eyes. One finger traced a design on the tabletop. It took Katharine a moment to recognize it as a dollar sign. Finally Dr. Flo came to a decision.

"Let me tell you a story about a princess who became a frog." She clasped both hands in front of her and spoke as if she were beginning a classroom lecture. "Have you ever heard that every woman is one man away from welfare?" She waited for Katharine to nod. "That worked backwards for me. I was born with two gold spoons in my mouth, as you probably know. Daddy left a small fortune and Mama's daddy left a considerable one. There are advantages to being the only grandchild in two families. Maurice made good money, too, so we lived well."

"And gave a lot of money away," Katharine reminded her. The generosity of the Gadneys had been legendary.

"Yes, but we still had far more than most people want or need. Because I had the degree in business, I managed our money, with the help of a good broker. We were all set for a wonderful retirement and a blessed old age." She stopped.

Katharine didn't break the silence. If Dr. Flo wanted to finish the story, she would. Katharine wasn't certain she wanted to hear the end, anyway.

At last the professor heaved a sigh that seemed bigger than she was. "After I retired, Maurice took a course on investing. He got so enthusiastic, he decided he wanted to manage our money for a change. He even asked me to cash in my whole 403-B plan. Like a fool—and because I loved him more than I loved money—I did." Her last dropped to a whisper. "There was so much money, you see. I never imagined it could disappear so fast."

This time she waited to make sure Katharine was listening. "But it did?"

Dr. Flo nodded. "He didn't know what he was doing, you

see, and it was the time of the great tech stock bubble. He was like a little boy, making thousands of dollars in an hour. I warned him, 'Honey, you know tibias, not technology,' but at that point, nobody could tell that man a thing." She came to an abrupt stop and pressed one hand over her mouth. "I should not have said that. I have sworn I won't bad-mouth him now that he's gone."

"You lost a lot?"

"Eventually, everything we had."

At Katharine's cry of dismay her mouth twisted into a wry smile. "It's over and done with now, but when I found out, I thought I'd go crazy. He hid it from me for a long time. When I'd suggest that we buy something or other to diversify our holdings, he'd spout his latest economic hero to me and tell me it had been years since I'd studied business. Me—who inhaled the *Wall Street Journal* every day and read economic journals like they were scripture. Still, like I said, I loved him and wanted him to strut his stuff. Besides, everything he spouted made sense if you applied it wisely. He just didn't know how to do that. I discovered that he had tried stocks, bonds, even real estate, but everything he touched turned to dirt. Our house was paid for, but he took out a big mortgage, arguing that it had gained so much value since we bought it that we ought to be investing that money instead of sitting on it. Some very sound economists think that way, so while I personally believe a paid-up house makes money for your future, I agreed. When he lost all the money from the mortgage, though, he finally told me how bad things were. Then, instead of keeping the little bit we still had, he started day trading. He cut back his practice to afternoons, and every morning he'd sit at his computer trying to figure out what to buy and what to sell. Then he'd put on his coat and go to the office to make more money to lose."

Her voice grated with sorrow. "Since he died, I have won-

dered whether he had a gambling addiction we never suspected or whether he was in the early stages of dementia."
Her lips trembled. She pressed them together for a moment,
but the pain in her eyes would not be contained. "I kick myself daily for not stepping in to stop him. I am convinced
that what gave him that heart attack was worry over how we
were going to live the rest of our lives." She pressed one
hand to her lips and blinked back tears.

Katharine was reeling. If that could happen to the Gadneys, it could happen to anybody. And Dr. Flo was right—it
gave new meaning to the old saying that every woman is one
man away from welfare. "But surely you had something
left," she protested. "I mean when you say it was all gone—
surely you at least had his life insurance."

"I had some through Spelman, but he didn't carry any. We
had no children and I had plenty to live on if he died first—
or so we thought. We agreed years ago not to spend money
on premiums we could donate to worthy causes. It all made
sense back then. Later, it was too late."

"So how are you living now?"

Dr. Flo managed a sad smile. "Frugally and by faith. After
he died, I went back to my broker and we decided this old
dog was going to have to learn new tricks. I sold the house—
and the furniture, and the exercise equipment, and his car,
and most of my jewelry, and even most of my clothes. How
could I have spent so much to cover my body? But when I
was done selling, I had enough to buy a condo outside the
perimeter, where things are cheaper. It's a studio so small I
can stand at one wall and practically touch the one across
the room, but it's paid for. The condo, Social Security, and
God are what I have left to see me into my old age. I am
coming to appreciate the power of that phrase in the Lord's
Prayer: 'Give us this day our daily bread.' That's what I ask
for these days." She reached out and covered Katharine's

hand with hers. "I haven't told many people this, so I'd appreciate it if you would keep it confidential."

Katharine put her other hand on top. "Of course, but do you really have enough to live on?" As soon as the words were out, she flushed. "I'm sorry, I asked without thinking. I don't normally pry into people's finances, but I handled the money for two aunts and got used to asking them questions like that. You are beginning to feel like family."

Dr. Flo gave her a grateful smile. "You, too. That's why I wanted to tell you. And yes, I have enough to live on if I'm careful. However, I know very well that I am one crisis away from disaster. Some days I get wobbly kneed thinking what will happen when I need to repair the car or fill a cavity. That's something people with credit cards and a cushion in the bank don't understand about people on the bottom of the financial ladder. An unexpected expense means less food or heat. It's also nice to have enough for a little luxury once in a while—a nice piece of meat, a good haircut, enough to take a friend to lunch. Our spirits need those things. That's why I said that this land could be a gift from God."

"And from Claude Gilbert." Katharine added.

Dr. Flo laughed. "Absolutely. Pretty soon I'll be talking to him like you do your daddy."

As she tried to take it in, Katharine was flooded with shame. What must it have cost Dr. Flo to eat salads while she wolfed down full meals with dessert? And no wonder she wore native skirts, cotton tops, and plastic flip-flops. "Why didn't you tell me sooner?"

"I couldn't. Our world—this world—" she gestured to indicate Katharine's house, her yard, places where the prosperous take beauty and comfort for granted "—is a world of reciprocity. We can go for weeks without spending a penny because somebody else is providing banquets, lake cottages, concerts, and plays. But we pay them back. Now I go almost nowhere, because I can't accept favors I can't repay. I loved going down to Jekyll with you, but I hated not being able to take you out to dinner . . ."

She took two deep breaths and looked out the window until she could trust her voice again. "That's why the prospect of owning eight acres of Bayard Island is not at all unpleasant. And I have to admit, in spite of Agnes's hopes for me, if it turns out I really own it, I will probably sell to Burch. When the rubber of your principles meets the road of need, you do things you never dreamed you would."

Katharine needed something to do. She rose and filled a pitcher with tea, arranged a plate with cookies and another with lemon and mint, then stood looking at the snack with humility. There was no reason on earth why she should have so much and others so little. In spite of the rhetoric, Tom didn't really work any harder than Anthony, or the men who carried away her garbage, or people who flipped burgers. He had invested wisely—both his money and his own talents—and added to what his parents and grandparents left him, but other people had smoothed his way. Nobody rises in the world unless somebody smooths the way. And she? She had come along for the ride.

Help me to share! she cried wordlessly. *Show me how to share with sensitivity.*

"I made these for Tom," she said as she set down the cookies. "Since he's not coming home, I'm glad you're here to eat some."

Dr. Flo smiled. "Me, too. They look delicious. And I really am trying to learn how to accept things graciously. That's a lesson I never had to learn before. But we've gotten ahead of ourselves here. We don't know if I have any claim on that land whatsoever. Shall we see what else Agnes sent?"

Chapter 25

Dr. Flo reached into the priority mail envelope and drew out a flat, dark object attached to an equally dark chain. "Here's the locket. Agnes didn't exaggerate when she said it was tarnished. It would take a lot of elbow grease to get this clean. I wonder if it has anything in it? Do you have a knife?"

Katharine fetched one with a sharp point, but Dr. Flo could not get it between the halves. "Do these things tarnish shut? Maybe I'd better take it to a jeweler. I don't want to ruin it." She dropped it reluctantly to the table with a faint *clunk.*

Katharine wondered how much a jeweler would charge to open it.

"Here's the baby shoe—what's left of it." Dr. Flo held up a tiny flattened object of faded brown leather. "Maybe you are sentimental about baby shoes, but I find it hard to get mushy about a shoe when we don't have a clue who it belonged to. I guess these are the letters." She slid out an inner envelope, mellowed by age to a soft gold. As she opened it and spilled its contents onto the table top, she began to slap the table frantically with the outer envelope.

"Silverfish! Oh, Katharine, I'm sorry. I never imagined I was bringing varmints into your house. And look at the condition of these letters! I don't know if we'll be able to read them at all." Still, her fingers stroked them reverently.

How must it feel, Katharine wondered, *to touch actual*

documents that belonged to your ancestors? She hoped she would get that chance one day.

She also hoped hers wouldn't have silverfish. Two fat ones wriggled toward her as if eager for a snack. She smacked them with her bare palm, then went to scrub her hands. She wetted two paper towels and handed one to Dr. Flo. "Here. Weapons, of sorts."

Dr. Flo grimaced. "I haven't touched any of them yet that I know of, but I don't think we ought to eat cookies while we go through this stuff, do you? Set the plate over yonder on the counter until we're done and have sanitized our hands."

The letters were yellow with age and stained with large jagged watermarks. Pieces of them had disintegrated. Other bits had apparently broken off in transit. The pile on the table looked less like history in the making than like a good fire waiting to start. Three more silverfish wriggled out as if escaping incipient flames.

Katharine smashed them with her paper towel and wished she had suggested they work on the patio table. It was a bit late now.

"We'll do the best we can," she said, as much to herself as to Dr. Flo. She smacked another silverfish and hoped none escaped to Tom's office. They'd find so much to eat in there, they would grow fat and multiply. She'd have to evict them with a shovel.

Dr. Flo scooped up the remains of two more off the table into her paper towel. "I think that's all of them."

"Good. Here's a trash can. And why don't you just drop the priority mail envelope on the floor for now while we see what we can make of the letters?"

Dr. Flo picked up a fragment containing only pieces of words. "Now I know how the folks who first tried to read the Dead Sea Scrolls felt. Let's start with the whole ones."

They sat across from each other and each chose a letter. Dr. Flo gave hers a good shake to make sure no creatures hid inside, then unfolded it. "At least whoever wrote them dated them. This one is from August 17, 1877, written to Marie." "This one is January 12, 1875, also to Marie."

"Here's one written on September 10, 1878, and it starts, simply, *Dearie*. Oh! Whoever wrote it has just heard of Françoise's death. Listen!" She read aloud.

Dearie,

I still cannot believe that our precious girl is gone. Since I got your letter today I have done nothing but weep. If only I could have held her to ease her end. I rejoice that you were with her, but the seas run high tonight, so much water flows from my eyes. This letter is damp and blurred, and I am almost too blinded to write.

Dr. Flo held out the page, and her finger traced its surface. "See the blots?" She continued.

My heart is so full of grief I want to throw myself into the sea, but I will not for your sake, that of the boy, and my dear captain. Take care of my boy! Please keep him safe until I can come for him. He is doubly precious now, being all that is left. Oh, my poor Fran-çoise. I pray that tonight you are with him for whom you were named, and that finally he clasps you to his bosom and knows your worth.

Does any mother hear such a letter without filling in her own child's name? Katharine's chest grew tight at the thought that Jon or Susan might die where she could not reach them. Why had she ever let them go so far away? On the heels of that her mind pictured the small forlorn stone at the edge of the Georgia marsh. She blinked back tears.

Dr. Flo cleared her throat several times as if something had lodged there. "I am intrigued by that 'for whom she was named' bit. Would you guess that Françoise was named for Francis Bayard? He died the year before she was born."

"Then maybe Claude Gilbert was named for Claude Bayard. You are going to turn out to be Burch's cousin after all. Just wait."

Dr. Flo's lip curled. "I wonder who would be more disgusted, me or—what's gotten into that cat?"

The large cat had crept from the utility room to the breakfast room unnoticed and was sniffing the priority mail envelope on the floor as if it held a mouse.

"Maybe he smells the silverfish," Katharine suggested as the cat rubbed his jowls against the envelope's surface.

"I'd guess he smells Agnes. Look at that."

He had caught it in his teeth and was dragging it off to his lair.

Katharine shrugged. "Anything to keep him happy."

"You said the little one is settling in a bit. What about that one?"

"He's still hiding out in the utility room. I'm afraid the little one is staking out Tom's library, though."

"That's good, since Tom isn't here so much of the time."

"Tell that to Tom."

Dr. Flo started unfolding the other letters. "Maybe we ought to begin by sorting these by dates."

In a few minutes the remains of nine letters lay in a stack on the table with unidentifiable fragments. The deed, blackened locket, and flattened shoe made a smaller pile at one end.

"Why don't you read them aloud?" Katharine suggested. "It's your family."

"Possibly," Dr. Flo reminded her. She took the top letter from the pile. "It's dated July 15, 1873, and this one, too, is addressed only to *Dearie*. I wonder who she was." She began to read.

Dearie,

I am sending you my most valuable treasures, Claude and Françoise. I know you will not blame them for what some have deemed my sin. With them I send dearest Marie, who has agreed to stay with them until I can fetch them. I pray you, make all three as welcome as you would me. You will soon learn what delights they are. Claude already reads, but speaks very little English. Please see that he is schooled. I send gold with Marie to pay for their keep. Do not ask about its source, nor reject it. We hear how difficult life is in Georgia at present. I am well, happy, and safe. Marie will tell you that my Captain is the best captain in the world—and she has known him longer than I! He promises we will come for them soon. I trust you are well, and send all my love.

Mallery

Dr. Flo laid down the letter. "We've found the pirate." Her eyes refused to meet Katharine's across the table.

"I wish I had him in this kitchen right now. I'd smack him so hard he'd see stars. How could he?"

Dr. Flo could only shake her head.

"Do you think Dearie was his sister? That could explain his talk about being welcomed back and the bit about being healthy, happy, and safe."

Dr. Flo gave a genteel snort. "That sounds to me like what a liar would tell his female relatives if he was endangering life and limb."

Katharine reached for her tea with an unsteady hand. Jon, over in China, kept assuring her he was fine. As she took a fortifying sip, she reflected that raising children doesn't get easier as they get older. Your worries grow with them.

"She has to have been his sister, though. To whom else could he send his black mistress and mulatto children?" Dr. Flo's voice was flat. Dead, even.

"How old were those babies at the time?"

Before Katharine could do the math, Dr. Flo answered. "Four and six. Can you believe it? All that malarkey about his children being his most valuable treasures. So why didn't he do the decent thing, and provide the poor little things a home where they wouldn't be oddities?" Her hand shook as she picked up the letter and re-read it, then she dropped it at the end of the table with distaste. "Be careful about researching your ancestors, girlfriend. You may not always like what you find."

Katharine wished she could think of anything to say that might alleviate Dr. Flo's shock. "I guess the only Bayards at that point would have been Elizabeth and her son, Claude. Francis died in 1870, didn't he? How old would Claude Bayard have been when the kids arrived?"

Dr. Flo reached into her purse, brought out her little notebook, and did a calculation. "Twenty-six. Old enough to be thinking of marriage."

"Didn't he have a five-year-old in the 1880 census?"

"That's right, he did. I wonder how Claude's wife liked having two mixed-race children in the household. And if Claude was anything like Dalt and Burch, I'll bet he had a conniption."

"But Elizabeth seems to have welcomed the children, and somebody bought marble for Françoise's stone. Maybe Claude never forgave his mother, and that's why he didn't put 'beloved' on her tombstone. Shall we read the next letter?" Katharine held it out.

Dr. Flo flapped one hand. "You read it. I have enough to digest from the first one."

As Katharine unfolded it, several loose bits floated down to the table. "This one is in such bad shape, I can't make it all out. It's addressed to Marie, dated November something—eleventh or seventeenth, I can't tell—of the same year. Here's what I can make out. The first paragraph is entirely blurred. The second begins—"

> *... cannot believe ... years of past fondness ... what he has done. Never did I expect ... I would never have sent ... had I known ... Captain is furious ... Claude a stern letter ... and urging him ... his namesake. Surely he can reconcile his wife ...*

"I told you his wife wasn't going to be happy," Dr. Flo growled.

"And I said Claude was named for Claude. Give each contestant one point." Katharine scanned the rest of the letter. "There's a long blurred bit, then the letter ends, '. . . *believe a separate residence is necessary, since we will be coming soon. However, do as you . . .*' That's all I can make out. Can you read it any better?" Katharine handed it across the table.

Dr. Flo looked at it quickly and laid it back down. "No."

"So how do you interpret the bit we've got?" Katharine retrieved the faded page and perused it again.

Dr. Flo's lips twisted in a wry smile. "That no matter how Elizabeth reacted, Mallery's nephew and his wife did not welcome his mulatto children and black mistress."

"Stop calling them that. Marie might not have been his mistress. Maybe he married her."

"Her name was Guilbert. The clearest point in that letter—and the only one that matters to me—is the fact that somebody was proposing to build a separate house for Marie and her children. That might help if Burch contests the deed."

"And Mallery didn't think the house was necessary, since he planned to come soon."

"But he didn't." Dr. Flo's voice was deep with disgust. "I

cannot forgive him for not checking to see how those children were being treated by their relatives."

"If Mallery's captain was also enraged by their treatment of the children, would you guess Mallery was an officer on the ship?"

"Probably. Mallery certainly admires the captain. But it's been several months, and the captain has not kept his promise to come back for the children. Those poor children. Pirating was obviously more important to their daddy than his offspring. I hate to think I've got his blood in my veins." She rubbed the inner part of her forearm as if she would press the bad blood out.

"Do you want to read the rest of the letters?"

"We might as well, but we could probably write the story without reading them."

As she had predicted, the letters held few surprises. Each letter promised to come soon. Most referred to letters received from Marie or the woman addressed as "Dearie"— whom they believed to be Elizabeth Bayard—describing the children's progress. Some expressed anger at the way Marie and the children were being treated by Claude Bayard. Several letters to Dearie, however, referred to what one called "your great kindness and that of Hamilton to Claude and Marie. I am so glad you love them as I do, and that the boys are becoming friends, as is right."

"That could explain the stipulation in Agnes's deed," Katharine concluded. "Remember how he called Claude 'my childhood friend'? If Claude went to Atlanta and never returned, Hamilton must have missed him."

"Unlike his own father." Dr. Flo refused to be swayed from her anger at Mallery. "Listen to this, written to Marie."

How I wish you were all with us. I never imagined so many years would pass. This morning we watched the sun rise over Hispaniola and agreed there is no love-lier spot in the world—although I would like for my Captain to see the Georgia marshes. They, too, are lovely. But I yearn for us to be together. He reminds me that we must do what we do—

She dropped the letter as if it were putrid. "Of *course.* Holding up ships is far more important than taking care of a small boy who has already lost his sister. And it must have made Marie real happy to hear about the beauties of home when she could not be there."

Katharine was getting sick of Mallery, too. "I wonder why he didn't just take another ship and come fetch them?" She picked up the last letter with a sense of weariness and in-completion. "I guess we'll never know. This last one is so folded and stained, here's the best I can do. It's written to Marie."

I entrust this . . . [something or other] . . . promises to see it delivered. How could Claude deny me the money? It is my own! I know you did your best.

"The next bit is either 'My God, . . . he'll,' or 'May God' something-or-other 'hell.' Wait! It's 'May God burn him in hell.' Whew! The next paragraph is really blurred, but here's what I think it says." She read slowly, stumbling over some of the words:

My heart aches that we never came as planned. The Captain . . . dedicated to his work. . . . I dreamed of a place . . . peace with the children . . . not criticize him now, especially to you. . . . heart breaks, as will yours. . . . He is gone. They shot him at dawn. . . . sick in heart and body . . . malaria has returned . . . with-out help from Claude, I shall not survive.

Katharine felt tears sting her eyes. She had never held the last letter of a dying man in her hands before. No matter what a rogue he had been, his despair touched her. "This is the last paragraph. Several words are blurred, either by water or by tears. It's written to little Claude."

My dearest Son, I fear I will never . . . again, but never doubt my love for you. You may never . . . choices I made, but no one can choose for another. Make your . . . in the world. And if I have hurt you, I . . . and God to forgive me. Obey Marie. God bless you both. M——

The last word wavered and straggled down the page, like the pen had fallen or been snatched from his hand while he was writing.

Katharine traced it with one finger, then slowly refolded the letter as someone had refolded it often before. As she handed it over to Dr. Flo, she mused, "He must have been brought home to be buried. I wonder who carved that pirate symbol on the stone."

"Probably little Claude—or Hamilton. It seems like a childish thing to do, doesn't it?" Dr. Flo didn't sound at all sentimental. In fact, she sounded downright angry.

"Or it could have been Claude Bayard. He sounds pretty childish, too. Mallery must have asked for funds to save the captain and himself, and Claude refused. I'd guess it was Claude Bayard who decided to bury Mallery outside the family plot, wouldn't you?"

Dr. Flo tapped the letter on one corner of the table, her mouth set in a disapproving line. "If it had been me, I'd have taken him out to sea and pushed him off a boat. Dropping off his poor children like that and never coming back. How could he do such a thing? And something else. Why does he keep harping on that captain? That's downright odd."

"I guess that's another riddle we won't solve." Katharine

rose and refilled their glasses to give Dr. Flo time to collect herself. She spoke from the refrigerator door. "But the captain could have simply been a good friend, somebody Mallery admired. The last letter sounds like the captain was very special to Marie. Perhaps he was her lover and the children had another mother, who died. Mallery does tell little Claude to 'obey Marie,' not 'obey your mother.' Marie may have longed to see the captain more than she longed to see Mallery."

"Yet both men stayed away for those children's entire lives."

Dr. Flo would obviously reject any attempt to excuse her ancestor's behavior, if that's who or what he had been. Katharine gave up and concentrated on slicing another lemon.

Dr. Flo pushed back her chair. "Speaking of the children, though, I meant to call Hayden Curtis when he got back this afternoon to see when Burch plans to move the graves. Do you mind if I make the call from here? I'll pay for it."

"Use my cell phone. I never use up all my minutes and long distance is free." Katharine retrieved it from her purse and handed it over.

She wasn't paying much attention to the conversation until Dr. Flo's voice rose.

"I can't make arrangements that soon for reburial. . . . That is unnecessary. I have already spoken with someone who represents a cemetery in Darien, but that's too soon. . . . No, that will not be acceptable. I insist—" He must have interrupted, for her face grew stormier by the second.

Katharine scrawled a note and held it in front of her: *Whenever we need to go down there, we will!"*

Dr. Flo read it, scowled at something Hayden Curtis was saying, then nodded at Katharine. "Okay. Hold on a minute."

"Can you go tomorrow?" she asked Katharine. "Burch is planning to disinter them tomorrow afternoon."

Katharine nodded without taking time to think.

Dr. Flo returned to her prior conversation. "We'll be there tomorrow. But you tell Burch that I insist on stipulating where the re-burials will be and he will need to pay for storage until I can make the arrangements. Otherwise—"

Hayden Curtis must have interrupted again. She listened, then said, "I don't care, you tell him that is my final word on the subject. Furthermore, I have the deed to Agnes Morrison's property. She mailed it to me before she died. It is very possible that her eight acres now belong to me. We can discuss that when I see you."

She paused.

"Wait until you have seen the deed before you make any rash statements, sir. I will see you at two-thirty tomorrow afternoon. Don't you disinter my relatives unless I am there."

She hung up and sank into the nearest chair, her eyes snapping with indignation. "They had arranged to move the caskets tomorrow and to re-bury mine in the slave cemetery behind the Church of God Reappearing." She pressed one hand to her heart. "Dear God, to think of relatives of mine being buried behind a church with that name! We've always been Episcopalians!" She took a minute to regain her equilibrium. "Mr. Curtis says if we can't be there at two-thirty, we will miss the whole shebang."

Chapter 26

"You look mad enough to chew nails. Chew a few cookies instead."

"After I wash my hands." Dr. Flo marched to the sink with such determination that Katharine sang the opening bars of "When the Saints Go Marching In."

Dr. Flo did not reply.

Katharine spoke to her back. "We can easily get there by two if we leave here by eight, and if you go get your things and spend the night here, we can get an earlier start. My niece finished one of my guest rooms last night. Why don't you call the Darien cemetery again and see if they can take the caskets tomorrow afternoon? If not, whoever Burch has digging them up will surely arrange storage until the cemetery can take them. At Burch's expense."

"They'd jolly well better." At the sink, Dr. Flo scrubbed her hands like she was scrubbing away not only silverfish but Hayden Curtis and Burch Bayard. As she reached for the towel, the doorbell rang.

"That must be Lamar Franklin. I forgot he was coming." Katharine headed toward the door. "He's interested in genealogy, and he's bringing me a book on Confederate privateers. Shall I invite him in for a glass of tea?"

Dr. Flo didn't answer. She was already looking up a number in her notebook.

Lamar stood with his back to the door, admiring the Murrays' front yard. "Nothing like the smell of new-mown grass and the look of freshly trimmed bushes," he said as Katharine opened the door. "I reckon you have a yardman, with your husband gone so much?"

His silver ponytail gleamed like he had washed it especially for the occasion, and he was dressed up in clean jeans, polished black Western boots, a wide belt with a silver buckle engraved with his initials, and another black T-shirt. When he turned, she read MY LIFE MAY BE WEIRD, BUT AT LEAST IT'S NOT BORING.

She wanted to say, "My life isn't boring, either, because I do all the mowing, weeding, and edging myself," but since Anthony was still working in the backyard and could appear at any moment to make a liar out of her, she admitted, "Yes, we have an excellent one."

Lamar gave a satisfied nod. "Woman needs a man around to take care of things." He held up a thick paperback. "I brought you that book you were wanting."

"I appreciate it. Won't you come in? Dr. Florence Gadney is in the kitchen. She's the one whose history we are investigating, and we've been looking at old letters she got today. We think they may have been written by one of her ancestors who was a pirate."

By the time she finished, he was halfway across the foyer. "Nice place you got here. Are you moving?" He peered into each room in turn, not the least bit shy.

She spoke to his back. "No, the place was trashed last month, and I'm still working on repairs. Dr. Flo and I are here, in the kitchen." She led the way.

Dr. Flo was finishing a conversation on the phone.

Katharine offered Lamar sweet tea or beer, and he chose tea. "I can buy a beer, but, since my wife passed, I've never gotten the knack of making good sweet tea."

After Katharine introduced them, Dr. Flo said, "Please excuse me for a minute, Mr. Franklin, but I need to give Katharine a report on a couple of phone calls."

He waved her apology away. "You go right ahead. I'll enjoy the view."

He wandered to the bay window and stared out. "Great crepe myrtles you got. I always liked dark pinks myself, but the light pinks are nice with the white."

Dr. Flo said softly, "The Darien cemetery can't bury the caskets until Monday afternoon, so I told Mr. Curtis to make arrangements for them until then."

"Which thrilled him, right?"

"Not exactly, but he said he'd see what he could do. Oh, and I called Rodney to fill him in, in case he thought he ought to be there. He was with a client, and asked me to call him back sometime tomorrow morning." She glanced over at Lamar, who was inspecting the window rather than the yard.

"Would you like some cookies?" Katharine asked him.

"Oh, that would be real nice, ma'am." He jerked his head toward the window. "I don't know who put this in for you, but they need to come back and re-seal it before you spend a fortune cooling the whole outdoors." He ducked his head in apology. "Forgive me for mentioning it, but you see, I'm in the building trade. Hate to see shoddy work." He ran his hand down one side of the window and Katharine saw that indeed, there were places where sunlight shone through.

When she wiped the table with disinfectant and set out the plate of cookies with napkins and tea, he took a seat and gave a satisfied smile. "That's what I call real nice. Don't get homemade cookies and good tea much since my wife died."

As he took one from the plate, Katharine thought, *Tom doesn't get them much anymore, either. This is the second batch he hasn't gotten to eat.*

Serves him right. Was that Aunt Sara Claire, acid even after death? Or her own voice in her head? *Dear God don't let me grow up to be like her.*

Lamar laid his book before Dr. Flo. "This oughta tell you all you want to know about Confederate privateers, but you may be disappointed. They didn't do much after 1861, and most only stayed out for a few weeks." His Adam's apple jiggled as he took a swig of tea.

Katharine couldn't remember why they had wanted a book on Confederate privateers. Who had brought up that subject? Dr. Flo seemed to share her confusion. She politely reached for the book and turned to the table of contents, but admitted, "Our pirate may have been a Yankee. Were any of the privateers from the North?"

Lamar dabbed his mouth with his napkin with excessive gentility. "Some. There's a chapter on them toward the end of the book, but they weren't official privateers—by which I mean they didn't hold letters of marque from the Union. Still, a number of private seamen armed their merchant ships and captured prizes. You think one of your ancestors sailed one of those?"

"We have no idea. We're just beginning this investigation."

"Well, I re-read the book last night, so long as I had it off the shelf, so let me summarize a tad. Then you can see if they's anything there you might be able to use." He shoved his chair back from the table, propped one calf on the other knee, swiped his ponytail off his shoulder, and spoke like a man accustomed to lecturing. Katharine was fascinated by the discrepancy between his appearance and how much he seemed to know.

"The very first letter of marque Jefferson Davis granted was for the *Triton*, which was owned by three men from Brunswick. It would have sailed out of Savannah, except'n a couple of Yankee ships got wind of its intent and blocked the mouth of the Savannah River. Charleston had a number of privateers. Two of them, the *Dixie* and the *Sallie*, were right successful, but neither of them stayed out long. The *Dixie* gave it up after four weeks, and even though the *Sallie* had a real lucky three-week run, her owners decided to auction their prizes and cargo and sell the ship. Both ships later became blockade runners."

Dr. Flo was making notes. "Are there lists of who sailed on them?"

He frowned in thought. "I suspect there would be, somewhere, but I'm not sure where. The only names mentioned in the book are captains, prize captains, and such, and men who were captured and tried." His face lit up. "The *Savannah,* now—that ship caused quite a scandal. Its officers and some of the crew were captured and taken to Philadelphia, where they were paraded through the streets and accused of piracy—which, traditionally, privateers were not. They were generally regarded and treated as prisoners of war. After the crew had been shamed by being put on parade, they were incarcerated as common criminals and kept in such deplorable conditions that Jefferson Davis protested personally to Lincoln. He claimed the Union was violating accepted conventions for the treatment of prisoners of war—not unlike our own day, in some respects, if you'll pardon my bias."

He reached for a cookie and took another swallow of tea, but it was obvious this was merely a pause for refreshment before he continued. Katharine and Dr. Flo waited.

"Davis never got a reply from Lincoln, so he sent word that he would take a similar number of Yankee officers who were currently being courteously treated as prisoners of war and treat *them* like common criminals, and if the prisoners up North were executed, he would execute one Yankee officer for each Confederate privateer. When he made good his threat by jailing thirteen colonels and captains, Lincoln decided maybe Southern privateers were prisoners of war after all, and ordered that they be treated as such. If I'm correct, those were the last trials on charges of piracy during the war."

Dr. Flo steered him toward the channel of their own interests. "Do you know anything about pirates down in the Caribbean *after* the War? The one we are interested in seems to have been in business well up into the 1870s."

"I don't know a thing about pirates, ma'am, just privateers, and I know damn little about them, if you'll pardon my French. My speciality is the War of Secession itself, not the merchant aspect of things." He flexed his biceps, to show off his anchor tattoo. "As an old Navy man, I am interested in naval battles as well as land ones, but privateers weren't engaged in what you might call real battles. Their captures seldom involved bloodshed, and they usually sent captured crews back up North with a passing ship. Besides, most privateers had converted to blockade runners by the end of 1861. Only one I read about that was still operating by 1863 was the *Retribution*. Most of the owners figured they could make a lot more money running supplies through the blockades. It was more certain, see?"

When he got blank stares, he explained. "A privateer might spend a couple of days chasing after a ship, then find she was loaded with something that wasn't worth the risk of getting it back to port. A blockade runner, on the other hand, could pick and choose what he carried and be sure of selling what he brought in."

He got a thoughtful look on his face. "That might be your Caribbean connection, now that I think about it. Blockade runners often sailed down there to cargo up with stuff from Europe. The Gulf Stream flows from Europe to the Caribbean," he made a big mark in the air which Katharine took for the Gulf Stream, "so European ships could easily bring stuff into a neutral port on one of the islands. St. Thomas, for instance, which was Danish at the time, I believe." He stopped and again searched his memory. "The *Sallie*—one of the Charleston privateers I mentioned that turned into a blockade runner? She was down around Nassau at one point, but I don't remember her having any connection with pirates."

"I read this morning that the Bahamas were the center of pirate society at one point," Katharine contributed. "I don't know if that was true as late as the end of the Civil War."

"I prefer the term War of Secession myself, ma'am," he corrected her gently. "The Bahamas reminds me of something. What was it?" He scratched his head, then slapped his thigh. "Got it! The *Retribution*. She was the last Confederate privateer, remember? She eventually sailed down to the Bahamas and was sold there. Do you reckon any of this he'ps you any?"

Dr. Flo shook her head. "Not yet, sir, but we appreciate your going to so much trouble."

"No trouble a-tall." He gestured to the golden envelope. "Is that the letters you said might be from a pirate or privateer?" He quivered with curiosity like a bird dog sighting quarry.

Dr. Flo filled him in briefly on what they had learned and deduced so far.

He stretched out one hand. "May I?"

"Help yourself."

He read slowly, rubbing his fingers on the edges of the pages as if he could absorb as much information from the paper and ink as from the words. "Mighty softhearted to be a pirate," he concluded when he'd finished. "All those tears over the dead baby, and looking at sunrises and such. Reminds you that even a pirate is still human, don't it? But that stuff about his wonderful captain—you don't reckon he was, you know, gay, do you?"

Lamar apparently had qualms about discussing that subject with women.

Dr. Flo gathered up the letters and replaced them in the

old envelope with the deed, the locket, and the baby shoe. "We thought about that, but from what he said to Marie about the captain's death, we concluded maybe they were dear friends and Marie was in love with the captain." Katharine was amused to hear the professor taking the opposite of the argument than she'd proposed before.

Lamar nodded judiciously. "Could be, I guess."

"But if that was the case, we can't figure out why the children had Marie's last name, Guilbert, instead of Mallery."

"Probably for their protection," he suggested, "once folks knew their father wasn't coming back."

"The Mallery family's protection, more likely, since the Mallerys were white," Dr. Flo said bluntly. "After all, Françoise died a year before that last letter, and her tombstone reads *Guilbert,* too."

"Well, if you've done a bit of genealogical research, ma'am, you know how it goes. Knowledge comes in small doses well seasoned with lots of guesses. I always get a real jolt when I have a piece of astounding luck, like those letters are for you. I wish you success in learning more about the feller who wrote them." His hand hovered over another cookie, then drew back.

"Have more," Katharine urged. "I've got a cookie jar full."

He obliged with a smile. "My wife has passed, like I said, and my girls never were much in the way of cooking."

"Then let me send some home with you, as a thank-you for bringing us the book."

Katharine found a plastic container and emptied the cookie jar into it. *Aunt Sara Claire would never have sent cookies home with him,* she commended herself. *She'd have figured it was only her due for Lamar to bring the book down from North Georgia.*

Lamar tucked the cookies under one arm and pushed back from the table. "I guess I better get on the road if I hope to beat the traffic up the mountain. I hope you'll find the book useful. And I sure do thank you for the cookies."

As Katharine watched his truck roar down the drive, she marveled. Now that she had entertained him in her home, Lamar no longer seemed odd. He was impressive, even rather endearing. And he certainly knew his Civil War—or, rather, War of Secession—history.

Chapter 27

While Dr. Flo went back home to pack and close up her condo, Katharine called Posey.

"Can you go to Jekyll tomorrow? I know it's short notice, but we got word that they are digging up Dr. Flo's relatives in the afternoon and she thinks she ought to be there."

"Is Tom going, too?"

"No, Tom didn't come home." Katharine explained his reasons, including the fact that he'd be accompanying the luscious Angela to the Saturday evening party.

"If you kill my little brother one day, I'll go on the stand and testify you had more than sufficient provocation," Posey vowed. "And I would be delighted to go to the beach with you tomorrow, except I promised Hollis we'd go to a spa. Wrens is in California."

What made Katharine suspect the spa had not been Hollis's idea? "Invite Hollis to come with us. She'd add a bit of life to the party."

"I doubt she'll want to go with three women, but I'll ask. Hold on." Katharine heard voices in the background, then Posey was back on the line, baffled. "She says she'd love to come. How long will we be gone?"

"We ought to stay at least until Tuesday, since the coffins can't be re-buried until Monday afternoon."

"What are we going to do with them until then?" She sounded alarmed.

Katharine wondered if Posey feared she was being asked to provide houseroom for three coffins as well as two guests. "That's not our problem. The attorney and the funeral home will take care of that." *We hope*, she added mentally. "But speaking of problems, Hollis and I will need to talk business part of the time. I've agreed to host a big party for somebody here in six weeks. Do you think she'll have any trouble with that?"

Posey's voice dropped, presumably so Hollis wouldn't hear. "Honey, you know as well as I do: Hollis *is* trouble. I swear, if I hadn't been awake and in a birthing center when she was born—"

"—you would think they had switched babies on you. I know. You've said it before. Is there anything bothering her right now I need to know about?"

"Nothing aside from the state of the world, the government, and the church, and the fact that her parents are stodgy old oppressors of the poor who vote wrong and don't have a speck of taste. She's after me to redecorate the living room in brighter colors 'Like Aunt Kat's' when she knows good and well I love it the way it is. Why we ever let her go to that artsy school—"

"It's a great school," Katharine said firmly, "and she has fantastic ideas. I thoroughly enjoy her company."

Posey sighed. "You aren't her mother. You don't have to worry that she will either marry a nut or be on your hands for the rest of your life."

"She'll take care of you in your old age."

"She'll dress me in purple and orange, tie balloons to my wheelchair, and dye my hair green."

"Think what fun you'll have."

"Speaking of fun," Posey grew serious and her voice resumed its normal pitch, "we aren't going to have to look at those bodies, are we? I mean, Dr. Flo will take it for granted that the people in the coffins are who they are supposed to be, right? She won't insist on opening them, or anything."

Katharine hadn't considered that, but now the picture was fixed in her head. "I sure hope not. I mean, of course not. We won't have to look at any bodies. But you will need to be ready to leave by seven in the morning, all right?"

"Isn't that awfully early?"

It was half an hour earlier than Katharine planned to arrive at Posey's back door, but given her sister-in-law's concept of punctuality, it was the latest possible time for Posey to aim for. "We need to get there early to be sure we don't miss the big event."

"I'll be ready. Do you think this is an occasion that calls for champagne? I'd love to bring some, if Dr. Flo won't be grieving or anything. Do you think she might want to celebrate having successfully moved them?"

Katharine was chagrined that she hadn't thought about honoring the occasion. "Champagne would be a lovely touch."

"And I'll run out and get some pâté with wonderful crackers and Havarti . . ."

Once Posey started thinking of delicacies, she was capable of prattling on all afternoon. "Bring whatever you like, but try to keep it to one or two suitcases. Dr. Flo tends to bring a lot of luggage, too. I'll get stuff for sandwiches and breakfasts."

"Before you go, I have one more question." Posey veered abruptly from cheeses and wines. "These are wooden coffins, right?"

"Probably."

"So are they going to fall apart when they are dug up? I mean, what's going to prevent us from having bones all over the place?"

"Oh, Mother!" Hollis moaned behind her.

Katharine shuddered. "You have a macabre mind, do you know that? You're going to make me nervous if you don't stop."

"Well, think about it. I've never been to a disinterment before, and I've been thinking about it for two whole days. This isn't like digging up the vaults we buried Mama and Daddy in, you know. Those were steel or something and came with lifetime guarantees, although I kept asking, 'Whose lifetime?' and nobody could answer. But if we dug them up, they'd still be sealed metal boxes. These things have had over a hundred years to rot, right?"

"Don't think about it. I'll pick you up at seven."

"I bought something to wear, by the way. I got a black chino pantsuit with a little white trim on the jacket. Do you think that will be all right?"

"You'll be utterly chic," Hollis said sarcastically in the background.

"Go pack," Katharine commanded.

"Okay. And let's stay until Thursday, to give us time to relax afterwards, okay?"

"Sounds great to me. See you all tomorrow."

As she was about to hang up, the big cat decided he'd had enough of the utility room. He peered out the door, and when he saw Katharine standing in the kitchen, dashed past her like an orange and black streak toward the front of the house.

To her mental grocery list for Jekyll, she added automatic cat food and water dispensers, then remembered they'd be gone nearly a week. She couldn't leave those cats alone for a week. They'd already been traumatized enough.

And what about the upholsterer, painter, and glazier she'd bludgeoned into coming next week? Why had she thought she could just waltz out of town?

She called Hollis back. "Do you have a friend who might

be willing to stay at our place this week, oversee some work-men, and be extra nice to two cats?"

"How about Misty?" Hollis replied at once. "Remember her? She helped you clean up after your break-in."

Short, petite, spiky hair, and a lisp from her tongue stud. Her only detriment was that she had referred to Katharine's old prom gowns up in the attic as "vintage clothing."

"I remember. She was a good worker. Is she available?"

"Yeah. She broke up with her boyfriend yesterday and slept over at my place last night. Staying at your place would give her some space to figure out what to do next. And she loves animals and her major was interior design. She's fabulous at getting folks to work."

"Bring her over, then, and let me show her the drill."

That night Katharine did not dream of vandals in her house. She dreamed she was standing in a field of bones, peering into a crumbling wooden coffin at a mummified pirate with a long black beard. Behind her, Misty was saying, "Ith that a thcool bell, Mith Murray?"

Now that she mentioned it, Katharine did hear a bell in the distance.

She came awake groggily. The bell was still ringing, and somebody was holding her foot.

She was terrified to open her eyes until she felt the weight on her foot give a stretch and utter a small *meow?* That's when she realized it wasn't a school bell she was hearing, it was the phone.

She rolled over, trying not to move her foot, and reached for the receiver, hoping whoever it was hadn't wakened Dr. Flo. If it was Hasty, she'd kill him. If it was Miranda, she didn't know what she'd do, but it would be terrible.

But what if something had happened to Tom? Or one of the children? She could scarcely get her tongue around the word *hello.*

"Stay away from Bayard Island. What happened to Agnes can happen to you."

"Miranda? This isn't funny." She yawned. Before she had finished, she heard a click.

Caught between annoyance and relief at being wakened from her bad dream, she snuggled back into her covers. The small cat shifted and began to purr.

Katharine was sliding back into sleep when something occurred to her. That voice had been too deep to be Miranda's.

Chapter 28

She decided not to tell Dr. Flo about the call. No point in ruining her day.

They ate a quick breakfast of cereal and fruit and were ready to go not long after seven.

"Did you sleep well?" Katharine thought to ask as they pulled down her drive. "Those mattresses are new and I haven't tested them."

"Tested them?"

"I always like to sleep on guest mattresses to make sure they are comfortable, but we just got that room pulled together night before last."

"The bed is wonderful. Your whole house is wonderful. Inviting and welcoming. You know, you were talking about how you hate fixing up the place for one. Why don't you consider that you are creating a sanctuary for people who need one from time to time? You are good at providing that."

"Me? I'm not a sanctuary person, whatever that is. The word conjures up images of unheated churches with stone walls and flickering candles."

Dr. Flo laughed. "To me it means a good bed and a place to unburden the heart. If I were to make a home again, that's the kind I'd like it to be. Maurice and I built a showplace. The only homey room in it was the den upstairs where we never invited guests. I wish now I'd taken them all up there and rented out the rest."

It was Katharine's turn to laugh. "Anytime you need a bed, come on over. I've certainly got plenty to spare."

"Think about it." Dr. Flo settled deeper into her seat and spoke seriously. "That's all I ask. Think about it. You're starting a whole new season. Make it your best one yet."

Posey surprised Katharine by being ready before they got there and by only bringing one large suitcase, one food hamper, and a thermos of coffee—along with three mugs, sugar, and real cream. Hollis threw in a duffle bag and her laptop and was ready to go.

During the journey, Katharine and Dr. Flo filled the other two in on the graves, the letters, and the reason for the trip.

Posey was fascinated. "I wouldn't have missed this for anything."

"I never heard of ancestry.com," Hollis said thoughtfully. "I'll bet I could find all sorts of skeletons in our closets, Mama."

"But no pirates," Posey said with regret.

Midmorning, Katharine's cell phone rang. "I've had an idea," Hasty said without preamble. "How about if I come take you to lunch, then come back to your place for a swim?"

"No can do. I'm on my way to Jekyll Island with Dr. Flo and my sister-in-law, with a detour past Bayard Island. We heard yesterday afternoon that they're doing the disinterments today."

"You be careful. Those people are mighty careless with guns."

"We'll be careful. Thanks for calling." She needed to get him off the phone. She felt vibrations from three sets of listening ears.

"Where will you be on Jekyll?"

"Her beach cottage. I need to go. I don't like to talk while

driving. Bye." She hung up. Too late she remembered she
hadn't planned to let Hasty know where she went at the
beach.

"Was that Uncle Tom?" Hollis called from the back seat
in a voice dripping suspicion.

"Probably regretting he didn't let you come up." Posey
contributed.

When Katharine didn't answer at once, Hollis muttered,
"It was her history professor."

"He's not my history professor, he's a friend."

"Yeah, right."

Posey was too busy fumbling in her purse to reply.

A few minutes later, Katharine's cell phone rang again.

"What's the emergency?" Tom demanded.

"Emergency?"

"I got a message—this number plus 911."

Katharine glanced in the rearview mirror. Posey was looking out the window.

"That was your sister being cute. Dr. Flo and I are on our
way down to Jekyll again with Posey and Hollis. They are
disinterring those graves this afternoon, so we're going to
attend."

"What graves?"

"I told you, the ones on the island. Some of them belong
to Dr. Flo and one belongs to a pirate." Actually, she wasn't
sure she *had* told him.

"Oh, yeah. Those." He wasn't sure, either. She could tell.
"Why are you going?"

"Dr. Flo wants to be present to be sure they re-bury them
where she wants them."

"And you are involved in this why?"

"I'll tell you all about it later. Are you ready for the party
tonight?"

"Almost, but I left my best studs at home. I had to buy
new ones."

"It never hurts to have two sets."

Why are we reduced to talking about tuxedo studs?

"So you all are going down to the cottage after the burials?"

"Yeah. We'll be there most of next week."

He sighed. "Lucky you."

She lowered her voice. "Wish you could come. Why don't you?"

"I might, if I get a chance. Wish you could come to tonight's party, too."

She wished he had made that possible.

She controlled her face for the sake of the others. "I hope you have fun." She managed not to add, *Watch out for barracudas.*

"My charming brother?" Posey inquired as Katharine closed her phone. "Finally regretting he didn't let you come up?"

"You know good and well why he called. But he might come down sometime this week."

"Good. Then I can beat him up in person. Listen, I've had an idea. We aren't due down at the cemetery until two-thirty—right, Dr. Flo? We've made such good time, why don't we drive into Savannah and eat lunch at The Lady and Sons? We're early enough that it ought not to be crowded yet." She added the last for Katharine's benefit. The last time they had eaten at The Lady and Sons, they had stood on the sidewalk for an hour waiting to get in. The food and ambiance were worth it, but not if you were on a tight schedule. To clinch the deal, Posey added, "My treat, to thank you for including me in the day's festivities."

Dr. Flo looked at Katharine and raised her eyebrows with a pained expression, silently asking whether she had told Posey about the Gadney financial woes.

Katharine shook her head. "Posey loves treating people to meals."

Hollis piped up from the back. "Daddy claims he works until June to pay Uncle Sam and until August to buy Mama's friends lunch and dinner. But let's take her up on it."

"Okay," Katharine called over her shoulder, "but you all needn't consider this trip a gourmet pilgrimage. Dr. Flo and I eat real light at the beach."

"I will after this," Posey agreed amiably, "but I can't pass Savannah without one meal at The Lady and Sons. I watch Paula Deen's TV show religiously, and have used lots of her recipes."

"What she means," Hollis translated, "is that she gives them to Julia to make."

"Besides," Posey added, ignoring her, "not only is the food delicious, but her sons may be there. They are hunks."

"Mama!" Hollis protested. "At least one of them is married. Besides, I lived in Savannah four years. If I'd been interested in one of them back then—"

"I'm not thinking of you, honey, I look for my own enjoyment. You wouldn't know what to do with a hunk if you got one. Everybody okay to go?"

"I could call Rodney while we're there," Dr. Flo put in her vote. "We need to set up a time to get together and discuss the legal aspects of this situation."

"Why don't you invite him to join us?" Posey offered. "If you all want to sit at a separate table and talk business, you can, but it's still my treat."

Dr. Flo borrowed Katharine's cell phone and Katharine headed to Savannah.

"I hope Rodney's on time," Dr. Flo said as they were walking to the restaurant.

"You sound a lot happier to be seeing Rodney than most folks meeting their husband's nephew," Hollis teased. "Is he a hunk, like Mama's hankering after?"

Dr. Flo laughed. "He's more than presentable, but actually I'm his godmother. When that child was twenty minutes old his mama put him into my arms and said, 'Flo, you gotta help me with this. I don't know a thing about babies.' I didn't either, but Mary and Horace lived not far from us, and Maurice and I were over there all the time. We stood up as godparents at his christening and saw him every week until he was six, when their family moved to Birmingham. That nearly killed us, but Rodney came and spent time with us every summer. We also took him to Disney World, Europe, and Japan, and we always got together for Christmas. Since he's moved to Savannah, I don't see as much of him as I'd like, so yes, you could say I'll be happy to see him. Besides, he's just gotten himself engaged to a beautiful girl his mama adores, so I need to give him a hug. There he is now!"

Rodney was waiting outside the restaurant door, a slender, well-built man about thirty with hair cut short to show a well-shaped head and the profile of a Roman emperor. Not drop-dead gorgeous, but certainly more than presentable.

"He gets his nose from his father's family," Dr. Flo confided. "It's his mother who was Maurice's cousin. More like a sister, really." The next minute, she was engulfed in a hug.

Hollis told Rodney, "You are mighty nice to spend your Saturday afternoon having lunch with four women."

His laugh was deep and rich. "What Auntie Flo wants, Auntie Flo generally gets."

Dr. Flo gave a happy little chuckle. "Right now, I want the best attorney in this area. But when you see the sleaze-ball you're going to have to work with, you may not thank me. He could give us a lot of trouble."

"When you swim with the sharks, you expect to run into scum. He doesn't scare me."

Over lunch, Dr. Flo and Katharine described what had happened in the previous week and what they had found in the letters. "I don't know if that's enough to win a case or not," he admitted. "But I'll be happy to check for you."

He waved them on their way, promising to bring his fiancée to Atlanta soon.

When they reached Bayard Island, Katharine noted as they crossed the little bridge, "We're still a bit early. Didn't Mr. Curtis say two-thirty? It's barely two."

"We might as well go on down there," Dr. Flo decided. "I'd like a chance to take pictures before they start digging."

Katharine turned in past the twenty-miles-an-hour sign.

"Are you all sure this is the right road?" Posey asked a few minutes later. "We've been driving through these woods for a very long time."

"We're sure. We're nearly there." Katharine glanced in the rearview mirror and saw Dr. Flo perched on the edge of her seat, as excited as a child going to Grandmother's. Katharine smiled. The professor seemed to have embraced her connection to this island and the cemetery, if not to Mallery or the Bayards.

The clearing was empty. No digging machines or men with shovels. No Bayards. No Mr. Curtis. "Shall we wait in the car?" Katharine pulled as close as she could get to the cemetery, in the shade of one of the big live oaks. It was a blistering day, with predictions that the temperature would reach a hundred.

Dr. Flo already had her door open. "I'm going to take my pictures. You all can do as you please."

Katharine handed her a spray can of insect repellant. "I want everybody to spray real good this trip."

Dr. Flo obeyed, then handed the can to Posey, who said, "As long as we're here early, I might as well look, too, if you don't mind my company."

"The more the merrier," Dr. Flo assured her.

"I've been sitting too long," Hollis announced, "but I'm not crazy about sightseeing in a cemetery. I'll walk around a little and come back in half an hour or so." She climbed out and headed for a path that led toward the marshes. Katharine hadn't noticed it before.

"Watch out for snakes!" Dr. Flo called after her, then crossed the clearing at a brisk trot.

"I'll be there in a minute," Posey said. "I just need to call Wrens and check in."

That was the second time she'd spoken with Wrens that day. Katharine never could figure out why they needed to be in such frequent touch, but Posey couldn't understand why she and Tom didn't. *Different strokes for different folks*, she thought as she covered herself with repellant.

Posey shaded her eyes with one hand. "Looks like they've put up a tent over some of the graves. Maybe that's where they plan to start?"

Katharine hadn't noticed the green canopy until then. "If they do, we may be here all afternoon. That's diagonally across the cemetery from Dr. Flo's graves. Have you sprayed yet?"

"Does repellant help with chiggers?" Posey stood on one leg to spray her other foot.

"I have no idea, but let's hope so." Katharine wished she had mentioned footwear when she and Posey were discussing clothes. Posey wore black sandal heels without stockings, which she was going to regret after walking through sandspurs and saw grass. Dr. Flo had changed into her laced walking shoes again while Katharine had worn black flats in soft glove leather, knowing they'd have to stand a while.

"We can leave our pocketbooks in the car," she said as Posey picked up her clutch.

"Do I look all right?" Posey peered down at her new black pantsuit. "I'm not overdressed, am I?"

"You look marvelous."

Perhaps a bit overdressed for an afternoon by the marshes on an all-but-deserted island in July, but they had all dressed for the occasion. Dr. Flo wore another of her broomstick skirts, this one patterned in dark brown and gold, and she had partnered it with a silky beige top and a gold linen jacket. If Katharine had followed her druthers, she'd have dressed like Hollis, in jeans, a long-sleeved T-shirt, and running shoes with socks. For once, Hollis's black jeans and black shirt looked exactly right. Instead, Katharine had put on white cotton slacks, a sleeveless black cotton shell, and a black-and-white-striped jacket with square black buttons. Dangling black earrings and a chunky black-and-white necklace completed her ensemble.

"More funky than funereal," Posey commented as Katharine settled a wide-brimmed black straw hat on her head, "but you look stunning, as always."

The heat and bugs were as bad as Katharine had feared. The cicadas made their particular brand of white noise in the background, and in spite of the repellant, mosquitoes dive-bombed them as they crossed the clearing. Before they were halfway across, Katharine felt drops of sweat rolling down her back and between her breasts.

In a few hours you'll be swimming, she reminded herself. *Focus on that.*

She paused to point out the remaining foundations of the old Episcopal church and to explain to Posey what had happened to it. Posey's eyes widened in indignation. "You mean the Bayards used wood from a church to fix up their barn? That is so tacky!"

"The Bayards do tacky real well."

"But Mona is supposed to have perfectly *gaw-geous* antebellum furniture."

"If she shows up, you can ask her if she wants to sell any of it. Watch out for those sandspurs."

The warning came too late. With a yelp of pain, Posey clutched Katharine for support while she lifted one foot and then the other to pull prickly little balls from her ankle. "You should have told me to wear hip boots," she grumbled. After that she minced her way warily toward the cemetery.

As they approached the green tent, Katharine was astonished to see three large floral arrangements that were only beginning to wilt in the heat. They sat near a mound of bare sand at one end of the four Morrison graves.

Dr. Flo had stopped nearby. "I think Agnes was buried here. These flowers had to have been placed this morning. In this heat, they'd be dead if they were older than that." As Katharine and Posey came up beside her, she added, "In case this is her, I think we should have a little prayer, don't you?" She bowed her head and offered thanksgiving for Agnes's life and kindness to strangers.

While Dr. Flo prayed, Katharine couldn't help thinking that somebody could have been praying that afternoon over two women shot by Agnes's shotgun in that very cemetery. Maybe Agnes was chuckling up in heaven at the identical thought?

When Dr. Flo finished, she headed for the Guilbert plot. As she stepped over the low tabby wall, she called back to Posey with a shade of pride, "That's my granddaddy."

She bent to touch the stone. At the same moment, a bullet whizzed over her head and took a chunk out of Mallery's obelisk. Katharine was never sure whether she even heard the shot.

Chapter 29

"Down!" Posey shouted.

Katharine hit the ground facefirst and got a mouthful of sand. She turned her head and laid her cheek on a sandspur, but stifled a yelp of pain. As scared as she was, she had a sense of déjà vu. Any minute they ought to hear Agnes's gruff laugh overhead.

Except Agnes lay under the green tent that now sheltered Katharine and Posey, as well.

Either their party had gotten in the way of a careless hunter, or—

The alternative didn't bear thinking about.

Where was Hollis? "Don't let her come back into this," she whispered a prayer.

Across the cemetery she heard the sound of Dr. Flo repeating softly, "Dear God, preserve us. Preserve us."

Another bullet hit a rail of the iron fence, eliminating any fantasy about a careless hunter. Somebody was hunting, all right. They were the prey.

After that, the only sounds in the clearing were the rise and fall of the cicadas' whine and the scream of gulls.

Katharine felt malignant intent all around them. Was someone creeping closer to the cemetery to finish them off, like victims in a horrid film? She was frantic to know whether the second shot had hit Dr. Flo, but when she lifted her head, Posey whispered, "Keep down and keep quiet!"

Katharine lowered her head. Sand caked her lips and got into the trough between her lower lip and her teeth. She slowly brought her hand to her mouth and scrubbed it with her fingers, but they were sandy, too. She dared not lift her head to spit. One part of her mind ridiculed her for worrying about sand in her mouth when she lay in peril, but small ir- ritants grow with time. Eventually she inched one side of her jacket up to her face and wiped out her mouth with that.

Emboldened by the continued silence and by no response to her little bit of motion, she considered her position. A large oleander bush grew inside the cemetery fence and pro- vided a flimsy shield between her and the sniper, its leaves long and narrow like fingerling fish. Moving slower than a snail, Katharine scooted closer and peered through the branches. To her right, the vista was eerily normal and lovely: marshes, hammocks like ranges of hills, a wide sky with gulls wheeling and swooping. To her left, the woods were mysterious, terrifying.

Dr. Flo lay on her grandfather's grave, pressed close to the stone. One hand stroked it. Katharine was so relieved to see movement that she started to sob.

Dr. Flo lifted her head a fraction. "Katharine? Are you all right?"

"You all keep down and hush!" Posey commanded softly. "He may not be through."

Katharine shivered, even though the heat was scarcely bearable. What was it like for Dr. Flo, exposed to the blazing sun?

"We've got to get out of here," she called softly to Posey. "Did you bring your phone? Mine's in the car."

"So's mine." Katharine regretted not letting Posey carry her bag. "But who would you call?" Anybody Katharine knew who lived within rescuing distance could be on the other end of that gun. "I don't even know if they have 911 down here."

"They've got a sheriff. The operator could find him." For all her frivolous appearance, Posey was competent in a crisis. In that way, she was very like her brother.

Oh, Tom, I didn't say I love you, Katharine grieved silently. *Why did I get mad about that stupid party?* She didn't want to die with that on her conscience. She didn't want to die at all.

She pictured Tom standing among Washington's elite and being approached by a policeman. Would they tell him there in the crowd that his wife had been shot? She was picturing his face going white with shock when she realized that Posey was demanding, in a voice that was half-whisper, "Lend me your *shoes*." She sounded irritated, like she was repeating the request.

"What?"

"Lend me your shoes." Posey shoved her sandals across the sand. Somehow she had managed not only to get out of them without lifting herself into shooting range, she had wriggled across Agnes's grave and close enough to reach Katharine. But Tom and Wrens would never forgive Katharine if Posey got shot.

She looked at the car, trying to judge how far away it was. "I'll go." She started toward it by pulling herself along on her elbows.

"You can't slither all that way on your belly," Posey protested. "You'll be full of sandspurs, chiggers, and who knows what else?"

"Have you got a better idea?" But Katharine herself suspected she couldn't make it that far. She wasn't dressed for slithering. Shards of shell were already cutting her palms and wearing out her shirt, and she was pulling a sandspur out of one forearm. Worse, once she got a few feet beyond the cemetery, her progress would be visible across the clearing.

"I'm going to run for it." Posey grabbed one of Katharine's flats and shoved her foot into it. "Good thing we wear the same size." When Katharine started to protest, Posey added, "I can run faster than you. I exercise."

"You can't outrun a bullet!"

"It's hard to hit a moving target." Before Katharine could question how she knew that and whether the information came from a reliable source, Posey had swiped her second shoe, leaped to her feet, and started speeding toward the car in a low, zigzagging crouch. Katharine hoped she was right about the moving target. She suspected Posey had heard that—and seen the crouch—on TV. Dumb, lovable Posey.

Still, she *was* fast. All that exercise paid off. Nevertheless, a bullet hit a tree as Posey passed it. She ran behind the wide trunk and stopped running.

Katharine held her breath and prayed. She waited for a fourth shot. She pictured someone moving stealthily in their direction, but dared not lift her head to see. She strained her ears for a telltale crunch or slithering sand and heard nothing except the rise and fall of the low-pitched cicada symphony and the whine of mosquitoes. She wriggled closer to the fence, heedless of the oleander branches in her face, until she remembered that oleander is one of the few plants that is poisonous clear through: leaves, flowers, stems, and roots. That sent her scuttling backward. She didn't want to dodge bullets only to die from oleander poisoning.

She lifted her head a fraction and saw Dr. Flo was still burrowed close to Claude Gilbert's stone. The low tabby wall gave her protection so long as she didn't lift her head. But could any of them survive long enough for help to arrive?

The sound of the car door opening sounded loud as a shot. With all her being Katharine willed her sister-in-law to be able to activate the cell phone and call for help before it was too late. "Please, God," she found herself whispering over and over. "Please, God. Please! Please! And keep your head down, Posey!"

The roar of the engine surprised her. She turned her head to see the SUV crossing the rough ground toward her. It stopped beside the tree and Posey jumped in the back.

"Good job, Hollis!" Katharine breathed. As the SUV neared, Hollis kept its wide body between her and the sniper's original position. Katharine ignored sandspurs and sawgrass and headed for the car in a running crouch, ready to spring inside. The SUV was still rolling when she heard an urgent command through the half-open window. "Jump in, Aunt Kat! Now!"

She fell in on top of Posey. Through the space between the seats she saw Hollis sitting low in the driver's seat, peering through the steering wheel.

"I forgot your sandals," Katharine remembered as they started to move.

"Too late now." Posey struggled beneath her.

"Where's Dr. Flo?" Hollis asked.

"Other side. Keep going." Katharine and Posey struggled to untangle themselves as the SUV pulled up beside the tabby wall. "Get in, Dr. Flo. Hurry!" Hollis called urgently.

Dr. Flo scrambled over the wall and through the back door. She fell on Katharine and Hollis took off. The back door hadn't latched. Dr. Flo grabbed for it, but Hollis said, "Get it later!"

The three women pulled themselves onto the backseat while she roared toward the road from the clearing. As she took the turn, the unlatched door swung open. Katharine tried to catch it, but missed. A bullet from the woods shattered the window.

Hollis floored the pedal. The SUV took off with the power of all its horses. Katharine had never been so glad to hear branches scrape paint. She didn't even mind when one smacked the door closed. Had she ever worried about anything so trivial as dents in her car? The only thing that mattered at the moment was catching her breath and hoping it wouldn't be her last.

Not until they passed the curve beyond where Katharine and Dr. Flo first met Dalt and Chase did Hollis finally sit erect behind the wheel. She exhaled a long breath. "I tried, but I couldn't get a signal on any of the phones." Her voice trembled.

Posey leaned up and clutched her shoulder. "You did good, baby. You did real good."

Katharine opened the back door, which had only partly caught, and slammed it shut. "You're our hero, Hollis." She peered at the forest through a hole where her window used to be and heaved a sigh. "I think we've made it."

Dr. Flo's voice shook. "I thought I was gonna see Maurice any minute there." She shook like she was sitting in an igloo.

"Turn on the heat," Katharine directed Hollis. "We're freezing back here." She had never expected to hear herself say that in July. She turned to Dr. Flo, "You do realize that somebody was shooting directly at you."

"Oh, yes. Dear God, yes!"

Katharine could have kissed Posey when she turned and hauled her big thermos of coffee up from the back. Steam rose as she opened the lid. "There's still some in here. Hand me Dr. Flo's cup, Hollis."

She flung the dregs out her window, refilled the cup, and stirred in four sugars. She touched Dr. Flo's arm. "Drink this."

Dr. Flo took the cup like an obedient child, but shook too much to bring it to her lips. Coffee sloshed out of the cup and onto her lap, but she didn't seem to notice. Katharine took it. "Let me." She held the cup to Dr. Flo's lips like a chalice. "Drink," she commanded gently.

When the coffee was gone, Katharine found a stadium

cushion in the back, with a blanket inside. She tucked the blanket around Dr. Flo's shoulders and circled her with her own arms. At last Dr. Flo stopped shaking enough to say, "You can sit back, now. I'll be all right. It was just so unexpected."

Katharine spread her fingers and shoved them through her hair, wishing she could comb out all the memories. "We walked straight into an ambush. They told you to come down at two-thirty, then they lay in wait to kill you."

Hollis called over one shoulder. "You got any more coffee back there, Mama? Pour me a little." As Katharine passed it over the back of the seat, she saw that Hollis was pale and shaking, yet she managed to keep the car on the sandy, rutted road.

Katharine kept trying both her cell phone and Posey's while they sped down the asphalt road, over the bridge, and off the island. She couldn't get a signal. When they neared the stop sign for the highway, she ordered, "Turn into the store on the right."

"*That* dump?" Posey demanded. "You think they'll have a phone?"

"You've led a very sheltered life, Posey. There's sure to be a phone, and I know the owners. Give me my shoes and you all wait here."

The shoes, warm from Posey's feet, felt like a hug. Katharine brushed off burrs and dried sprigs of grass that clung to the front of her shell and pants. She straightened her striped jacket, pulled a comb from her purse and dragged it through her hair. She refreshed her lipstick.

"Who the hell are you getting dolled up for?" Posey demanded. "Get out of here and call the sheriff, or I'll do it myself."

Like Katharine, Posey seldom swore. Katharine gave her a comforting pat as she climbed down from the car. "You did good, lady. Hang in there. I'll be right back."

Posey clasped both hands over her mouth and nose and rested her head on the back of the seat ahead. Fat tears oozed between her lashes and made tracks of mascara down her cheeks.

Katharine didn't wait to see if someone would console Posey. She was too busy trying to get her legs coordinated enough to march them both into the store.

A dusty black radio blared. Behind the counter, hands up and in front of her and eyes closed, Miranda swayed to the beat. With her pale hair rippling over her thin arms like leaves in a breeze, she looked like a wood nymph freed from her tree.

When she heard the door slam, she opened her eyes. "Hey!" she greeted Katharine, stopping her gyrations. "Chase said your friend was coming today, but I didn't know you were coming, too. Did you come up with something to stop them digging up them graves? You gonna stop Burch from building?"

"Maybe, but right now, I need a phone. My cell won't work down here." To her relief, she spotted a phone hanging on the wall behind Miranda.

"Mine won't, neither. Ain't enough towers or something. I can't let you use ours, though. Granny's real strict about that. Otherwise we'd have every Tom, Dick, and Harry in the area running in here all the time to use our phone, getting in the way of the customers."

Katharine could hear Iola loud and clear in that sentence. She also saw no customers to get in the way of. "This is an emergency, Miranda. Please!"

"You figuring on calling the Bayards?" The sharp little face brightened. "I could call 'em for you. You wanting 'em to know you're on your way?"

It was a start. "Yeah, let me speak to somebody at their house." Maybe she could identify the shooter by a process of elimination, and then call the sheriff.

Miranda dialed the number without looking it up and turned her back while it rang, a revealing gesture that insisted on privacy for the first precious moments after the ring had been answered. She rose on her toes and stood that way until somebody spoke on the other end, then her whole body slumped. "Hey, Miz Bayard. It's Miranda, up to the store. That woman from Atlanta is here for the digging up of the graves, and she wanted me to tell you—wait a minute." She cupped a hand over the mouthpiece and asked Katharine, "What was it you wanted me to tell her, again?"

"Let me talk to her." Katharine reached for the receiver. Miranda hesitated but finally handed it over.

"Mona? This is Katharine Murray, Dr. Flo Gadney's friend. Is Burch there?"

"No, he's gone to fetch Hayden. Hayden's car's in the shop." Did Katherine imagine it, or was Mona out of breath? She certainly breathed twice before adding, "They ought to be there not long after you all get there."

"Is your father-in-law at the house?"

"He's out and about somewhere. What did you want with him?"

Katharine ignored the question. "How about Chase?"

"He's gone down to feed Agnes's animals. What's this about?"

"Are you coming down for the disinterments?"

"Of course. I wouldn't miss it for anything."

"Well, listen, there's somebody shooting down there. We arrived early, and nearly got killed. Could you call the sheriff and ask him to send a deputy to Stampers?"

"Somebody got shot at Stampers?" Katharine couldn't tell if Mona had heard wrong or was deliberately misunderstanding. "You'll need to call him yourself. I'm busy getting together a few things for—you know, digging up the graves." She hung up.

Katharine handed Miranda the receiver, picturing Mona collecting shovels and spades.

"Would you call the sheriff, please?" She added, to satisfy Miranda's blatant curiosity, "We got to the cemetery early and somebody shot at us. We need for the sheriff to get down there and see if he can figure out who it was."

Miranda dropped the receiver like it was a dead thing. It hit the floor with a clatter. "How come you asked Miz Bayard was Chase there?"

She was no dummy, this child.

"I was trying to find out who might be out with a rifle."

"Chase don't shoot people." Miranda's eyes glittered like chips off a green bottle. "He don't shoot nothing if'n he can help it. 'Sides, he's a terrible shot. I swear it."

Katharine had no doubt whatsoever that Miranda would swear black was white if it would help Chase Bayard. However, there was no point in upsetting her. "I wanted to know who was at the house. Call the sheriff, Miranda! This is important."

Miranda picked up the cord and pulled the receiver up hand-over-hand with deliberate slowness. "You ain't gonna tell him Chase shot at you."

"I'm not going to tell him anything. I'm going to ask him to go down to the cemetery and look for casings or whatever they look for to identify a gun. Are you going to call him, or shall I?" Katharine started around the end of the counter.

Miranda held up an imperious hand. "Nobody's allowed behind this counter."

A voice spoke at the door. "Make that call and make it fast, you hear me?" Hollis could have been a rock star as she stood there in her stark black clothes, mahogany hair, and sunglasses. She was certainly somebody whose authority Miranda respected more than Katharine's.

She dialed and spoke rapidly into the mouthpiece. "Hey.

This is Miranda Stampers down at the store by the road to Bayard Island. Yeah, that's right, Iola's my granny. Listen, I got somebody here who says—maybe you better talk to her your own self." She handed Katharine the phone with a pout.

Katharine explained who she was and what she wanted. The woman on the other end dithered. "The sheriff's at a convention this weekend and most of the deputies are handling a crisis down in Darien. Major White's the only person I've got in that area right now. If you can wait an hour or so—"

"The major will be fine," Katharine told her. "Please tell him to hurry."

She returned to the SUV with four cold Cokes and climbed in front beside Hollis.

"You want to drive, Aunt Kat?"

"You're doing just fine, honey. Keep it up."

Chapter 30

When the cruiser pulled into the lot ten minutes later, Katharine had immediate regrets. It arrived with siren blaring and lights flashing and turned into the parking lot so fast it spun out and stopped inches from her car. The deputy climbed out with a smirk on his face, hitched up his pants, and headed her way. He was chunky and sloppy, his uniform shirt untucked, his badge crooked. He didn't look more than thirty, but a brass plate on his chest read MAJOR WHITE. She wondered what he had done to get promoted so high so young.

When he saw a car full of women, he shoved the thick fingers of one hand through his greasy brown hair and his smirk widened to a leer. "Well, hell-o." He drew out the last syllable. "You the ladies what got shot?"

Katharine was appalled. She had met a number of law enforcement officers across Georgia. They had been invariably courteous and literate. This man went to show that stereotypes have to come from somewhere.

"We were shot at," she corrected him, "out on Bayard Island."

"That right?" He turned his head and spat. "What was you doing on Bayard Island, if I may ask? That's posted property and the Bayards don't take kindly to trespassers."

"We're supposed to meet them at two-thirty for a disinterment. We got there early."

"And you got in the way of a hunter or something?"

"No, we think somebody deliberately shot at my friend."

"I doubt that. We don't run to many murders down this way, except'n' when somebody gets likkered up on a Saturday night. Most likely an accident, if you ask me."

"I'm asking you to investigate."

"Exactly where did this purported attempted murder take place?"

"At an old cemetery on the island."

He shrugged. "I can take a look. Got to go thataway, anyway. Burch is shifting graves today so he can fix up the place, and he asked me to be present." He grinned down at Hollis. "You follow me, sweetie, if you can keep up."

"I can keep up," she assured him grimly.

"Wrens is never going to believe this," Posey said to nobody in particular.

At the turnoff into the woods, the deputy stopped parallel to them and rolled down his window, motioning Hollis to do the same. "Why don't you go in first, sweetie, so you can show me exactly where the purported incident took place?"

"It was no purported incident," Hollis snapped. "Somebody fired four bullets at them, including one at my mama, and shot out our back window."

He gave her a wide smile. "You're mighty cute when you're mad."

"Please hurry," Katharine urged him. "And we'd rather you went first, in case the sniper is still there."

With the grunt of a henpecked man, he lurched down the road faster than he should.

As they followed, Posey reminded Katharine, "Somebody's gonna have to find my shoes when we get there. I've got more in my suitcase, but none of them match this suit, and I'm not changing clothes in that clearing with a madman loose. I don't want to get shot half-naked."

That picture diverted Katharine for the rest of the drive.

When they got to the clearing the second time, they found what they had expected earlier: two men in a truck with a backhoe chained to the bed. Between the backhoe and the cab was a double stack of large wooden boxes. Nearby, another man sat in a black Lincoln with the engine running. Katharine supposed he was using his air conditioner, but marveled that anybody needed it. They had driven all the way back with the heat on and still her bones felt cold.

The deputy went over and parked next to the Lincoln, but Hollis circled and parked facing the clearing exit. "In case we need to beat it out of here," she explained.

As the deputy climbed out of his car, the man from the Lincoln sauntered to meet him. "I pity his dry cleaner," Posey said softly. "He's gonna have trouble getting sand out of those cuffs and sandspurs out of silk pants without picking them."

"Those shiny shoes are going to be a mess by the end of the day, as well," Dr. Flo added.

Katharine silently blessed Posey for distracting her for at least a moment.

The funeral director was a handsome man with iron-gray hair above a face that reminded her of Humphrey Bogart, but Katharine wondered if anybody in America ever looked at him and didn't know immediately what he did for a living.

The deputy stuck his thumbs in his belt and strolled over to the SUV. When Katharine lowered her window, he said, "Nobody's shooting at the moment, but let me check out the situation and get back to you. I recommend you stay in the car."

"Do you want me to show you where the bullets hit?"

"Just tell me." When she had, he said, "Let me take a look first. I'll get back to you if I have any questions."

As he swaggered toward the cemetery, Posey cracked her door and yelled after him, "Hey, while you're over there, would you look under the green tent and bring back my shoes when you come? Black sandals. They're there somewhere."

"Oh, Mama," Hollis groaned.

Major White gave no sign he had heard either one.

The funeral director followed the deputy, and the two men from the truck climbed down to join the parade. From his gestures, the deputy was explaining what had happened. The workers and the funeral director began to walk with uneasy glances around them.

Posey mimicked the deputy. " 'I recommend you stay in the car.' Can you all think of any reason on God's green earth why we ought to get *out* of this car? But I sure feel like a sitting duck."

"Me, too," Katharine admitted. "Let's sit low in our seats." She slid down, every muscle in her body tense to fling her into the floor at the slightest provocation. "Dr. Flo, I'd feel a lot better if you were to go ahead and sit on the floor."

"I'm not climbing down on that floor. Let him shoot me if he wants to."

"You can't think like that," Posey admonished her. "We don't know that he wanted you in particular. People are crazy these days, shooting other folks for no reason whatsoever except pure meanness."

"This wasn't random, honey." She called up to Katharine, "Which of them do you suppose it was? Do you think it was the same one who shot Agnes?"

"That would be my guess," Katharine agreed.

"Wasn't Agnes the woman with the cats?" Hollis asked.

Katharine nodded.

"She was shot?" Posey demanded.

Katharine sighed. "Yes, she was."

"You didn't say a word about her getting shot. You think it was on purpose?"

"Yes."

"You all were crazy to come back down here!"

Nobody gave her any argument about that.

In her side mirror, Katharine watched while the deputy and his companions circled the fenced cemetery. As they approached the Guilbert plot, a buzzard rose and joined companions circling in the sky. One of the shots must have hit something. She felt sick. She hoped Dr. Flo hadn't seen the bird.

The deputy motioned the others to keep back, then stepped over the tabby wall and made a cursory examination of the site, including bending over the obelisk to feel the nick the bullet had made. Katharine wondered why he bothered to keep the other men outside the plot. He himself was tromping over whatever evidence might be there although the sniper had been so far away, there probably wouldn't be any clues in the cemetery to disturb. The deputy reached for his phone. As he talked on the phone, he turned and watched the clearing in a 360-degree angle, so he must have had at least a niggling worry that a sniper was still around. She had never before appreciated the courage it took to be an officer of the law.

The two men and the funeral director stood to one side, having a discussion. When the deputy closed his phone, the flatbed driver's voice boomed over the cemetery. ". . . gonna be able to lift these graves this afternoon, Major? Or had we just as well go on home and come back another day? I could be playing ball with my kid about now, you know. It's not how I'd rather spend a Saturday. And are they gonna want to lift the one we buried this morning? If'n they'da told us earlier, it could've saved us a lot of trouble."

The deputy stretched and flexed his biceps. "Everything is

still go, Ned. I just talked to Burch, and he said folks from town was out here huntin' around noon, but they're all gone now. What we had here was clearly somebody shootin' at that rabbit over yonder that the buzzard's been picking on. Those ladies just got excited and thought they were the targets."

"Got excited?" Posey gasped. "He'd get excited, too, if somebody shot at him three times and then shot out his window on the road."

She said the same thing a few minutes later when the deputy came back. Katharine noticed he was holding in his gut—probably for Hollis's benefit.

"Yes, ma'am, I can see they got your window, but you *were* trespassing and the property is clearly posted. The Bayards don't take kindly to people coming onto their island uninvited."

"I told you, we *were* invited,"Katharine said, exasperated. "Besides, there is a possibility that Dr. Flo is the legal owner of this portion of the island."

He peered into the back at Dr. Flo, and narrowed his eyes. "What you folks tryin' to pull? The Bayards have always owned this island. I'm sorry you all got in the way of a stray bullet, but that's why they put up all them signs. They don't want people gettin' hurt."

"Those weren't stray bullets!" Posey insisted, indignant. "Two of them were aimed straight for Dr. Flo and one was aimed at me!"

"Can you prove that in a court of law?"

One by one each shook her head.

"You didn't see anybody, right?"

"We were too busy saving our hides," Posey reminded him hotly.

"Well, I'm real sorry for your inconvenience, but in the future, I'd suggest you stay off posted property." He turned and lumbered over to where the other men were standing beneath a sycamore.

"Of all the nerve!" Posey sounded like she was ready to climb out of the car and wallop him.

Hollis muttered, "If we were men, he'd be taking this seriously."

"What can we do?" Dr. Flo asked.

"Nothing at the moment," Katharine replied. "We didn't see a soul and you haven't proven a claim to the land, so I guess we were technically trespassing, since we got here early."

Burch Bayard drove into the clearing in the old black truck Katharine and Dr. Flo had seen first at Stampers and then parked in front of his house. He wore a dark suit, a white shirt, and a yellow power tie. He looked real happy until he saw the green tent—then he headed straight for the funeral director's car.

He leaned out his open window and yelled, "What the hell's that tent doing here, Sykes? So help me, if you buried that bitch on my land . . ."

Mr. Sykes spoke in a voice the women in the car could not hear. Katharine wondered if the ability to speak so only a few could hear was something they taught in mortician school.

Mr. Sykes might be inaudible, but Burch wasn't. He spewed out a stream of profanity which boiled down to, "I don't care where she requested to be buried, you knew good and well we were planning to move this cemetery this week and she had no right to be buried here."

More murmurs from Mr. Sykes.

"On Wednesday?" Burch sounded flabbergasted. "She waltzed into your office this past Wednesday, showed you a deed, and asked to be buried here? Then came home and shot herself to be sure it happened before I got my digging permits in order? I'm not paying for her removal, I can promise you that." He opened the truck door and, shouldering Mr. Sykes out of his way, stomped over to the SUV. "Did you all have anything to do with that?" He pointed toward Agnes.

"Heavens no," Katharine assured him. "We don't shoot or bury people. I'm not convinced she shot herself, though. She was chipper when we talked with her Tuesday night." She knew she shouldn't bait him, but the temptation was irresistible.

Out of the corner of her eye she saw Hayden Curtis clambering down from the passenger seat of the truck. He was sweating so profusely that he had circles at the armpits of his blue seersucker suit, which looked as out of place in the clearing as the funeral director's black. The pudgy attorney did not look happy.

"Let's not get carried away." He flapped his little paws in Burch's direction.

Burch ignored him. "Why were you were down at Agnes's on Thursday messing up the place?"

"We didn't mess up a thing. We were looking for letters she promised Dr. Flo. As it turned out, she mailed them before she died."

From the backseat, Dr. Flo added, "She mailed a copy of the deed to this property, too. It's very explicit that if Agnes's family doesn't have heirs, the land reverts to the descendants of the family for whom the house was built. That may well have been my family."

Burch glared at her, but it was Katharine to whom he spoke again. "That is flat-out impossible. I've already told you—"

Dr. Flo spoke again. "Who was Mallery?"

He blinked, then shrugged. "How the hell should I know? The relative of one of my ancestors, Elizabeth Mallery Bayard, is all I can figure out. I'm gonna re-bury him near her in a little family plot up near our house. It's going to be real picturesque."

That word again.

It grated on Katharine's sensibilities, but she said nothing, steeled for Burch's next attack. Instead, he clutched his head with both hands and cried, "I'm trying to do the best I know how, here. Why do folks keep interfering?"

He stomped off toward the other men. As he approached them, Major White nodded toward the SUV and said, "Those are the ladies making the complaint about getting shot at."

"Let 'em complain. Wish somebody would finish them off."

The funeral director came over to their car. "Which of you is Dr. Gadney, who wants the three re-burials delayed until Monday?"

Dr. Flo identified herself, but before she could say more, Hollis demanded, "Sir, how did that deputy get to be a major?"

A smile flickered across his face. "That's not his rank, it's his name. His mother thought it would give him something to live up to. Mostly it's been something he's had to live down. If you could step over to my car, Dr. Gadney, I have papers for you to sign."

"That deputy never did bring my shoes," Posey complained.

"I'll get them," Hollis volunteered.

Posey backpedaled. "Do you think it's safe, Katharine?"

"I think so. The sniper isn't likely to be taking shots with everybody here."

"He's so nasty, maybe Burch was the sniper," Hollis suggested.

"He wouldn't have had time to shoot us and fetch his lawyer from Darien."

Katharine spoke automatically. Her mind was busy with another problem. She had been wondering how Burch would manage to move Agnes and her family, since she seemed to have no kinfolks, when she had remembered that Agnes's grandfather had been a cousin of Miss Ella Bayard. Would that make Dalt Agnes's nearest relative?

If a judge agreed, Dr. Flo hadn't a hope of proving a claim to the land.

Chapter 31

While they waited for the disinterments to begin, Katharine moved the SUV closer to the cemetery, in the shade of a live oak. They opened all the windows to catch what stray breezes they could, and Posey insisted they all reapply repellant. "We don't want to get carried away bodily by these mosquitoes or come down with West Bayard Island disease."

Around two-thirty, Mona and Chase arrived in her Mercedes and parked near the church foundations. Chase climbed out, wearing fresh khaki slacks and a long-sleeved blue shirt. Mona was celebrative in red slacks, a red-and-white-striped tank top, and a floppy red hat.

She waved to the men, who had gathered in a herd under a sycamore tree. "Hey, y'all. Give me a minute to set up, then we're gonna have a hell of a tailgate party." From her trunk she unfolded a small table and set out bowls of shrimp, platters of wings, platters of sandwiches, and trays of crudités. A galvanized tub in the trunk held champagne on ice.

"Martha Stewart in the marsh," Dr. Flo muttered. "You'd think we were here to christen a yacht."

Katharine figured Mona was there to christen a dream come true.

"Her outfit's not as stunning as yours," Posey told Katharine.

"Her sunglasses aren't as expensive as yours."

"Meow, meow," Hollis said. "The question is, can she shoot?"

"Somebody said she's as good a shot as her husband," Dr. Flo told her, "but I don't know how good he is."

Mona contemplated her work with pride. "Okay, y'all. Soup's on. Come get something to eat. Don't be shy!"

The men ambled toward her like cows heading to the barn.

Posey opened her door. "I think I'll see if I can find out where she was earlier this afternoon." She got down from the SUV, calling, "Aren't you Mona Bayard? I'm Posey Buiton, and I was so sorry to miss your house on the last tour."

"Oh, Mama," whispered Hollis in disgust.

"Don't knock her," Katharine advised. "Posey's got her methods and they usually work."

While Posey was accepting a glass of champagne and being charming to Mona, Katharine, Dr. Flo, and Hollis watched the others fill plates and glasses. The clearing had taken on the feel of a carnival.

Katharine herself was beginning to relax. She took deep breaths of marsh-laden air and looked across the slough and grassland to hammock islands on the horizon. She knew that mud and ooze, dead sea creatures and birds, plastic bottles and aluminum cans were part of the marsh's reality, but at a distance the grass, water, and sky looked pristine and fresh.

Burch, Hayden, Major White, Mr. Sykes, and his workers carried their food back to the sycamore and continued their democratic male bonding experience. It consisted, as far as the women could hear, mostly of baseball talk. Katharine wondered what they were waiting for. Nobody seemed in any hurry whatsoever.

"Chase, take those women some food," Mona commanded. She sent glasses of chilled champagne and plates of cold boiled shrimp, chicken wings, cream cheese and crab sandwich wedges, carrot sticks, raw broccoli, and olives.

Hollis offered a toast. "To champagne. If you gotta wait, it's a great way to pass the time."

They heard another car, and Nell's gray van bumped into the clearing. She pulled up near Mona and unloaded Iola and Miranda, then jolted to a shady spot not far from Katharine where she could watch the proceedings without climbing down. Iola wore a long red skirt with a white tank top that displayed more wrinkled neck and chest than was prudent. Her hair was beauty-parlor fresh: bright yellow and cascading from her crown in those improbable curls. Miranda wore white heels and a white strapless dress that she spent the next half hour tugging up. In the time since Katharine was at the store, she had painted her nails black and applied so much lipstick, blusher, and mascara that she looked like a clown.

Mona was disconcerted to see the Stampers. "You aren't here to protest or anything, are you?" she asked Iola.

"Would it do any good? I figure you all are gonna do what you want to with your part of the island and we'll do what we want to with ours."

At that reminder that outsiders owned part of the island, Katharine could see the struggle within Mona to make a sharp retort. Good manners won. "Well, come on over here and get food and a glass of champagne. Chase, carry a glass over to Nell along with something to eat."

She ignored Miranda completely.

Miranda spotted the SUV and came over. "Hey," she greeted them. "I didn't know we were coming when I seen you earlier, but Granny said we might as well."

She gave Chase a furtive look and smoothed her white skirt before she eyed Hollis's glass. "You got champagne, too?"

"Yeah." Hollis opened the door. "And I think I'll get more. Come on."

She marched Miranda over to Mona, held out her glass,

picked up another glass and handed it to Miranda. "Enjoy the party."

Miranda gave her a shy, pleased smile over her glass and took a sip, then wrinkled her nose and laughed. Hollis laughed with her.

"Looks like Hollis has picked up a disciple," Dr. Flo said as she watched them.

Katharine had been thinking how like Hollis it was to notice that Mona hadn't offered the girl anything to drink and take steps to rectify that.

"But that poor child," Dr. Flo continued. "Wanting so desperately to be sophisticated, and instead looking like a refugee from a Halloween parade. Why don't young girls put on pretty clothes and enjoy the fresh, lovely looks God has given them instead of covering themselves with all that guck? They'll have enough years to be garish later."

Katharine didn't have an answer. As a teen, she had tried out various looks, and suspected Dr. Flo had done the same thing. Miranda might get it right one day.

While Chase was carrying Nell her food and drink, Mona kept a close eye on Miranda. In Mona's place, Katharine might have done the same. When Chase started back to the car, Burch called from under the tree. "Come over here, son." Chase ambled over to the men. Burch grabbed his elbow. "It's finally happening, boy! It's really going to happen!"

"Looks that way," Chase croaked. He gave the path to the woods an anxious look.

Miranda's eyes followed him yearningly, but he ignored her and stood watching the woods. Then he gave a start and took off toward them at a lope.

Katharine looked out her back window and saw the man named Cooter stepping from between two cabbage palms. He held Dalt Bayard by one elbow. Both men wore overalls, long-sleeved shirts, and straw hats, but Cooter's clothes looked fresh and pressed. Dalt's looked like he'd lived in them a while. He also staggered like a man who had done serious drinking that day.

Chase remonstrated with them, pointing back into the woods. His granddaddy threw back his head and laughed, then pushed past Chase and dragged Cooter toward the other men. Chase frowned as he followed.

When they got closer, Dalt called, "Running a bit behind, aren't you, son? Thought we'd be late."

"We're about to start," Burch called back. "Did you know Agnes was buried here?"

"Yep. Watched the whole shebang. Not much of a turn-out. A few folks from town."

"You might have seen fit to mention it to me."

"Didn't want to ruin the fun." Dalt stumped toward the cemetery gate, calling over one shoulder, "Have you paid your respects to all these fine relations of ours before you start hauling 'em up?"

Burch ignored him.

Dalt gave a high-pitched cackle and informed the other men, "That boy never could abide cemeteries, ever since he nearly fell into his mama's grave when he was six. Scared him so bad he wet his pants."

"Oh!" Dr. Flo exclaimed in disgust.

When Burch didn't rise to his bait, Dalt peered into the broad branches that shaded the cemetery. "Never did cotton to the notion of lying out in this godforsaken spot, myself. You plant me in town, you hear me, son? Some place where they's a bit of life going on."

"I'm gonna drop you in the marshes and let the fish eat your gizzard."

The old man cackled again and hobbled into the cemetery. With Cooter's hand to steady him, he wandered along the rows of graves.

"Hey, Dalt," Major called. "Some folks claim they got shot at earlier this afternoon in your cemetery. Wasn't you who shot at them, was it? You been huntin' today?"

"Been hunting for my liquor. Mona hid it and I had the dickens of a time finding it. They didn't get hit, did they? We gonna get to bury bodies as well as dig 'em up?"

"Forget it, Daddy!" Burch burst out. "Nobody got hurt."

The others resumed their desultory conversation. Dalt shuffled back through the cemetery, out the gate, around the fence, and climbed over the tabby wall. "These here don't belong to us," he said loudly to whoever might be listening. "I'm sayin' it and I'm sayin' it real loud. These folks have nothing to do with us. You ever hear of any Guilbert's around here, Cooter?"

He gave it the French pronunciation.

His companion bent to peer down at Marie's stone. "Nossir, Mr. Dalt. Never heard of anybody with that name 'round here. Sure didn't."

"I've got champagne, Dalt," Mona called. "Come get you some. You, too, Cooter."

Dalt's head shot up and quivered. "Is she offering me a drink? Hurry, Cooter, before she changes her mind." He staggered out at an impressive speed, but as they passed the obelisk, he glanced down, saw the name, and stopped. "Mallery? Well, I'll be. I been coming to this cemetery all my life and never saw a name on that shaft before."

Chase glowered. "I told you Tuesday that those women found Mallery."

Dr. Flo and Katharine exchanged a look. Chase spoke like it was a familiar name.

"I thought you were funning me, boy. Or maybe I was too drunk to listen good."

"What's new?" Chase kicked a twig buried in Spanish moss and sent it high into the air.

"Dalt, are you coming or not?" Mona held out a bottle that glinted in sunlight.

"I'm coming." He shuffled across to the impromptu bar.

When she gave him a glass, he raised it to the sky. "To Mallery. We've had real hell *raisers* in this family, but that's one who deserves to burn there."

Posey drifted back to the car to report. "Mona's so keyed up about moving this cemetery, she can't talk furniture right now, but I did find out she's been driving around alone all day picking up food. She could have stopped by here long enough to shoot at us."

Dr. Flo opened her door. "Looks like we're fixing to start, anyway."

Ned was driving his backhoe off the truck.

Chapter 32

"We'll move those graves over yonder first, then these women can leave," Burch called over the motor's clatter.

Katharine started to object that they had better not move Agnes without somebody's permission, but she bit her tongue. That was none of her business and wouldn't matter to Agnes. As her mother used to often remind her father, *You cannot fight all the battles in this world, only those you are given.*

The three women positioned themselves at one edge of the Guilbert plot where they had a good view of the proceedings. Hollis elected to stand with Miranda and Iola by Nell's van.

Ned maneuvered the backhoe into position to take down enough tabby wall to get to the graves. His partner brought four wooden boxes and laid them outside the Guilbert plot with their lids open. "Sometimes there's not much there except dark soil, after so many years." Mr. Sykes sounded like he was apologizing for that. "But we bury the soil where they were, just the same."

Katharine sipped tepid champagne and wished it were ice water. Sweat tickled her skin as it rolled down her torso. Her hair lay hot and heavy on her neck. She checked her watch. Three o'clock. *Three more hours to Jekyll and a swim,* she promised herself, hoping it was true.

As the backhoe chomped its first bite of wall, she regretted that one more piece of the region's history was being erased. On the other hand, she was fascinated by the transformation in Ned. Walking around, he was a chunky man of little grace. On his backhoe he was as delicate and precise as a ballet dancer, moving the machine and its scoop with a skill that was beautiful to watch.

She would have appreciated his performance more if she hadn't been wondering which of the others had been taking shots at them earlier.

By now, they formed quite a crowd, but not a soul wore a guilty expression. Burch was keyed up—a man finally getting what he wanted. Major White and Hayden Curtis remained under the sycamore, settling in for a boring afternoon. Mr. Sykes strode around the perimeter of the cemetery rubbing his palms together like the coach of a winning team. Nell sat in her van in the shade while Iola, Miranda, and Hollis leaned against the front fender, apart from the others, yet very present. All three Stampers wore the expressions of those who are attending a public execution because it's the weekend entertainment in town.

While Ned positioned his backhoe to dig up Françoise's grave, Dalt stumbled around to the other side of the cemetery and got his first glimpse of the Stampers van. "What you doing here?" he shouted. "Burch, did you know the Stampers bitch is here with her brats? They ain't family. I told her then and I'm telling her now, she ain't family. Git out of here!" He waved a hand as if to shoo flies, lost his balance, and toppled in a heap. "Now look what you made me do," he complained.

"You always were more attractive prone," Iola called from beside the van.

"Hush your mouth, woman. I ain't taking no notice of you."

"You did once."

"Never did and never plan to. Now git out of here. *Git!*"

Iola placed both hands on her hips. "We ain't goin' nowhere, Dalt, 'til we get what's owed us. That woman over there ain't the only one with a claim on this island. Nell's owed a piece of it, too." She expanded her audience to include the rest of them. "Look at her! Just look at her! Who does she look like? I ask you that." She flung out one hand toward Nell in the driver's window of the van. Nell's face was white, her eyes wide and disbelieving. But it was an oval face with wide cheekbones and blue chip eyes. A Bayard face. Bayard eyes.

Katharine hadn't noticed the resemblance before. Shocked, she did the math. Nell was what, four or five years younger than Burch? Born before his mother died, certainly.

Had he ever looked at Nell before? Not the way he was looking now—from her to his father and back again. "Daddy?"

"She's not owed a blessed thing," Dalt insisted, still on the ground. "I gave her a store and a prime piece of land for that youngun. She's not owed another thing. Cooter, help me up."

"I'll knock you down again!" Burch raised a fist and headed for his daddy.

Mona dragged on his arm to hold him back. "Get him out of here," she screamed at Cooter, who was helping Dalt up. "Get him out of here!"

"You'd better!" Veins stood in Burch's neck like wisteria vines, "or so help me, I'll kill him!"

"I'll kill him first!" Iola jerked Miranda by one arm and pulled her into the van. Hollis jumped out of the way as Nell started the engine. As they pulled away, Iola stuck a rifle out the window and fired at Dalt. If the van hadn't hit a rut and lurched at that moment, he could have died. Nell gunned the motor and they roared away.

"Get her! That was attempted murder!" Dalt yelled. "Don't you let her get away with that!"

Major White took this shooting seriously. He lumbered toward his cruiser as fast as an overweight, out-of-shape deputy can run in sand.

"I ain't hurt," Dalt shoved Cooter away and stood unsteadily to his feet. "I'm fam'ly and this is a fam'ly event. Don't need all these—these strangers around." He waved toward Hayden, Dr. Flo, Katharine, and Posey. He hadn't noticed Hollis.

Hayden, still under the sycamore, had turned his back and was staring over the marsh like he'd never seen one before. Mr. Sykes was advising the man who was setting Françoise's headstone beside one of the wooden boxes. "To make sure the right stone gets on the right grave," he called over to Dr. Flo as if he were giving a lecture in mortician's school.

"We appreciate it," she told him.

He gave her a small bow. "We try to do the best we can for your loved ones."

Somebody needed to do something for Chase. He was staring at his grandfather with an ashen face.

"Come on, son." Mona joined him and jiggled his elbow. "They are starting to dig, and I want us with your daddy if he watches. You know how he feels about cemeteries. Burch, you do want to watch, don't you?"

"Not particularly, but I will." He moved to stand beside his wife and son.

"Why, let's all pretend nothing happened here," Posey drawled softly to Katharine.

As Mr. Sykes had predicted, the machine uncovered nothing in Françoise's grave but a patch of soil that was darker than sand. Nevertheless, that soil was carefully gathered and deposited in the wooden box. When the lid was secured, Mr. Sykes copied the name from Françoise's stone onto the lid of the box in permanent black marker. Katharine wondered what a future archaeologist would make of that.

This generation of humans buried earth in wooden boxes marked with hieroglyphics of undetermined meaning.

"That wasn't bad at all," Posey whispered.

Katharine said nothing. The backhoe was scooping Marie's grave. What had the day been like when the woman was buried? Who had attended? Had they come to mourn, or simply to make sure that she was good and buried? Had Claude made the trip back from Atlanta?

Again, nothing turned up except dark earth, a few scraps of black cloth, one shoe sole, and a string of crystal beads on a golden chain. When Dr. Flo didn't move, Katharine stepped forward. "I believe that ought to belong to Dr. Flo."

"It may be gold," Mona objected.

Burch touched her arm. "Let it go, hon."

Nobody else spoke as Katharine retrieved the jewelry from the backhoe before the dirt was lowered into a second box. Mr. Sykes copied MARIE GUILBERT onto the lid.

"Thank you," Dr. Flo said softly. "It looks like a rosary."

"Marie must have been Catholic."

Posey passed them a small bottle of hand cleaner. "Use this. Some of that stuff on your fingers might not be dirt."

Katharine cringed. She scrubbed her hands and wiped them on a tissue, but as Ned moved toward Claude Gilbert's grave and carried his tombstone over beside the two boxes, she found she was wiping them once again down the side of her pants.

Claude had been buried in a metal casket. The backhoe dug a hole around it, then Ned and his assistant jumped into the hole and shoveled out the sand around it. Carefully they lifted one end and inserted a chain, then repeated the procedure at the other end. The chain was attached to the backhoe, which lifted the coffin and gently placed it beside Claude's tombstone.

Posey gave a little puff of relief. When Katharine raised a questioning eyebrow, she gave a little shrug. "Okay, I'm silly," she whispered, "but I'm still glad there haven't been any bones."

Ned turned his bucket toward the obelisk. "Do you want this one, too?" he asked Burch.

"It's just a stone," Dalt called, stumbling a little as he headed toward the backhoe. "Yank it out and don't bother digging."

"Nonsense," Burch objected. He lifted one hand toward Katharine and Posey. "You all can go now. The rest are ours. Mr. Sykes will take care of your relatives for the weekend, then put them wherever you arranged for them to go on Monday. The rest of this is family business."

"That one is mine, as well," Dr. Flo said as Ned's backhoe bit the dirt.

"No, it's—" Burch began, but his daddy interrupted.

"Don't make such a fuss over it, y'all. It's nothing but a marker." Dalt jerked his head and one grubby thumb toward the marsh. "Carry it over there, Neddie, and dump it in the slough." He shuffled closer and peered blearily at it. "I'd a done that before, except I didn't know where it was. Granddaddy never said. Not inside the fence, though. That figures."

"It has a pirate on it, Papa Dalt. Did you see that?" Chase circled and pointed to the back of the shaft. He was clearly uneasy and kept darting anxious looks at the women.

Dalt inched around to have a look. "Well, I'll be damned."

"Very likely," Posey murmured. Katharine coughed to cover her laugh.

Burch looked from his son to his father, puzzled. "What are you two talking about?"

"Mallery," the old man said.

"Who's Mallery?" Mona demanded.

He leered at her. "Burch didn't tell you about the fine family you married in to, gal? Didn't describe all the skeletons in the family closet before you signed on?"

Her nostrils flared.

"I don't think you ever told Daddy, either," Chase told him.

"Lotsa things I never told your daddy."

"Obviously," Burch muttered, not looking at him.

Mona whirled to glare at her son. "Do *you* know what he's talking about?"

He shrugged. "Sorta. A bit of it." Again he slid a quick look at the women.

"Mallery was a pirate," Katharine called across the plot. "Down in the Caribbean." Then Dr. Flo gasped and Katharine stared.

The backhoe had carefully lifted the obelisk from the sand. It had sunk deeper than any of them had realized. As it rose into the air, the name appeared not as one line, but two:

MALLERY
BAYARD

Chapter 33

"It appears that the pirate was both your relative *and* Dr. Flo's," Katharine told Burch.

"He has nothing to do with the Guilberts. Nothing to do with pirates, either. I'm sure that skull thing was a schoolboy prank."

Chase's sarcastic laugh was rough like his voice, not yet mellow or mature. "Family's only got one pirate. We ought to be proud of the fact."

Dalt whirled on him. "Hush your mouth, boy! Mallery disgraced our family and went straight to hell. Don't you ever forget it, and don't ever tell." He recited the jingle like an affirmation of faith. Had it been passed down through generations of Bayards?

Not to all of them. Burch was still demanding, "Who was Mallery?"

Mona put a hand on his arm. "Talk about it later. Posey and her friends need to get on the road." She turned to them. "You've seen what you came for, and you've got a long drive ahead."

She sounded so gracious, a stranger might think she actually cared.

Dr. Flo tilted her chin. "I have letters Mallery wrote to Marie Guilbert, making it clear that Claude and Françoise were his children."

"His children?" Papa Dalt guffawed. "That's a good one,

isn't it, Chase? This lady thinks these Guilberts were his children." If he was making a joke, most of the others missed it.

Burch threw manners to the wind. "Shut up, Daddy!"

Katharine felt sorry for him, having to deal with an irascible old father determined to wring as much drama as he could from the day. However. . . . She stepped forward.

"Dr. Flo does have letters, which were in Agnes's house, that make it clear that those children were Mallery's. They also make it likely that the house was built for Marie and the children. I don't know why your father finds that so funny, but we're staying for this disinterment. You and Dr. Flo will need to agree on where to bury those remains."

"Remains?" Dalt's mirth had dissolved into exasperation. "I keep telling you, there are no *remains*. All that *remains* is to throw in the towel and give up your fool idea of building on this land, Burch, or there won't be anything *remaining* of our whole damned family."

"Dig it up," Burch ordered Ned with an impatient flap of one hand.

"I'm telling you, smart-ass," Dalt tried desperately, "there is no body in that grave. Never was, never will be. Give it up!"

"That's interesting," Dr. Flo murmured. Katharine nodded.

Ned nodded at Dr. Flo. "If you'll step aside, ma'am?"

She backed as far as the tabby wall. Katharine and Posey stood beside her.

Gently Ned scooped out dirt to a depth of three feet. The blade struck something that rang in the air. He backed, dug deeper on one side, and peered into the sandy hole. "It's a box of some sort, but not as big as a coffin. You want it lifted?"

"No!" roared Dalt.

"Yes!" yelled Chase and Burch. Chase was bouncing on the balls of his feet like the child in him was dying to break out.

Ned nodded toward his partner. They jumped into the hole and worried the box in the sand until they could get under it and hoist it out. It was green metal, three feet long, two feet wide, and one foot deep.

Chase's gruff boyish voice cut the silence. "Oh, boy! Treasure!"

Burch scratched it with a coin. "It's copper. I'll bet Francis Bayard made it. He liked to work with copper—remember, Mona? He made that jewelry box you've got, and the chest in the living room. Maybe we can put the three of them together like a display or something."

Mona didn't answer. Her eyes were fixed on the box.

Chase bent over it. "What you reckon he put in it?"

Katharine could think of a number of things. Many Southern families buried their silver as war came nearer. If stories were believed, unclaimed silver caches dotted the Southern landscape. At the other end of a long spectrum, this box was about the size of an infant's casket. Had Mallery blotted the family history before he departed for the Caribbean?

"Whatever it is, I also have a claim on it," Dr. Flo reminded them loudly, stepping up beside Mona. The Bayards were massed around the box like it was the altar of a new and precious god.

"No, way," said Burch. "Mallery was a Bayard. Whatever is in that box belongs to me."

"Us," Mona corrected him.

"Whatever is in that box belongs in the bottom of the slough," yelled Dalt. "I keep telling you, Burch—"

"Mallery was the father of Claude Gilbert, my grandfather," Dr. Flo pressed on. "I have more claim on the contents of that box than you do."

Nobody was listening. The only thing the Bayards had on their collective mind was the box.

"The padlock is rusty," Mona complained. "I don't know how we'll get it open."

"I got a crowbar in the truck." Ned looked toward Burch. "You want I should go get it and have a look-see?"

"No!" shouted Dalt.

"Might as well." Burch pretended to be casual, but he was bent toward that box like it held the Holy Grail.

Chase knelt at one end, running his hands over the edges, caressing the box with his fingertips. "This thing is so well made."

"Chase is a woodcarver," Katharine informed Posey. "He's really good."

Ned's wide shoes trudged heavily through the sand as he returned with the crowbar. The Bayards moved back slightly to give him space.

Mona glared at Dr. Flo. "If you think you have any claim on this box, you can think again. This box was found in our grave and on our property."

"It may not be your property," Dr. Flo reminded her. "That is to be determined in a court of law."

Burch's laugh was ugly. "Then get yourself a lawyer."

"I have a lawyer."

Burch looked around the clearing. "I don't see him anywhere. You can take us to court over the land—not that you'll win. But that box is ours."

"That's right. Don't give it to her, son!" Dalt commanded. "Drop it in the slough!"

"I am her lawyer," said a clear voice from the edge of the crowd.

Katharine watched dumbfounded as Posey stepped over the wall and marched up to the Bayards. She might only be five foot two and look like an expensively dressed blue-eyed bottle-blond bimbo, but nobody could question her dignity at the moment. "I represent Dr. Florence Gadney in this, and I state in the presence of these witnesses," she gestured to include Hayden Curtis, Mr. Sykes, and his men, "that Dr. Gadney has a legal claim on the contents of this box, whatsoever they may be."

"Bull!" Mona's laugh was as rude as Burch's laugh had been a moment earlier. "You're no more of a lawyer than I am."

Katharine held her breath. Could Posey maintain her bluff?

Posey's lips curved into her sweetest smile and her drawl was so soft you could have spread it on toast for breakfast. "Emory University Law School class of 1976, hon. When and where did you graduate?"

Mona blinked. "Are you serious?"

"Absolutely." Posey now addressed Ned. "We have no objection to your opening that box, so long as it is clear that Dr. Gadney has an interest in the contents."

"Don't let her get away with this, Burch," Mona begged. Any camaraderie she might have felt for Posey over antebellum beds was consumed in the fire of her determination to own the copper box.

Burch looked over his shoulder at Hayden Curtis. Mr. Curtis came plodding up, sweating as heavily as he was panting from the heat. "Might as well open it and see what's there if it's all right with Mrs.—what was your name?"

"Buiton. Persephone Buiton."

"Mrs. Buiton. We have no objections to opening the box if you have none."

Katharine blinked. *Persephone?* What was Posey up to? Could you go to jail for impersonating an attorney under a false name?

"No!" Dalt grabbed Burch's arm. "I keep tellin' you, son. Don't open it!"

"Do it," Burch told Ned, then jerked his head toward Cooter. "Get Daddy out of here."

Cooter dragged Dalt to the back of the small circle around the box.

Ned maneuvered the crowbar into the rusted lock and put his considerable strength behind it. "Here, boy, come help me," he called to Chase.

Katharine had no idea whether he needed added muscles or not, but Chase jumped forward with alacrity. "Yessir!"

Dalt pulled loose from Cooter and flung himself across the box. "No!" He pounded his fists on the box, practically sobbing. "Boy, listen to me. At least listen to me! That's all I ask. Listen to me!"

Cooter started to pull him off, but something in his daddy's voice finally reached Burch.

"Wait a minute," he held up a hand to stop Ned and Chase, then dropped it to his father's shoulder. "Okay, Daddy, I'm listening. What do you want to say?"

Dalt grew still. "Not here." He jerked his head to a private spot under a distant live oak. "Over there."

Burch helped him up and steadied him as they walked to Dalton's chosen confessional. They spoke for several minutes, heads close together. At several points Dalton waved his hands toward the women. At one point Burch stepped back and let out a strangled cry. When the story was finished, he stood with his back to the assembly, staring over the marsh. He turned to look for a moment at Dr. Flo, then asked Dalt a question. Dalton nodded. Burch spoke and Dalton nodded again. Burch draped his arm around his father's shoulders and Dalt draped his around Burch's waist. As they returned, it was hard to tell who was supporting whom. Burch motioned for Hayden Curtis to join him in a private spot. After consultation, they came back to the group.

"We're not going to open the box," Burch announced. Mona opened her mouth, but he held up his hand to silence her protest. "Daddy and I have agreed that it ought to go to Dr. Gadney. We will give you the box if you will sign a statement that you will never make public the contents of this box or use it in any way against our family."

"But that will not invalidate any claim she may later make against this property," Posey warned. "Such a claim would be based on documents she already holds."

Burch looked at Hayden, who nodded. "Agreed."

Dalt took a step forward, so furious Katharine expected flames to shoot from his nostrils. "She can make all the claims she wants, but this island belongs to me. Me and Burch," he conceded. "Now take the damn box and git off our land."

"Not the box!" Chase stumbled across the plot and fell to his knees beside it. "It was made by my great-great . . ." He stopped and looked helplessly toward Dalt.

"Your great-great-great-great-granddaddy," Dalt coached him.

Chase nodded. "He made it," he repeated helplessly. He rubbed his hand over its surface and tears glistened in his eyes.

Posey had reached into her purse for a notebook and was busy writing out a receipt.

Dr. Flo called to Ned, "I have no objection to your opening the box right now. We can put the contents into one of Mr. Sykes's boxes, if he will provide one, and I will be glad to leave this box for Chase. It is possible that his own considerable talent has come down from the one who made it."

"Don't you open that damn thing here," Dalt warned. "You take it somewhere else and open it in private. You can send the box back to Chase if you want, but don't you dare open it here." On the word *here* he waved one hand to encompass the clearing. He wasn't refering to geography. He didn't want any of the local men to know what it held.

"Okay, here's your receipt," Posey told Burch, "with both our stipulated disclaimers."

Before they left, Dr. Flo shook hands with Mr. Sykes. She would have shaken with Burch and Mona, but they were engrossed in conversation.

Ned and Chase carried the box to the SUV and slid it into the back.

"I thank you so much," Dr. Flo told them.

"You going back to Atlanta tonight?" Chase asked, his voice cracking as boys' voices do.

"No, we're going down to Jekyll for a few days," Posey told him. "I've got a cottage there."

"Have fun." He turned to Katharine. "I'm sorry about somebody shooting at you." With the resilience of youth, he changed the subject. "Miranda's granny took Samson, Agnes's dog. Did you know?"

Katharine was as glad as he to have a happier topic to discuss. "No, I hadn't heard. The cats are doing well. I'm calling them Phebe and Savant, and they're beginning to settle in. My niece's friend is feeding them this weekend."

"That's good." He took an uncertain step toward the cemetery. "Well, I guess I ought to get back. Mama wants me over there while they dig up all those folks." He didn't sound thrilled by the prospect.

As she started her engine, Katharine wondered if she would have insisted that Jon and Susan attend a similar event. Her last mental picture of Bayard Island would forever be Chase standing in the clearing, his hand raised in a final salute.

Chapter 34

As they jounced toward the asphalt road, Katharine admonished Posey, "Don't you know you can get in trouble claiming to be a lawyer when you aren't?"

Posey's blue eyes widened. "But I am. Didn't you know? I graduated from law school right before I married Wrens, and worked until the babies started coming. I even keep up my license to practice in Georgia." She patted her golden curls. "If Wrens ever throws me out or loses all his money, I want to have something to fall back on."

"Which is about as likely as a snowstorm on our way to Jekyll," Hollis pointed out from the backseat, where she sat with Dr. Flo.

Katharine vowed to warn Hollis privately never to take economic security for granted. If rapid poverty could happen to Dr. Flo, it could happen to anybody.

At the moment, she still had a bone or two to pick with Posey. "Why didn't you ever tell me?" She could not have said why she felt so put out, but she did. "And is your name really Persephone?" Twenty-seven years they had been friends as well as sisters-in-law. Why would Posey, who chattered constantly, have kept both her name and her profession secret all that time?

Posey glowered. "Why that popped out this afternoon, I'll never know. If you ever mention it again, it will be *me* shooting *you* across a clearing. I have never understood how

Mama could saddle me with such a name." Her giant sigh was a plea for sympathy.

Katharine wasn't feeling sympathetic at the moment. Posey had ripped off a mask and turned into somebody else. "I still can't understand why you never told me you were a lawyer."

Posey shrugged. "I guess it never came up. I quit about the time you started dating Tom, and after that I was busy with the girls, then you all were getting married, and we've always had other things to talk about. But it's never been a secret. The whole family knows."

"Except me." Finally Katharine identified why she was so hurt. She had no brothers or sisters, and no cousins. With her own parents gone, Tom's family was the only one she had. She resented "the whole family" knowing something she didn't.

Posey—often quick to understand what others were feeling—laid a soft hand on Katharine's arm. "Don't look at me like I'm a criminal. I wasn't deliberately keeping secrets. I don't mention being a lawyer because I don't want people thinking they can call me for free advice, but I'm not ashamed of it or anything. My name, now—I don't let that skeleton out of the closet very often. Nobody, and I mean nobody, has called me by it since I was six. How I could have blurted it out this afternoon . . ." She shook her head in disgust.

"You know what they say," Dr. Flo contributed from the backseat. "The best-kept secret is one everybody knows."

Katharine wondered what other secrets the Murray-Buiton clan might have in their joint closets, but now was not the time to ask. She had one more concern, far more serious.

"One secret I wish you had kept was where we are headed. You told Chase flat out that we're going to Jekyll, and he and Mona know exactly where the house is. If he tells somebody else—well, one of those people was shooting at Dr. Flo a few hours ago."

Posey pressed one palm to her cheek in consternation. "That didn't cross my mind. Chase is such a nice boy, I answered without thinking." She turned around to face Dr. Flo. "Do you want us to skip Jekyll and go on back home?"

Dr. Flo considered. "I'll admit I'm a bit nervous about staying this close to the Bayards, but I'm also so weary that all I want is a good night's sleep. They're going to be busy at that cemetery pretty late, so I doubt they'd come after us tonight. Could we go home tomorrow? Mr. Sykes seems competent to handle the re-burials without me. I'll come down later to visit Rodney, and I can see the new graves then."

They inevitably drifted into a discussion of the mysterious box. "You all really don't know what's in it?" Hollis climbed on her knees to examine it.

"No idea," Dr. Flo assured her.

"But Dalton did," said Katharine.

Posey drew her eyebrows together until she remembered that caused wrinkles. "Why did Dalton laugh so hard he nearly wet himself when you said the Guilberts were Mallery's children? They were, weren't they?"

"We thought so from the letters," Dr. Flo said in a thoughtful tone, "but I'm beginning to wonder if they could have been Marie and the captain's children, whom Mallery was trying to keep safe."

"He called them his greatest treasures," Katharine reminded her. "Besides, in that case, you wouldn't be related to the Bayards."

"Hooray! I'm all for that."

"I thought it was real rude, that old man telling everybody about his son falling into his mother's grave," Hollis said fiercely.

"I was surprised to hear that Burch's mother died when he was six," Katharine added. "Imagine being raised by that old curmudgeon. It's a marvel he turned out as well as he has."

"He's not too bad," Dr. Flo admitted. "Caught between a rock and a hard place, with Mona urging him to sell the land and his daddy yelling bloody murder if he does."

"Not to mention a lifetime of having it hammered into his head that Bayard Island and Bayard Bluff are the center of the universe."

Posey turned around so she could watch Dr. Flo and Hollis's faces when she asked, "What about the scene when that woman claimed her daughter is Dalt's?"

That occupied them for several miles. "Her poor husband," Dr. Flo said thoughtfully. "He must have believed Nell was his little girl, don't you think? I loved that picture of him taking her with him on his tractor."

"A tippy tractor," Katharine reminded her. "We'll never know what he knew or didn't. Like you once told me, the dead don't take their money, but they take their stories."

"The one I feel sorry for is Chase," mused Posey. "That child is so gorgeous, I wanted to take him home and help him forget he's a Bayard. You don't reckon there's anything we could do for him, do you?"

"I hope he or one of his kinfolks doesn't try to do something to Dr. Flo," Katharine said softly, for her ears only. "I still wish you hadn't told him where we'd be."

Posey's eyes grew dark. "You think somebody might still want to hurt her?"

Katharine shrugged. "She still has a valid claim on Agnes's property, and you saw how fierce the Bayards are about that island. I won't feel safe until we're back in Atlanta."

Posey slumped back in her seat and didn't say another word.

Dr. Flo called up, "Remember what Nell said about Chase, Katharine?"

"Chase isn't out of the woods yet," Katharine intoned solemnly. "The sins of the fathers are visited on their children to the third and fourth generation. It's Nell I feel sorriest for in that regard, though. I don't think she knew before today that Dalt was her daddy, and Burch sure hadn't suspected. The only good thing from Nell's perspective is that after this, the Bayards may increase their pressure on Iola to leave the island."

"You don't really believe all that stuff about kids suffering for the sins of their parents, do you?" Hollis asked Dr. Flo. "I'm not going to suffer for Mama's sins, am I?"

Everybody laughed except Posey, who was staring out the windshield with her brow puckered in spite of wrinkles.

Dr. Flo pulled a pillow out of her carryall and tucked it behind her back. "Actually, that thing about the generations is in the Bible, except what it says is 'I, the Lord thy God, am a jealous God, visiting the iniquity of the fathers upon the children unto the third and fourth generation of them that hate me.'"

Katharine was impressed. "How do you know that by heart?"

"I grew up memorizing the Bible. Used to win all sorts of prizes for it. It took me a few years longer to get it from my head to my heart, though. That was when I started trying to get to the root of things. Do you care to know what I found out about that particular verse?"

"I do," Hollis said promptly. "Does it give me a loophole out of suffering for Mama's mistakes?"

"Maybe. What I discovered is, Hebrew has different words for sin and iniquity. Sin is a temporary or one-time lapse into immorality—mistakes, if you will. Iniquity is general all-round wickedness, an evil condition of the heart, an attitude toward life and toward others. God defines iniquitous people as 'them that hate me.' But before you get too paranoid about that, Hollis, there is a chapter in Ezekiel where

God promises that if the child of an unrighteous person turns around and does right, they won't be punished for their parents' sins."

"Whew." Hollis gave an exaggerated sigh of relief. Posey turned to make a face at her.

Dr. Flo went on as if uninterrupted. "Still, the effects of iniquity can definitely be felt three generations down. I have a theory—"

Katharine was feeling too muggy for a coherent theological discussion. She should never have drunk three glasses of champagne. She certainly should not be driving. Spying a restaurant sign ahead, she said, "Before you share your theory, does anybody besides me need a cup of coffee and a piece of homemade pie? Buckhead's coming up."

The sign advertised THE BUCK HEAD ONE MILE. HOME-MADE PIES.

The Buck Head, when they reached it, was a seedy wood-and-glass building surrounded by a sandy, unpaved lot occupied by two cars.

Katharine pulled in. "The *Open* sign is lit. Shall we give it a try?"

Posey looked at the establishment and wrinkled her nose. "Lordy, Katharine, the places you have taken me today."

"Stick with me, baby. I'll show you the world."

The restaurant had a floor of red vinyl tile, yellow walls hung with the heads of four wistful looking bucks, chartreuse booths, yellow tabletops, and yellow, green, and orange striped curtains. "Shades on," Posey said, pulling hers down from the top of her head as they entered.

"Stop it!" Hollis hissed. "You're embarrassing us."

"Hiss at Katharine. She may be giving us all ptomaine poisoning. But law, look at the meringue on top of that chocolate pie. It must be three inches thick!" She instructed the waitress, "Cut me as big a piece as you can for the price."

She turned to her companions and whispered, "First, I need a lipstick break. Do you think the bathroom will be clean?"

"I aim to find out." Dr. Flo started toward a set of doors labeled DOES and BUCKS.

Katharine's phone rang. "Maybe that's Tom!" Posey exclaimed.

"Tom's getting ready to go to a party," Katharine reminded her. While Posey followed Dr. Flo, she stepped outside so her call wouldn't disturb the three other customers.

It was Hasty. "I don't want to be a pest, but I've been worrying about you all afternoon. How did things go down there?"

She opened her mouth to say a brief "Mission accomplished" and found a cataract pouring out. Her energy rushed out with the story until she felt so weak she had to sit on the curb to finish. It reminded her of times in high school when she had carried the phone out the back door (as far as the cord would reach) to sit on the steps and talk to Hasty.

He whistled when she described the sniper, fumed when she told him the deputy was dismissing the incident as a hunting accident, and interrupted before she finished telling about the aftermath of lifting Mallery's stone. "You all are coming straight back to Atlanta, right? There are currents in all this I don't like at all."

"I know that, and part of me wishes we could. I'm so tired I could sleep a week. But Dr. Flo is wearier than I am, and she's wanting to stay down here, so we've decided to proceed as planned. We may be coming back tomorrow."

"But none of the Bayards know where you will be, right?"

"Not exactly." She told about Posey's slip to Chase. "And he and Mona were there Tuesday night."

He was silent so long she thought she had lost the connection. "Hasty? Are you there?"

"I'm here," he said soberly, "but I don't like this, Katie-bell. I don't like it at all."

On that cheerful note, she went inside to join the others.

"Tom?" Posey inquired, her eyes so wide that her eyebrows met her fluffy bangs.

Hollis didn't say anything, but her head was cocked to one side like she was ready to pass judgment without hearing the case.

Katharine was too tired for the hassle. "Did you order for me?"

"I did," Hollis told her. "I ordered you warm blueberry pie with vanilla ice cream on top. Dr. Flo and I got peach, so we can swap if you like."

"Blueberry's fine. Let me go wash my hands." She had never trusted those waterless sanitizers.

She returned to find that the pie and coffee had been served. Posey, back to her usual cheerful self, was tucking into an enormous piece of chocolate. Hollis and Dr. Flo were engaged in their earlier discussion.

"But you don't think God *punishes* folks, do you, Dr. Flo? God can't blame a kid for what its parents and grandparents did."

Dr. Flo laughed. The discussion seemed to be rejuvenating her. "God is God, honey. God can do whatever God wants to do. But if a child lives in a family that is prejudiced, dishonest, selfish, or violent, chances are good the child will grow up that way, too—and get punished for it. Ask kids in juvenile detention center where they learned to lie, steal, shoot, hit, or do drugs."

"They're being punished by society, not God," Hollis argued.

"Who created society? God is big on delegation." She took time to eat some pie and sip her coffee. "Aside from children picking up iniquity from their parents, there is also the matter of natural consequences. They frequently take three generations to mature. It wasn't the folks who wrote Jim Crow laws who had to deal with race riots, Civil Rights marches, and burning cities. It was their grandchildren."

Katharine hadn't been listening closely until then, but she took a break from pie to point out, "A lot of blacks suffered, too—in all three generations." Her dad had been a Civil Rights lawyer. She had heard a number of horror stories.

"Of course," Dr. Flo agreed. "Wherever there is iniquity, other people suffer. But it was the third generation of whites who suffered the consequences of their grandparents' iniquity."

Hollis abruptly switched sides. "Or look at the environment right now. Folks who are paving over forests, warming up the atmosphere, and spewing gases into the air—they aren't the ones who will suffer the consequences of their carelessness. It's their children and grandchildren. Pretty soon we'll all be walking around in gas masks and living in bubbles."

Posey tried to interject humor into the proceedings. "No more trips to the beach cottage."

Hollis huffed. "Get real, Mama. There won't *be* a beach cottage. Augusta will have ocean-front property by then."

Dr. Flo shied back from their confrontation with a self-conscious little laugh. "Did I start all this? Maurice would be saying around now, 'Flo-baby, if the ladies had wanted a sermon, they'd have gone to church.' Sorry. I didn't mean to get carried away."

As Katharine finished her pie, she thought about her SUV. It had gotten pretty beaten up all that week. Maybe it was time to listen to her daddy and trade it in on a hybrid car.

"It works both ways, doesn't it?" she mused. "Parents and grandparents can also pass on virtues to their children. I figure one reason I'm a relatively moral, law-abiding person is that I had moral, law-abiding parents."

Dr. Flo swallowed a bite of pie as she nodded. "Me, too.

Every time I read a story about somebody going bad, I think 'There, but for the grace of my upbringing, go I.'"

"Oh, sure," Hollis protested. "I can see you now, shoving a needle into your arm or having a string of illegitimate babies. You're too smart for that."

Dr. Flo snorted. "Of course I am. I'd have cooked corporate books instead. I could do that. I've got the know-how. But I also have a conscience, thanks to my parents."

"We were all lucky to have good parents," Posey agreed. She added with a sideways look at Hollis, "But you have to choose to decide to follow their values."

Hollis wrinkled her nose. "The good ones."

Posey signaled for the bill. "I need another potty break after all that coffee."

Dr. Flo slid from the booth behind her. "May I join you?"

"You've been mighty quiet these last few minutes," Hollis told Katharine. "Are you tired? You've done almost all the driving so far."

"It's not that. I've been wondering what it is that Dalt knows and we don't. As soon as we get to Jekyll, I want to use Dr. Flo's laptop to look up the Bayards in the 1850 census. It occurs to me that Mallery Bayard could have been Francis Bayard's older son. That might mean that his descendant—Dr. Flo—could own the whole blessed island. Maybe that's why they were so willing to give her the box and get rid of us."

"This place has a wireless connection."

Katharine stared. "How do you know that?"

Hollis pointed to a back booth. "That kid over there is checking e-mail on his laptop. Want me to go get my computer?" Katharine handed her the keys, marveling at Hollis's attention to details around her.

When Hollis returned, Katharine logged on to ancestry. com and pulled up the 1850 census for Chatham County.

Her eyes widened as she read the entry for Francis Bayard's household. "Look at this." She pointed and Hollis followed her finger.

"Cool! Is Dr. Flo in for a surprise!"

When the other two came back from the restroom, Hollis welcomed them with a grin. "We've found Mallery. Come look."

She turned the computer around to face them.

In 1850, Francis Bayard was thirty-two. He lived in Savannah. His occupation was "Planter." The value of his real estate was eight thousand dollars. Others in his household were Elizabeth, twenty-seven, Mallery, nine, and Claude.

Dr. Flo's brows rose above her glasses. "Oh, my!"

In the next column, Mallery's sex was marked with a large *F*.

"A girl?" Posey squeaked. "The pirate was a girl?"

Dr. Flo slid onto the bench and peered closer at the screen. Her lips twisted this way and that while she thought that over. "By the time the war came, Mallery would have been what? Twenty? Maybe she ran off and joined a privateer. There were a few women pirates. Maybe there were women privateers, as well."

Katharine did a calculation. "Claude would have been thirteen. Maybe he was good with a chisel and proud of his big sister at that time."

Dr. Flo reached for the keyboard. "Let me look at something else."

She called back up the McIntosh County census for 1880. This time, she requested a blank census form and enlarged it. When it appeared on the screen, she gave a grunt of satisfaction. "I thought so. By then they were listing where the parents of each person were born, as well as the person themselves. Let's look at Claude Guilbert again."

She found the listing for Marie Guilbert and moved the

cursor to the far right. "Now we know why Dalton laughed." She pointed. "We could have found this earlier if we'd thought to look. Claude's daddy was born in Haiti, but his mother was born in Georgia."

"The unforgiveable sin," Hollis said with a grimace. "Mallery Bayard had a black man's babies."

Chapter 35

Katharine, Hollis, and Posey could scarcely wait to get to Jekyll and open the chest, but Dr. Flo said little on the drive. As soon as Katharine pulled into the garage, Hollis and Posey wrestled the box out of the back and Hollis started scouting for something to break the padlock.

In the middle of that, Katharine's cell phone rang once more.

"That will be Tom," Posey said confidently.

"Tom's heading to a party." Besides, the screen said it was Hasty again. "I'll go out in the courtyard where I can hear better."

"Or something." Hollis sounded incredibly cross.

Katharine went to the far side of the courtyard, out of earshot.

"Are you at your sister-in-law's yet?" he demanded.

"Just got here. We're about to open the pirate's chest, if we can find something to open it with. The padlock's rusty. Can I call you back?"

"How about your tire iron?"

"You are an angel." She could have bitten her tongue. Hasty was so prone to take things more seriously than she meant them.

"Do you need an angel flying to your rescue? You may, if you are staying in that house."

"The place has a great security system." She said it as

much for her own reassurance as for his, and didn't mention that the whole back wall was glass. "We'll be okay."

"Your house had a great security system, too. People still got in. Twice."

Her temper flared. "Keep talking like that and your angel badge will be revoked. You're already losing your halo."

"I prefer to be a realist. Why don't you all go to a motel?"

It was tempting, but Dr. Flo would never let Katharine pay, and she couldn't afford a motel. "We'll be all right. Now let me off the phone so I can fetch a tire iron."

"You really ought to bring the chest home and let qualified people open it. You could do all sorts of damage." His warning reminded her that Hasty the friend was also Dr. Hobart Hastings, the historian.

"We'll be careful. And Hasty? Don't call again. It's making Hollis nervous."

"You're making me nervous. You could be in real danger, you know."

"I know," she said soberly. "We'll be careful."

He grew cheerful again. "Go see what's in that trunk. And call me if you find anything of intrinsic historical value."

She hung up wishing Tom was that interested in things that interested her. Immediately she felt guilty for the thought. Tom would be interested once he got home and had time to listen properly. He was a real good listener when he wasn't preoccupied with business.

She was tempted to call him, but when she checked her watch, she calculated he'd be on his way to pick up Ashley. "May you break out in spots and have a terrible hair night," she muttered to the woman as she went back in the garage, where Hollis was attacking the lock futilely with a large screwdriver. "Let's try my tire iron," Katharine suggested.

"Smart lady," Posey exclaimed.

If I'm so smart, why do I enjoy Hasty so much when I'm married to Tom?

Hollis was eying her with narrowed lids. "Whose idea was the tire iron really?"

Katharine shrugged. "What difference does that make? It might work."

Dr. Flo watched while the other three strained and heaved. At last the lock snapped. Katharine stepped back. "It's all yours, Dr. Flo."

Hollis held up one hand. "Before you open it, let's each make a guess what's in there. Dr. Flo, you go first."

Katharine was startled to hear the professor echo one of her own fears.

"I'm betting on the bones of an illegitimate baby. I'm trying to like Mallery, but I have a very poor opinion of a woman who has children by a lover, then abandons them to her prejudiced brother. I hope we'll discover she had a real good reason to leave home."

"Maybe the baby was the child of incest," Hollis suggested.

"Whoa!" Posey lifted crossed forefingers to ward off evil. "You all are freaking me out. I'm hoping for pieces of eight, whatever they are."

"I'd be very happy with that," Dr. Flo agreed. "Katharine?"

"I suspect we'll find Mallery's effects, sent back home after she died."

"No fair," Hollis grumbled. "That's what I was going to say. It's the only things her parents had to bury."

"That is the most likely." Dr. Flo reached for the top of the box. "Here goes."

The lid creaked in protest as she lifted it. The others held back and let her look first. "Katharine and Hollis win. It's mostly clothes."

"Fantastic!" Hollis bent over the box. Dr. Flo pulled out a stack of letters tied with faded red ribbon and what must have once been an exquisite doll with painted golden hair and a pink satin dress. The head was still intact.

"Let me get something to lay the stuff on," Posey suggested. "Hollis, fetch that tarp."

"Let *me* get something to lay the stuff on?" Hollis repeated as she unfolded the sheet of yellow plastic and laid it on the floor. "You need to get this straight, Mama. I am not you. Handle the clothes carefully, Dr. Flo. They could fall apart when you lift them."

"You lift them out, then." Dr. Flo laid the doll on the tarp and climbed stiffly to her feet, holding the letters. "Maybe these are the ones Mallery got in answer to those we already have. Some could be from Marie."

Katharine had a growing suspicion Dr. Flo wasn't interested in a trunk full of a white woman's possessions. That was confirmed a second later. "I keep hoping we'll find something to prove the children were Marie's and the captain's, and that Mallery was just real fond of them, like I am of Rodney."

"Then what was the scandal?" Katharine asked.

"I don't know. Nothing in here seems to shed any light on anything—especially why Dalt was so determined to get rid of this stuff." Instead of reading the letters, she watched Hollis lift out a blue cotton bodice with dainty flowers.

"This would have been part of a dress. And this was a skirt, and this a petticoat. See? It has a place for her hoop. These are marvelous! Look! Ball gloves!" They fell like snakes, stained white gloves long enough to cover the elbow.

"Did pirates have balls?" Posey asked. Hollis snickered. "I meant dances," Posey protested.

A few garments later Hollis announced, "That's it except

for a book and something flat. They're both wrapped in oil-cloth, and the book looks real heavy."

"Might as well see what they are." Dr. Flo handed Posey the letters. Posey untied the ribbon and began to read the first one.

Hollis lifted out the flat parcel and unwrapped it. "Oh!" It was an oil portrait showing the head and shoulders of a girl in her late teens. She wore a white dress that bared her shoulders, and long white gloves. A red camellia was tucked in her bodice. She had an oval face, wide cheekbones, eyes like chips of sapphire, and blond hair curling to her shoulders.

"You beauty!" Posey breathed.

"I'll bet she was a flirt," Katharine guessed. "She has the smile of an imp."

Posey held up the letter she had been reading. "She went to school in Charleston. This is all about boys she was meeting at the Citadel. I'll bet she broke some hearts."

Hollis reached for the painting. "You think this was Mallery? Why would they have buried her portrait?" She propped it up against a tire so they could all look at it.

"They wouldn't want it hanging in the family gallery if those children were hers," Dr. Flo pointed out. "She's certainly not what I ever expected to hang on my family wall."

Hollis lifted out the book and sat cross-legged on the garage floor with it on her lap. As she began to unwrap it, Posey bent over to watch. "It's a family Bible, looks like. Does it have one of those family pages?"

"You look at it, Dr. Flo." Hollis hoisted it above her head. "It belongs to you, and after it has been buried so long, I don't know if it will fall apart. I certainly don't want to damage it."

Dr. Flo took the Bible and laid it on the hood of the SUV. "It's been buried over a hundred years while nobody cared a thing about it," she snapped. "I don't think we have to worry about hurting it. Katharine, would you get my reading glasses from my pocketbook?"

With them perched on her nose, she turned past the first pages. "Here's the family page. The Bible was presented to Francis Bayard and Elizabeth Mallery on the occasion of their marriage by her parents, but the first entry is for William Bayard, who was born in 1720 and who established Bayard Bluff in 1754. Looks like Francis was a typical Bayard. Elizabeth's mother may have given her the Bible, but he used it to record the Bayard family history. Here at the tail end are Francis, Elizabeth, and—oh, my!"

She looked down in dismay. Hollis climbed to her feet and they all went to surround Dr. Flo. Beside Mallery's name were a birth date—June 19, 1841—and her date of death: August 14, 1870. The whole entry had been crossed and recrossed with a heavy, unforgiving line.

"She didn't die in 1870," Katharine objected. "She was alive eight years later."

Posey had retrieved a piece of paper from the garage floor. "Did this fall out of the Bible?"

Dr. Flo opened it, read it, laid it on the Bible, and crossed both hands over it. "Thank God."

"What is it?" Posey could hardly contain her curiosity.

"A marriage certificate." Dr. Flo picked it up again. "It's in French, and says, 'I certify that Mallery Frances Bayard and Henri Guilbert were married before me this fourteenth day of August, 1870.' It's signed by Father Reynauld Achilles, priest of St. Pierre's Catholic Church, Port-au-Prince, and one of the witnesses was Marie Guilbert. Marie must have been Henri's sister, the children's auntie—and my great-great aunt." She pressed her lips together and blinked back tears. When she could control her voice she looked up at Katharine and whispered, "They were married. The children's parents were married."

Until that moment, Katharine hadn't realized how much that mattered to Dr. Flo.

"They buried everything that belonged to or reminded them of her." Hollis burned with indignation. "Her doll, her clothes, even her picture!"

Dr. Flo fetched the portrait and looked long and gently at the face of Mallery Bayard. "Your papa disowned and buried you before your time and your brother refused to save you from death, all because you married a man they would not accept. My poor, poor great-grandmother."

"Francis died the following year," Katharine said somberly.

Dr. Flo gave a short, unpleasant laugh. "Probably had a stroke when he got this news."

Chapter 36

Posey, coached by Katharine, insisted that Dr. Flo sleep downstairs. After they carried in their bags, the professor said, "If you all don't mind, I'd like to boil an egg and make a cup of tea and some toast, then I'd like to go to bed and read the rest of the letters in private."

When she had retired, Posey rummaged in the freezer and put together a supper of jambalaya, rice, turnips, and corn-bread. "See? I can cook," she told her daughter.

"As long as Julia leaves stuff in the freezer for you to thaw."

"Hush your mouth and set the table. At least I made corn-bread."

"From a Jiffy box."

"If you two don't behave, I'm sending you both to your rooms," Katharine warned.

Posey and Hollis were laughing as they sat down to eat. Katharine didn't want to worry them, but she eyed the glass doors warily. When Posey suggested they carry wine outside for a while after dinner, she objected.

"We've got close neighbors," Posey reminded her. "I think you're being silly."

"The Bayards must guess that we know all about Mallery by now."

"So what? They gave us the stuff, for heaven's sake. And Dr. Flo signed that paper agreeing not to spread their family sins all over. Besides, there are still people on the beach. If you want to sit up all night with a gun in your lap, Wrens has one in the bedroom safe, but I'm taking my wine out on the deck." She picked up the bottle and her own glass and marched out. Katharine and Hollis followed. What else could they do?

Seeing the citronella lamps, the woman next door called, "Is that you, Posey?"

"Sure is. Come on over and have some wine." Posey added in a low voice, "What did I tell you? I never worry about the house when we're not here because if anything happened, Jenny-Jill would call me right away."

"Can we take a rain check?" Jenny-Jill asked.

A man's voice added, "We're waiting for a call from our daughter. She's due to have a baby any minute and I can't get my wife more than twenty feet from the phone."

"I don't blame her one bit. Let us know when the baby comes."

Katharine's cell phone rang. "It's probably Tom," Posey said again. "Third time's the charm."

"Tom is busy," Katharine said firmly. Still, she didn't recognize the number. Perhaps a stranger was calling to tell her he'd had an accident on the way to the party. She carried the telephone out on the boardwalk for better reception.

"Miz Murray, this is Lamar Franklin. I learned something you might be interested in." What Katharine was most interested in was how he'd gotten her cell phone number, but the man seemed to be a master at finding information.

"I got a friend online who specializes in seafaring history, so I asked him about pirates down around Haiti after our War of Secession. He said there weren't many, piracy having pretty much died out in that area by 1850, but there was one feller whose name was—here, let me spell it: H-e-n-r-i G-u-i-l-b-e-r-t. Wasn't that the name you were looking for?"

"Yes, it was."

"Well, he was something of a hero around those parts between 1860 and 1879, when he was captured. He was executed for piracy, and he did take a number of ships, but what he did mostly was sail down to Brazil and help slaves escape. They didn't get around to abolishing slavery down there until some time after we did, and conditions were apparently appalling on the big plantations. Henri Guilbert would take his boat down around the horn of Brazil and pick up slaves who had made it to the coast, then he'd take them back to Haiti. Apparently his wife was something of a nurse and sailed with him. I wondered if these could be the ones Dr. Gadney was looking for."

"They have to be." Her heart was beating fast, and she could hardly wait to tell Dr. Flo. "She's already gone to bed. We've had a long day. But this is so important, I'll wake her up to let her know. Thank you so much."

"You're welcome. I wish I'd found this sooner, but I was up on a roof all day and just got to my computer a little while ago. I've printed out everything I can find online about the feller, plus the e-mail from my friend. I could drop it off by your house sometime tomorrow afternoon, if you like."

"That would be wonderful. I'm not in town, but there's a young woman staying there who is feeding my cats."

"I already spoke to her. She gave me this number. Okay, I'll leave it with her. Hope this is helpful."

"It's amazing," Katharine assured him. "Thank you so much."

Katharine hurried in and found Dr. Flo sitting with the letters in her lap. "Mallery did sail with a privateer," the professor announced. "She wrote her mother and father that she couldn't stand it that their cousin John was going to sea and she had to stay behind because she was a woman. Later she wrote that she had cut her hair and signed on with the *Retribution,* and nobody knew she was a girl until after they sailed. Apparently after that, they accepted her as part of the crew because she had some nursing skills. One letter was written from the Bahamas. I'd guess that's where she met Henri Guilbert."

"Wait until you hear what I've just learned from Lamar."

When Katharine finished, Dr. Flo clasped her hands on the bedspread. "They rescued slaves? No wonder my daddy was tediously adamant that his people were never slaves. And no wonder Mallery's daddy was furious. Right after he'd lost his slaves and his livelihood, his daughter marries a man who is foreign and black, and whose life's mission is helping slaves."

"What a wonderful heritage!" Katharine reached out and hugged her.

Dr. Flo's eyes shone. "It is, isn't it? I'll proudly hang Mallery on my wall, and I'll sleep well tonight. Good night." She lifted one hand and touched Katharine's cheek briefly.

Now that she knew the whole story, though, Katharine returned to the deck and looked around apprehensively. If Mona had feared the paper getting wind of blacks buried in their family cemetery, how much more would the family fear the whole truth coming out?

The sky was growing dark. The dunes loomed as large shadows. While she could hear the ocean, she could barely see it. Normally she would have been suggesting a walk at that time of night. At the moment, all she wanted was to get everybody inside and arm the security system.

She sat down again long enough to tell the others what Lamar had discovered.

"Freeing slaves!" Hollis said the words like she had discovered a new world. "That ought to make Dr. Flo like Mallery better."

"It has. In time, Dr. Flo may even forgive her for leaving the children in Georgia while she sailed with her husband."

They sat for a few minutes chatting about the new discovery. Then Posey cocked her head. "Was that the phone?" Nobody else had heard it. Posey hurried inside and came right back out. "I guess it was my imagination. Katharine, aren't you going for your usual walk on the beach? I see people out there still. You ought to be perfectly safe."

Katharine's first impulse was to demand, "Are you crazy?" But then she realized, *She's so used to Wrens doing all the worrying for her, I think she's forgotten how.* Oddly, Katharine felt grateful to Tom for helping her learn to stand on her own two feet.

If Posey wouldn't take their danger seriously, though, Katharine needed to take it seriously for all of them. Maybe it would be wise to leave the house and check it all the way around from the outside on her return.

Or was she just rationalizing what she wanted so badly to do?

Accustomed to being alone most of the time, Katharine was feeling antsy from too many hours at a stretch in the close company of other women. She could use some solitude. Besides, it was a lovely night for a walk. The surf was pounding in her ears like a lover's call.

"I don't like leaving you all alone," she made one more half-hearted protest.

"We'll be fine," Posey insisted. "We're going in as soon as I finish my drink."

"Will you promise to arm the security system?"

"Of course. I'm not dumb. I'll even get out Wrens's gun and put it where we can get to it easily, if necessary. And you take your cell phone. Take a key, too, in case I turn in before you get back—and don't go too far."

Katharine was half afraid Hollis would want to come along, but Hollis yawned and said, "I think I'll go on up to bed. I was sewing real late last night."

Katharine fetched her phone and a key and made her way along the darkened boardwalk to the beach. *I won't be gone long,* she promised Tom silently. He'd never forgive her if she let anything happen to his sister or his niece.

She walked at the water's edge, enjoying the sudden flash of a wave in the dimness, the hard sand under her feet. There were enough other walkers—both people and dogs—for her to feel safe. Worry trailed off her like beads of water. When a wave rolled higher than she had expected and splashed her to the knees, she laughed. "I am so glad I got to do this!" she said aloud. "It's exactly what I needed at the end of this day."

She went much farther than she had planned. Only when she saw a house that was the landmark for her long morning walks did she realize she ought to be getting back.

As she turned, the moon went behind thick clouds and a gentle rain began to fall.

Next door to Posey's, Jenny-Jill Roberts was uneasy. The thought of her daughter having that baby without her was driving her crazy. Why had those kids decided to do this on their own?

"We'll call you as soon as the baby is here," her son-in-law had promised, "but we want this to be a bonding experience for the three of us."

Lordy, those kids had no idea of all the things that could go wrong with a birth. Jenny-Jill, who had dropped three children so easily her husband teased she had "textbook deliveries," imagined every single complication happening to her only daughter over in Valdosta, with her mother miles away. What if the baby was breech? What if the contractions wouldn't strengthen? What if they went on and on, leaving poor Jennifer too weak and limp to push?

As was her custom, after she had watched the Jay Leno show on the bedroom TV, Jenny-Jill stepped out onto her back deck for one last look at the ocean. A light rain was falling, almost a mist. She lifted her face to greet it. The sky was a flat charcoal and all color had drained from the earth. Between their house and the ocean, the dunes were a drab, mysterious gray. She could not see much of the water except an occasional flash of white, but she knew it was out there, and she could hear its relentless approach to land. *Splash! Suck. Splash! Suck.* Jenny-Jill took a deep breath to fill her lungs with salt air and winged her nightly prayer of thanksgiving for the ever-fresh miracle that she and Jeff had been able to buy a house on the ocean for their retirement. Some people took oceanfront property as their due. Jenny-Jill never would.

Back in the house Jeff snorted and then resumed a low, steady snore. The den TV was still showing *High Noon*, but he was sprawled on the couch sleeping not like a baby—no mother ever coined that expression—but like the friendly drunk he tended to become when Jenny-Jill got grumpy. She'd have to rouse him to get him to bed.

As she turned to go in, she saw movement on her neighbor's deck. Hadn't she heard them drive out some time ago? Maybe Posey's daughter or sister-in-law had been out on the beach. Maybe they'd like to come over for a glass of wine.

She opened her mouth to call, but hesitated. The figure was dressed all in black and peering in Posey's sliding glass doors, keeping to one side so it could not be seen. As it shifted, Jenny-Jill saw something glint. Dear God in heaven, was that a rifle?

Weak in the knees, Jenny-Jill hurried inside. She locked her door and pulled the vertical blinds. Then she rushed to shake Jeff.

"Hon? I think there's somebody trying to break in next door. And I think he's got a gun."

"What? Huh?" Jeff sat up and rubbed his face. "Is the baby here?"

"No, I saw somebody on Posey's deck. Do you think I ought to call 911?"

"They've got a houseful of people over there. It was probably one of them." He pulled himself to his feet and lumbered toward the bedroom. "Come on to bed."

"In a minute."

Jenny-Jill went to the sliding glass doors off the living room, the ones nearest Posey's house, and pressed her ear to the glass. Was that glass breaking? She strained to listen. A minute later, she jumped. Had that been a shot?

She went to the phone and stood in painful indecision. She didn't want to make a fool of herself. Should she call 911?

Chapter 37

Walking on the beach in a light rain was normally one of Katharine's great pleasures. She took deep breaths of the salty air, lifted her face to the misty rain, and enjoyed ripple waves tickling her toes while breakers boomed out of sight.

Gradually, however, her contentment dissipated. As scenes from the afternoon replayed in her mind, she felt rain seeping through her clothes and the dark night seeping into her soul. When she looked about her and realized all the other walkers had vanished, she grew uneasy.

The cell phone in her pocket was a connection to the house, but Posey was probably in bed. Besides, Katharine disliked getting calls from people waiting at airports or stuck in traffic, who called to fill their own empty moments. She toyed with the idea of ringing Tom at his party, but Ashley would think her pathetic. She stood ankle-deep in water for a moment of indecision, then punched the buttons to redial Hasty's number. Because she was nervous—she wasn't in the habit of calling him. Would he make too much of the call?—she began without preamble as soon as he answered.

"I said I'd let you know what we found in the box." She walked up onto firm sand and strode briskly home while she filled him in on the box's contents, the letters, and what Lamar had said. He was suitably impressed—and, being Hasty, pontificated about what Dr. Flo should do with the contents of the box because of their historical value.

Katharine, however, felt curiously flat. "I keep wondering. Has a single thing been accomplished this week besides adding a couple more branches to Dr. Flo's family tree?"

"They are pretty impressive branches."

"I know, but there still seem to be an awful lot of loose ends. Agnes's murder, if that's what it was, is unlikely to be solved. It has officially been declared an accident. Dr. Flo's claim to part of Bayard Island isn't likely to be settled without a legal battle she—" Katharine stopped just before she blurted "can't afford." "—doesn't need. And what about the island itself? It's probably going to get covered with garage Mahals, just like the rest of the coast."

"You're in a lovely mood, Katie-bell. Are there any nails around you could chew?"

Her foot hit something sharp. "Ow! I think I just stepped on one."

"Are you bleeding?"

"I don't know. Let me see." She grabbed the injured foot and rubbed an exploratory finger along it. "I guess not." She felt around in the sand for the offending object. "It was just a conch. But it's a good symbol of Bayard Island: perfect on one side and broken on the other."

"Where are you?" His voice was suddenly sharp with concern.

"Walking on the beach. Posey's lights just came into view."

"You have been telling me all day what danger you've been in, and you're walking on the beach at this hour? Who's with you?"

"Nobody, but there were lots of other people out walking when I started." Again she peered around, but saw no other walkers. She picked up her pace, glad of his company even if it was just a voice. "Did I tell you about what happened at the cemetery, when Iola informed the world that Nell is Dalt's daughter?"

"Twice. It seems to have made a big impression."

"It embarrassed Nell to death. Then Iola started shooting, and they raced out of the clearing like the proverbial bat out of hell. I wonder if Major White ever found her. I hope not, but she can't hide forever. Then Dalt will haul her into court, and she may lose her business and wind up with nothing. I wish Burch had left those graves alone and never started this mess."

"*He* started the mess?" She could picture Hasty's eyebrows rising. "It sounds to me like Francis Bayard started it, disowning and burying his daughter before she died."

"Not to mention Claude, who refused to acknowledge Mallery's children or send her the money to save her life," Katharine agreed.

"Hamilton sounds like he may have been all right."

"Yeah, and Asa might not have been too bad, but he fathered Dalton, who fathered a daughter he refused to claim and who hid the family's dirty linen from his own son." She clenched her fist around the broken conch. "The family record on taking care of their children has been abominable— even Mallery's. Not to mention Iola's, who never told Nell who her father was, but who has been flaunting Dalt's daughter in front of him all these years while refusing to leave the island. Why did I have to get mixed up in their business?"

She hurled the shell into the sea with a silent imprecation: *May you be crushed and broken until you turn to sand.*

"Exactly what I've been asking. Are you at Posey's yet? I won't hang up until you are."

"I'm almost there." Since she didn't have a key to the glass doors at the back, she took a path up to the street. It was reassuringly well lit by halogen lights, and she saw cars passing. "Thanks for listening. I'll let you go, now. I'm out of danger."

"Call anytime. And Katie-bell? Speaking of danger, I want to tell you something. I don't much care what Hollis thinks, but I don't want *you* to see me as a danger. I like you. Hell, I may even still love you. But I don't want to break up your marriage. I don't even want to break up mine, as rotten as it is at the moment. The problem is, I don't want to lose you again, either. Do you hear me?" His voice was as soft and silky as the dry sand sliding between her bare toes.

"I hear you. I even agree."

"So what are we to do?"

"Be friends?"

"More than that. Is there a word for 'more than friends and less than lovers'?"

"Liends?" she tried. "Frovers? I guess there isn't."

"Well, I just want to be there for you when you need me, and to be with you when I can. Is that too much to ask?"

"I don't know," she admitted.

"We'll work it out." He sounded as confident as he used to when they were hopelessly snarled in a geometry problem.

She smiled in the darkness, feeling a blessed sweet lightness of release.

"One more thing," he said. "I once heard your dad say that no lie remains hidden forever—that truth inevitably comes to light. I think he'd say that this week, you've been walking beside Dr. Flo while her family went through the painful process of birthing truth. It wasn't just bodies buried on Bayard Island, you know. There were a lot of underground secrets and lies, waiting for somebody to look hard at those graves. I think your dad would be real proud of what the two of you have done."

She was so touched, she could hardly speak. "That's nice! Thank you. Good night."

As she reached the walk to the house, she lifted a happy face to the misty rain.

She let herself into the house with her key. Because the downstairs lights were still on, she called softly, "Posey? I'm back."

"It's about time."

It was not Posey who came around the staircase. It was Iola Stampers. She was still dressed for the disinterments, but her red skirt was bedraggled, her curls coming down in places, and her mascara smudged. And she held a black pistol like she knew how to use it.

She gestured with the gun. "Come on in. I found this lying real convenient on the kitchen counter."

Dismay rose in Katharine like a tide. "What do you want? Where's Posey?" How and why had Iola chosen their house as her hideout from the sheriff?

"She was gone when I arrived. I been waitin' for you 'n' her. Come on in here." Iola gestured again with the gun.

Katharine walked toward the living room, but under the overhead bridge, she stopped. The vertical blinds had been pulled and loosely closed, but they were rattling in a breeze. A splash of glass littered the floor. And a blood-brown smear marred the tiles near Dr. Flo's door.

Iola saw her notice the stain, and gave a brutal bray. "Your niece was feisty. I gotta give her credit for that. Come on in and sit down."

Katharine's knees turned to mush.

Was feisty? Was Hollis dead? Was Dr. Flo gone, too? Oh, Posey! Thank goodness you weren't here! Or was she? Had she been surprised by the intrusion, pretended to be away, and hidden herself upstairs until Katharine's return?

Katharine brushed raindrops from her hair while she strained to hear any sound in the house, however faint. All she heard was the soft purr of the air conditioning. She raised her voice. "I've been out walking on the beach and I got soaked. Just let me go change my clothes."

Iola shook her head. "You ain't going nowhere. Get in here and sit down." She backed to the couch and settled herself among its cushions, still covering Katharine with the gun. "Fancy place you got here. Must be nice. Sit down, I said!"

Katharine stumbled to the nearest chair and perched on the edge. "It's my sister-in-law's house. We came to visit for a few days." She could feel her soaked pants oozing into the cushion.

"Planning your next move to take over Bayard Island?" Iola inquired.

"Nobody's planning to take over Bayard Island. What gave you that idea?"

"Agnes. She said that friend of yours might inherit her property, and that she'd never sell. I'm curious. How could a black woman own part of the island?"

Katharine sucked saliva to moisten her mouth, which felt very dry. "It's a long story."

"Go ahead. We could have a while before your sister-in-law gets back." The woman was edgy, peering off to each side and then quickly back to make sure Katharine hadn't moved.

Chills ran up Katharine's body that had nothing to do with air conditioning and damp clothes.

When she didn't speak at once, Iola gestured with her gun. "Tell the story—and make it snappy!" Then she gave a raspy bark of laughter. "Sorry. I ain't had a cigarette for a while, and I'm feeling a bit edgy." Katharine looked at the gun and saw it wobble. That was not reassuring. "I don't suppose you got a smoke, have you?" Iola added hopefully.

Katharine shook her head, and although she didn't smoke

and deplored the habit, she heard herself giving the standard well-mannered Southern apology. "No, I'm sorry."

"Well, we might as well have the story, then. Go ahead." Iola lolled back against Posey's cushions, her skirt like a wide bloodstain on the white couch.

"It started before the Civil War, with a girl named Mallery Bayard."

Katharine could usually tell a good story, but it was hard, facing a gun. She kept thinking about that small round hole. She drew the tale out as long as she could, but eventually she ran out of breath and story at the same time.

When she finished, Iola was grinning. "Don't that beat all? Dalton so high and mighty proud of his precious family, and they ain't no better than the rest of us." She scratched one cheek with her free forefinger. "Will your friend sell Burch her part of the island, if she can get a judge to give it to her?"

Katharine was relieved to hear the present tense, but where was Dr. Flo?

And Hollis? Just the thought of Hollis made her throat clog with tears of fear.

She was shaking hard inside, but Katharine willed her voice to be steady. "She hasn't proven her claim yet, so I don't know what she'll do. What do you think she *should* do?" She was as surprised by the question as Iola, but it seemed to relax the woman, put a patina of a normal chat on the bizarre conversation.

Iola settled herself more comfortably among the cushions and dropped the hand holding the gun into her lap. "I think she ought to sell and let Burch bulldoze the whole damned island. Bury it in stucco houses and Yankees." She brayed a laugh. "That'd kill his daddy quicker than anything, and send him straight to hell where he belongs." She puckered her brow and said in a frustrated tone, "I told Agnes—only she wouldn't listen. The only way to get at Dalton Bayard is through his land. He never loved man, woman, or child the way he loves that island."

Katharine stared at her blankly. *Was that what Agnes's death had been about? Revenge on Dalt?*

"When . . .?" She had to stop and clear her throat. "When did you talk to Agnes last?"

"Day after Miranda told us she and Agnes had found a deed proving she owned her land. I took the motor launch from our dock and headed over to her place, and I told her to sell the cemetery bit to Burch and keep her house, but she wouldn't."

Iola added, a touch of regret in her voice, "Agnes was a tough old bird. I always respected her. Your friend's tough, too. I thought I'd scared the living daylights out of her this afternoon. I sure never expected to see you all back at that cemetery."

"That was you shooting at us? You could have killed us!" Too late, Katharine remembered this was no time for indignation. *Dear God, help!*

Iola gave her a rueful grin. "I tried, but she moved. Besides, my dadgum rifle kicks a bit to the left, and I failed to compensate. I really need to replace that thing." She nodded toward the kitchen. Katharine looked over her shoulder and saw a rifle lying on the counter. It looked like the one Iola had aimed at Dalt that afternoon. "Guess I keep it for sentimental reasons, you might say. Dalt gave it to me years ago—it's older than Nell. But like I said, it ain't real accurate. Pulls to the left. I tried to compensate for that when your friend was running for the car, and I nearly got her, too, but it's hard to hit a moving target, and she's fast for an old lady."

"That was my sister-in-law. She exercises a lot." A voice in Katharine's head said, *Keep her talking. Keep her talking.* "But why on earth did you shoot my car?"

Iola grinned again. "For the hell of it. Messed it up right

smart, didn't I? Never did like it that Cadillac started making SUVs. Seems to cheapen the whole line. I've always driven Caddies, and—"

Something crashed on the deck outside.

Iola leaped to her feet like a cat. "What was that?" She headed for the wall of glass, gun cocked and ready.

Katharine didn't wait to find out. She was sprinting for the front door.

Chapter 38

Katharine dashed down the walk and toward sea grape bushes between Posey's and Jenny-Jill's, aware of the open door behind her. Any second she expected a bullet to stop her.

The rain had strengthened. It plastered her hair to her face and her blouse to her chest.

When a cruiser glided to a stop at the curb, she swerved to meet it.

The driver rolled down his window. "Are you the woman who called 911?"

Katharine gasped for air. "No, but I was fixing to. There's a woman in there with a gun." She jerked one thumb toward Posey's.

He climbed out and opened his back door. "Get inside out of the rain, then we'll talk."

She huddled on the vinyl seat, shivering, while he explained, "A neighbor called. Said there were two women in the house and one had a gun."

She spoke through chattering teeth. "I was the other one. Something crashed on the deck and startled us, and when Iola jumped up to check on it, I ran out."

The officer in the passenger seat gave her a keen look. "You know the woman with the gun?"

"Slightly. But listen, my niece and my friend are still in

there somewhere and at least one of them is hurt. You need to get them out!"

The driver reached for his radio. "Possible hostage situation." He asked for help. The officer in the passenger seat shrugged out of his jacket and handed it to Katharine. It was warm from his body. She clutched it gratefully around her as the three of them waited and watched the house. It sat white and solid, keeping its secrets.

Police, fire, and emergency vehicles appeared on the street. None used sirens or flashing lights, but as if a silent message had gone through the neighborhood, people began to creep from nearby houses and crane their necks to see what was going on. A few held umbrellas, prepared for the duration. Two held the hands of small children.

Some faces were avid for excitement as they inched closer to the scene. Katharine wanted to scream at them, "Go to bed! This is not late-evening entertainment!"

But she also saw white, worried faces—expressions that said, "I wish I could help, but all I know to do is stand here in support."

Jenny-Jill was one of those. She had come out without an umbrella, and she was dripping wet, but she stood in her yard with her eyes fixed on Posey's house. Under the halogen streetlight, her hair looked purple and her face sickly white. Her eyes were wide with terror.

"She must be the one who called. Could I go over to thank her?" Katharine asked.

"You'll get soaked," the officer warned.

"I'm already soaked."

She hurried across the squishy St. Augustine grass. "Jenny-Jill? I'm Katharine, Posey's sister-in-law."

That was as far as she got. Jenny-Jill flung her arms around her in a cushiony hug. "Thank God! I hoped you could get out. Did the plant help?"

"Plant?"

"I threw one of the plants off my deck onto yours, hoping it might distract the woman with the gun. It made a gosh-awful mess, but—"

Katharine squeezed her tighter. "You saved my life."

They stepped apart and looked at each other in the rain. "Where are the others?" Jenny-Jill asked anxiously. "Did they all go out? I heard the car leave not an hour ago."

"I'm scared Posey's daughter and our friend may still be inside."

Jenny-Jill pressed one hand to her cheek. "I should have called sooner. I just couldn't decide if anything was wrong or not. Jeff is always saying I have a vivid imagination, but I saw somebody on the deck, then I heard something that could have been a shot. I waited and waited, trying to make up my mind, and finally I decided to go over and just peek in the living room. I didn't mean to pry or anything—"

"I'm so glad you did."

"Me, too, because I saw you and the woman sitting there, and she had a gun. I couldn't think of anything else to do but throw that plant. I hoped it might distract her enough so you could get her gun."

Jenny-Jill had clearly been watching too much television. However, silly as the idea sounded, it had worked.

"Then I called the police." Jenny-Jill's teeth chattered. The rain had a chilly edge. She clutched her arms around her to keep herself warm.

One of the officers spoke behind Katharine. "You should go back inside now, ma'am," he told Jenny-Jill. "The police have the place surrounded and you could be in a line of fire."

Jenny-Jill nodded, but she did not move.

Katharine took her arm and pulled her deeper into her yard, behind an oleander.

The police held a consultation, crouched behind their cars. Among the newcomers was a tall man in civilian clothes who seemed to be in charge. Katharine heard him say, "Where's the woman who got out of the house?"

She left Jenny-Jill and hurried toward him, keeping behind the cars. She arrived breathless, but she hadn't breathed well since she first saw Iola.

"Did you want me? That's my house. Are you planning to go in?"

"Not yet. We hope to talk her out. What can you tell me about the situation?"

"My niece and my friend are in there with a woman and a gun. My friend is over seventy." She filled him in on who Iola was and as much about her as she knew.

He began to talk on a megaphone, his voice calm and persuasive. The neighbors crept closer. Katharine moved over to the shadow of an oleander bush, watching the house.

Suddenly Katharine thought she saw movement in one set of French doors. Was somebody standing in the left-hand pair? She crouched and ran to tell the nearest officer, "I think somebody is looking out of that upstairs room on the left."

"Get down!" he said urgently. "You're visible in the street-light!"

He pushed her down so fast, she fell forward and skinned her knee and palm on the rough street. For long minutes, nothing happened. Her legs began to cramp and her scrapes stung. She sent up silent, desperate prayers.

Down the block a car screeched to a stop. A door slammed and someone pounded up the block. In the streetlight Katharine saw the gleam of Chase's hair. "Daddy! No! No!" he shouted, gasping for breath.

From the other direction, Burch shouted, "I'm okay, son. I'm here." He ran to meet his son.

Katharine saw the French doors open an inch and the glint of a rifle. She yelled, "Chase! Go back!"

The Bayards met where Katharine crouched. A shot rang out. Chase, on the left, fell to the ground.

Another shot. Katharine felt a spurt of blood, sticky and warm, as Burch crumpled on top of her.

An officer dragged her free as a team of paramedics dashed toward them. Mona came pelting down the sidewalk. For once she was not beautiful. She was distraught. "Chase? Chase!" She fell to her knees beside her son and began to scream.

Chase's eyes stared at her but could not see.

Paramedics held her and pinned her arms, but she struggled and fought them. "Not Chase. Not my baby!" They carried her to shelter behind a fire truck.

Katharine was dimly aware of police storming the house, but the officer who had rescued her from Burch was tugging her hand. "Come on! Can you get as far as the bushes over yonder?" Crouched, they scuttled to the shelter of the sea grapes between Posey's and Jenny-Jill's.

Katharine's skinned knee and palm burned like fire. She tasted salt on her lips. She was shivering from shock and rain-soaked clothes.

She could hear Mona speaking disjointed words and phrases. ". . . down here to supper . . . Burch left . . . waiter said hostages . . . this street . . ." Her voice strengthened with anguish. "Chase was scared it was his daddy. He made me come. I drove as fast as I could, but it wasn't Burch. Thank God, it wasn't him. Oh, Burch! Chase!"

Katharine could not bear to hear Mona's anguish and do nothing. She started around the bushes as Mona shouted angrily, "Somebody get my child and husband out of that street!"

As Katharine watched, Mona's knees buckled and she collapsed onto the asphalt, face down and arms spread out.

She lay there, sobbing. Her white neck looked very vulnerable in the rain.

Katharine ran and held her until paramedics came to put Mona on a stretcher and carry her to one of the rescue vehicles.

A shout came from the front door. "We've got her, but somebody get an axe in here!"

Chapter 39

Katharine knelt in the street, her face in her hands, while rain fell around her like a robe. It took her several moments to recognize a familiar voice.

"What in heaven's name is going on here?" She turned her head and saw her SUV creeping slowly down the street. Posey was calling through the driver's window.

An officer stepped to the car and explained.

"My child is in there!" Posey abandoned the car in the street and slid to the ground. With no regard for the rain or the gaping crowd, she dashed up the walk. Several officers stepped forward to hold her, but she wriggled away like an eel and dashed through the open door.

Katharine was trying to summon the energy to stand up and move her car when she saw someone slide over from the passenger seat. She gasped. "Tom?"

He jumped down and hurried toward her, lifted her up, and held her close. "Are you all right? If anything has happened to you—"

Joy took wings in her heart. Tom was here. Not at a party in Washington being charming to Ashley. Here. When she truly needed him, he had come. "I'm fine now." She clung to him.

He held her close for another second or two, but Tom was a pragmatist at heart. "Let's get you in the car. You are soaking wet."

He fetched the stadium blanket she always carried in the back and wrapped it around her before he pulled the car down the street out of the way. When he had turned off the engine, he turned to face her. "The policeman said there's been a shooting. Were you in there? How did you get out? And is Hollis still there?"

"I'm afraid so." In an instant, the adrenalin that had sustained her evaporated. She felt so faint she had to lay her head on her knees for a few seconds.

As she managed to sit erect again, he flicked on the interior lights. "What have you got all over you?" He reached over and touched her forehead and cheeks.

She rubbed one cheek with her hand. "Blood, probably. Not mine. A man got shot—"

He pulled out his handkerchief (Tom always carried handkerchiefs), held it out in the rain, and washed her thoroughly. "That will do for now." He gestured toward the hole in the backseat window. "Posey told me how you got this. Rough day, wasn't it?"

"It has seemed like a week. Can I tell you about it later?"

"Yeah. I've heard Posey's version. I can wait for yours. Right now I'm worried about Hollis."

"Me, too. Do you think—?" She had been about to suggest they try to get in the house, but two men came out just then with Iola, hands cuffed behind her and head down.

A stretcher followed. Hollis's eyes were closed, but her face was uncovered.

"Thank God," Katharine breathed. "She's alive."

Posey trotted behind the bearers, her face white.

Tom jumped out and intercepted his sister. They were near enough for Katharine to hear.

"How badly is she hurt?"

"Bad. She took a bullet in the chest. They think it missed vital organs, but she's lost a lot of blood and they won't know anything for sure until they check her out. I'm going with her." She started toward the ambulance, calling over her shoulder, "If you find Katharine, tell her Dr. Flo's hurt, too. I can't stay to see about her."

Tom and Katharine ran hand in hand to the front door.

Dr. Flo lay on the couch with a host of EMTs around her. Her lids fluttered when she saw Katharine. "Hollis saved us," she whispered.

"What happened?" Katharine demanded.

"I don't know. Asleep . . ."

"Don't talk," one of the medics commanded. "Save your strength." They prepared to move her onto a stretcher.

"Mary . . . Rodney . . ."

"I'll call them," Katharine promised. "And then we'll join you at the hospital. How do I get the number?"

Dr. Flo recited it drowsily. Katharine waited until the paramedics had carried her out before she cried to Tom, "I didn't have a pencil!"

"Get one now." She fetched one from Posey's telephone and he dictated it. Tom had always had a phenomenal memory.

They couldn't stay in the house, of course. It had become a crime scene. They couldn't even pack up Dr. Flo's things, since that room was sealed off, but under police supervision they gathered up suitcases for Katharine, Posey, and Hollis and headed to a hotel.

"I want to go be with Dr. Flo," Katharine said when they had checked in.

"You'd better shower first, or the emergency room will think they ought to admit you."

He made calls while Katharine cleaned up. She threw her white slacks and striped jacket in the trash. She could never bear to wear them again, even if someone could get out all the stains.

When she returned to the room, Tom looked up from his

book and smiled. "You look better. Rodney and Mary are on their way from Savannah, Wrens is on his way from California, I persuaded Molly and Lolly we do not need them down here with four small children, and Posey says both patients are doing as well as can be expected and are headed to ICU. Do you still want to go to the hospital?"

He was already standing and reaching for his keys. He knew she wouldn't sleep until she saw Hollis and Dr. Flo for herself.

Several hours later they returned to the hotel. Katharine expected to lie awake for hours and have dreadful nightmares. Instead, as soon as Tom climbed in beside her and pulled her against his chest, she fell asleep and didn't wake until the sun was high in the sky.

After checking with the hospital again, they ate breakfast and lazed beside the hotel pool.

Back in Atlanta, they'd have been in church by then. Katharine felt like a child given permission to play hooky.

"I'll need to find someplace to get shorts and shirts," Tom commented as one of the teens in the pool splashed water close to his legs. He hadn't had any casual clothes in D.C., so for the time being he wore black suit pants and a white shirt, but he had rolled up the sleeves and left the collar open and had borrowed a pair of sandals from Wrens's closet while they were still at the house. He wasn't as handsome as Hasty, she thought fondly, but he was familiar and dear.

"You look very nice," she told him.

"Shall I buy a bathing suit? You're going to want to swim, aren't you?"

"Another day. Today, I'm too tired to put on a suit."

He read (Tom never left home without a book) while she dozed in her lounge chair.

"How did you get here?" she finally thought to ask as the waiter set drinks before them.

"Posey called from some restaurant where you all were

eating pie. She said she thought you were in danger and I ought to be here. She sounded pretty worked up, so I figured I'd better check things out. I called another fellow to take Ashley to her party—which, frankly, was a relief—and told the pilot to gas up the company jet. We got here as fast as we could. When I called the house to say I had arrived, Posey said you were out for a walk, so she came to get me."

Bless Posey. She must have suspected Tom had come when she had answered the telephone, then had sent Katharine out to the beach to make his arrival a surprise.

Katharine shaded her eyes with one hand and looked out to sea, hating to ask but needing to know. "How long can you stay?"

"As long as you need me. I'm sorry I've been such a beast since the break-in—going back to work so soon and leaving everything to you. Posey raked me over the coals on our way in from the airport. She told me how hard you've been working, you and Hollis both."

"You needed to go," she reminded him.

He reached for her hand and played with her fingers. "Well, I can stay a while this time. I have enough accumulated vacation time to take a couple of months, if I need to."

"You know you can't be gone that long!"

He gave her a rueful smile. "No, I really can't. There's an important Senate hearing in a couple of weeks. But I could manage ten days. Why don't we stay down here and rest a little?"

She couldn't afford ten days at the beach with all she had to do at the house, but she wasn't worried. Tom would be content for a couple of days. Then he'd get antsy to work on the house. They'd go home. By Friday he'd be on the phone most of the time checking on the office, and he'd be off the next Monday. That's how Tom was made.

She smiled. "That would be nice." At least he was here now.

* * *

Hollis sat up in bed with tubes and wires running in several directions. "I'm wired," she announced. "Somebody take a picture for the nephews. They'll love to see me looking like a space monster."

"I'm glad to see you at all," Katharine told her soberly. "We can only stay a little while, but can you tell us what happened?"

Hollis had already given her statement to the police. She looked wan and tired.

"Dr. Flo was asleep, so when Mama left, I went upstairs to watch TV. I heard something downstairs that I thought was a knock, so I started back down, thinking it was you and you'd gone out without your key. But it wasn't you."

Hollis's voice dwindled and her hands twisted on the blanket. Posey reached over and caught them between hers. "Just tell it slowly, honey. You're safe."

"It was the woman from the cemetery, the one who shot at the old man. She had broken one of the doors and gotten in, and was standing there with her hands behind her. When she saw me on the stairs she said something like 'Nice place you got here.'" Hollis's voice deepened and rasped, like Iola's. Before textile arts, she had considered majoring in drama. "She said, 'Could I talk to the black woman for a minute? It's real important.' I told her Dr. Flo was sleeping and I didn't want to wake her, but she said, 'I don't give a dog's rear end what you want or don't want, you go wake her up and tell her I want to talk to her.' And she brought her hands out from behind her and pointed a rifle at me."

Hollis's voice wobbled. She paused to look out the hospital window for a moment while taking Posey's recommended deep cleansing breaths. Finally she was ready to continue.

"I figured she had come to kill Dr. Flo. Mama had left Daddy's pistol on the countertop, and I thought if I could get to it before she saw it—but I didn't." Her voice wobbled. "She got it first, and laid her rifle on the counter. After that, I didn't know how to stop her. I decided I could do more behind her than in front of her, so when we got to the door, I stepped back and said, 'She's in there. You wake her up if you want her.'"

Katharine smiled. Hollis had probably used exactly that snotty tone.

Hollis paused to sip water. "She went in the door and I opened the hall closet to get one of Daddy's golf clubs. They weren't there."

"He took them home the last time we were down," Posey told the others. "Wanted to get them refinished or something."

Hollis gave a little snort. "Now you tell me. Nobody ever tells me anything in this family. All I could find was a stupid badminton racket one of the kids had left. So I grabbed up a racket and tiptoed after her."

"A badminton racket?" Tom looked flabbergasted. "Against a gun?"

Hollis grimaced. "Yeah. Not real smart, huh? But it was all I could find. When I got to Dr. Flo's door, the woman was standing halfway across the room taking aim. All I had time to do was hit her arm and deflect her aim. But at lcast the shot went wild and didn't hit Dr. Flo. She fired real quick again and did hit her, then she turned on me. I tried to run, but she shot me." Her voice still sounded surprised at that. "I thought I was a goner. I screamed 'Mama!'—which was dumb since I knew you'd gone after Uncle Tom . . ."

Posey got up and drew Hollis's head to her chest. "Everybody cries for their mama when they are in danger, baby. I'm sorry I wasn't there."

For once, Hollis didn't pull away. She rubbed her cheek against her mother's soft blouse. "But the woman must have thought you were upstairs or something, because she ran past me. I had just enough time to pull myself into Dr. Flo's room and drag a chair under the doorknob before I fainted." She gave Katharine a wobbly grin. "I won't laugh at you again. That chair trick really worked. Even the police couldn't get in until they chopped the door down."

"Time for visitors to leave," a nurse announced in the door.

Hollis was already closing her eyes for a nap.

From there Katharine and Tom went to see Dr. Flo.

Rodney and his mother occupied the two guest chairs, but he immediately rose and offered Katharine his seat next to the bed.

"She's awake, but a little groggy," Mary whispered.

Katharine took her hand. "Dr. Flo? It's Katharine." At the enormous bandage around the professor's small chest, she felt a lump rise in her own. "I am so sorry I wasn't there."

Dr. Flo made an impatient gesture with her other hand. Most of her words were inaudible, but Katharine made out a few. ". . . bad enough Hollis . . . never forgive myself . . . if you . . ." Her eyes closed.

"She comes and goes," Rodney murmured.

"We want to thank you for all you are doing for Florence," Mary added. "You are so kind. She's coming home to us when she gets out of here, and Rodney will drive us back to Atlanta when she's able."

Katharine made polite noises and stayed a few minutes longer, but all the time she was wondering what she had ever done for Dr. Flo besides drive her straight into danger.

When they were alone in the elevator, she said, "Tom?"

He was engrossed in reading the safety certificate. Tom read cereal boxes if there was nothing else to read. "Yeah?"

"Could we cover Dr. Flo's expenses while she's here? I can't say much without her permission, but Maurice left her badly off. Her money—it's all gone."

He finished reading the certificate before he nodded. "I heard something about that."

"When? From whom?"

"People were talking about it all over town right after the doctor died."

"People meaning men in clubs and locker rooms?"

"I suppose so. The rumor was that he'd gotten too heavily invested in tech stocks back at the turn of the century, and never recovered."

"Why didn't you tell me? Why haven't we done anything for Dr. Flo before?"

"We scarcely knew the woman. You can't walk up to a casual acquaintance and offer her money."

It was so reasonable. It was so wrong.

"What about now? Can we pay her bills?"

The door opened. He stepped back to let her off first. "We already have. I arranged that last night while we were here. But I need to stop by the business office for a minute and sign a few more papers."

She looked at him in fond exasperation. "Tom Murray, have I ever told you that sometimes you drive me crazy?"

"Occasionally." He smiled. "Why don't you wait on that couch by the door? You look a little peaky."

She tottered toward the couch. Now that Tom had mentioned it, Katharine *felt* peaky. Seeing Hollis and Dr. Flo had made her aware how close they—and she—had come to death.

She discovered, however, that she wasn't quite done with the island. Mona Bayard sat in a wheelchair by the curb, awaiting pickup.

Katharine regarded her through the glass wall beside the automatic doors and wondered what she should do. Her impulse was to go to Mona and express how sorry she was for everything that had happened, but how do you offer comfort to a woman whose entire world has exploded? Especially when you have been one of the agents of destruction? Would Mona want to speak with her, or did Mona never want to see her again?

Two women came up the walk. One looked with open envy at Mona's navy pantsuit and matching pumps. As they came though the door, she said to her companion, "What do you reckon she paid for that outfit? The shoes alone cost her four hundred."

The other heaved a big sigh. "Some women have all the luck." They laughed as they headed to the elevator.

Katharine pressed one hand against the glass. It was no more solid than the events that walled her off from Mona. There was no point in offering her condolences. Some stories have no happy endings.

Mona's cream Mercedes pulled up to the curb, and a tall man got out. He wore a black Western shirt with black slacks, and had thick gray hair. Katharine knew without seeing it that he had a black Western hat in the backseat. He came around the car and took Mona's arm like she was made of porcelain. Other visitors came in then, so Katharine heard him say, "Come on, Sugah. Let's get you back to Texas where you belong."

Maybe for a Texan that would be happy ending enough.

But to lose your son, and your husband . . . Katharine shivered and could not stop.

Then Tom strode across the lobby—sturdy, familiar, and very dear. "Are you cold?" He immediately stripped off the jacket he'd worn to the hospital, and wrapped her in it.

Katharine looked up, memorizing his face for his next departure. "Have I ever told you I love you?"

"Not often enough." He held out his hand. "We're done here. Let's go take a nap."

She put her hand in his and gave it a squeeze. "Or something."